Rebecca Alexander fell in love with all things sorcery, magic and witchcraft as a teenager and has enjoyed reading and writing fantasy ever since. She wrote her first book aged nineteen and since then has been runner-up in the Mslexia novel-writing competition and the Yeovil Literary Prize 2012.

Trained in psychology and education, and having researched magical thinking in adults for her MSc, Rebecca met some really interesting people in some very odd circumstances, which she could no longer resist writing down.

She lives in a haunted house by the sea with her second husband, four cats, three chickens and the occasional rook.

'[*The Secrets of Life and Death*] is a fine addition to the urban fantasy genre and marks Alexander as an author to watch'
Independent on Sunday

'Finely observed, beautifully written' *Daily Mail*

'Heartfelt but complicated rather than subtle, this novel offers plenty of suspense' *Kirkus*

Also by Rebecca Alexander:

The Secrets of Life and Death
The Secrets of Blood and Bone

REBECCA ALEXANDER

The Secrets of Time and Fate

DEL REY

1 3 5 7 9 10 8 6 4 2

Del Rey, an imprint of Ebury Publishing
20 Vauxhall Bridge Road,
London SW1V 2SA

Penguin
Random House
UK

Del Rey is part of the Penguin Random House group of companies whose addresses can
be found at global.penguinrandomhouse.com

First published in the UK in 2016 by Del Rey

www.eburypublishing.co.uk

A CIP catalogue record for this book is available from the British Library

ISBN 9780091953263

Typeset in India by Thomson Digital Pvt Ltd, Noida, Delhi

Printed and bound in Great Britain by Clays Ltd, St Ives PLC

Penguin Random House is committed to a sustainable future for our business, our readers
and our planet. This book is made from Forest Stewardship Council® certified paper.

To the men in my life: Steve, who died;
and Russell, who didn't.

Chapter 1

'She couldn't possibly have survived.' The young doctor handed Felix Guichard a sheet of paper.

Felix took it, his hand shaking. 'How was she found? What happened?'

The doctor consulted a slim package of notes in front of him. 'She was noticed by a security guard watching a camera on Vauxhall Bridge. She climbed over the edge and he called the police. He saw her jump.'

Felix stared at the list of numbers in front of him – a lot seemed to be highlighted. They meant nothing to him.

The man softened his tone. 'She was in the water at least twenty minutes. The police said she was struggling, at least at first. They brought her in but—'

'She was—' Felix swallowed hard, his eyes stinging with tears.

'We managed to get a pulse eventually, and put her on full life support. Then we got the first blood results back and as you can see they are grossly abnormal.'

Felix glanced again at them. 'What do you mean, "abnormal"?'

1

'We only see people like this in multi-system failure, close to death. Her electrolytes, chemicals in the blood, are disturbed. There's evidence of liver, kidney, gut failure.'

'And this condition is always fatal?' The numbers in front of him shimmered and he closed his eyes.

'Not necessarily always fatal, not if we catch it early enough, but that's the odd thing.'

Felix recalled Jack turning to laugh at something her adopted teenager Sadie had said. The memory was so painful he lifted his hand to his stomach to ease it without thinking. The doctor's words seeped into him. He cleared his throat. 'Odd?'

The young man frowned a little as he leaned over the paper. 'These issues don't result from drowning. They happen over hours or, more likely, days. Was she chronically ill or suffering from some serious condition?'

Felix's mind faltered over the explanation of borrowed time. How did you discuss being held back from death by magic, by sixteenth-century sorcery? 'No, not as far as I know. She seemed fine. We were just up in London for the night.'

'Did she seem depressed?'

Felix thought back to the agonising moment when Jackdaw Hammond told him she was possessed. Not just possessed – the sorcery that had extended her life had allowed a creature that fed on human blood to infiltrate Jack's being. She must have realised she would become a predator, ruled by her supernatural partner, and thought this was the only way to save the ones she loved. Heroic, that was Jack. He bent his head under the weight of the agony released inside him. Heroic, yes, but stupid. He knew something about the myths and beliefs of possession and exorcism. It was one of his areas of research as

2

a professor of social anthropology, for God's sake. He could have tried—

The touch of the man's hand patting his shoulder brought him back under control. He dashed his sleeve across his wet eyes. 'Depressed, no, but she had just got bad news. Look, can I see her?'

The doctor stepped back half a pace. 'They didn't tell you?' He inhaled sharply. 'I'm sorry, but she's missing.'

'Missing?'

'She was breathing by herself but in a deep coma, so we moved her into a high-care side ward, until—'

'What?'

'Well, in intensive care she was supervised the whole time, but here in high care the supervision is a little lower. The staff were preoccupied with another patient when . . . we don't really know what happened.'

'She just walked out?'

'No, no. I mean, she couldn't have, not with these blood results.' He reached for the paper. 'This is end-stage organ failure, unrecoverable, I'm afraid. Maybe a member of staff moved her in error, we're searching the hospital. Or possibly she was moved to a private clinic, I don't know. Hopefully the paperwork will turn up somewhere.'

Felix's mind raced through all the possibilities. His brain seemed to have slowed down with grief, half-realised ideas piling up in his mind. 'But she was just – gone?'

'She had had her airway removed, and all her drips and monitors were disconnected.'

Felix stared through the window at the ward, lit by flashing lights and monitors. The patients were all heavily sedated. 'Maybe she did just walk out.'

The doctor shook his head. 'I think that is highly unlikely, close to impossible. She was dying.'

Hope flared in Felix like a small flame. She had spent almost twenty years at the point of death. 'The alternative is that someone took her. But the police aren't treating it as suspicious?'

'Well, we think it's much more likely to be that she's been transferred, we have a hospital-wide search out looking for her. Papers get lost in the middle of the night . . .'

The man's voice faded as Felix marched through the ward, slamming open the double doors, and started to run as he reached the corridor. She could have survived. The thought made his heart race and fill him with energy. He ran through the hospital, only stopping when he hit the air outside, pausing to catch his breath. She was still alive. Looking out across London he began to realise the enormity of the task ahead, finding one desperately sick young woman who was possessed by a demon.

'Professor! Professor Guichard!' The police officer was out of breath when he reached Felix.

Felix turned to look at the man. He had called the police originally when he couldn't find Jack after she ran off, only to be told she had been brought to the hospital.

'Yes?' His voice was hard, trying to control his emotions.

'We think we have footage – can you come and identify a person on the hospital's CCTV?'

He reluctantly followed the young man back into the building, and into an office marked security. A woman, surrounded by banks of monitors, looked up in the eerie light from the screens.

'This person left the hospital just over an hour ago,' she said, glancing up at Felix. She tapped a keyboard and a figure appeared, shuffling along in oversized clothes, leaning one hand against the wall for support. 'This is the corridor outside the medical assessment unit. Here she is again, going past urology.' She switched to another camera. 'And here, she's crossing the lobby.'

'But . . .' Felix squinted at the picture. 'Can you enlarge the image?'

'I've been working on it.' She leaned in to the screen, pointing at a shadowy image advancing down a corridor. 'She looks up about . . . here.' Stopping the image, she zoomed in on the fuzzy mess, which then sharpened.

It was hard to make out the features, but he recognised her easily. Narrow face, blond hair, wide eyes over broad cheekbones. 'Jack,' Felix whispered.

The police officer sighed. 'Well, that's good news. I thought we were looking at an abduction.' He tapped Felix on the shoulder. 'She didn't have any ID on her. For my records, is that Jackie, or Jacqueline?'

Felix stared at the image for a moment longer. 'Jack – Jackie.'

'And a surname?' The man was persistent, obviously keen to close the case.

Felix thought fast. 'Grey. Jackie Grey.' He knew the name she used, Jackdaw Hammond, had no official standing.

'We have her belongings here. Not much, just a few wet clothes, they cut them off. A purse but no cards, just cash, no phone or ID. Is that right?'

Felix thought quickly. 'She doesn't carry cards on her if we're going out for the evening.'

'And you don't know why she jumped off the bridge?' The policeman was relaxing, making notes.

'No. She just got some bad news, I think. That's all. She's been under a lot of strain.'

The man underlined something in his notebook. 'Well, if you just give me your contact numbers we can keep you informed of our investigation, and if we have any other questions—'

'Investigation?'

'There's a suicidal young woman out there.' The man looked across at Felix, sharp eyes watching his response. 'We will be looking out for her, of course. We will process this as a vulnerable missing person.'

'Of course. Thank God someone's doing something. Let me know as soon as you hear anything, will you?'

He left the policeman with his information, but doubted whether they would find Jack. She was used to being invisible, living quietly in the shadowy world of sorcery and magic.

He walked out into the cool air. It was just April, but the night was already stretching towards dawn and was mild. How much longer could she fight off the possession of Saraquel – the same possession that had driven Elizabeth Báthory to be one of the world's first serial killers four hundred years before?

Phoning Maggie, Jack's foster mother, was the next thing he should do but all he wanted to do was keep running, keep shouting her name. She could be dying somewhere, wrapped in clothes she must have stolen, sick from – what did the doctor call it? – multi-organ failure. The only lead he had had came from the surveillance cameras. When Jack left the hospital, she turned left. He followed.

Chapter 2

Journal of Eliza Jane Weston, Prague, 23 November 1612

I hardly know how to pen words of such calamity. It had begun when a visitor came to the door of our house in Jánský Vršek, Prague. My manservant Tomáš showed a veiled woman to my upper apartment, despite my command that none be admitted because of my advanced pregnancy. I was shamed, my feet upon a stool as they were swollen, and a shawl around my shoulders. But the embarrassment was swallowed within a moment as she spoke.

'Stay, madame,' she said, seeing me struggle to rise. 'I know what it is to bear a child.'

That voice, a voice I had not heard since childhood. She was taller than I, slender, veiled and dressed in green. She swept back the lace from her countenance.

I could feel the cold seeping into me. It was the Countess Elizabeth Báthory, a revenant escaped from her imprisonment where the nobles of Transylvania had walled her up in her own castle. All my father's journals, which I had so carefully translated for him, came back to me.

She leaned forward and fixed me with her blue eyes. 'Tell me of your father, Edward Kelley. Tell me of the sorceries he learned in Alexandria.'

Edward Kelley, Prague, 1586

Franco Marinello, my sea captain friend from Venice. As I sat at table, listening to his adventures in our hall in Prague, I scratched at the half-healed rat bites I had collected in prison. Marinello had written for an introduction to the emperor, a gift that my mentor John Dee could easily grant, even though we had fallen from favour. So Marinello had come to the Holy Roman Empire court.

My little daughter Eliza, just seven years of age, sat upon my knee. 'Father, why does Lord Marinello have an earring?'

Marinello heard her, and leaned forward so she could see the ruby in his earlobe. 'The court ladies prevailed,' he said. 'One took it from her own ear, and with a bodkin – there! Her favour was for all to see. Unfortunately, her jealous husband also saw. I shall need a discreet withdrawal from court, soon. Venice – and adventure – beckons.' No great thinker, nor politician, the sea captain's powerful figure, his handsome face and tales of voyages upon the seas made a glamorous impression upon the ladies. We too welcomed his company. When he arrived he beguiled us all with his stories and promises of wealth. The house seemed too small to hold the man, who stamped about the rooms making the children laugh and the women preen a little. Even my own wife, rather Calvinist in her dress and behaviour, laughed at his jokes and his worse German. Dee's sons competed to hold his sword, or examine his cloak and velvet doublets. The daughters of the house blushed and giggled at all of his good-natured advances. Madinia, Frances, Katherine and Margaret Dee wore their prettiest kirtles and gossiped about him, talking of his beard, his ruff, his thick curls, his black eyes. Even my own little Eliza let the other girls rag her hair into ringlets, and was permitted to serve him wine at dinner.

'Where do you go?' said Dee, always interested in travel, as he was a great mapmaker.

'I have a ship in Candia, which I can sell in Alexandria where there is a demand for deep-drawing vessels. I will pay the taxes upon my main carrack there.'

Dee stroked his beard and looked across at me. 'It would be prudent to sail down the Italian coast from Venice, and re-victual your ship at Brindisi.'

Marinello shrugged. 'I have no business in Brindisi; I make straight for Candia.'

'If I had the money I would ask you to take us there, nevertheless,' said Dee. 'I have a correspondent in Brindisi who has an insight into a great mystery that has bearing on our work.'

'What business, Master Dee, if I might ask?' said Marinello.

Dee paused, studying his hands for a moment. 'We go upon business concerning a lady, one noblewoman of Transylvania with whom you are acquainted. A lady touched by death. Countess Báthory.'

I held my breath a moment, remembering that Marinello had an entirely different view upon the countess, being her past lover. But Marinello merely took a cake from a platter before him and held it lightly in his hand. His eyes were sharp upon Dee, and he held his silence.

'Lord Marinello had some affection for the countess, Master Dee, having met her in Venice,' I said. 'Perhaps he knows a kinder lady.'

'Nay, little man,' Marinello said to me, with a gentle tone. 'You warned me about the countess. I know that lovely face hides the nature of a beast. Touched by death, you said? And now that death has touched me.'

He put down the cake and rolled up his embroidered sleeve, secured with a bunch of ribbons at the wrist. He revealed the inside of his forearm. There was the knife wound he had shown me in Venice a month before. The countess had drunk his life blood from the fresh wound but now the bandage oozed with pus. I undid the end of the binding and gently unwound it. It stuck to the gash but Marinello gave no sign that it hurt. Dee walked to the door, opened it, and called down the stairs to his wife. He returned to see the injury laid bare.

It was as if someone – the countess – had bitten the flesh through several times, each bite overlaying the next around the slash in the skin. Everywhere her little teeth had broken through was raw, the flesh angry red, the skin oozing with pus. In the centre of the bitten area lay a circle of dead flesh, grey as a pigeon's wing, bisected by the knife wound. The stink of infection and decay rose in the warm room.

Jane Dee put her head around the door and advanced into the chamber. 'Oh, sweet Jesu,' she said, in her musical voice, then blushed at her outburst and covered her mouth for a moment. 'Dear Edward, please call for hot water and my medical kit.' Jane Dee, no mean scholar herself, had studied medicine privately while in Prague. 'How did this happen, my lord?'

I went to the door to call for Dee's man.

'I was savaged by love,' he answered, making a comedy of it, but he still winced when she touched his arm with gentle fingers.

'This part is dead,' she said, brushing the grey area within the bites, 'and infects the rest. It should be excised. If not, you risk losing the limb.'

10

Marinello grimaced at the sight. 'So my surgeon says. But he shakes his head and says he should amputate below the elbow and, lady –' he smiled '– 'tis my sword arm.'

I commanded the man bring supplies for Mistress Dee, and some stronger wine.

Dee studied the area, oblivious to the smell. 'It is not truly *gangraena*. Look here, Edward, Jane. There are no red lines advancing up into the armpit, nor is it blackened. This is death, yet retains some characteristics of life. Like the countess herself.'

I covered my face for a moment with my sleeve, sickened by the stink of decay. But Jane sat upon a stool and folded her long hands in her lap. Almost thirty years younger than her husband, who had reached his sixtieth year, she was a tall woman, her flaxen head just touched by a silver strand here and there. One for each child, she had joked with me, seven strands weaving through her closely braided hair.

'We might persuade a surgeon to try to remove the dead tissue,' she speculated, but with a doubtful tone in her voice.

'Or you might do it,' said Dee. He turned to Marinello. 'My wife has a very gentle touch and healing hands, my lord. Your wounds may mend if the cause of the suppuration is removed.'

Marinello held out his healthy arm, and after a long moment, Jane placed her fingers lightly in his. He weighed them, while her colour changed to pink and she looked away. I was momentarily jealous that she should trust him on so short an acquaintance.

'The hands of a mother, Master Dee, and a healer indeed. An angel's fingers.' He raised up her hand to his lips and released her. She jumped up.

'I would need to examine it more closely, and in a better light,' she said, still flushed. 'But if it does not corrupt the muscle it would

11

be no worse than a sword wound. It could be cleaned and poult-
iced.'

The course was set. Jane would clean the dead flesh from
Marinello's arm, he would recover as a guest of Dee as he could
not sustain the high cost of living in the court, then he would set
out upon his adventures with us before the end of May.

Chapter 3

Present day, Shoreditch, London

Jackdaw Hammond woke, as she did a dozen times a night, to the sound of a rat gnawing something close to her face. Days had stretched into weeks, she wasn't sure how long she had been squatting in the old building. She brushed the rat away, but it stood its ground until she batted it with a shoe. She was herself again, an increasingly rare event as Saraquel, her possessing spirit, seemed to take her away for hours at a time. She would walk out of the back of the abandoned restaurant where she was sleeping, and would find herself on the steps of St Paul's in the dark, many hours later. She had no idea what Saraquel had been doing with her body all day but, judging by the scratches and bruises, nothing good. As her world returned, she sometimes sensed him, or caught a word or two thrown in her direction, as he passed the 'vessel' back to her for essential maintenance. Her pockets were often filled with cash and notes and she hated to speculate where he got them from. But today her mind was her own, and she tidied herself up as well as she could, and headed out for an early breakfast.

Barbara, the owner of a more successful cafe, had a soft spot for Jack and would sell her hot coffee and some fresh rolls. On occasion she offered Jack the use of her shower room, but Jack was worried about Saraquel taking over while she was naked and vulnerable. She did accept the use of Barbara's washing machine on a couple of occasions, and it made her feel more normal to smell like soap powder. Grief or depression: whatever Jack named it, it felt like the rats were gnawing at her insides. Felix, Sadie, Maggie, Charley: family, but so far away. Even Ches, her beloved wolf-dog hybrid, would have hated living like this. A few times she had been driven to a phone box but Saraquel always intervened, and she would wake up hung-over in a shop doorway, or spinning along the pavement like a child. Jack raged against him, but he just threw the switch and she was gone.

'You're early,' Barbara said, just opening the back door. 'You look brighter. I'll put some bacon on, shall I?'

Jack searched her pockets for money, and came up with a roll of tightly packed twenty-pound notes. Jack stared, her mouth open with astonishment.

'Did you rob a bank?' Barbara stared at her, and all Jack could do was shake her head.

'No—' her voice was rusty, she rarely spoke, and she had to cough. 'Maybe I found it.'

'Look, love, it's none of my business, I know, but you should get some help. Alcohol rots your brain, ruins your memory. I should know, my brother Jimmy . . .'

Jack let the familiar lecture roll over her. She didn't drink, not while she was Jack, anyway, and she didn't think Saraquel was pushing her into alcoholism.

'There's a shelter off Cheapside. They could help you.' Barbara sizzled two slices of bacon in a pan, and Jack's attention immediately sharpened. She felt the dizziness of Saraquel's approach, and tried to put it off.

14

'A shelter?' she said as Barbara pushed the sauce bottle closer. Jack rarely ate anything as Saraquel usually took those moments, and the next thing she knew she was sipping her milky coffee, the rolls gone. She chased a stray crumb with her finger.

Barbara was holding a piece of paper. 'St Jude's shelter, there's a map on the bottom. It's on the way to St Paul's, and I know you like it down there.'

Jack took it cautiously, not sure a homeless shelter for alcoholics had much to offer her, but some discomfort inside made her pay attention. Saraquel didn't want her to go near St Paul's for some reason, the great church made him uncomfortable.

'Thank you,' she said, with real gratitude. She rummaged in her pocket for the money, and peeled off a couple of notes for herself. 'Here, take the rest of these. I must owe you a fair amount.'

'That's OK. I'll hold it for you, all right? I'll put it in the safe.' She smiled at Jack. 'I know you're a bit of a nutter sometimes, but I like you.'

Jack knew she was overcome by Saraquel sometimes – the real nutter. She twisted her face into an awkward grimace approximating a smile, and nodded. She turned to go, and Barbara called after her. 'There's a case worker down there, Hazel. Tell her I said hello. She used to help Jimmy.'

Jack made it into the street before Saraquel started to flicker her life into moments snatched between the possession. It was late afternoon before he tired of the game he was playing and she came to abruptly, again on the steps of the landmark cathedral. She looked through her pockets, but the paper was gone. He didn't want her to go to this shelter. She struggled to remember where it was.

'Cheapside, Gutter Lane, Carey Lane . . .' she muttered to herself as she walked, startling a couple of tourists. 'Yes, I'm a fucking nutter,' she grumbled at them. She wondered if her sanity had been eroded by Saraquel, but walked the length of the road anyway, then started looking down the various side streets. A few abortive turns and backtracks brought her past a man looking as shabby and unwashed as herself and smelling considerably worse.

'Hey,' she said, but he turned away. 'Wait! Wait, I've got money.'

He stopped and looked over his shoulder at her. 'What do you want?'

She realised with a jolt that he wasn't a man at all, but a boy, maybe seventeen or so. 'I'm looking for St Jude's.'

'Why?' He looked around and stepped closer, his eyes searching for pockets, as if he was going to mug her. She stepped back, putting a hand out.

'I need to speak to someone there.' Her dodgy memory spat out a name. 'Hazel – a case worker or something.' She reached into her pockets and pulled out a handful of change. 'Here. Get yourself a drink and a sandwich.'

She knew the money would go on drugs, but she wasn't going to judge his methods of dealing with his own demons.

'It's just there. St Jude's.' He pointed at a large stone basement with bars on the windows, under some offices. 'Downstairs.'

She watched him walk away, wishing she had asked his name, as if she could help him when she couldn't even help herself. The hall had steps down one side to an open door. She stuck her head in, looking around at a shabby corridor. Saraquel squirmed inside her, and she expected him to take over, but he didn't. No, she realised. Couldn't.

Chapter 4

Present day, Dublin

Jackdaw Hammond. The cryptic message on Robert Conway's phone meant one thing: the Vatican wanted to speak to him, now. The instructions were in an email, which could wait.

He struggled with the key in the lock. It yielded with a squeak that sounded as reluctant to get on with its day as he was. He pushed his way to the counter at the back of the shop, past the displays that Judith, one of the shop's two part-time managers, would put out on the Dublin street later. But not until he was ready for customers.

Italy had been wonderful, rejuvenating, a chance to relax and connect with old friends. He had been part of Florence's world long enough to have visited all the museums and galleries many times, but sometimes the gesture of a sculpture or the colour of a painting still left him breathless in a way that people rarely did any more.

Booting up the computer gave Robert time to make a pot of coffee and open the narrow window at the back of the shop. The musty smell of old books might attract some of his customers but he had little time for the past.

He sipped his black coffee and stared over the street, watching leaves unfurl and glow in the first greens of spring, before opening his work emails. Two hundred and thirty-three, and they were just the personal messages. Judith and Kate had been dealing with a lot more, two thousand or so by the look of it. Many were requests to look out for something very rare or difficult to source; a few offered books for sale, all at ridiculous prices no doubt. They could wait.

Kate had been to auction nine times while he was gone, and bought less than a dozen books. But what books, he thought.

He turned and unlocked the book safe, a sealed walk-in cupboard at the back of the property that held a couple of hundred volumes in a moisture- and temperature-controlled environment. The total value of the stock was not immediately apparent, but they were insured for several million. Kate had left the eleven new books at the front for him to examine, each in its own case. He lifted the top one, knowing she had left it there especially. Richard Knolles, *The Generall Historie of the Turkes*, 1610. Not the most valuable of her acquisitions at just under three thousand pounds, but a beautiful copy. He had owned one before, but this one was a better imprint, every plate was as crisp as if it was new. He lifted the calfskin cover, Victorian replacement probably, maybe 1860s, with garish marbling on the endpapers that had just stained the first page. He leafed through the book carefully, checking for water-staining, insect damage, clumsy repairs. Beautiful, the pictures jumping out at him from time to time. His phone beeped again.

He placed the book in its polythene cover, and looked through the more valuable acquisitions.

The bell rang, and Judith's voice floated over the bookshelves. 'Hi, Robert. Lovely to have you back.'

He leaned over to see her advancing to him with her hands held out, and submitted to a hug, a kiss on his cheek. He knew she would have liked more from him, but it was the best he could do.

'I'm just drooling over the latest gems,' he said, uncasing another.

'Have a look at the Agricola,' she said, pouring herself a coffee in a mug that claimed to belong to the world's best mum. 'Or, better still, the Robert Hooke. A first-first.'

He opened the box containing the Hooke, *Micrographia: or some Physiological Descriptions of Minute Bodies made by Magnifying Glasses*, unfolding one of the amazing plates. An image of a flea, drawn from one of the earliest microscope studies, was as clean as if it had just been pressed. First edition, first issue, in excellent condition from 1665.

'Shame about the cover,' he said, closing the plate gently and looking at the binding.

'Modern, I know. Not all that good, either, but with a value of fifty to sixty thousand pounds we could re-cover easily.'

He cradled the book for a moment, checking the box for defects that might leave the cover exposed, then repacked it gently in a layer of acid-free tissue paper. 'How much did she pay?'

'Forty-seven thousand and change. She's been panicking ever since.'

He nodded approval. He already had a buyer in mind, a German collector, and he would enjoy the trip over to Dresden.

He returned with some reluctance to the emails. Invitations to social occasions, antiquarian book events, and a few friends keeping in touch. Finally, he opened another email account, this one with very few emails in it, all addressed to *Esorcisti*. Exorcist. He opened the first one, glancing over the text, translating from the mixture of Latin and Italian as he went.

My dear friend, I hardly like to ask you to intervene, but we have a situation developing that leaves us concerned. It regards the revenant Jackdaw Hammond. It would be helpful if you were to contact me at your soonest convenience—

Naturally, Monsignor Andreotti was referring to the work of the papal department Robert was semi-retired from. He sighed and scrolled down, hoping he would actually give details rather than require him to phone the Vatican. In truth, he was getting to the point when his semi-retirement needed to be extended into actual retirement, with maybe an occasional teaching role. He had no taste for the work any more, and the internal politics were brutal. No doubt it was some crisis that would turn out to be nothing, like the last few emails from his colleagues at the Congregation for the Doctrine of the Faith. He would just have to call the Inquisition and find out what they wanted.

The name in the email intrigued him though. The revenant. The woman living on magic and sorcery who had somehow killed the creature he had spent his whole life trying to avoid. At the moment when Elizabeth Báthory's body had been consumed by fire, Saraquel would have had to possess another host, a half-dead thing that was close by. That had to be the revenant Jackdaw Hammond. It seemed a shame to destroy the woman who had rid the world of one of the deadliest hosts of a five-thousand-year-old curse named Saraquel.

He called to Judith, saying he would get more coffee, and stepped outside. The number he phoned was diverted through another service. He waited patiently, trying to remember the right alias with the right password, then was put through to Cardinal Andreotti.

'Ah, you got my message at last. Where were you, Siberia?' Andreotti's baritone words were flawlessly Italian, although to

Kelley's knowledge he was born in Austria. Working in the Vatican gave one a peculiar precision of diction.

'Just around the corner in Florence.'

'You should have come to see us.'

Conway laughed. 'It was the "us" that stopped me. What of this woman, the revenant?'

He could hear Andreotti sigh. He wasn't exactly sure how old the cardinal was but he looked like a very active eighty-year-old. He reminded Conway of Christopher Lee, a comparison that Andreotti sometimes played on.

'The office will be sending a team to neutralise the new revenant, of course, but I am concerned about the consequences. Listen, Robert, this is beyond something we can discuss on the phone. It concerns our old friend.'

Saraquel. 'When can we discuss him, then?'

'I shall be forced to go to London. Incidentally, there is a young man you might usefully contact, a Stephen McNamara. He was present at the . . . retirement of our old rival.'

The battle with Elizabeth Báthory. Conway knew an inquisitor had been injured but had survived what must have been an epic fight.

Andreotti sighed. 'He is struggling with the stress of being present at the end. He appears to be off the radar, I'm afraid. Perhaps someone who knew our mutual enemy could help counsel him. He may also know more about this Jackdaw Hammond. Come to Rome, my friend. We can discuss this with fewer listening ears.'

Conway knew the most watched and bugged office in the Vatican was Andreotti's. Hardly anyone knew him well, and he had lived a secretive life within the walls of the enclave under a number of aliases, including Andreotti.

Conway took down the details and rang off. Another revenant, and so close, just a short flight away. For a moment he made a mental audit of his aliases and security. No, he should be safe in Ireland but going to London would be dangerous. Damn it, he should have retired when Báthory was killed. Now someone else was tormented by Saraquel and, worse, he was expected to do something about it.

Chapter 5

Journal of Eliza Jane Weston, 23 November 1612

Saraquel had found me.

The countess stared at me, her blue eyes as dispassionate as if I were a dog, nay, even less dangerous. 'When your father performed the spell that bound me to my body,' she said, and I could not look away, 'I felt such energy, such power. But after time, it seeped away, and I felt my health failing. Only blood seemed to sustain me.'

Father, I thought, what do I do? In that moment, the babe wriggled inside me, and I resolved upon that instant to fight the creature – perhaps destroy it. I thought back to all my father had told me.

'I know something of the nature of revenants,' I said, choosing my words with care. 'My father warned me against such.'

'Souls held back from heaven by sorcery,' she mused, quoting Father Konrad of the Inquisition.

'Or hell,' I said.

'You correct me?' Her smile was that of amusement, but also wonderment. 'Does the mouse so offend the cat?'

'You shall kill me, or not,' I said, with more bravado than truth. 'The mouse cannot care about the outcome, since it is not his to determine.'

Edward Kelley, Prague, 1586

As we packed provisions for the journey to Brindisi, Dee and I spoke most urgently about the position of our families. While Marinello rested, feverish after his surgery, Dee wrote letters to the Emperor imploring him for his patience. But the Holy Roman court was quiet and lawyers' letters fluttered around us like bats.

It was with hope of a reply that Dee's steward allowed a nobleman into the house at the very moment at which I walked into the hall to see what was happening. My heart was filled with fear, nay, terror, when I saw a tall man in robes standing there, speaking German to the servant.

'Ah, I see your master,' he said, with some grim pleasure.

'Father Konrad,' I stammered, when I took in the red robes of the papal emissary. 'What . . . what business do you have here?'

'I come, strangely enough, on a matter of sorcery that does not involve you. For a change,' he added, flashing his long, white teeth from his great height. It was my destiny to be surrounded by men a foot higher than I, and I was no dwarf. But in his robes Reichsritter Johann Konrad von Schönborn, knight of the Holy Roman Empire, seemed seven feet tall. I was intrigued by what he said, however.

'Sorcery, my lord?' I said, stepping back from the doorway into Dee's study. 'I would like to know more.'

Konrad made a gesture to his two guards, and they fell back to watch the door. My mind raced to how we could escape from the Inquisition as my family were all around, and Protestant to a soul. He followed me into the study, ducking a little at the doorway, and looked around. There were charts upon the wall and books on the table. Without being asked, Konrad sat in Dee's chair, and I upon my usual stool, praying that we were not his targets.

'I have been asked to investigate a strange tale,' he said, still looking around the room. 'The story of a mythical golem, a man moulded of clay from the river, animated by a rabbi of Prague.'

All the town was buzzing with the tale; indeed, my master hoped to learn more. Perhaps the spells that animate clay might shed light on the mysteries of revenants such as Elizabeth Báthory, the countess whose unnatural and unholy survival we regretted and sought to end.

'I have heard of such,' I said cautiously.

'And I have heard of worse tidings for you,' he said quite affably. 'The very creature you held back from heaven has become a monster and, for some reason, is a guest of Emperor Rudolf's court this very day, having travelled from Transylvania in search of some answers of her own.'

If fear had struck me cold at seeing Konrad, the very blood froze in my veins at the thought of the countess here, in the same town as my children, and those of Dee. 'We must leave at once,' I said, my voice quivering. 'For she has tried to get me to work for her. She claims—' I swallowed hard, a lump bobbing in my throat like a mouthful of dry bread. 'She claims to be ensorcelled by some demon that makes her crave blood.'

Konrad stopped looking at Dee's books and stared instead at me. 'I tell you this because you may be able to help the Inquisition.'

I nodded without speaking. If I was on the Inquisition's business I was safe for a little while, perhaps long enough to find refuge in a Protestant country.

'For some years we have suspected that a few of these revenants roam Europe, and they share one thing in common.'

We were interrupted by Dee's man, who entered with a tray of cups and a jug of wine. When he left, Konrad lowered his voice.

'It may be that she has spies here already,' he said. 'It is common knowledge that you were freed from incarceration.'

'I am under house arrest,' I said. 'Following some irregularities in Venice. I am but one month released from prison. Some trumped-up charges of heresy, soon resolved.'

He cast me a look of scepticism. 'I want you to use Dee's knowledge to find out about this golem story from the Jews.' He sipped the wine, and grimaced. 'We will pay you to travel with Marinello, who goes to Alexandria where the rabbi Judah Loew has fled from Prague.'

My thought flew to Dee's request to go to Brindisi. 'We would need a heavy purse to travel so far,' I demurred.

He smiled. 'The Inquisition has deep pockets. And agents everywhere, my Protestant friend.'

'And the countess?'

'Here I cannot move against her, though she be Protestant. She and her husband are holding the Turks back from Vienna and who knows? Even Prague. She is under the Emperor's protection here.'

I relaxed a little. This was foolish.

Chapter 6

Present day, St Jude's refuge for homeless men and women, London

Inside St Jude's was dark with a corridor leading to a number of doors. The whole place smelled of stew. Jack pushed open the first door, marked 'Reception', which had a murmur of female voices behind it.

A young woman looked up and smiled. 'Hello, you're new. Can I help you?'

Jack looked around at two desks covered with files and two old computers, a couple of middle-aged women seated against a wall and a youngish man at a filing cabinet. She opened her mouth but nothing came out, strangled, she realised with indignation, by Saraquel.

The woman stood and walked over to Jack, talking a little slower and louder. 'Can I get you a cup of tea, at least? And maybe you would like to sit down. You look tired.'

After battling for a long moment with her stifled speech, Jack managed a single nod.

An older woman pulled out a chair by her desk. 'I'm Hazel. Can we help?'

The other woman smiled. 'And I'm Claire. Milk?'

What – oh, tea. Jack nodded. She shook her head at sugar. She looked around the room as she waited. There were leaflets and notices layering the walls, from libraries for the homeless to pamphlets about health care.

'Thanks, Claire.' Hazel perched one mug on the corner of the desk and handed the other to Jack. 'I can see you're having trouble talking. Is that new?'

Jack managed the tiniest of nods then tried to speak. It came out as a squawk rather than a word, so she nodded again. Her fingers were shaking, a dribble of tea spilling over the edge. She balanced the cup on the desk.

'Well, don't worry, just communicate however you feel most comfortable.' Hazel pulled her chair away from the computer. 'We offer a completely confidential service here. Unless we think you are going to hurt yourself or someone else, we don't even ask you for your full name, and we would never let any other agency know about you. We're just here to help, OK?'

Jack's eyes filled up with tears. It had been so long since she had fantasised about getting help, yet the presence inside her seemed to be struggling.

'How long have you been—?' The woman sipped her own drink, eyeing Jack over the rim.

Jack thought back. The days had started to blur into each other but it must be three weeks since she ran from the hospital. It was amazing how quickly her desperate struggle for survival had made real life seem like a dream, or a book she had once read. A book about a man called Felix. Tears started gathering, then dribbled down her face.

'A while, huh?' Hazel nodded slowly. 'I'm guessing you've left someone important behind?'

Jack covered her face in her hands and started to sob. It was a strange sensation, blotting out Saraquel and even the others in the room. It was as if it was just her and Hazel. The woman did nothing, didn't speak or comfort or interfere. When Jack looked up a large box of tissues had appeared and Hazel was waiting.

'Better out than in.' She smiled at Jack. 'Can I offer you some accommodation for the night? We have a bed in the women's dorm. I can't guarantee it's quiet but at least it's warm and cleanish.'

Jack strained a nod, Saraquel heaving on her neck muscles. Here, at least, he seemed to lose some of his power over her.

'We have a three-night policy, after that you have to be assessed by the team for a more permanent place.' Hazel's voice had taken on a more business like tone. 'You can sign up for benefits if you want.' She paused, seeing Jack's reaction. 'But you don't have to.' She handed Jack a leaflet. 'These are our guidelines. They're simple: we don't tolerate alcohol or drugs on the premises. They are too much of a problem with some of the clients.'

Jack clutched the leaflet, feeling the relief of being in control of herself, even under restraint. 'Thank – thank you.' She managed to squeeze out the words.

Hazel grinned at her. 'There you go. Can you tell me what you like to be called?'

Jack struggled with the words, finally closing her eyes and forcing Saraquel down. 'J – Jack.'

'Thank you, Jack. Let me show you where you can stay.'

29

Hazel took her to the women's bathroom, complete with a shower and a token-operated washing machine outside the door. She gave Jack a bag of donated clothes, including new underwear, and showed her the room with half a dozen beds, each separated by screens, with a small locker beside each.

'Try not to lose the locker key,' Hazel said, grimacing. 'You wouldn't believe how many we get through in a year.'

Jack was allocated number 4, a bed by the window, and Hazel quickly stretched a sheet over it and added a ready-covered duvet and pillow from a large pile in a cupboard.

Jack spent some time revelling in a long, lukewarm shower, and dressing in new clothes. It was a relief to throw away the men's things she had stolen from a locker in the hospital weeks before. She kept the rest of the money close. For some reason Saraquel was becoming more and more muted, and she had time to consider what would happen next. She could contact Felix, Maggie, Sadie, but something stopped her. Nothing had changed. She was the agent of a monster who could, for all she knew, hurt or even kill them while Jack was absent. This was a conundrum she had to solve for herself.

Part of her had had enough. She had fought death for more than twenty years, each day a battle against the torrent of cold that stilled her breath in her throat and slowed her heart to a funerary drumbeat. Another part of her just wanted to put one foot in front of the other until something better came along.

'You're new.' An elderly man stared at her behind a grizzled beard that seemed to compensate for his lack of hair. He swatted at his head, as if there was a fly. He looked pointedly down at her plate. 'You goin' to leave that?'

Jack pushed her half-eaten food across the scratched, laminate table. 'Help yourself.'

'Not for me.' He winked at her, and passed the plate down where the head of a border collie appeared and licked the plate clean. 'For Roly.'

She smiled, enjoying the hours without Saraquel. True, she felt tired and sick, and the cold was sneaking back in, all signs of her magical energy banks being low. She should try and find the herbs she needed, but she was afraid that if she left the building Saraquel would return.

'Not hungry?' One of the volunteers, Patsy, had obviously been watching. 'And, Terry, you know you're not supposed to feed Roly off the plate. Use one of the dog bowls.'

Jack watched the two banter, Patsy crouching down to make a fuss of the collie. A pull, almost like pain, reminded her of her own animals. Food tasted like ash, that was another problem, just bitter and dry. Saraquel was putting huge pressure on her to go out for the type of food he wanted. Steak, maybe, barely griddled, dripping with blood. With a lurch in her abdomen she realised that was what Saraquel wanted to feed on. Blood.

'You all right, love?' The woman smiled at her. 'You look a bit peaky. Can I?' She put her hand on Jack's forehead. 'You're very cold. Do you want me to get a fleece from the stores?'

In Jack's vision, time slowed down as the woman's thin wrist approached, the veins fuzzy with proximity, blue under the skin. She smelled like fresh, hot blood—

Jack jumped back. 'No! No, I'm fine, I'm just . . . it's sitting still.'

'Blood,' mumbled the bearded man, swatting again at his ear as if plagued by a swarm of insects.

'Well, let me know if you change your mind. How about a cup of tea?'

Jack swallowed down the blood thirst as her stomach roiled. 'Yes, thank you. Sorry—' She turned back to the man, now running his hands down his bald head as if trying to wipe something off. 'Did you say something?'

'You've got blood, I've got these liars.' He shouted into the room, making Jack jump. 'Liars, all of you!' His hands stalled, and he lowered them. 'Bastard liars,' he mumbled.

'What do you mean?'

'The voices. They talk about blood. Your ghost wants blood.' He cackled a laugh, revealing just three black teeth.

'You can hear him?' Jack leaned forward and asked again. 'My – ghost?'

But he was already mumbling to the dog, crooning something to it, lifting it onto his knees and letting it slobber over his mouth and nose.

Patsy returned and put the tea on the table, away from the dog's inquisitive snout. 'Don't mind him, Terry's harmless. He's just bothered by a few voices from time to time.'

'Liars!' Terry cackled again.

'Unreliable voices, apparently,' Patsy continued. 'You ever have any problems with voices you can't explain, love?'

Jack was quiet, but something about her stillness made Patsy nod, and smile sadly.

'We have a mental health outreach programme here,' she said, pointing at the noticeboard overhead. Jack craned her neck around to read it. 'No pressure, no hassle. You can accept any level of help you like, from just talking right up to medical treatment. OK?'

Jack nodded, and picked up the tea. It tasted like hot water but the warmth was comforting.

'OK. Thank you. But I think I'm all right.'

As the woman retreated, she turned back to Terry. 'What do the voices say?'

Terry swiped at his head again. 'They're lying.'

'Well, what lies are they saying, then?'

Terry looked at her with so much compassion in his eyes that Jack teared up. 'They say you are haunted by an angel.'

Chapter 7

Present day, Rome

The restaurant Robert Conway had chosen looked over the Piazza Navona, the fountain of Neptune playing on the water, the sound overwhelmed by the tourists, and vendors setting up the market. Andreotti made his way carefully over the paving to Conway's table. Robert shaded his eyes to watch his progress. The cardinal was very tall, very thin, and a little stooped over a flat document case. He was leaning on his cane but Conway suspected he was sprightlier than he made out. He sat and propped his stick against the table.

'My dear Robert,' he said, smiling at the waiter who rushed to serve him. Andreotti, for all his secrecy within the Vatican, spent a fortune on his street clothes and looked like a millionaire. He asked for an espresso, being very specific about the bean and the degree of roast. Conway enjoyed watching Andreotti charm the man. He decided to add to his stature.

'I'll have whatever His Eminence the cardinal is having,' he said.

When the man had gone, Andreotti opened the leather case and pulled out a slim file. Conway studied the papers before him.

The pictures of two revenants stood out. One was just a teenager, her pinched features and white skin declaring her frailty, common to revenants. Sadie Williams, the caption said, just fifteen. Most successful sorceries to create the undead were performed on young people, their life force was at its strongest. The other picture was labelled Jackdaw Hammond, the woman who had defeated Elizabeth Báthory by some means. Conway couldn't believe she hadn't used sorcery, but who really understood sorcery nowadays? He believed that only the voices from the fifteenth and sixteenth centuries could really capture the essence of magic, and his search for books and documents from that period gave him a unique breadth of knowledge.

'Interesting,' he said, turning over the page to gather the scant information. The child, Sadie, had a mother, a woman whose many trials had softened her with drink. 'The easiest way to find the child is to follow the mother.'

'We know where the child is,' Andreotti said, and nodded to the man bringing the coffees. 'So does our opposition.'

'So why delay? The child – send her on to heaven.' Conway turned to the Hammond woman's picture. 'There was an inquisitor present when Báthory was killed. What does he say?'

Andreotti grimaced. 'There we have a problem. Inquisitor Stephen McNamara is *simpatico* to the revenants. His own sister was cursed and one of Báthory's victims. When she – this Jackdaw Hammond – took Báthory's life, McNamara let Hammond go. Now we have a woman loose in London attacking prostitutes and drinking their blood. I think it is not a coincidence.'

Conway looked at the photographs in the middle of the file. There – the forensic pictures of the twisted, charred outline of what had once been a beautiful woman from the sixteenth century. The police had buried her remains as Sadie Williams. There had certainly been enough DNA of the child's spread about the site, it was easy for the inquisitors to plant a little on the charred remains. Elizabeth Báthory was really dead. Another wave of relief hit him – he had been tracking her most of his adult life but it was too dangerous to get close to her.

Conway put the papers away and closed the file. 'So where's the problem? The child's officially dead, the mother is already impaired. And this Jackdaw Hammond . . . who would miss her outside her own circle?'

'That circle includes Professor Felix Guichard. He was there at the *conflagrazione* of the countess.'

Conway leaned back in his chair and looked down at the folder. He had no doubt that Andreotti would destroy its contents after the meeting rather than risk losing them.

'Guichard had access to pages from Edward Kelley's Polish journal,' he said slowly. 'He is also well connected.'

'Not in our world.'

Felix Guichard. Not only was he a scholar of Dee and Kelley's writings but he was an expert on magical beliefs around the world. If he knew something of the nature of revenants, he could possibly shed light on questions Conway had been researching most of his life.

'And our competitors?' Conway asked. The Inquisition watched not only individuals but also big corporations. What medical research company could ignore the possible effects of magic? Even big banks had sorcerers on staff – the successful ones, anyway.

'Bachmeier and Holtz? They have been very quiet since the death of Báthory.' Andreotti slid the folder into the case. He drew out another photograph. 'Let us worry about them. What I need you to do is find McNamara and make sure he neutralises Hammond.' He handed over the picture of McNamara.

'Shame.' Conway looked at the stern features of the inquisitor, his iron-grey hair making him look older than his date of birth would suggest. 'He succeeded where even Konrad von Schönborn had failed.' The legendary knight and inquisitor had followed Elizabeth Báthory and other revenants throughout the 1500s and eliminated more of them than any other agent. But Elizabeth Báthory eluded him and he had almost died in the pursuit of her.

'And Edward Kelley.' Andreotti smiled. 'Even the great Dr Dee failed.'

Conway smiled back and toasted Andreotti with his coffee. 'Indeed. Let me talk to McNamara, see if I can bring him into the fold. And between us we will eliminate Jackdaw Hammond.'

Andreotti leaned back, threw a few notes on the table and flicked a crumb off his suit. 'I am following the investigation but I wanted to run one scenario past you.'

Conway tensed. 'Yes?'

'Is this the opportunity we have been waiting for, my friend? When Saraquel is weakened. Is this not the moment an *esorcisti* waits for? To crush him while he is off guard?'

Conway shook his head. 'I am sorry. I don't think it is possible.'

'If it were possible, it would be you who could do it, old friend. Never mind. We'll continue to eliminate the hosts and weaken him further. Perhaps we will find some advantage in that.'

Conway found his hands were trembling, the coffee slopping in the bottom of the small cup. He put it down with care. 'No one has ever succeeded in exorcising Saraquel.'

'I heard that it happened just once.'

'But the host was utterly destroyed in the attempt.'

Andreotti put his gnarled fingers over Conway's smaller hand for a moment. 'You know what they say about me in the office,' he said. 'The cardinal is going a little . . .' He circled a finger above his ear. '*Demente*. It is why I keep secluded within the Vatican, it is why I walk in disguise at night in the great churches.'

Conway smiled. 'You are no more demented than I am. All that experience came with a lot of years, that is all. No, I intend to retire. Soon.'

Andreotti looked him over briefly. 'You don't look old enough. But this job would wear anyone out. We'll get this inquisitor McNamara and track down this Hammond woman. God knows what evil Saraquel is wreaking through her.'

Chapter 8

Journal of Eliza Jane Weston, 23 November 1612

I watched the creature within the countess gain control.

'Saraquel,' I said, 'she seeks a way to remove you.'

'She dare not, lest she falls into a dead, empty husk.' The creature laughed, but it was a cracked sound like pain, as if he was unused to being amused. 'She suits my purpose as she is. Beautiful, ever young, and a viciously carnal creature.'

'She seeks freedom, nevertheless.' It was easier to treat with the creature than the aloof countess. 'What do you seek –' some instinct made me add '– my lord?'

'You humans have no idea of the gifts you have been granted,' it said, moving its head around strangely, like a lizard. 'Sensation, touch, smell. You have pleasure, pain, your senses drown in it. She shares the pleasures of her body with me. They all do.'

I thought rapidly. My father had told me a story that I hardly believed at the time, but it was so outlandish I thought him almost mad. 'My father—'

'We had some times together, Edward and I. Such adventures with Marinello.'

Edward Kelley, Prague, 1586

I conferred with Dee and Marinello as soon as I could. Dee was worried about working with the Inquisition, but Marinello was more concerned about the money. When assured he would be paid a sum to arrange our passage, and with his own plans to profit from the sale of his ship, he at least was easy.

Having been warned about the countess's presence in Prague, we were still unprepared for her visit. Dee was at Konrad's lodging in the court planning the journey, Marinello was sleeping, still weak from the surgery, when she appeared. She came, not with her own attendants, but eight Imperial guards and a signed order from the Emperor. I was bundled up by a soldier and muffled by a brawny forearm before I heard the shrieks of the women.

My children and Dee's were at their letters in an upper room, and were soon gathered into the hall with no time to put on more than their outside boots and cloaks. I fought, though my toes barely touched the ground, and managed to bite hard upon the fellow's forearm. A glancing blow sent me sprawling before the guards but the distraction gave Marinello, in his nightshirt and still half dazed with fever, an opportunity to lay about him with his sword. Unable to swing it properly in the small room, certainly not without hurting the children, he used the hilt upon the helmets of the guards to send three sprawling beside me, and I pulled a further one down with a blow to the knee. But then, the inevitable. The remaining men held Marinello fast, and bound him with a veritable suit of ropes.

Only then did the heavily veiled countess advance into the room. 'Franco,' she said, to his sweating face. 'My erstwhile lover. In a room with my enemy?' I knew her voice instantly.

He shook off one of his handlers, leaning against the wall. 'I know you,' he said, throwing back his black curls. 'I know what you are.'

'I am a woman,' she said. Her hand caressed his cheek, then moved to the ruby in his ear. 'But as our mutual friend will confirm, I am also overshadowed by a spirit, a spirit that causes me to indulge the worst impulses.' With a quick movement, she ripped the jewel from his ear, leaving a thin trickle of blood down his neck. With a strange expression on her countenance, she leaned forward, her tongue already out, but he spat in her face and she recoiled. It seemed to me as if confusion reigned within her for a moment, then the sardonic look was back. 'As your friend could confirm, you would be advised to go gently, Franco. Lest my appetites take me towards the . . . tenderer flesh.'

She looked at the small group of children, huddled between their mothers and a maid.

I stood and stepped forward. 'I have known a gentler lady,' I said, 'who showed mercy.'

Then her voice changed, as if she were herself transformed into that creature. 'A queen,' she said softly, 'in mine own kingdom.'

Dee intervened. 'My lady, we are your mortal enemies however gentle we speak. It was your destiny to lie underground, and we broke the laws of God to save you. We can only work for your release from this terrible state. Your survival only darkens your soul further.'

She spread her hands out. 'And yet – if I die, or fail to bear Lord Nádasdy a son, the last boundary against the invasion of the Turks will fall and the roads to Rome, Vienna and Prague are open.' She shrugged. 'We Transylvanians have borne the brunt of the invasion. If we give way Europe – and Christianity – lies helpless before them. The troops Lord Nádasdy commands stand guard, funded largely by my family and our allies. If Lord Nádasdy falls without an heir, that money is lost to the cause.'

Dee bowed. 'That destiny must be defined by God alone, my lady. But what we did together was manifestly wrong, only achieved through our weakness and intimidation after you kidnapped us.'

'My spies tell me you seek knowledge in Brindisi, from the Jews there. They report that you seek to understand the secrets in order to undo the spell that gives me life. I need you to make that spell, remake it if you need, to lift the curse that haunts my family. For the Jews know the mystery of life and death.'

Dee glanced at me. Gold is a powerful master, one of our servants must have betrayed us.

She sighed, the breath just reaching her veil. Her musical voice was persuasive, now we knew we stood in no danger. 'Gentlemen, I respect your convictions even as I grieve the necessity of the coercion I must apply.'

Her words, while losing none of their softness, rang through my head like a bell. Coercion?

'What can you mean, my lady?' Dee's voice was sharp.

'I carry an edict issued by the Emperor. Your families are under arrest and will be held at the Emperor's command. You are no longer welcome in Prague, or anywhere in the Empire.'

My little son John and daughter Eliza, snatched up to be held in the rat hole I had only just been released from?

'I will go to his Imperial Majesty immediately, and plead mercy.' Dee looked pale, his hands shook. He had feared this moment, I knew, but now that it was here a suspicious seed took root in my brain.

I turned to the countess. 'It is no coincidence that you arrive here to tell us this terrible news.'

'Certainly I would like you to have a most urgent reason to work on my difficulty. In four months I shall give birth to my son, for surely heaven would not be cruel enough to taunt me with a daughter. My son shall not be borne to a mother who seeks his destruction even as he passes from her body.'

Dee's face was as resolute as I have ever seen it. 'If my wife or my children are harmed I shall send you straight to hell, if I have to speak every word backward and undo every action that shackled your black spirit to your body.'

'And my child?' The woman seemed unmoved by his anger. 'You would condemn an innocent along with me?'

'It is the child of a monster who squats in your carcass,' I managed to say.

She turned to face, it seemed, the entire room. 'Your presence in Prague is no longer welcome. Your families will be safe under house arrest, and will remain so while you are on the business of an ally of the Empire.'

'How did you know our business?' I said.

She made to leave, then stopped. There was laughter in her voice. 'Do not blame me, Master Kelley, but Marinello. If his letters were not so casually sent in the hands of merchants I would never have known where to find you, nor how to control you.'

'If harm comes to my family—' Dee was as angry as I had ever seen him.

She bowed her head a fraction. 'None shall. But be certain, gentlemen, that if aught happens to me the same shall befall your families. For you must know—' She paced along the floor, her skirts brushing up the herbs placed there not a few days ago. 'There is a voice inside my head. A monstrous presence.'

Dee looked at me, and I knew he had some concern about my strange speech in my sleep. 'Does this presence have a name? Is it Saraquel?'

Her eyes stared into mine, deep blue in the candlelight. 'It prevents me speaking its name.'

'Like a demon,' I asked, afraid of the answer. 'Would that we knew his nature, my lady, we might exorcise him.'

A shiver through her whole body confirmed my suspicions. When she had first been saved, a magical ritual binding of her soul to her failing body, she had spoken to me. *Go, Edward. But remember me as Saraquel*.

Dee answered her. 'Saraquel. Which is not the name of a demon at all, but one of the sacred angels of the first book of Enoch.'

I knew it was one of the earliest religious texts. I had opened my mind to angels, and those that had spoken to me had been just whispers compared to Saraquel's voice. Yet he, a supposed angel, had spoken to me through an impure creature born of death and sorcery and sustained by witchcraft and spells.

Dee stepped forward, and she was forced to look up into his face.

'An angel is a creature of light, not darkness and death,' he said. 'We go, not to prolong your unnatural existence, but to understand what we did on that day, in captivity, in your diabolical castle.'

'I too need to know what you did to me,' she hissed back. 'You were tasked with saving my life, healing my body. My sickness, unnatural though you call it, was passed to me by my mother, and to her from her mother. All I asked is that you sustain my body as Zsuzsanna the witch had done for me. But you did far more than save me from death. I am overcome with such thoughts, such longings that I cannot deny them.'

'You must resist them,' Dee said. 'For they are thoughts of great cruelty and destruction. Your own people—'

She stepped back, and I watched her face change, a slow smile dawning as she turned to me. 'Why should I save them?' she said, baring her teeth. 'Am I not their overlord?' I shuddered as I saw the look in her eyes. Then a cloud came over them, and some confusion, and she held out a hand to me. 'Am I possessed?' she asked me. 'Speak truthfully, Edward, for I know when you lie.'

'I fear it, my lady,' I said. 'I fear we have both been.'

She turned to Dee. 'Then hasten upon your journey and find a way to get this demon from my life lest I feast upon my own newborn child. That is my nightmare, Dr Dee. My servants find me blood from young girls, bled like cattle so I might be sustained. Young men open their veins for me. But soon I know I shall need more.'

Dee looked at her. 'Lady, if you are to be saved, you must seek penitence and prayer. You must seek refuge within an abbey.'

She snapped her head back to him. 'How dare you speak thus? I, a countess of the royal house, to be confined to a convent like an adulterous housewife?' She slashed her hand down as she spoke.

But Dee stood firm. 'And you must abstain from taking blood.'

'Without it I will weaken. Perhaps endangering my babe.'

I took one small step towards her, driven to speak from some voice within. 'My lady,' I said, my voice shaking like a leaf in autumn. 'You know the herbs will sustain you. And prayer will weaken this – demon – within you. Blood fortifies him.'

I could not be sure our arguments had worked, but we had given her the idea that strengthening her human nature would protect the child. She ensured we had enough gold for the journey, being generous even. I knew we should hold her prisoner and exorcise her of her devil, allow her soul to be judged in heaven – but I knew in my heart that the creature that flamed in the countess's heart was no demon.

Chapter 9

Present day, London

Jack felt better. Three nights of sleep, proper sleep, and three days of being herself had given her time to get some perspective. She found herself crying, grieving for her old life, for the promise of a relationship with Felix, but now she felt more able to deal with Saraquel.

She had tried to engage Terry in conversation again, but he was incomprehensible in his delusions. At breakfast on the third day, she left half a bowl of porridge and pushed it across the table towards him. After a long moment, he snatched it and passed spoonfuls down to the dog. In between, he ate some himself, making Jack wince as he shared the same spoon.

'Tell me more about angels,' she said, in a casual manner. 'I don't know anything about them.'

He screwed his eyes shut. 'I'm not supposed to talk about the voices.'

'But I have voices of my own,' she said softly, so it didn't get anyone else's attention. 'I'm sure it's OK if we both have them.'

'I used to be a teacher,' he said, quite out of the blue. 'I used to teach English. Shakespeare, Chaucer.'

'Oh. Really? Do you miss it?' Jack watched him start humming to himself, until his eyelids started to droop. 'Terry?'

When he looked back, he was sharper. 'Your angel is a hundred times bigger than you,' he said, his tone matter-of-fact. 'If he spread his wings out, they would go right across the road. And into the car park.'

'So, angels really do have wings,' she prompted. 'I did wonder.'

'And he's in a hundred places at once. Or a thousand. I forget which.'

She sat back and digested that. 'But why is he in me, when he's a huge angel with wings and can be in a hundred places?'

He leaned down to stroke the dog, and mumbled something.

'What, Terry?'

He shrugged a shoulder up, as if warding her off. 'I've got lots of liars, me. They don't like your angel. You should go.'

She nodded slowly. 'I was hoping to get rid of the angel. He's – too big for me.'

'He wants blood, that's what's wrong. He wants to eat me and my dog Roly. To drink our blood.'

Jack put as much calm into her voice as she could manage. 'Well, I won't hurt anyone, Terry, I promise.'

He shook his head, swatting again at the invisible voices. 'You're going to hurt me like you did those girls.'

'What? No—' She put out a hand but he slapped it away. 'I haven't hurt anyone.'

'Those girls! I saw you, at St Paul's, I remember now. It was you!' He jumped to his feet, rocking the table. One of the bowls fell to the floor and shattered, making the dog bark.

A helper was already on hand. 'Go away, please. We'll look after Terry.'

'I was just—'

He waved her away, and she walked to the door feeling more isolated than she had for days. She went out to the quiet reception, where Hazel was making herself a cup of tea.

'Hello, Jack.' She yawned and stirred her drink. 'Do you want one?'

'No.' Jack tried to make sense of the man's ramblings. 'Have there been any assaults on girls around here lately?'

Hazel stopped stirring. 'I suppose you haven't caught up with the news. There have been a couple of girls, sex workers, who have been attacked by some man who cut them. The police have been all over the area interviewing people. They talked to some of our men yesterday.'

Jack shook her head. 'I had no idea.'

'I wanted to warn you – well, all the women. Be especially careful out there when you leave.'

'You said I had three days, then you might be able to arrange more.' Panic surged into Jack's chest.

'First we have to talk about what happens next.' Hazel reached across her keyboard for a sheaf of forms. 'You are entitled to some benefits, and we think it would be in your best interests to apply.'

Jack shook her head. 'I can't.'

Hazel smiled, but it was a sad grimace as if she had heard it too many times before. 'Isn't there anyone out there who is missing you? Who would help? I know it's hard to go back—'

'It's impossible. I hurt someone. I'm afraid I would do it again.'

Hazel's voice was soft but it cut into Jack. 'Nothing you could do will hurt as much as you disappearing, Jack. At least let them know you are OK. We use an anonymous system—'

Hazel's image blurred and Jack sniffed. 'I can't. I have to sort this out myself.'

49

Hazel pushed a box of tissues across the desk, and Jack dried her eyes, fighting back the images of Charley and Maggie, Sadie and Felix.

'Well, can I suggest something?' Hazel's voice was kind. 'There's a rehab and retreat centre called St Francis's, they take volunteers there. It's in the country, in Hampshire. No questions asked, just hard work and good food. You might find your feet there. I phoned yesterday to see if there might be room for you. The woman that runs it used to work here, she said she could find a place for you. It's pretty basic and they work in silence all day, but that might suit you.'

Jack knew she couldn't let Saraquel loose in the city again. Maybe if it was a church retreat like St Jude's Saraquel would be suppressed. 'Let me have the details,' she said.

'It's a Christian community. The place used to be a convent so there's a chapel,' Hazel said. 'I know you like the cathedral. I could arrange to get a lift out there, if you want.'

The quiescent Saraquel lurched inside her with discomfort. 'How long was it a convent?' Jack asked, feeling inside herself for the reaction.

'A couple of hundred years, I think. There aren't enough nuns left to run it as a religious community, though a couple of elderly nuns still live there.'

Again, the compulsion to run, the discomfort of the thing banked down inside her. 'Give me the details, I'll think about it.'

Of course, Saraquel took over when she left the shelter. She sat outside against the wall for several hours, feeling him fight for dominance, and when he won she was dragged away from the shelter down to the river. For a long hour she fought with him, ranting and arguing, making walkers step around her and a couple of kids jeer at her. They distracted her – and she was gone.

When she was aware again, she was lying at the base of some statue or other in a park. She didn't recognise where she was, but every muscle ached. Her face was sore, bruised, as if someone had hit her on the cheekbone, maybe even cracking it. Her lips were swollen and split, and when she looked around she saw a bundle of rags a few feet away. Sitting up shot a stabbing pain from her chest into her abdomen, and she crawled over to the shape, cradling her ribs with one arm.

An old woman lay on her side, blood trickling from her face and neck. Her eyes were black and swollen shut, and her toothless mouth was open as if in a protest. Jack tentatively touched her throat, to feel the flicker of a pulse there.

'Help!' Jack croaked, then tried again. 'Help – over here.' She buried her face in her arms and wept. She could feel a pull towards the blood on the old woman, the agony of knowing what she had done. Saraquel lapped up her despair, she could feel her sanity dripping away—

'Are you OK?'

She looked up to see a man with a spaniel staring at her.

Saraquel muted her tongue, but the man crouched down close to her, close enough to make her flinch away. 'I've called the police,' he said. 'I think you've been mugged.'

Jack pointed mutely at the bundle of clothes beside her.

He leaned in to see. 'Oh, God, is she dead?'

Jack shook her head, taking one of the old woman's hands in her own.

He took a phone from his pocket and dialled. 'Ambulance – and police, I think. Yes, police. There are two women here . . .'

The words drifted over Jack. The dog's nose touched her face and she put out a hand, but the man must have pulled the animal back. Saraquel swept towards the pain and the world faded. The next time she was aware, she was confronting a female police officer at the gate of, she assumed, the same park.

'It's all right, love, I'm not going to hurt you.'

Jack flickered in and out of awareness, then an arm swept around her chest and lifted her off her feet in blaze of agony, greedily fed on by Saraquel. The next sensation was of lying restrained amid bright lights and sirens and finally, the oblivion of sedation.

Chapter 10

Present day, Bee Cottage, Lake District

Felix sat at the kitchen table, reading an article on his laptop. The house was comfortable, and few people knew of Jack and Sadie's connection to it. Sadie slumped onto a chair next to him, still in her pyjamas. She had taken Jack's disappearance worse that he had expected. Sadie and Jack had bonded since the fifteen-year-old's abduction the previous autumn.

'How are you feeling, Sadie? Can I get you anything?' He knew he couldn't do much, but Maggie was out shopping. Jack's foster mother, sick with worry, had turned all her concerns onto Sadie, and he had almost pushed her out the door for a change of scenery.

She shrugged a shoulder, although he had heard her retching upstairs again. She was haunted by nausea which would, had nature taken its course, have been her cause of death.

'Bored. I hate this.'

He winced, there was nothing he could say to comfort her. She was too ill to go out, too ill to enjoy much indoors, even inside the protective circle of symbols in every room. She covered her mouth as her abdomen cramped again, then curled up on the chair, the other arm over her stomach. Her wrists, sliding out of her sleeves, were so thin he could see every tendon, every bone under the pale skin.

'What are you reading?' she asked, but didn't look very interested.

'I'm looking into the condition that the hospital thought Jack had. There are articles on "multiple organ dysfunction syndrome" that suggest treatments.' He could see her hand shaking over her mouth. 'Do you want me to get you a bowl?'

She shook her head, but she was shivering. 'I just can't get warm today.'

He reached around to the back of the chair where he had hung his fleece.

Sadie stood and wrapped herself up in it before curling into a ball on her seat. 'I feel worse every week,' she said in a conversational tone. 'When Jack was my age, she was really weak too, but at least she was getting better.'

He scanned the rest of the article, then sat back. 'I wonder – how would you feel about having a blood test?'

'Why?' She glanced at him from between her long fringe and the collar of the jacket.

'I just wondered . . .' he started. He thought through the ideas the article had raised. 'Borrowed time, that's what you all call it. Somehow you survive your death—'

'Through sorcery,' she prompted.

'—through sorcery,' he said. 'You have been caught at the point of death and suspended there. But from a biological point of view, what's really happening? Jack was abducted when she was a child but she still grew, she still functioned for nearly twenty years. Yet the hospital said she had a recognised condition they had seen before.'

Sadie sighed, rolling her forehead on her knees. 'I just wish the sorcery made you healthy as well as kept you alive.'

He leaned back in his chair, looking at her paper-white face, the deep shadows under her sunken eyes. Sadie wasn't improving, she was deteriorating despite all the magic Maggie, the witch who had saved her, could do.

'Just before terminally ill people die, their organs start to fail. There's a sort of avalanche in the body, one cell dies, it gives off signals and more start to fail.'

'OK,' Sadie said into her knees.

'Suppose that's what borrowed time is?' The idea started to get exciting. 'Suppose that process is arrested by the symbols and the herbs? That would mean the person is always weak, always dependent on the magic, but isn't dead, they are still alive. Some people get better from this medical condition, at least, if it's not too advanced.'

Sadie lifted her head enough to look at him from under her fringe. She didn't shrug, which was close to a sign of interest from the teenager. 'Do they?'

'There are treatments for multi-organ failure.' He sat back, rolling the concept around in his head.

She stared at him for a long moment. 'Is there a cure for being possessed by a demon?'

He opened his mouth but the words wouldn't come. His mind raced on with speculations. 'Maybe Jack is possessed because she is so weak, her body is barely her own. Maybe there was room for Saraquel because she was hardly inhabiting her body, because it was so close to death.' Thinking out loud, he carried on. 'Which means we could try treating you and Jack. If we can make you both stronger, we might be able to help Jack fight whatever it is.'

'If you can find her.' Sadie then lifted her head up, as if she were listening to something.

'What is it?'

She shrugged. 'I don't know. Something in the garden.'

'What do you think about my idea?'

'What do you expect me to say? You've found something on the Internet and you want to experiment on me so you can help Jack. Great.'

He smiled down at her. 'I'm trying to help you too.'

She sighed again, exaggerating the wince that accompanied it. 'OK, so you want to stick a needle in me and take blood. I hate needles.'

Seeing the dog, he patted his leg. Ches, who had been listless since Jack had gone missing, slumped against his knee, a little whine expelled as he sagged to the floor. 'I was going to ask a doctor friend of mine to look at a small sample, that's all.'

That made her sit up. 'Which bit of me living in hiding did you not understand?'

He smiled again. 'You sound just like Jack.'

She clamped her hand to her mouth again, fighting down the nausea, while he fetched her a bowl. She pushed it onto the table. 'There is something in the garden, I can feel it. The garden feels it.'

Felix didn't question her intuition about the acre of barely tamed wilderness that surrounded the medieval cottage; Sadie seemed to have a psychic connection to it. He followed Sadie as she pushed herself off the chair and shuffled her way to the kitchen door. She stepped into Jack's boots. He reached over her shoulder to draw back the bolt, and followed her over the rough grass.

He'd mowed the ground a number of times, but the wild lawn seemed to grow back overnight, and he had to steady the girl as she stumbled along the path.

'Stay in the circles,' he warned, barely able to see the symbols carved into the ground. He scanned the deep hedges and stands of elder trees, draped in ivy. 'I can't see anything,' he said, looking into the bushes along the back wall.

'Listen.' She looked around at ground level, at banks of resurgent nettles, and pointed at the elder trees that dominated the centre of the plot, interlaced with brambles as thick as his thumb. She put her head on one side. 'There's something here.'

A deep cawing came from an upstairs window, followed by a knocking sound. Jack had left a half-tamed raven behind, and even with Sadie's efforts to give him attention, he was getting more destructive. Apart from that, the garden was silent, even the squabbling from the rookery behind the house seemed to have abated.

'Felix – look!' Her voice was more animated that he'd heard it since Jack had disappeared. 'It's a cat.'

Cat, no, he corrected mentally. It was a tiny black-and-white kitten, maybe six weeks old. It shrank down as they approached, but then its nerve broke and it scampered back into the leaves, dragging a leg behind it.

'Oh, you have to rescue it,' Sadie said, wobbling at the edge of the weeds and peering in. 'It's hurt.' Some of the nettles were shoulder high, and woven among them were the most vicious brambles and blackthorns he had ever encountered. He still had scars from reaching through them once before.

'Let's try a less invasive approach,' he said. 'Get back inside the circle while I get some meat.'

He went into the kitchen and put a few forkfuls of dog meat on a saucer, pacifying Ches with the rest of the can, then locked him into the hall. Sadie had crouched down in the wet grass, careless of her pyjamas and, for that matter, his fleece. She was crooning to the invisible kitten.

He could see the movement of the black ears and white chin as it scented the air. Sadie took the saucer.

'Get ready to catch it,' she said, and tapped the saucer gently, waving it close to the nettles then putting the dish down. 'Come on, little kitty. Come on, baby cat.'

Slowly, the rustling and movements became more purposeful as patches of black fur and white fur wove their way through the dense foliage. A head, with black down to the eyes making it look like a bandit's mask, poked through the grasses and sniffed the meat a few inches away.

Keeping an eye on Sadie, the kitten crept forward, belly to the grass, then hooked a paw full of meat onto the ground. When no one moved it bent to eat and Felix's hand shot out, scruffing the tiny creature and lifting it up. It seemed to weigh almost nothing. It squealed, provoking a protest from Sadie, and before it could get one of its starfished claws into his hand, he cradled it against himself. It was bird-thin and stank. It was also wide-eyed and panting with panic, and every claw had shot through his thin shirt into his skin, but he got the impression it wasn't completely feral. It relaxed, curling against him.

Sadie picked up the saucer and held it up to the kitten, who sniffed the air again. 'You have to come in, now,' she murmured to the cat. 'We rescue people here.'

Chapter 11

Journal of Eliza Jane Weston, 23 November 1612

I put out my hands in supplication to the spirit before me.

'When I am gone,' I said, 'the secrets will die with me.'

A look flew across the face of the countess, still beautiful, still young although I knew she was in her fifties. It was an expression of determination, as she fought down the intruder to find herself again.

'So there are secrets?' she breathed, and turned to the fireplace, alas, empty. 'You look cold, madam, let me summon your man that he may light a fire.'

I declined since we had no wood, but she divined the problem and called Tomáš to the chamber. She spoke to him, an imperious lady, and threw him a gold coin that flashed in the air as it travelled to his hand. He ran off bowing and I heard him clatter down the stairs to buy fuel.

She turned her attention back to me. 'Tell me, what of your father?'

'My father is dead, my lady,' I said, 'these fifteen years.'

Edward Kelley, on the road to Venice, 1586

And so we went upon the errands of the Inquisition and the monster Báthory. We made a strange band of travellers. I, in my round cap and new cloak, carried a lot of the baggage. Dee had only packed books before I made him leave some behind to make room for clothes, and Marinello was still recovering from the fever after his surgery. One of Konrad's guards, a man called Márton, proved to be a good companion and travelled with songs as well as bags. Marinello's servant made up the last of the party, a weasel-faced fellow called Giuseppe who was much occupied with Marinello's vast wardrobe, which had a mount of its own. But the hired horses were good, paid for by Konrad, and a heavy purse from the countess rested within Dee's doublet.

I had sent a letter to Konrad's quarters at court, and he pledged to ensure the safety of our families. The morning after the countess had come to us, he sent a guard to escort us to a large house on the outskirts of Prague where our families were held in some comfort at the order of the Emperor. Jane Dee was tearful, she had not expected her greybeard husband to go adventuring again, but he filled her ears with reassurances. We would simply travel under Marinello's protection to Brindisi, and thence to Alexandria. With his seafaring experience we would be soon be home. Four months, no more. He even jested that the hot sun would make him heartier, and burn his face as brown as a Turk. Mistress Jane took me aside and begged me to use my influence to remind her husband to eat, to sleep, and not to return to her as close to death as he had after his expedition to Poland.

I promised to do my best, and in gratitude, Jane touched both her hands to my face and kissed my cheek. Marinello, seeing the embrace, demanded a kiss too, then one from every female in our household from the children down to the servants. Jane Dee declared him cured, and sent us on our way at least with the appearance of complaisance. Konrad had promised to offer support to the two women, and our expedition set off in grand style, with all the women, children and servants waving. Marinello postured upon his horse, making it capriole in the cobbled yard, casting sparks from its metal shoes with each jump to the enchantment of the children.

Our journey to Venice took thirteen days over good roads. At each stage, Marinello paid out of the Inquisition's purse for a group of fresh mounts and two grooms, the men both as protection and to return the horses. At night, we tired travellers slept in inns and farms, somewhat better housed that we could have afforded without the countess's and Konrad's money. It seemed strange to all to be funded by the very agencies which sought our deaths.

Finally, the floating towers and domes of Venice hove into sight, and we exchanged dusty horses for shiny boats and were ferried with our luggage to Venice. I was as enchanted by the view as ever; the houses appeared to rest directly upon the shimmering water.

My previous landfalls on Venice had been difficult, however – on one I had been beaten unconscious and robbed; on the other occasion I had been in the custody of the Inquisition. I clung to my bags, one hand on the hilt of the dagger stored in a secret pocket there. Dee, who was a better traveller, was fascinated and exclaimed at every sight, demanding of Marinello information about everything he could see.

Marinello took us straight to the docks where he leaped ashore then visited the wharf where lay his ship. He had not paid his crew's wages and they were angry at first, but soon appeased by sight of gold. They went back to work on the two-masted vessel, very small in my eyes against the storms of the Mediterranean. After inspecting it thoroughly, showing us its many strengths, Marinello announced himself satisfied. He gave the master of men a long list of repairs and tasks to perform against our journey, speaking in liquid Vèneto, the native language of the Venetians. Dee found it interesting, having a smattering of Italian, that the Venetians had their own dialect, and questioned Marinello through the streets as Márton, Giuseppe and I struggled with the baggage.

Marinello called out to acquaintances as he strode to the door of his own palazzo. Here, I was surprised to see his wife in residence, a black-haired beauty much shorter than Marinello, and inclined to hurl a great deal of Vèneto abuse at her husband. He pacified her with a hearty kiss and called for his children, two boys and a baby girl, to be presented to their 'honoured guests'. The elder boy, a grave young man of nine or ten, was much impressed to meet a mathematician, and spent some time quizzing Dee about navigation. The younger boy, a merry seven-year-old, made much of his father and demanded to know of his adventures. He wished, in broken Latin, that he was old enough to travel to Candia, but Marinello soon sent the children back to the nursery and took us over to a cabinet filled with maps.

He brought out a great scroll, and laid it upon a table in the corner of the room beside a window two yards high, filled with glass panes gathering sunlight. 'Here,' he said, rolling the vellum out with care, dropping his heavy gauntlets and his purse on the corners to keep it flat. 'This was my grandfather's map of the Mediterranean seas.'

It was a long scroll, and coloured with faded inks. The coast ran down one side, and the opposing coast of Albania and Greece wriggled along the other. The islands were sharply defined in darker ink. Venice was a single red figure of a church on the top left-hand corner. Lines of navigation, shoals and smaller islands were all marked in tiny script. Dee's eyesight was insufficient to decipher them without his eyeglasses, so he called on me to read them out.

'Napoli, Malta, here on the other side, Brindisi – Candia, beside Greece. Many leagues by ship from Venice.'

Dee looked up at Marinello. 'You say this ship will get us to Brindisi?'

'Easily. I have a half-share in a ship at Candia, and my own carrack rests at Alexandria under distraint. I can take you and Master Kelley to Brindisi, then on to Candia to regain the larger craft.'

Dee nodded. 'If the situation was different I would love to explore the islands, but our families must be our first concern.'

I was still curious. 'How can you make your fortune if your ship is under distraint?'

'I will trade salted fish, wire and glass with the Candians, then buy their wine and oil to take to Alexandria,' Marinello said. 'I can sell it at market there, and pay off my debts to relieve the ship. I shall release my goods in storage, if the lazy, thieving bastard I left in charge has not sold the lot, and I shall return to Venice with both ships full, a rich man. If not –' he shrugged and grinned at me '– I shall sell the smaller ship to gain the larger. My partner will understand.'

He made it seem easy, but his wife, who seemed to understand Latin, rolled her eyes and left the room.

Marinello pointed to a tiny blot upon the scroll. 'Here I know the captain of the pirates. I think he will help me through the straits here, and through the Ottoman areas.' His finger stabbed an area south of the Grecian mainland. 'My father kept *routiers*, I have added my own notes to them with each voyage. I know these seas well, I have been sailing them since I was a boy.' He smiled a little ruefully. 'At least, I hope the pirate captain is still allied to Venice. Gold may be needed to buy his assistance.'

I bent over the map. 'Could you not outrun or fight him if this pirate has a thought to take your ship?' I knew little of warships but had some experience of trading vessels plying the Irish Sea and English Channel.

'Fully laden, I can't outrun them. And fighting would be impossible. I have seen these corsairs sting trading ships like hornets: dart in, hole the craft below the waterline, dart out, all while guns fire overhead. In the end, the crews spend all their time trying to save the ship from sinking. And any resistance to boarding is met with certain, savage death. I have seen pirates behead every sailor on board because just one raised a dagger to them. They are the terror of the seas.'

I felt my stomach tighten, and my mouth filled with acid liquid. I have a healthy fear of armed ruffians on land, on sea they seemed the creatures of nightmares. 'But there is little danger just going to Brindisi?'

'Do not fear, my little sorcerer.' He laughed and ruffled my hair much as he did his son's. 'I'll keep you safe from the godless Ottoman pirates.'

Chapter 12

Present day, Royal London Hospital

Robert Conway sat in the chair the nurse had set beside the young woman in the hospital bed. She stared resentfully back at him.

'I'm an investigator—'

'Why should I talk to you?' she snapped, running a hand through her bleached fringe. She had spots and greasy hair, he estimated her age as her late teens. 'If you're a reporter I want money.'

He smiled back at her as he assembled his lies. 'I'm not a reporter, Ms Hillman, but if you are eligible I am authorised to pay you a small sum for expenses. I represent a not-for-profit organisation that is doing research into—'

'How much?' she said, the lies rolling off her indifference.

He could see that she was in the grip of addiction and would only speak to the promise of drugs or the money to buy them. He sighed. She was so young.

'I can give you a hundred pounds.' Which was a nuisance, because he only had a small amount of sterling on him. He would have to go to a bank, which was difficult as it was easy to trace, and his bad leg was painful after the flight from Rome and the taxi ride. Still, the Inquisition was generous with his expenses and she might hold the key to the rash of attacks on women.

'I've got a kid,' she whined, the sunlight making her look even younger, as if her skin was transparent, veins tracing their way across her forehead and cheek. 'A baby girl.'

'One hundred and twenty pounds,' he said, mentally counting all the notes he had on him. 'Now, can you describe the person who attacked you?'

She leaned back against the pillow, which crackled as if it was covered with plastic. She touched a hand to the dressing on the side of her neck, swallowing awkwardly. 'There was a woman, she spoke to me first.'

'First?'

The girl hesitated, then lowered her hand to touch her other wrist, the one with the drip. 'She was nice, at first, but she was funny. I thought – you, know, she was high.'

'Can you describe her?'

The girl's face changed, as if she was trying to remember. 'I don't know. About your height, a bit shorter maybe, thin, scruffy. I think light-haired. All I remember is her eyes, really. They were green. Then I don't remember anything until he jumped out.'

'He?' Conway was impressed as few people recalled anything from an encounter with a possessed revenant. They had a hypnotic power they used to influence people.

'There was this man, he shouted at me. He grabbed me, put his hand on my neck to stop the bleeding.'

'Your neck?' Robert glanced at her as she pulled the top of her gown down gently, revealing more dressings. 'Can you unwrap it?'

She rolled her eyes, but peeled back one edge of the dressing. There was a clean cut, neatly held together with adhesive tape strips, but around it were purple bruises in semicircles that looked like toothmarks. It also looked infected.

'He pressed his hand on it, to stop the bleeding,' she said, carefully replacing the dressing and pulling her gown up over it. 'Then he sort of prayed over me.'

'Did he tell you his name?' Conway smiled at the girl, watching her expression change as she pushed her hair back again.

'What's it worth to you?' She licked her lips, momentarily looking towards the window.

He pulled out his wallet. 'One hundred and twenty pounds and . . . eighty-three euros. That's it, that's everything I have on me. But—' he pulled his hand out of the reach of her outstretched fingers. 'I will give you nothing unless you tell me everything you know.'

She opened her mouth to protest, but her eyes were fixed on the notes. She started talking.

The man had visited her in hospital, claiming to be a detective, she didn't know or care who he was. He had paid, too, and showed her a photograph of a woman who might be the one that attacked her. He never gave his name but she described him as forty, tall, thin and 'scary'. Finally, he had written down a number for her to call if she remembered anything else, and she reluctantly allowed Conway to jot it down.

She stretched out her hands for the money, her cold fingers brushing his when she took the bundled notes and held out her other hand for the change. A moment of compassion flared in him. He had seen addiction before, and had a sense that this would be one of the children who would fall to its claws. He hoped she didn't really have a child to leave behind.

'If you would like, my organisation can help you get into rehab,' he offered but he could see she was already shutting down, thinking of the moment when she would get back on the streets and buy her drugs.

He walked away, leaning more heavily on his cane than usual. Clearly, this agent was Stephen McNamara investigating the attacks in the area. Perhaps he was already regretting letting Hammond go. The press had dubbed the attacker the 'Shoreditch Vampire'. He just hoped they weren't right.

Outside the hospital he tried the number the girl gave him. The number rang through to an answerphone of a company claiming to provide insurance, a cover, Robert had no doubt. He had time to withdraw more funds from his bank under one of his pseudonyms, just hoping there would be no connection back to the name Robert Conway. He enjoyed an excellent lunch at a new restaurant on the South Bank. As he got older, the one pleasure that had intensified was that of food.

The phone rang back and he spent a few moments preparing to speak, as he watched the London Eye creep around its fixed pivot.

'Robert Conway,' he said, showing his willingness to be open. He allowed a hint of his Irish accent to creep over the words.

The voice was crisp and very English. 'I know who you are.'

'Maybe you do, Mr McNamara. Do you know why I'm calling?'

There was no reply, and Robert leaned back in his seat on a bench in front of the river.

'I assume you went to see Layla Hillman,' was the eventual reply.

'I did.' Robert waited until a courting couple had passed out of earshot. 'I was interested in the possibility that there is someone in London attacking prostitutes. I was even more interested that someone who recognises my name is investigating. You haven't kept the office informed, in fact, they think you are a rogue agent.'

'I'm on sabbatical but I realised these assaults might be related to a revenant. I'm not even sure there is one person responsible,' the man said, his tone less certain. 'I was going to report to my superiors when I knew for sure. They could be independent incidents.'

'Oh, I think not.' Robert allowed the man a few breaths before he added, 'Which I think you already know. In fact, you showed a picture of a woman to young Layla, a picture of someone you suspect to be a revenant. Jackdaw Hammond, the woman *you* released.'

The man at the end of the phone was curt. 'So you know about Jack.'

'Monsignor Andreotti is rather concerned about you, Mr McNamara. In fact, we had a short conversation about the fact that your supervisors have not heard from you in some weeks. Your absence is hardly seen as a sabbatical.'

'So I'm under suspicion?' The man's voice hissed out as if he was afraid of being overheard. 'What do you want?'

'My orders are to help you do your job, Mr McNamara. Despite her heroic destruction of our mutual enemy, Jackdaw Hammond is now a threat in her own way. Or should I say, in a similar way.'

He could hear McNamara breathing at the other end of the phone for several moments before he answered. 'You're asking me to kill the woman who saved my life and that of two others. How many have been saved from Elizabeth Báthory since?'

'Yes. But Hammond has now become a danger.' Even as he said it, Conway wondered for a minute whether this Jack could lead them to the bigger threat of Saraquel – maybe he was weakened . . . Damn Andreotti and his heroic ideas.

'And your department can help . . . remove the threat?'

Conway half-smiled at the waiter as he brought him a plate of seafood. 'My role is strictly advisory. I am an exorcist who specialises in these odd cases. And I am somewhat of an expert on the rituals of necromancy that create revenants. If you break the magic as well as the body, the revenant is released from their bondage.'

'This is no ordinary revenant,' the man finally said.

'But still, Mr McNamara, she has a soul kept back from heaven by the agency of sorcery, and against the will of God. We need to retrieve her before she does any more harm, and then track down the sorcerer that made her.'

There was a long silence. 'The man who helped us kill Báthory will fight for Jack, and he has a much higher profile.'

'This professor?' Robert reached into his pocket for his notebook.

'Felix Guichard. He's a good man.' The younger man wavered. 'And has more knowledge about Edward Kelley's journey through Eastern Europe than I even knew existed.'

Perhaps this Guichard had access to the lost journal, Edward Kelley's diary of the ensorcellment of Elizabeth Báthory. Conway's fingers hesitated over the keypad. 'I see. Which university is he teaching at?'

'Exeter. But I don't know where he is now. I tried to contact him but he's taken a leave of absence. I believe he's looking after Sadie, the child. Who is blameless in all this, and no threat.'

Robert let his words hang for a few seconds. 'I'm aware there are special cases,' he said, although the Inquisition would have never agreed. 'But there have to be very exceptional circumstances for leaving a revenant in the community. They are targets, for example, for unscrupulous . . . let's call them researchers.'

McNamara sounded far away. 'Jack risked her life to kill a — *obiettivo principale*: Báthory.'

Conway lowered his voice as a man walked by with a Labrador on a long lead. The dog snuffled at his shoes for a moment. He cupped his hand around the phone. 'How did she vanquish Báthory?'

McNamara took a deep breath. 'Does it matter? She did it.'

'Tell me, man,' Conway snapped back.

'She drank some of the professor's blood, then used the extra energy to turn the monster's own spells against her. A fire elemental—'

Conway thought the implications through. Báthory was one of the manifestations of a creature so dangerous he had shivered to think of even being in the same country as it.

'McNamara, if she was there when Báthory was killed she could have become infected with the same blood cravings,' he said with more urgency. If only that was all. More likely she had picked up the parasitic possession of Saraquel, with all the consequences that would follow.

Stephen McNamara sighed down the phone. 'I owe her my life. She hasn't killed anyone.'

'Not yet. But she will.' Robert lowered his voice. 'At this moment she is blindly feeding while not in her right mind. I understand that. But soon she will be driven to the worse physical and sexual excesses, killing her victims, maybe torturing them.'

'I just want to give her a chance—'

'Then the first of the slaughtered children will be on your conscience, my friend. And you will drive the stake through her heart out of guilt as well as revulsion.'

Chapter 13

Present day, London

Jack woke in a room painted a soft green, and in a warm bed that crackled under her as she moved. A hospital bed. She tried to sit up before she realised her hands were restrained by padded straps attached to bars on either side. Her heart lurched at the captivity, but she was too weak to fight it. Her muscles softened. She had almost slipped back into sleep when a tall woman dressed in scrubs and with frizzy hair opened the door.

'I've got an extra shift on Saturday—' the woman said over her shoulder. 'Oh, hello. You're finally awake.'

'Where am I?'

The woman gave her a long, assessing gaze, then undid the straps. 'You're in Leigh Farm's acute assessment ward. You seem to have lost it in a public park and attacked the policeman trying to help you.'

Jack shifted up and the woman leaned forward to put the end of the bed up so she could sit.

'Ouch.' Jack carefully touched her side.

'I'm afraid you have a couple of cracked ribs. Do you remember anything?' Her voice was full of sympathy.

Every muscle seemed to ache. 'Did I—' Memory crept back. 'Did someone hurt me? A mugger?'

'The police will want to talk to you about what happened. But the attack seemed to set off some sort of break in your mind. Now, I'm not judging, but we need to know. Did you take any drugs last night or drink any alcohol?'

'Last night? Was it only . . .' She thought back feverishly to the previous day, to leaving St Jude's. 'I was at a shelter. I left and then—' She leaned back into the pillow.

'Drugs? Alcohol?'

'No. I don't think so. Maybe, I don't really remember.'

'Before the police come here and interview you, can you give me your name?' She pulled out a pen from her pocket. 'We don't want you treated as a missing person.'

'No, of course not.' Jack thought quickly. 'Charley Slee, I mean, Charlotte Slee.' Using her foster sister's name might put the police off looking into her real identity. 'Look. I was trying to get to this retreat, I can't remember what happened next.' Saraquel seemed completely dormant, although she was sure he was still there. 'St Francis's retreat, Fleet. It was suggested to me by the shelter I was in.'

The woman, Jo by her name tag, nodded slowly. 'Look, you were unconscious when you came in, and we were waiting to see how you were when you woke up. The police brought you in on a section 136, to a place of safety. We won't hold you if you are lucid and well. But the police really do need to talk to you about the assault.'

'I just want to put this behind me.'

'You are covered in bruises,' the woman said gently, 'and have a cracked cheekbone too. Not to mention a concussion. You were attacked.'

Jack shook her head. 'I just got into a fight with . . . someone. I remember now. I might have been drunk.' She looked down the front of her hospital gown. The tattoos of the circle of symbols that kept her alive were almost obscured by bruises in every shade from blue to violet to red. 'I'm really sorry to have caused such a nuisance.' She just hoped Saraquel hadn't hurt anyone else. The memory of the slack face of the old woman lanced through her. 'There was someone else who was attacked. What happened to her?'

'She wasn't brought here so I don't know. The police might be able to give you more details. Is she a friend?'

Jack looked at her hands, at the split skin over her knuckles. 'No. I don't know her.'

The woman sighed, and tucked in the sheet at the foot of the bed. 'I'll get the doctor to talk to you, then you are going to have to speak to the police. I'll look into getting you into that retreat, OK?'

The rest of the morning was taken up by lying to psychiatrists and nurses, and then lunchtime was interrupted by two police officers. They didn't believe her story either, no one did. There was a resigned attitude which she realised stemmed from their belief that she was just another drunk, abused woman who had been beaten up. Her anger rose at the thought of anyone being accepted as passive victims when they had been attacked, but understood how it happened. Three days in the shelter had been an eye-opener.

Finally, the evidence. The female officer met her male colleague's eye, then launched into a catalogue of Jack's injuries. 'Bruises, cracked ribs and cheekbone possibly from a weapon, concussion –' Jack put a hand up to stop her speaking '– and boot marks on your back from being kicked. And you have no idea who attacked you and the woman you were with?'

Jack's eyes filled up with tears.

'I don't remember.' She squeezed her hands together. 'What happened to the old lady?'

The male officer leaned forward. 'Fortunately, she was too drunk to remember a lot of it. She said she put up a fight too. She carried a large spanner and a hockey stick for protection. We'll be taking more statements from both of you. Can you remember anything at all?'

Jack opened her mouth to say 'no' but the word 'yes' slipped out, on a wave of outrage at the creature who would target a vulnerable, apparently homeless woman. She wiped her eyes on her sleeve. 'It was dark, I just got an impression . . .' She thought fast. Saraquel somehow gave her a moment of awareness of his own form when he took over. 'Someone really tall,' she finished lamely.

The two officers looked at each other. 'That's not much to go on,' the female officer said, a half-smile on her face. 'I think we'll put that down to the concussion, then.'

'I just want to go.'

'We don't want to let you back on the streets. You were twenty kinds of crazy last night,' the man said, rubbing his chest as if remembering. 'One especially high kick,' he admitted, his mouth quirking into a lopsided smile. 'I suppose you had every reason to be fighting off strange men.'

'I'm sorry. I really am. I wasn't myself.' Her tone of quiet sincerity seemed to convince them.

'Well, technically you have been a victim of a crime, we can't hold you on anything you've done,' he said. 'But we strongly advise that you stay in hospital until they find out why you lost it so

75

spectacularly, and you can contact us if your memory starts to return.' He handed her a card.

She shook her head vigorously, setting off a pain over her eye. 'No, I want to leave. I think I have somewhere to go.'

'St Francis's Retreat, Fleet, apparently. One of the nurses is sorting it out with them. We may have more questions for you.'

'That's where I'll be,' said Jack, not having any idea how she was supposed to get there. 'Did I have any money on me?'

'Nothing. Nor watch, nor phone. No ID either.' He smiled again, sadly. 'A bit of a mystery woman.'

Jack looked from one to the other. 'So, can I go? To Fleet?'

The woman put her head on one side. 'I'll take you myself. Rob's going to cover the rest of my shift.'

Jack fell asleep in the car, lulled by the warmth and the motion. The policewoman, Vicky, left her in peace. She awoke abruptly as they turned into a gravel drive, feeling her chest tighten and her heart racing. She recognised it as Saraquel's panic, and grimly held herself rigid until he was squashed back down by the approach to the building. It must be a religious site, she thought, because they were the only ones that he couldn't cope with.

A woman opened the wide wooden door and came out. She appeared to be in her sixties with short silver hair, jeans and a sweatshirt with 'In Retreat with St Francis' on it.

'Charley Slee, I presume?' she enquired in a deep voice with more than a hint of a Scottish accent.

Jack nodded, and took the proffered fingers. The woman didn't shake her hand, but held it with both her own as if trying to divine something. When Jack glanced up, she saw tears in the older woman's eyes. 'You poor dear,' she said simply. 'You've been through enough these last few days. Come and rest with us.'

Jack sighed, her shoulders sagging with relief. Here she could continue to push back against Saraquel.

Vicky spoke to the woman for a few moments, then said her goodbyes. The whole time Jack clung to the older woman's hand, feeling the warm strength in the fingers.

The car door slammed, the car moved away, and Jack dared to let go.

'I'm Bea. I'm one of the centre managers, and I'm the only resident one. That makes me Queen Bea around here.' She smiled at her joke. 'I'm guessing you're not really Charley or Charlotte Slee, but I'm happy to use that on our paperwork. But I think you and I need to start out on an equal footing, knowing each other's first name. How about it?'

'Jack,' she whispered, feeling a relief to have someone know who she really was inside.

Bea stared at her through narrowed eyes. 'You look like you've been through all kinds of troubles.'

Jack felt an impulse to tell the woman the truth, but didn't dare.

'Go on, I'll bet I've heard it before,' the woman prompted. 'In your own time. Shall we go in for a cup of tea while you work up to it?' She led the way inside the building and through a heavy wooden door.

Jack found herself seated at a table in a surprisingly modern kitchen within the walls of what looked like a medieval building. The tea came with a slab of chocolate cake, which she demolished in a few bites, and Bea followed it up with a cheese sandwich.

'You looked hungry. Are you cold?'

Jack shook her head, halfway through the sandwich. The wholemeal bread was home-made, and finally filled her up.

'Go on then. Tell me your story. Abducted by aliens? Hearing the voice of God? Think you're Napoleon?' Bea said, smiling, while her keen blue eyes stared at Jack.

'Possessed,' Jack said, without an answering smile.

The humour on Bea's face faded. 'By what?'

'I don't know what, not for sure. But by something that makes me crazy.'

Bea looked quite serious. 'You're really convinced, aren't you?'

Jack welled up again, and sniffed back tears. 'Look, I'm not well, that's all. Don't listen to me.'

Bea sighed and reached for her own tea. 'What we can offer here is hard work, good food and peace. Quiet, in which you can work out your own problems. We observe silence between seven a.m. and seven p.m., bedtime is at nine. No television, no computers, no drugs or drink. You can attend services if you want, but they are very low-key.'

Jack was surprised. 'Is this still run by nuns, then?'

Bea smiled warmly, and put her hands together at the table. 'Nuns and ex-nuns, yes. The ex-nun will be me. Resigned, but couldn't quite get out the gate. We cater for men and women who need space in their lives to sort themselves out. And you, Jack, are very welcome.'

Chapter 14

Journal of Eliza Jane Weston, 23 November 1612

'Kelley – dead? So you say,' the countess said, standing and perusing the picture upon the wall. It was a sketch of my eldest son, now gone to heaven, alas.

'He fell out of a window, and died of his injuries a few days later.' I knew not what else to say, such a grief had it caused.

'I have made enquiries,' she said, still staring at the portrait, a good likeness. 'I travelled to Most, to Hněvín castle, and found the people there could not agree upon your father's fate.'

Edward Kelley, Venice

The small ship, *Il Delfino*, had a single cabin, home to we three travellers. Canvas awnings were rigged over the deck for the eight sailors and the cook. We left Marinello's man and Konrad's guard behind. I trusted neither, but wondered if without his manservant Marinello would expect me to serve him. I need not have worried. Away from Guiseppe Marinello seemed happy in shirt and britches.

He wore the shabbiest soft boots I could have imagined, sewn about with strips of gut. He grinned at me when I challenged him about it. 'Look here,' he bade me, 'look at the soles.'

I could see nothing special about them, except the wear, in places they were so thin they almost showed the soles of his feet.

'Watch,' he cried.

The captain sprang to the side of the ship and, to my horror, grasped a line above his head with his good arm. He leaped onto a taut rope restraining one of the heavy sails, which was billowed out by a lively breeze. He walked along it, his feet gripping the halyard almost like a monkey, feeling it between his great toes and the others.

'My lord,' I called out, fearful for his safety and, indeed, my own. I misliked the look of the swarthy, muttering sailors who had no love, it seemed, for Englishmen. 'In God's name, be careful.'

'I cannot afford to be sliding around the ship,' called out the laughing Marinello, now standing beside a mast, one hand lightly around it for balance. 'I must be as secure as on land, especially if I am to wield a cutlass in your defence, my friend.' He bounded back onto the deck. 'I have them resoled with the finest lamb leather I can afford, several times a year.'

'Lamb leather?' I had only heard of such being employed in ladies' shoes. My father – or rather, the man who married my mother – had been a cordwainer in London, making boots for the merchants and their wives there. I had often finished their high shoes for him.

The ship hit a wave and shuddered. I staggered but Marinello seemed glued to the deck.

'Come, my cautious friend,' he said, grinning. 'Let us drink fresh wine while we still have some, and talk of our adventures. You still have to tell me how you did the countess such a disservice, yet she engages us to put it right.'

Indeed, I thought, why does she? It was simple. We were the only people who could unravel the enigma of her existence.

We went below, ducking into a tiny doorway and down steps as steep and narrow as a ladder and black with sea damp. Marinello eased his broad shoulders in and hailed Dee.

Looking as relaxed as he did ashore, sitting at the single table by the light of a tiny window, Dee smiled up. 'We make good time?' he asked. He spread his hand out over a piece of parchment that was covered in tiny marks. 'I am calculating our present course. I anticipate we will reach Candia in no more than eleven days or so, based upon your *routiers* and my notes from your grandfather's map.'

I sat with some relief on one of the fixed benches that I reasoned could also play a part as a bunk at night. My stomach rolled in my belly as if it were filled with round-shot.

Marinello laughed at Dee and perched his hip upon the other bunk. 'I swear, if my men take more than ten days I'll heave them overboard. The wind, the tides and the season are with us.' He pointed to an area on the map. 'Here we make a small diversion to avoid the Sultan's ships, but essentially we shadow the coast, then sail across at Brindisi to Kérkyra. The city is heavily defended but they should let us land for fresh supplies under the Venetian flag – I am well known there.'

Dee folded his hands in his lap. 'I have contacts at Brindisi. But what of these Barbary pirates?'

Marinello looked rueful. 'Well, the corsairs are a threat to any shipping. They are well organised and well manned. They mostly travel with xebecs, but also sail captured Spanish and English ships.'

I shook my head. 'Xebecs?'

'Fighting ships, with lateen sails and many pairs of rowers, all slaves. I can run out four pairs of oars, five if needed, but sailors row for money, slaves for their lives. I cannot outrun xebecs in this bucket.' He motioned at the map. 'There are pirates – slavers – out of Naxos, ruled by the pasha at Constantinople. We need to pass at night, if possible, under cover of darkness but also with a good following wind.'

I was thrown forward by a lurch of the ship, and grasped the fixed table for support. 'I think I shall stay atop,' I said.

'You'll find your sea-legs in time,' Marinello said, not without sympathy. 'And we'll need your young eyes and excellent sense of danger on deck, soon enough.'

Chapter 15

Present day, Exeter

Felix turned over piles of letters and assignments and groaned. Even working part-time, he was being swamped by work at the university which had built up during his weeks of absence. Rose, his assistant, pushed the office door open with another box.

'I thought you ought to have a look at some of the journals before they put them out in the library.' She stopped, staring down at him. 'Felix, really, you look terrible.'

'I know. I haven't been sleeping.' He lifted the first journal out of the box onto the desk. A couple of magazines fell to the old carpet.

She disappeared for a few minutes and returned with two mugs. The fragrant steam wafted off the top and straight, it seemed to him, into his brain. 'Let me help,' she said, pulling up another chair.

'Thank you.' He sipped the coffee – black and fiendishly strong – with gratitude. 'But I can't take you away from the rest of your work.'

He didn't mean it. If anyone could cut through the mountain of papers, it was fifty-something Rose, mother of three and full-time department assistant.

'Yes, you can.' She pulled a bin over and started glancing through the letters. She began throwing them in, putting a few aside, mumbling what they were about while he tried to sort the assignments by the date they had to be back. 'Funding refused, department rubbish, student numbers blah, blah. Oh, and something from Harvard.' She added a page to the slim pile on the desk. The next letter stopped her.

'What is it?' Felix looked over his reading glasses.

'A Professor Alicia Dennett, who has written to you before about a connection of Edward Kelley's.'

'Where's she from?'

'Uh – Cambridge, UK not US. Literature fellow of one of the colleges. She wants to meet you about some poetry by Edward Kelley's daughter, Elizabeth Jane Weston. She thinks it's urgent.'

Felix stopped his reading and thought back. 'Weston was his wife's child from her first marriage, I think. Wasn't she a poet?'

Rose frowned and sipped her coffee. 'Mm. It does ring a bell. She wants to see you pretty badly. There's a phone number and an email address.' She looked up. 'Has this anything to do with what you've been researching on your sabbatical?'

Felix sighed, dropping the journal onto his desk. 'It's about . . . do you remember that woman that came to the university? She called herself Elizabeth Bachmeier.'

She shuddered. 'I'm not likely to forget. She hypnotised me or something.'

'She hurt a friend of mine, who has since had a sort of breakdown.'

Rose looked up, her eyebrows raised. 'I'm so sorry, Felix. Is this the young woman you were helping?'

'Jack, yes.' It was a relief to talk to someone about Jack. 'But she's gone missing.'

'God, you must be worried sick.' She frowned. 'Hang on a minute.' She scoured the letter, then started reading a passage out. '"Recent purchases of original *Westonia* drafts and books by a company called Holtz and Bachmeier have created an increased demand for the folios in my possession, and I am concerned about their security." Isn't that the same company?'

'It is.' It was hard to think with all the emotional baggage about Jack in the way. But Bachmeier and Holtz were the medical research company that Elizabeth Báthory had used as cover for her business – and her extended existence. 'I'll speak to her.'

She passed the letter over. At the top, written in ink, was a scrawled mobile phone number. While Rose continued pruning his correspondence, he dialled it.

'Hello?' The voice seemed wary on the phone.

'Professor Dennett? My name is Felix Guichard. You wanted to talk to me?'

'Oh, thank God. I was so worried, things here have been so hectic. I can't talk right now, but can you meet me? I need to talk to someone about what's happening, and I don't feel safe talking on the phone.'

He was taken aback at the urgent tone. 'I don't really have time at the moment, maybe—'

'Then I'll come to you, where are you?'

He shook himself mentally. 'Actually, I'm at the university in Exeter. I'm on my way back to London tomorrow. If we could meet there some time . . .'

Her voice was lighter with relief. 'British Library, Thursday, two o'clock? I have to come in for another appointment. That would be so helpful. Oh – I have to go.' She rang off abruptly, leaving him staring at his phone.

Rose was gazing at him. 'You're really going back tomorrow?'

He rubbed his hands over his face. 'I have to. I've been asked to speak to the police about the last sighting of Jack. I can be there by lunchtime. Then I can sleep over and make it to the British Library the next day. I'll see Professor Dennett there.'

'All very cloak and dagger stuff, I'm sure.' Rose dropped another pile of papers in the bin. 'I don't want to be nosy but you're – you're in a relationship with this Jack, aren't you?'

He smiled without humour, and looked up at her. 'Jack would argue with that, but yes, I really am. I can't bear the thought of her lost in London. I have to go back, I have to find her.'

She sighed, throwing the last letter on to his desk. 'How about this: you go sick, and I get some of the PhD students to look at these undergraduate assignments? Janet can take the last couple of lectures before the summer break, and I can probably cobble together an exam paper from previous years.' She smiled wryly. 'It's not like I haven't done it before.'

He stared at her, seeing her compassion. 'Thank you, Rose. I don't know what to say.'

She shrugged, putting the letters in the top of the box. 'Just let me know you're all right. And good luck.'

It was a long journey to Paddington station the following day, the London train was airless and packed with commuters. Felix had downloaded some research about Bachmeier and Holtz to read, but was constantly interrupted. It was a relief to make his way by taxi to Shoreditch police station and be ushered into a small office at the back of the building. A tall man with receding reddish hair stood up and extended a hand.

'Professor. I'm Inspector Marshall. We have a mystery we were hoping you could help us with.' He smiled and sat back in his chair. 'Do sit down.'

Felix leaned forward, breathing faster. 'Have you found her?'

'Jackie – Grey? No. Can you tell me how you know Ms *Grey*?'

For the first time, Felix realised the man wasn't as sympathetic as the smile would suggest. 'She's a friend, that's all. I haven't known her very long, I suppose about six months.'

'And where did you meet her?' The tone was cool but there seemed to be an agenda.

'In a pub in Exeter, which is where I live – look, what's this about? I thought you had news.' Felix looked around the room. There were a number of photographs on a board behind the inspector's head, some of them from the CCTV at the hospital. 'Where is she?'

'When she was pulled out of the river no one expected her to survive. We routinely take photographs and fingerprints of dead and dying people to help identify missing persons. Since she doesn't match anyone with the name of Jackie or Jacqueline Grey, we processed the information further and something very strange came up.'

Felix sat back, suddenly realising what had happened. He tried to look as if he didn't. 'And? Isn't Jack her real name?'

'The fingerprints exactly match those of a Melissa Harcourt who went missing twenty years ago.'

Felix stared at the man. 'What happened?'

'She was abducted from an equestrian event in Yorkshire as a young child. She hasn't been heard of since, and then she turns up in your company. And tries to kill herself, then runs away from the hospital when she recovers. Can you explain that, Professor Guichard?'

Felix stared around the blank room. 'No, of course I can't! I told you, I've only just met her. I only know her as Jack.'

'If we look into your movements on the twenty-second of August, twenty years ago, we won't find you in Yorkshire, I suppose?'

'Twenty years ago – how can I remember? Wait, I can tell you where I was. I was in Africa, probably in Mali or Benin. I was doing research there into local belief systems.'

The man looked disappointed, but he dropped the cold stare. 'You can understand our interest.' He jotted down the information. 'I am going to have to follow this up, sir.'

'Look, Jack never said anything to me about – well, anything from her past, really. I don't even know where she lives.' Not true, but Felix was an expert on body language and hoped he could fake sincerity well enough to convince the police officer. 'I'm just trying to find her.'

'Well, I can tell you a lot of people are trying to find Melissa, including her parents. I was hoping you would know something.'

'I'm sorry, I really am. Look, I would be happy to go over everything I know,' he lied, 'if you can think of anything that will help.'

The officer sat back in the chair. 'We will be in touch, Professor. Let me know if you hear from your friend, anything at all. OK?'

Felix slept badly at his hotel. He hadn't thought about Jack's parents, even though he knew she had been abducted – or rescued, as Maggie described it – as a child. The relationship between Maggie and Jack was so natural he'd grown used to it. Jack's parents had gone through losing a child to abduction, they must have imagined her in the hands of a predator. They must have thought she was dead.

He set off for the British Library in good time and did a search for Elizabeth Jane Weston in the catalogue. She was a prolific Medieval writer in Latin, and the library had a number of pamphlets and books in several editions. He had just decided to ask for the 1606 *Parthenicon* when an elderly woman approached him. He stood up as she advanced.

'Felix Guichard?' She looked over her shoulder, and smiled back up at him when he nodded.

He took her small hand in his. 'Alicia Dennett?' She had a vibrancy about her that belied her white hair.

'Perhaps we could go for a cup of tea somewhere.' She shot another look around the quiet lobby. 'People know me here.'

Despite his worries, he was momentarily amused at her reluctance to be seen with him. Once they sat at a table in a nearby tearoom, though, it became clear things were not funny for her.

'I think I'm being followed. In fact, I know it.'

Felix checked around the room himself, such was her conviction. 'Why would anyone follow you, Alicia?'

'I have a copy of the fifteenth folio.' At his look of incomprehension, she put her bag on the table. 'You do know who Elizabeth Jane Weston *was*?'

'She was Edward Kelley's stepdaughter, a poet who wrote in Latin and who died young. That's it, I'm afraid.' He had looked her up in the library catalogue but couldn't see anything in his research to suggest controversy.

Alicia's voice was reproving, as if he should know more. 'Eliza was the family breadwinner after Kelley died. Or rather, after he disappeared, because the evidence for his actual date of death is based more on rumour than fact. But she stopped writing to him around October 1597, so I assume he died shortly after that. She was only a teenager at the time.'

'And she was well published, I know that. I'm sorry, I'm more focused on Dee and Kelley.'

'But she's *central* to Kelley's story.' She leaned back. 'This English girl wrote in Latin, the lingua franca of her era, and had a substantial following in Europe. She married a local lawyer and lived the rest of her life in Prague.'

'And Kelley corresponded with her?' Despite his fears for Jack, the thought of another insight into Kelley's mind lit a candle of interest.

'We don't have his letters, unfortunately. But we do have some of her responses to questions he posed. My research was into her poetry itself.'

'Poetry?' He couldn't see where this was going, and allowed his attention to drift out of the window momentarily. Two men were standing on the opposite side of the road and looking in.

'I started looking at different versions of the same poems, published in different editions and over several revisions. Weston changed her poems regularly. What interested me is that the words she changed seem to spell out fragments of messages. As if she was encrypting ideas within her published poetry.'

Now his interest was really caught. 'Kelley was a famous cryptographer in his time.'

'Kelley often created cyphers and puzzles, I know. I think he taught Eliza to do so. Dee and Kelley often communicated in code too. I have discovered partial messages, I think about some monster Kelley was looking for. Of course, I didn't mean monster in a literal sense, but once I published my first hypothesis, people started buying up the manuscripts and books. Ten years ago you could pick up an original Weston pamphlet for a few hundred or a thousand pounds. Now, they are all bought up for many times that.' She looked around. 'Were those men there a minute ago?'

'Yes.'

She shivered and drew her scarf around her ears. 'Then I'd better explain quickly. The biggest problem is identifying the order she wrote her poems in. The publication order is subtly different. But if you compare each version of a poem, for example "Mortem Non Gustabunt", there are elusive differences. A word added, a word taken away. If you arrange all the omitted or additional words in the order of publication they spell out a sort of message.'

'"Mortem non gustabunt"? They shall not taste death?' Suddenly the older woman's ideas came sharply into focus. 'What do these messages say?'

'Well, they are only fragments so they didn't make sense.' She glanced again at the window. 'I searched for other versions of each poem to fill in some of the gaps. I found an unpublished draft of eighteen of her poems in the library at Cambridge University. They were misfiled, thank goodness. I now have that folio. Folio fifteen.'

'Why unpublished?' Despite himself he looked at the teashop window as a waitress brought their teas. The men appeared to have gone. 'You took it from the library?'

'I'm looking after it. Why it was never published is one of the mysteries, along with why it was here in the first place. She never came back to England to my knowledge. But in 1708 the manuscript was rescued from a house fire in London along with a number of other rare books and papers.' She poured her tea, her hand shaking. 'I'm a bit spooked, to be honest. I'm now fairly sure where the poems fit in the sequence of publication so have been able to decode eleven of the works.' Felix looked at the shaking hand as she poured his tea. A little slopped into his saucer. 'Oh, I'm sorry,' she said. 'It's just that I think – that is, I know that someone else is looking for the folio. That's why I need to get it out, get it published. That way the whole world gets the information, not just these people that are trying to buy it.'

'Why don't you put it out online through the university library, or the British Library?'

'There's a question of ownership to consider,' she said, and sipped a little tea. 'And there's a massive backlog, as you can imagine. Less than one per cent of our antiquarian documents are online.'

'Still—'

'I think it's also about money,' she added. 'They offered the university more than a hundred thousand pounds for it, can you imagine?'

'Who did?'

'Some drug company in Germany or Romania. Bach something, I wrote it down.' As she fumbled in her bag Felix spoke.

'Bachmeier and Holtz?'

'Yes. Do you know them?'

One of the men Felix had seen earlier was now in a parked car on double yellow lines, on the opposite side of the road. 'I know of them.'

'Of course we couldn't sell the folio, it was donated by a benefactor. But I have made a copy for you.'

Felix met the man's eye, and after a long exchange of glances, the car slowly moved off. He turned back to Alicia. 'Benefactor?'

She pulled out a flash drive and thrust it into Felix's hands, watching the window anxiously. 'Put it away before they come back.'

He slid it into his laptop case. 'Have you had a chance to complete the message?'

She nodded. 'I think I have the information to put them in order, at least, although I'm struggling to understand the sense. They are subtly numbered within the text. When you lay them out in order, you can exclude all the words in the canonical poems, and what is left spells out a cryptic, coded message about a sealed document and how it can be used. Maybe not cryptic to you. And now people are following me.'

'But why would someone be following you? Surely the folio was available for them to read.'

'Since their offers to buy the manuscript were refused I've kept the folio hidden. The library's been burgled but nothing was stolen, my own office was broken into and ransacked. I have it safe but I don't know for how long.'

There was something believable in her fear. He had been thrown into the world of supernatural conspiracies when he met Jack, and he recognised that confusion. 'What do you think this message means?'

Her eyes were bright with interest. 'From that single poem – "Mortem Non Gustabunt" – it seems to be about some creature – she calls it an spirit – that haunts the royal family. I don't know which family she refers to—'

'I do.' A cold feeling started to creep through his chest. 'The family of Elizabeth Báthory.'

'The "Blood Countess"? I thought that was all hyperbole.'

'Definitely not. Elizabeth Báthory, in her own way, was a genuine monster. And Bachmeier and Holtz are in some way connected with her . . . legacy.'

The old woman's eyes sparkled. 'Now I am intrigued. I know they were prominent researchers during the Holocaust.'

'Really? You mean they were part of the Nazi experiments?'

Alicia nodded. 'They were involved in research into hypothermia, forcing people into ice baths to study their metabolism.'

'That's – interesting. Kelley wrote about people at the edge of death.'

'And you learned this from Kelley's own writings? I had no idea he published that much.'

Felix leaned around her to scan the street. There was no one obviously staring into the tearoom like there had been a few minutes ago, but he was sure he'd seen the same man walk past before. He returned his attention to Alicia. 'Kelley didn't publish much except for his alchemical work, and he died relatively young. But he kept at least one journal, it was auctioned to an American university last year.'

'Let me guess. They mysteriously sold it on.' She took a deep breath. 'To these people, these researchers?' She looked at her cup. 'My employers – the university bigwigs – seem more interested in getting the money than understanding the messages in a few old poems. But I think they are important.'

'Bachmeier and Holtz are a medical research and drug corporation.' He typed the name of the company into his phone. 'Look, they are a big deal.'

She adjusted her glasses to the end of her nose and peered into the small screen. 'Oh, I see. But –' She touched the screen to bring up the menu items. '– this man, this Pál Bachmeier, I've seen him before.'

'You have? Where?' The man on the screen was stocky, in his fifties, with a big smile for the camera.

She frowned for a moment, then gave him back his phone. 'He was very charming, I recall. It was when they came to try and buy the folio. He even offered to give me a grant to study the poetry, as long as the original went to Prague.'

Something scratched at the back of Felix's memory. He entered Elizabeth Báthory's name into a search engine and brought up the details of her family. There, children Anna, Orsolya, Katalin, András and Pál. By 1610 only Anna, Katalin and Pál were living, which would make Pál her heir. He sat back in his chair, the horrible possibilities multiplying. Surely the German would be Paul. The name was Hungarian, like Báthory's last surviving son. This might well be her distant heir.

He saw Alicia safely into a taxi, although he realised as it pulled away that a young woman was watching them and a car had followed the cab. As he finally sat in his own taxi he was able to pull the flash drive and laptop out and load the images. There were eighteen sheets in the folio, single-sided, with some hand-written notes on the front cover. The printed type was very small and hadn't scanned well but he could see it was from the sixteenth or seventeenth century. The notes were in English, a surprise since Weston wrote Latin and must have spoken Czech, but the words were hard to read. Felix had to enlarge them to decipher them. *For my father, that he may rest in peace in Heaven.*

In the corner was a library stamp. It included the name of the pamphlet's donor.

Robert Conway.

Chapter 16

Present day, London

Robert Conway had started his second coffee of the morning, black with a dash of hazelnut syrup. He shivered a little in a chill breeze drifting off the Thames. A younger man approached, six feet, cropped greying hair, bright blue eyes. He stood looking down at Conway as if his considerably greater height might intimidate Robert.

'Stephen McNamara, I presume,' he said affably, 'mysteriously absent from his duties tracking down our missing revenant. Coffee?'

After a long moment of gazing down at Robert, the man sat, looking around at the street beyond the tables.

'We're quite alone,' Robert offered, then finished his own drink. 'Have something, the pastries here are excellent. As you get older, food is really the last pleasure you enjoy.'

The man ignored him, turning the laser gaze onto Conway instead.

'Well,' Robert said. 'It's nice to meet a colleague. You've caused some concern in higher circles.'

'I'm told the circles don't reach much higher than you,' McNamara said, his voice as flat and grey as his appearance.

'Given your success last year, I'm surprised we haven't met before.' Robert reached into his jacket for his vibrating phone, noticing McNamara's body tense as he did so. What did he expect, Robert to pull out a gun? He quickly checked the screen. 'It's just a query about my business. So, last year—'

'You want to know about Elizabeth Báthory's death.'

Robert waved at the waiter, finished his drink and threw a note on the table before standing up. 'If you don't want coffee, shall we walk?'

He didn't give McNamara time to refuse, simply stepped slowly along the street, hearing the quiet pad of the man's shoes behind him. They strolled in silence up to the zebra crossing, and waited for the traffic to stop. Robert walked to the steps of St Paul's Cathedral and looked up at the columns.

'I love this church,' he said with satisfaction. 'Better even than the Duomo, which I adore. I'm fascinated by St Paul's construction. Now, tell me everything you can about the revenant that's biting people before I call for a full extraction team,' he said, with genial authority.

'I know little. I'm not even certain it's her.'

'Well, *my* intelligence tells me she was seen here, several times, acting very oddly.' He had a number of pieces of CCTV information from the department's contacts in the British police. A slight, average height, blond woman had been seen fighting and arguing, apparently with herself, until reaching the steps of St Paul's where she would fall asleep. It wasn't typical behaviour for a possessed person, but in the early days the possessing spirit had an incomplete influence, until the taking of blood made it stronger and gave it the advantage. Then the possession would be complete.

'I know.' McNamara finally met his gaze. 'What do you know about her situation? When I first met her she was sick, frail. Then she took blood and – she was different.'

'She became vulnerable, a vessel, a dead body filled with the blood of the living. And she was there when Báthory died, a corpse possessed by a creature thousands of years old. He had a vessel waiting to transfer into.' He paused in the foyer of the great church, looking up at the carvings. 'You are quite sure the countess is dead, I suppose?' A shadow seemed to pass over Robert's soul at the thought. 'I know the press reported the death of a child.'

'The child survived, the body we left in the church was that of Elizabeth Báthory. I'm certain.' The man spoke with conviction.

'Then tell me about this revenant, the one who helped you. Tell me what you know.'

The man hesitated before answering, but then sighed, as if he knew he had to yield to the Vatican's authority. 'She calls herself Jack, Jackdaw Hammond. She was taken as a child, and saved by a necromantic ritual to tie her soul to her body. They used Dee's sigils. She took a dying teenager last year and saved her by making her into a revenant. Báthory was then drawn to the girl.'

'This Sadie Williams. Yes, of course. Cardinal Andreotti tells me you attempted to retrieve her last year.' Robert allowed his voice to become sterner. 'But she eluded you?'

McNamara's face developed a slight flush across his cheekbones. 'Sadie is very resourceful, but she was then kidnapped by Báthory. We – Jackdaw, her friend Felix Guichard and I – managed to follow her and defeat the countess by turning her own infernal creation back upon herself. And we saved the child.' He followed Conway into the church as he undid a rope barrier and held it for McNamara.

'Who is still a revenant, unnatural in the sight of God,' Robert said softly, and smiled at one of the guides approaching him. He showed him some kind of ID. The man moved on to another visitor.

McNamara was silent for a long moment as the two men stared up at the imposing ceiling of the cathedral. When the younger man turned, Robert glanced at him.

'Is that even true?' the man said, his face creased in some hint of confusion. 'What is done is God's will, surely? The child has a soul, as much as you or I do. Who are we to take her life, however fragile, however it is preserved?'

Robert found himself nodding slowly. 'You are attached to this child and this woman.'

McNamara shrugged. 'My own sister was one of them – as much a human as you or me. When we intervene with medical science, don't we prolong life unnaturally?'

Robert stepped up to the altar of the cathedral, confident that McNamara would follow. 'Revenants are different. They have passed over that divide between life and death. You know their bodies are less connected to their souls which leaves the possibility of possession.' For a moment he crossed himself and lowered his head as if in prayer. He looked up, watching McNamara, his eyes closed and his lips moving. *A believer. Interesting.* 'You are naturally biased by your own sister's experience.'

'Jack is different.' Stephen McNamara turned his head sharply, staring at tourists snapping photographs. 'There's something . . . do you ever wonder if some people are just destined to do something that changes the course of history?'

Robert took a hissing breath. Just the words he had hoped not to hear. An evangelical was a dangerous as a cynic in the world of exorcism.

'No single person has that power,' he said mildly.

The man looked indecisive, which Robert suspected was unusual.

'It's not just Jack, it's the child,' McNamara said. 'I've seen a few revenants in Eastern Europe, mostly sick children enchanted by their families to give them a few extra years. They are invalids, often haunted by their unholy state. But my sister – and Jack – have lived full lives, have people that love them, that they love . . .'

Robert shoved his hands into his jacket pockets. 'You know I am an *esorcisti*, a senior Vatican exorcist.' He lowered his voice as a school party chattered past like a cloud of starlings.

'I do.'

Robert looked at his feet for a moment, wondering how much he could give away to this man with the piercing gaze. 'More than half of these revenants – their bodies only tenuously connected with their souls, remember – become possessed. They become colonies of spirit entities, which you might call *daemons*.'

The younger man narrowed his eyes, the gaze becoming more intense. McNamara leaned in and lowered his voice to a rumble. 'What would you call them, Mr Conway?'

How much do I tell him? Robert considered the consequences of what he was doing, but now, dear God, he was as exposed as he'd ever been and it would be reassuring to have this young man at his side.

'What we are dealing with, what inhabited Countess Elizabeth Báthory, is much more than a mere demon, one of Satan's dung flies. It – he – calls himself Saraquel, and possesses many hundreds of people at the same time.'

After a long silence, McNamara frowned. 'That doesn't sound like any demon I've ever heard of.'

'I understand your confusion. But do you truly believe in angels and demons, my friend?'

McNamara turned away from him and waited until a party of schoolchildren had moved on. 'I'm not sure I do. No.'

'Yet you saw such evil – and such power – in Elizabeth Báthory that you were prepared to risk your own life to kill her. A woman who was essentially immortal through some system of magic you don't understand. That magic was given to mankind by angels. Enoch was taken into heaven and shown the role of magic in our lives, what it could be.'

'I don't understand.' The younger man's shoulders were tight around his neck.

'Setting aside your faith for a moment, imagine that there was once a great energy that infused the forming matter in our universe. Some of that energy – I call it *spiritus* – became part of all living things, and the greatest part of that energy was shaped by the beliefs and fears of man into what we think of as God.'

The man shrugged. 'So you say.'

'But other energy was formed into other beings – angels, demons and all the lower creatures mythology gives names such as undine, fairy, goblin.'

McNamara turned to stare at him. 'You are a priest and you believe in fairies?'

'Of sorts.' Conway smiled up at the younger man. 'When you have seen what I have seen, you have to broaden your belief system to account for things like the blood countess.'

'Angels, demons – a metaphor for man's part in the universe.' McNamara took a step away. 'I can't believe in them literally. My own sister . . .'

'Listen to me. They are terrifying beings, filled with the intelligence of a thousand men, the bodies of giants that they can change at will. Yet they lack the ability to feel, to love, to be embodied in a physical sense. These are demons and angels.'

'I can't imagine that. You say they are formed by belief. But if millions of people like me don't believe in them, how can they exist?'

Conway stepped closer to the man. 'Angels and demons are not formed by the beliefs of men.'

'Then – by what?'

Conway watched the expression of disdain be followed by confusion. He smiled at McNamara. 'They are formed by the convictions of God.'

102

Chapter 17

Journal of Eliza Jane Weston, 23 November 1612

Despite myself, a little curiosity wakened about the story of my beloved father, for I did not know his fate. 'I know only that he was a captive of the Emperor.'

The countess swept her skirts away as she sat down. 'Some say, as you do, that his leg was so badly broken in an escape attempt he died the following day.'

I nodded. 'That is the story I have heard, lady.' I smiled. 'He had escaped thus before.'

'Yet there is no grave. There is not one person who can say to me that they saw his dead body, nor can they agree on a date of his death. Some say May, some say July.'

All I knew was his very last letter came to me in April, smuggled out of Hněvín castle by a visitor, who went to treat for his release on behalf of my mother. I remember every word.

'My dearest child, I write in despair that I might not see you again. Please God that you, your brother and mother get safe back to England. Seek out Dee, who will take you in even if he does not forgive me. And keep that which we dare not discuss, at all costs, by concealing it in plain sight. Your loving, foolish father, EK.'

103

Edward Kelley, the voyage to Brindisi, 1586

After a few more days at sea I felt along the prow carving to its painted smile. I had, as Marinello prophesised, found my sea-legs, and in the warmth of the summer skies had burned brown as an acorn. I could see creatures, dolphins as lively as children, swimming and leaping under the prow of the ship as it raced under sail before a favourable breeze. My fellow crew members muttered that they would not stop for me should I fall but I found the movement of the sea soothing and, having learned to swim of necessity in my earlier adventures, knew they only had to throw me a rope should I tumble in. Indeed, the dolphins almost called me to join them, their flashing bodies sporting alongside, and they seemed close enough to touch.

The rowers lay on deck under two brightly coloured awnings that bleached in the sun as the men darkened. Only César the cook worked, apart from Marinello at the helm. The Portuguese man laboured over a brazier in the open sun, sweating and swearing in equal measure, but since he was the only sailor of his country, few knew what he meant. The scent of his cooking made my mouth fill with water.

Dee was in his shirt and hose, sat upon some bales of cloth packed in oilskins, and made mathematical observations in his journal. He had long been interested in navigation, and his prodigious talent for numbers was helping him construct a better map than Marinello's own. The coastline was too dangerous to approach. It was defended from Ottoman spies and pirates by flotillas of armed fishermen. The long view down the distant shore and islands gave Dee a perspective that he sketched every day, building his observations and drawing his charts. The colour of the water, the fish and birds, the shape of the land were all meticulously noted.

I found Dee elusive on the question of Saraquel.

'I merely thought that some things, fragments really, that you mumbled within your sleep might be worth pursuing, Edward. We need to understand more about Saraquel if we are to undo the evil that was done.'

I knew he was dissembling; he would hardly go on a journey of nearly a hundred leagues to investigate a few mumblings in my sleep. I withdrew to the prow with my journal, watching Marinello and Dee drawn into more discussions that I was excluded from. I started to feel that I had lost both my master and my friend.

On the fifth night, Marinello called his crew on deck, and put the rowers to work. He ordered the brazier put out and the men to work in silence, slowly drawing the oars through the water so as to reduce their rippling and splashing. He brought the sails down by half, and *Il Delfino* cut softly through the water. Then, I heard what Marinello's sharp ears had detected, laughter and speech, rolling over the water.

'Barbary slavers,' Dee whispered in my ear. 'We shall not change course, we are already in favourable currents and the wind is good. We shall come quite close to them.'

As the voices got louder, Marinello stilled the rowers with a hiss, and let the wind slide the ship within a furlong of two ships, only visible because of their cooking brazier's dull red light and a few lanterns.

The wind caught the edge of one of the sails and it flapped. I fumbled in the dark until I caught the edge, and clung to it. I was almost lifted off my feet over the water but my waist was gripped by strong hands and I was pulled back into the boat with the stilled canvas. Marinello, for it was he, eased the sail back into its curve. Other men reached for bows, spears and swords, the tiny metallic clicks reaching me as I clung to the gunwale, pushed down by Marinello's strong hand. I understood – in a fight in the dark I was as likely to be killed by our own men as by pirates. Voices stilled over the water, and every man aboard the ship held their breath. Then a man made some garbled comment, and another laughed, and the ship passed without being detected.

When we had gone another mile, Marinello had the whisper passed around to put out oars and even he and the cook took one of the giant blades while Dee steered the ship. I stood watch, straining ears and eyes for the threat. It was not until we had gone a whole league that Marinello called quietly to put out full sail. He trusted two of the sailors to keep watch while we and half the crew rested upon deck, an ear of each no doubt cocked behind them.

After another hour I relieved Dee at the helm, using a tiny shielded lantern to see the compass and Dee's precise instructions. It was not until dawn when I could see all around that there were no ships that I allowed a crewman to take over.

Marinello was just rolling out of his blanket when I went below. 'A taste of adventure, little man,' he rumbled.

'I mislike being useless in such trials, my lord,' I said. I had never liked Marinello's appellation 'little man', but beside the giant captain it was easy to see his mistake.

'Then it is time you learned to sail and row, my friend.' He clapped me on the shoulder as he passed, and murmured so as not to disturb Dee. 'We'll make a seaman of you yet, my sorcerer.'

Chapter 18

Present day, Bee Cottage, Lake District

Felix looked at Sadie, hunched over the papers she had spread all around her, determined to break Elizabeth Jane Weston's code. He was researching something quite different.

Ten years or so before, his ex-wife Marianne had befriended a couple new to Exeter, a doctor and his wife. Marianne had had some fleeting but rare condition, and they had met George and Petra socially afterwards. Marianne, a Scandinavian import herself, had some fellow feeling for Swedish Petra, and the two men shared an interest in the boundary between science and belief.

He had sent Sadie's blood sample to George. The email that returned was worrying.

Hi Felix. Where the hell did you get these samples? I'm assuming whoever gave them is now dead. Electrolytes shot to hell, acidosis, her potassium and calcium are desperately low, liver's shot, kidneys are crap, clotting's all over the place. Why did you want me to review a patient who's already dead, is this one of your court cases? I can't give an official opinion, I'm not a pathologist, but I'd be certain this patient will die within hours or days, if they haven't already. They need intensive care and a miracle.

Sorry to hear about you and Marianne splitting up, but she seems happy. She says you've met someone too? Find a night we can go down the pub and gossip like girls. G.

He fired off a reply, while glancing over at Sadie occasionally. The skin of her neck clung to each vertebra, as if the bones were trying to cut through. He could see her deterioration, and Maggie had warned him she didn't have any further ideas about saving her.

'Listen to this,' Sadie said, still bent over her notes. '"The traveller – something, something – protects you yet haunts – something – his multitude." What does that mean?'

'I have no idea.' Felix sat back and thought about it. 'Maybe Saraquel has possessed other people before.'

A message popped up in his inbox. *Ring me.* And George's number. He tapped the number into his phone.

'George?'

'Felix! What's this all about? Can I help?'

'Would you believe me if I told you the person that the blood belongs to is right here, talking to me? That they have been ill for a long time but are nowhere near dying?' I hope, he added silently.

Sadie frowned and turned away from him. Bandit, the kitten, which had been asleep beside her, yawned and stretched.

'No. I mean, OK, yes, if you say so, but honestly that's something I've never heard of. It's hard to see how they can survive. You should get them straight to a hospital.'

Felix took a deep breath. 'They wouldn't go. They have a very specific belief system.' As the kitten limped towards him he put out a hand to stroke it.

'They believe they should sit there and die? Come on, Felix, are they really able to make that judgement, in that state?'

'Absolutely.'

He could hear the frustrated sigh at the other end of the phone. 'Look, I work at a private hospital in Manchester now. We see a lot of religious people there, and people with very specific requirements. We recently dealt with a millionaire with very difficult OCD, who believed he had to breathe filtered air. Can we at least see her? I'm serious, Felix, this patient is dying, no doubt about it.'

Felix thought quickly. It was the very opposite of what Maggie or Jack would agree to, but he felt responsible for Sadie and he could see her fading every day. The kitten batted his finger and then jumped away, sliding onto Sadie's notes.

'Stop it, Bandit!' Sadie muttered, picked him up under his fat belly and put him on her shoulder.

Felix turned away, to murmur into his phone without Sadie hearing. 'What would you be able to do for her?'

'Hydrate, oxygenate, feed. Aggressive life support, balance up those numbers. Maybe treat possible infections, dialyse to give her kidneys a chance. There's a number of new protocols that can help in some cases. It's not really my area, let me look into it. But will you consider getting her here?'

Felix thought for a long moment. Sadie stroked the kitten on her shoulder and rested her head on the back of the sofa. The white fur of the cat was almost the same shade as the cheek it rested against. Bandit purred. Sadie closed her eyes, they were so shadowed in darkness her skull seemed visible.

'Let's try it. Where is this hospital?'

'I'll email you the details. I can swing the tests on the charitable arm of the hospital, but a bed will cost something. Can you cover it?'

Felix looked over at the kitten, so vibrant next to Sadie despite its difficult beginning. 'Definitely.'

Maggie had come home from the shops in Ambleside and was putting sandwiches on plates when Felix pushed open the kitchen door.

'I don't know why I bother,' she said, 'she never eats it.' Her voice sounded shaky.

'That's what I'm worried about.' Felix balanced one hip on the table. 'Sadie's getting worse.'

Maggie glowered at him. 'And you're an expert on borrowed time now, are you?'

He knew she was worried sick about Jack and let it pass. 'A friend of mine, a doctor, has some ideas that might help. He's been looking at the blood we took from Sadie. Her test results are as bad as Jack's were.'

'You shouldn't have told a stranger about her.' She paused in what she was doing. 'What did he say? Can he help?'

'Maybe.' He looked at the floor. 'Look, I know you're worried about the circles and the herbs . . .'

She shook her head. 'I'm also worried because to the whole world, and the press, Sadie is an abducted child. Or a murder victim. We can't just turn up at a hospital, she doesn't have a legal identity.'

'Would anyone even recognise her now?'

She bent her head for a moment. 'You haven't seen the news today, have you?'

'News?'

She nodded towards an open newspaper on the work surface. He walked over to it, nudging Ches out the way as he went. There was a picture of a child at nine or ten years old, fair curls drifting across her face as she laughed. 'Missing child located after twenty years' the headline screamed, followed by the picture from the CCTV at the hospital. It was Jack.

DNA confirms the identity of a suicidal woman as that of Melissa Harcourt, abducted from a gymkhana twenty years ago. The article went on to describe the lengths the police and family had gone to to find the missing child, the men that had been questioned, and the vehicles police had traced after the incident. But Melissa was supposed dead after years of silence, and the British press had moved on. The police had issued a statement. They were reopening the inquiry into Jack's abduction, following up new leads about a white car, a red van and a horsebox seen leaving the gymkhana. The article included a message to Melissa – Jack – to contact the police on a confidential number.

Felix felt sick. Jack could be reading this, more emotions for her to handle. How much longer could she cope?

Maggie had tears in her eyes. 'Where is she, Felix? What did you say to her—' Her face was twisted with anger at him.

'I didn't say anything. I left her alone with Ivanova, the other borrowed timer, then she came out and told me she was possessed. That's it, she ran away. That's all I knew before I found the hospital.'

She covered her eyes with a shaking hand. 'I should have been there.'

'Look, Maggie.' He dropped his voice. 'Right now, I know Jack would want us to do everything we can to save Sadie. Everything. That's all I can do for Jack right now, until we find her. OK?'

'I just need to know she's safe.' Maggie reached for some kitchen roll and tore off a sheet to wipe her eyes. 'I know you don't understand but I love her like I love Charley, she's like my own daughter.'

'She was alive when she left the hospital. She'll get in touch if she can, eventually. She thinks she's protecting us.'

Maggie gave him a stern look before she sighed. 'I suppose you're right. I know – I'm just not used to having help.' She managed a small smile. 'I'm not used to needing anyone else. I've been on my own for a long time.'

'What about Charley's father?'

She shrugged. 'I was forty-two, I wanted a child. He was a sorcerer I knew – we did a deal.' She stared back at Felix. 'Then she was diagnosed with leukaemia, and I found out Jack – Melissa – was going to die on a certain day. Roisin saw her, she's a seer as well as my midwife and healer. And we did manage to save Jack, just to give my baby a chance. I never thought what I was doing to her parents. She was going to die anyway, that's all I thought. We never expected Jack to survive more than a few days.'

'They would have lost her anyway. They would have had nothing.' He could feel her guilt, he knew the uncertainty must have been unbearable for the Harcourts. 'Without the sorcery she would have died, she needed your expertise. Maybe now they will have some time with Jack. If we can save her.'

'If we can even find her.' Maggie took a deep breath, closed her eyes, and breathed out.

He kept his voice low, in case Sadie overheard. 'If my friend is right, we may be able to reverse some of the effects of this multi-organ syndrome. Perhaps we can find a way to strengthen Jack and Sadie, give Jack a chance to fight off whatever this Saraquel really is.'

Maggie bent her head forward for a moment as if thinking. When she raised it, she had a different expression on her face, more determined, more positive.

'OK, we'll try it. But if I say we have to leave, we leave, OK? I'm looking at a lifetime in prison for abducting Jack, and without me and the magic, Sadie will certainly die.'

When he returned to Sadie, she was frowning at her notes. 'There's too many words missing,' she mused. 'But I think that this is about something that haunts you, like you said, but more than one person at a time.' She looked up. 'Felix, I know this sounds crazy, but wouldn't the Inquisition know more about this stuff?'

He sat down, thinking about it. 'I don't know if we want the Inquisition to know anything about you, they have a commitment to wipe out borrowed timers. But Stephen McNamara might help.' The inquisitor had helped them before. 'Actually, they know the most about possession of all the Christian sects.'

'Possession? Ugh. I saw this old film once, with my friends. It was horrible, we switched it off.'

He leaned back against the back of the sofa. 'I've seen exorcisms in Africa, they are stressful for both the exorcists and the possessed people. I don't even want to think about Jack going through something like that.'

'But if it saves her it would be worth it. Assuming you can even find Mac. I mean, he's part of this mysterious Inquisition cult thing.'

'Well, that's the problem, isn't it?' He thought over his admittedly small knowledge of beliefs about possession. 'I could try to contact him, if the phone number is still up to date.'

'Go on, then.' Sadie was still frowning, but darted forward to highlight another few words. 'I think this Eliza Weston woman knew all about Báthory. If you take out all the words that appear more than once between all eleven versions of "On The Name Of Jesus", for example, you get "the", "thousand", "souls" and "torments" and the words "Sarah" and "Quell". That could be—'

'Let me see.' He slid on to the floor next to her, following her claw-like finger. It trembled, and he could feel her bony arm against his.

'Sarah-quell torments the thousand souls,' murmured Felix.

'Exactly.' She pulled over a computer tablet she was resting her pages on. 'Only I remember Saraquel from those old pages you were translating. I looked up Saraquel on the Internet, and it said he was like an important angel. One of the Seraphim or something, in the book of Enoch. Kelley wrote about him, didn't he?'

'He was supposed to be an angel of death. Maybe that's shorthand for a demon. Or maybe there isn't much difference, demons were supposed to be fallen angels.'

'And,' she said, holding up a hand dramatically and disturbing the cat, 'there's this magic paper that was called Zadok's something.'

'All I know about Zadok is that Handel wrote a piece about him.' When Sadie shrugged he added, 'Handel, composer? He wrote *Messiah*?'

'Oh. That guy. Where did he get Zadok from, then?'

'You'll have to look in the Bible for that. We've got one somewhere . . .'

She rolled her eyes and showed him the tablet. 'Or we could download a searchable one?' She scrolled down a list. 'He was some sort of seer, and he looked after the ark. The ark?' She showed him the screen.

'Of the covenant, I assume, not the boat.' Felix scanned some of the references. He glanced at her, wondering how to broach the subject. 'My friend, the one I sent the blood sample to, thinks he can help you.'

'Mm?' She scribbled something in a margin. 'What did he say?'

'You have the same problem Jack has. Multi-organ failure. They can treat it.'

She shook her head. 'Ches, get off my feet – get that page before he sits on it.' She retrieved the papers in danger of being covered by the dog as he lay down, and looked up at Felix. 'You mean, really treat it? What about the herbs and the circles?'

'We'd use those as well.'

'What would I have to do?' She stroked the dog's head as he rested in on her leg.

'They would put you on drips and monitors, all while you were asleep. They would get some nutrients into you, give you medicines like you were actually dying and they could save you.'

'And this would work?' Her voice suddenly sounded five years old.

'I don't know. But Maggie and I would be with you to make sure you didn't get any worse. Maybe you would get a rest, maybe you could even put on a bit of weight. Your mum could come up for a while as well.'

Sadie's lip trembled, but she tilted her head down as if she didn't want him to see her cry. 'Ever since Jack left – I just get so cold. It's depressing living like this.'

'I know.'

'Anyway, where is Jack?' She sounded as if she had found a low-banked flame of anger. 'You must have said something to make her run off.'

'It wasn't something I said. It was something another, very old, borrowed timer told her about being possessed.'

'I know.' Sadie dashed a hand over her face and leaned against his arm. 'Well, go and find her.'

'Can we try and make you better as well?'

She shrugged. 'I suppose so. At least I'll be able to sleep. I can't stand the nightmares any longer.'

'Nightmares?'

She looked at her nails, split and dry since she had lost so much weight. 'I keep dreaming about weird voices and strange views, like looking through stained-glass windows. All wobbly glass. And someone sings my name. It happens when I get really sick, mostly.'

In one horrible moment, the idea coalesced in Felix's head. Saraquel was trying to possess Sadie.

Chapter 19

Present day, London

Robert Conway lined up the last things to pack. Plane ticket in the name of one of his aliases, wallet with matching ID, passport in new name. He would have to hunch his shoulders and slow down going through customs – the alter-ego looked fifteen years older than he did. He'd grown used to switching between identities. He was ready to go.

Yet something stopped him. His whole life he had lived in terror of Elizabeth Báthory and her supernatural passenger. Maybe no one alive knew as much as he did about Saraquel, not just from his research into ancient books and texts, but from avoiding Báthory and her spider's web of contacts all over the world. Maybe Bachmeier and Holtz did some good in the world of pharmaceuticals, but with Báthory at the helm he could never be sure of their motives. All he knew was that he had barely kept one step ahead of them at times, and the threat of contact with Saraquel – again – terrified him. Stephen McNamara and Jackdaw Hammond had survived an encounter with Saraquel, then helped annihilate his host. Now they had the advantage, and Saraquel had not yet completely consumed the new vessel.

Why should he risk his life to save some young woman he didn't even know?

Because, his better side argued, *Saraquel is on the run. This might be the chance we – the church and I – have been waiting for. Without his powerful stronghold in Elizabeth Báthory, maybe Saraquel would be vulnerable for a time.*

Many had attempted the exorcism of Saraquel, just one had survived. No one had kept Saraquel at bay for more than a few days, except this Jack. Perhaps, with the poetry becoming understood, Saraquel really was at a disadvantage. Maybe, if Andreotti had that information . . .

His old friend answered the phone on the second ring. 'I thought I'd hear from you soon,' the voice rumbled down the phone in precise Latin.

'Talk me out of it.'

He could see almost the lazy smile on Andreotti's long face. 'You know I won't. Your legendary reputation for self-preservation may be dented, though.'

'What makes you think now is the time?'

'My whole department is gathering information on known hosts. They seem to be converging on the UK.' He had switched to German, maybe someone was within earshot back in Rome.

Conway shook his head. 'That just makes it harder. I'll be exposed, I'll be the primary target. Saraquel's been after me for years.'

'I'm sending a full team. It will be a chance to eliminate a score of revenants. That will weaken Saraquel further.'

Conway sat down again. 'It will be a mass slaughter. Some of these people are innocent.'

'Saraquel is in charge, they are probably helplessly watching him live their lives, you know how it works. Death might be preferable. Saraquel exploits their worse impulses. Báthory's worse instincts were just more violent than most.'

'I'm afraid . . .' He swallowed the next few words, because the bottom line was that his fears were huge. 'I'm afraid he'll consume me and then we are really lost. If Saraquel gets me he'll know everything I know.'

There was a long pause. Andreotti switched to English. 'I'm coming to London. I'll coordinate from there. If you need me, old friend, I'll be there. I don't know how much help my old bones can be . . .'

The thought of Andreotti at his side was tempting but he knew the old man's body was fragile. 'You organise the team. I need to keep the safe house separate for this showdown. One thing.'

'Just ask.'

'If Saraquel gets me, gets inside me . . .'

'I think you can do it, and think this is the time to exorcise him.' There was resolve in Andreotti's voice but he could not disguise the catch of emotion in his voice. 'But if he overcomes you, it will be quick and painless, my old friend, even if I have to do it myself.'

The drive to the safe house on Dartmoor took five hours. The place was in a deeply wooded valley right on the edge of the moor proper. The main building was on the road, a late Victorian farmhouse rented to a nice couple who respected his privacy and provided a front for the property. But the old place, just a one-roomed medieval cottage, was forgotten even by the county surveyors and the old maps.

He took a few moments to speak to his tenants at the main house. As far as he knew they had never breached his security, but he still had alarms around the perimeter and a security company in London had reported no trouble. He parked the car at his gate, out of sight of the road, and walked back down the drive.

'What a lovely surprise, George!' Mrs Tenant waved at him with a pair of secateurs where she seemed to be pruning something. Mrs – Chilcott, Maria Chilcott. He creased his face into a smile. *George, I'm George here. So many names to remember.*

'Maria! I just thought I would check the old place out. I'm having a few friends over – work colleagues, you understand – and I thought I would just check it out.'

She walked a few steps nearer, towards the car. 'Would you like a few teabags and a jug of milk? Just to get you started?'

'I'm fine, thanks,' he said, 'I stopped in town for a few supplies.'

'Well, I hope the place is OK,' she said, going back to her vegetation. 'It's been a bit blowy recently, we lost a few slates.'

He walked back to the gate and punched in the security code. The electric barrier swung open, and he drove through, the gate closing behind him. He checked again that he hadn't been followed, and started down the overgrown track towards the house at the end.

Open up to the rafters, the single room was taller inside than wide. Robert had rebuilt it over successive seasons, camping out in the hand-built wooden studio beside it. There was something satisfying about restoring the stone and cob walls, even though it took several years. The thatch was beyond restoration, and Robert had replaced the roof timbers himself in one hectic summer, trying to get the tiny house at least watertight by winter with local slates. Of course, he was younger then, more energetic. But the complete isolation was satisfying, and he had recently installed a generator for electricity. When life off the grid got tedious, he could drive into Moretonhampstead for a coffee, a slice of cake and to commune with his online contacts.

What made the cottage's energy special was that it was set on a flattish rise, the underlying granite just a foot or so under the short, springy grass. Someone had placed stone blocks directly on to the ground, tapping into the energy of the mass of volcanic rocks that lay deep under the moor. The walls continued up, stone rubble and blocks set in cob, finally lime-rendered. But the energy was fantastic. It felt, to a sensitive like Conway, as if a bell struck on the other side of the rock formation would vibrate in the cottage miles away.

He unlocked the door to find the only invaders were a few small rodents. Fortunately, emergency supplies were all stored in metal tins on the shelves that ringed the walls at head height and there was nothing to keep them in the house. The wooden studio was in better order and a shed behind it housed the generator. It took a few minutes to get it started, but once it did it was easy to get the well pump to run some water through the dry pipes in the cottage and to fill up the storage tank. He switched off the generator and the sound faded, leaving the birdsong to fill the silence. He took off his jacket and started the process of cleaning from an old sink in the corner that was all the kitchen he needed.

As sparse as a monk's cell, the single room of the barn had one metal cupboard containing his most precious books, a table for everything from eating to food preparation and reading, and three wooden chairs hung on the wall. He only ever sat on one, but kept the others to put things on. A simple bunk was built into a cupboard, barely long enough for him to lie down in. The mattress was hung up in the wooden cabin next door to keep it from going musty. He swept out mouse droppings and set the live traps. He surprised a young rat in the back porch, and let it out. He could see that was where they were getting in, through a chewed hole in the bottom of the door. He swept out the mess and went into the studio to get tools and wood to repair it. The physical work was satisfying. To air the place, he opened both the doors and the deep-set windows, climbing the ladder to reach the roof lights. By late afternoon he was ready to light the small woodburning stove with bone-dry logs, grind some of the coffee beans he had stored, and hand-pump well water to brew it, the mechanism stiff after its long rest.

He leaned against the sawhorse outside, feeling intensely aware of his surroundings, of the blanketing energy from the granite that suppressed entities, mobile phone signals, everything but his satellite phone was turned off. The trees leaned over the house, one almost touching the chimney at one point, and he made a note to trim it before he remembered this was not a time to relax but to prepare for the biggest challenge of his life.

He finished the coffee and went inside, shutting the door against the cooling evening. The metal cupboard – an especially adapted gun cabinet – had a large deadbolt. The key was on his key ring, and it slid easily into the lock. Inside, wrapped in protective layers, rested his most precious books, never to be sold. One box, inscribed with old Hebrew inscriptions and protection charms, he didn't touch at all.

He chose one book instead, uncasing it gently, and laid it on the table. It was the size of a paperback, with carved wooden covers wrapped in decaying leather. He opened it, gently, revealing the frontispiece.

The account of travels into the world of the Moorish, by Candia unto Alexandria, upon pain of death by our enemy Báthori Erzsébet, for the exorcism of that creature which we dare not name. He looked down the page to the author's handwritten name, almost illegible after centuries of stroking with a finger, much as Robert was tracing it now. Edward Kelley.

Chapter 20

Journal of Eliza Jane Weston, 23 November 1612

'But you, his loving daughter, must know of Kelley's secrets,' said the countess, 'and hold his books, his journals since his death.'

I caught my breath at the ache in my back. I stood, leaning heavily on the arm of the chair. 'Forgive me, lady,' I said, with natural politeness, hardly knowing if I spoke to Saraquel or the countess. 'I sit too long.'

Again, that expression of one woman's sympathy for another. 'I have borne children, Eliza. Your baby comes.'

I opened my mouth to protest, but none came forth. Instead, Tomáš came in and made up the fire. My eyes followed him, wondering if I could call out for him to get help, my husband, anyone. But I knew to do so would herald their deaths, and maybe my children's.

'His journals died with him,' I said, in truth. 'They were lost upon his adventures.'

Edward Kelley, the voyage to Brindisi, 1586

I found that while I had little skill as an oarsman – and none of the required heft – I did have a knack with the sails. Sometimes

I sought the smoothest, fastest ride to calm my delicate stomach. Other times there was pleasure in finding the best breezes at the right moments, until the ship scudded along like a swan trying to fly. I found some joy, too, in the sounds of the rigging, listening for loose lines, the beginning of a flap, the creak of a halyard taking up the strain.

Dee watched me with some amusement. 'Tell me, Edward, will you sign on as a sailor rather than scry for me?'

I smiled but did not take my eye off the horizon, except to glance at the compass. When I took the helm and Dee plotted our course we ran fast and straight for our goal, leaving Marinello to snore in the shade or look over our shoulders at Dee's new charts. He added notes and sketches to his own *routiers*, recording winds and the shape and colour of the waves. The little leather books were wrapped in sharkskin and locked away when not in use, lest one of his men steal one. The books were of great value to merchant ships, the condensed knowledge of generations of master navigators.

'I calculate we shall reach Brindisi early tomorrow,' I said, sparing a look at Dee.

'God willing.' He stared at the rugged coastline. 'There Marinello hopes to discover news of pirates and sell some goods. He will take on fresh food and water, also. Edward, look at those seabirds, do my old eyes deceive me? Are they feeding in a great flock?'

Dee had good eyesight for distances, and I could immediately see what he meant, the white birds in such abundance they looked like sea foam. I called out to Marinello, who dozed in a makeshift chair on deck, his feet up on a bale. The captain hailed the youngest of the men to stand watch, and then stared over the water, his jaw hard with disgust or anger, I could not be certain of which. The youngling called down something in his native tongue.

A brightly coloured piece of fabric bobbed in the water ahead. It was only as it approached that I realised it was the shirt of a man, billowing around the headless stump of his neck, the flesh grey. He rolled in the waves, his bloated belly telling of a day or two at sea.

Marinello called out a new heading – away from the flock of gulls, away from the corpse. Dee spoke in quiet tones to him, then came back to sit beside me at the steering oar.

'Edward, we have found the site of one of the corsairs' massacres. I will plot it on our maps, the sailors of Brindisi must be warned that pirates are operating so close to the port.'

'How can you be sure they were pirates?' I asked, in equally low tones, looking at the disquieted men, several of whom knelt to pray.

'The corsairs behead their enemies.' Dee made a face of disgust. 'Marinello says, should the pirates attack, we will fight with bows. But if they board, we must lay down all our arms immediately. If one man hold a sword against them, they will kill us all.'

The following morning, somewhat against the wind but under oars, the ship arrived at Brindisi and was allowed in after a healthy exchange of shouted oaths and promises. The port was heavily guarded against intruders, and even the Venetian flag and the small size of the ship did not induce trust in the port guards. Finally, we were berthed alongside a ship from Rome, and the authorities searched the ship for stowaways. They were persuaded by Marinello to break open a small barrel of wine he was carrying, and were thus reassured of the provenance of the crew, along with a letter from Konrad. A few coins changed hands, and most of the men were free to disembark and go into the town to enjoy the many pleasures of the port.

'They will all be drunk and destitute by morning,' Marinello said to Kelley and Dee. 'Hopefully, none will be inside the prison, I have little money for ransoms.' He took out his better cloak, and dragged a comb through salty tangles in his hair and beard. 'I should get a barber to attend this thicket of a beard,' he mused, before stepping onto the gunwale of the boat and swarming up the side of the larger Roman vessel. 'Before I present myself to the ladies,' he observed merrily over his shoulder as he crossed the deck, a jaunty word to the watchman of the larger vessel.

'Master, must we go into the town?' I asked, uncertain of the place. Shouts and raucous laughter from the quayside seemed to suggest a rough, dangerous town.

'I have never been to this part of the world,' Dee said, 'but it seems a rare place. Here also lives my correspondent. He is a man who may help us in our quest, a fellow mathematician.'

One of Dee's network of contacts, I guessed, and valuable to add to my own. I went below for my short cloak, and slipped a slim-bladed dagger into the belt at my waist. When I followed Dee on to the Roman ship I was aware of eyes watching from the land. Immediately I stepped ashore, the smell of cooking pork hit me and my stomach growled. It had been some days since we had tasted fresh meat. Dee paid for two great slices of the meat, wrapped around a hot apple and covered with charred rosemary. We juggled the food as we walked past inns, shops, and a few houses, most with half-dressed girls leaning from the upper windows. Dee seemed to be looking for something, and by the time the meat was gone and our fingers licked, he had found it.

'Ah, Edward, here we are!'

I looked at the worn and grubby sign outside a battered door down one of the narrow alleys. I hung back, but Dee rapped a tattoo on it with his cane.

A youngish man peered from the door as it opened, long hair curling about his face, his beard almost as long as Dee's.

'What?' He stared at Dee, then at me. 'I do not treat Gentiles.' He was closing the door when Dee answered in some language I did not know but guessed was Hebrew. The man opened the door again, then looked up and down the alley before ushering us in.

'I'm sorry,' he said, in good Latin, 'but I get fined if anyone sees me treating a Christian. What may I do for you?'

Dee bowed most politely to him. 'We are not in need of your medical services, but we are in need of information.' He waved at me. 'This is Edward Kelley, and I am Dr John Dee, late of the court of her Majesty, Queen Elizabeth of England, and of his Imperial Majesty, Emperor Rudolf.'

'I care nothing for your kings,' the man said, his eyes darting over us. 'But I know of you, Dr Dee, and your kindness to me in replying to my letters makes me humble. I also have a pamphlet by Giordano Bruno, who mentions you.'

Dee bowed. 'And he has mentioned you, also, as a Jewish doctor who lived under the protection of a priest of Venice called Brother Lorenzo.'

The man nodded his head twice, sharp as a bird, and beckoned to us. We had passed some mysterious test, it seemed.

Dee followed the man through a narrow corridor, across a tiny kitchen with a smouldering fire and into a courtyard. A tiny woman, no larger than a ten-year-old child, silently appeared with a tray of cups and, a few moments later, brought some sort of hot infusion within a kettle. Despite the heat of midday, it was refreshing, and

Dee and I sat side by side on a bench in the shade and I laid aside my cloak. The man and woman had gone.

I looked Dee in the eye. 'Tell me,' I said, 'on our friendship. Why are we here? Tell me what it is you fear.'

Dee finished his drink. 'I have grave concerns that you are a mouthpiece, perhaps one of many, for the being called Saraquel. You know that is the name of one of the angels in Enoch, the very text we have been guided towards.'

'This much I know.' I sat back, looking around me but we were still alone. 'But since our days at Csejte castle, I have not sensed his presence. I thought him possessing the countess.'

'Yet in those days, when we wrestled with conscience, we were guided by Saraquel, believing him to be benign.'

I thought back to the many 'spirit conferences' at Dee's house in Mortlake, the ravishing of my mind by beings so great, so dazzling, that I could not hear their voices for the ringing in my very soul. But Dee had written down their speech, and asked them questions. No angel was as powerful, bright or loud as Saraquel, his presence like molten gold within me.

'And now—'

'Now, Edward, a great angel beyond our expectations has been guided to us, not in the conferences, but gently in your sleep. Uriel, an archangel, has spoken to me. Not once, but thrice, and I have followed his instructions. We are to seek the book of Enoch, those wisdoms given directly to a man, no more than seventh in line from Adam, by angels in heaven.'

'In the house of a Jew?' I stammered.

'Remember, Jesus was also a Jew. And the books of Enoch are Jewish texts, they hold them and interpret them for us. They are not written in Hebrew or Greek, nor in Latin. None but Jewish scholars still hold the knowledge of reading the Aksumite scripts. In these we may find the secret of Saraquel's possession and save our families from the countess.'

The man returned and holding his hand pressed to his heart, bowed. 'What exactly can I do for you?' he asked.

'How are you known here, first?' said Dee courteously.

The man hesitated before speaking. 'I am known here as Izaak, the doctor.'

'We seek explanation of the sacred books of Enoch. What do you know of them?'

Izaak shrugged. 'What everyone knows. They were given to man by the angels.'

'I seek a Hebrew translation of it, and a reliable man to interpret it for us.' Dee smiled back at me. 'For I am sure the wisdom we seek is hidden in those words.'

The man spat some words over his shoulder, and the little woman, who must have been standing in the shadows of the house, came forward. She hissed something back, and rolling his eyes, he said: 'My wife has something to say. She understands Latin, but speaks it poorly. I will translate for you.'

Dee turned to the woman and bowed low. After a moment, wondering why I had to be polite to a poor Jewess, I did the same.

She started speaking, and Izaak translated.

'A copy of the ancient text of the books of Enoch is held by my father, the rabbi. He is the scholar you seek, and Izaak will translate for it you. But we are poor, and the Jews here are barely tolerated. A new Pope, an attack by the Turks or the corsairs and we will be under suspicion again. Money will give us the freedom to travel when we are outlawed again.'

Dee stood and bowed to the woman, dwarfing her completely. 'Madam,' he said in sonorous Latin, 'we would not dream of taking your husband's time and not rewarding it.'

I spoke in English to Dee. 'I have a few crowns and a handful of scudi only. Have you gold to pay him?'

Dee furrowed his brow at that, then turned back to our hosts. 'I have little money with me,' he said, smiling. 'But I have the map I have made of our journey. I will be happy to make a copy for you.'

This was inspired – maps changed hands in seafaring nations for enormous sums and Dee was a renowned mapmaker. Immediately, the man turned to his wife and spoke to her, then listened to her rapid speech.

He turned back to Dee. 'A map would be of great value to us,' he conceded. 'The Jews here are forbidden the routiers and maps of the sailors, lest we start trading ourselves.'

The woman disappeared, and returned with a tray of simple foods: fruit, bread and more of the strange tea.

I leaned over to top up my cup with the round, spouted pot. 'You have a wife of some wisdom,' I said to Izaak.

'Wisdom, yes, some. But it is women's wisdom, not given to men to understand fully.' The man threw a glance at the woman who stood again in the doorway, quiet but watching us. 'She is also, as are many of our women, a witch.'

Chapter 21

Present day, Hampshire

Jack was so tired she had little time to worry about Saraquel. She washed up until her hands were raw, she weeded until the convent garden was tidy, did laundry, peeled potatoes. She found some small comfort in the evening prayers, sat at the back of the chapel, sometimes dozing, and sometimes letting tears roll slowly down her cheeks. By each evening she was exhausted, and for the first time since she left Felix she wasn't haunted by terrifying dreams.

Every day, Bea checked in with her, but otherwise Jack made no effort to connect with any of the nuns or the 'guests', fellow retreaters as haunted and hollow-eyed as herself. For five days she just rolled on the surface of a wave of chores, routine, prayer. It was as if time had stopped, as if there were five days outside of time where she could just be Jack for a while.

On day six, everything was different.

She woke up feeling ill, and her neck was sore. Jack's cause of death would have been a shattered cervical vertebra, and she knew she needed to rest in the magical circles and drink some of the decoction that had kept her alive for twenty years. She realised that Saraquel, the source of her previous good health, was damped down by something, maybe the consecrated ground or the chapel. Jack had never believed in God, nor ever been part of any religion, but she had a feeling Saraquel did. She pushed herself a little harder, but also lightly inscribed two circles of symbols, one under the rug and the other over her head in the narrow cell she was sleeping in. It helped her to have a sanctuary to retreat to, and a little investigation of the convent gardens brought up one of the herbs she needed. Cooking it in the kitchen aroused some stares from one of the other retreaters, but she ignored it, and stored it in a washed-out jam jar. The warm decoction, though underpowered, was a relief.

So she was starting to feel positive when the real Charley Slee walked in. Jack dropped the peeler into the potatoes and gaped.

'What – How did you find me? Is Maggie with you?'

There was a chorus of shushing, but Charley shook her head and smiled. Always a fashion original, she was dressed in a denim catsuit with strategic tears all over it, and suede ankle boots. At twenty-two she could get away with it. 'Mum's looking after Sadie with Felix,' she murmured.

Jack dried her hands off and gestured for Charley to follow her outside.

In the garden, Jack turned and fell into Charley's arms. The longing for home, and for Maggie and Sadie and Ches, surged up and Charley just hugged her as she cried. She didn't say anything, just stroked Jack's hair and waited.

Jack finally let go and dived into her pocket for a tissue. 'Oh, God, I'm so pleased to see you.'

'You could have called,' Charley said in a mild voice. 'Mum's been an absolute wreck. We all have.'

'How did you find me?' Jack sat on a bench under a tree heavy with apple blossom.

'Roisin. Maggie finally thought about asking the seer that found you in the first place. She didn't tell Mum, though, just me. Roisin said that was who you needed.'

'Did she tell you – I'm possessed?' Jack barely dared look up at Charley.

'Of course they did! Felix and Sadie are working on it. I don't care if you're possessed, I just want to help you get un-possessed or whatever it is.' She caught Jack's bigger hands in her own, and squeezed them. 'Look, lots of things have happened. Felix is researching this Saraquel and he's quite a character.'

'This schizophrenic guy I met said he was an angel.'

'Yeah. Well, there's a bit of information about angelic possession. Kelley was into it, he used to channel angels. Then he started putting clues around about possession by an angel that had gone bad. His stepdaughter sneaked his ideas into her poems, very secret codeish stuff.'

'Is that even a word?' Jack smiled at Charley, feeling her face stretch into a smile as if it was the first time.

'It is now.' Charley's answering smile faded. 'We think Báthory was possessed by this angel. Once she drank blood it got inside her.'

'And I drank Felix's blood when we fought her.' Jack's head was ticking over the memory of that day. 'When she died – when her body died, I mean – did that allow Saraquel into me?'

'That's our current theory, according to Felix and Sadie.' Charley leaned over and squeezed Jack's hand. 'We've missed you so much – all of us.'

'I'm sorry.' There didn't seem much more Jack could say. 'Saraquel makes me crazy.' Which was a half-truth at best, because it had been Jack who threw herself in the Thames, and Saraquel who had swam to the boat.

'We have to get you out of here.'

'I can't leave. Saraquel grabs me the second I'm outside. He . . .' Jack gulped back the nausea. 'I think he's dangerous. He took me over.' She squeezed her eyes shut at the thought. 'I think I've been hurting people.'

'Oh, Jack.' Charley's eyes filled up and they sat, hand in hand, for a long moment.

Jack stretched her legs out, enjoying the sense of well-being that came with being genuinely tired rather than sleep-deprived. 'Have you told Maggie where I am?'

'Not yet, but I'm going to. She's climbing the walls looking for you. She's even called Pierce and asked him to speak to all his contacts. Sadie's upset too. She's playing up for all of us except Felix.'

Jack looked at her feet, stretched out in old trainers against the short grass. She couldn't ask the question, but Charley answered it anyway.

'Felix hasn't stopped looking for a cure, or looking for you since that night. He's let go of his work, his life in Exeter, everything. He has even considered asking Stephen McNamara to see if this has happened before, or whether exorcism would help.'

'OK.'

Charley squeezed her fingers. 'And he's come up with a plan.'

Jack let go of Charley's hand and fumbled in her pocket for a tissue to blow her nose. 'I'm OK. So, what has Felix come up with?'

Charley rubbed her own eyes and sniffed. 'He wants Sadie to be looked after in a hospital with all the circles and herbs she needs, just with intensive care as well. There's this treatment they want to try. Think of it as –' She narrowed her eyes '– if the moment of death was the low point, this is supposed to help you climb back up.'

'And this treatment can help?'

Charley grimaced. 'There's one catch.'

'Go on.' Jack looked down at the ground.

'The company that have developed the treatment say it helps, but only in a small percentage of cases. It's pretty new, untested.'

Jack sighed. 'Better to try it on me first, then. Only I can't leave here without Saraquel turning me into a monster.'

'Felix is worried about the company that evolved the treatment.' She seemed to be trying to say something.

'Spit it out, Charley.'

'It's Bachmeier and Holtz, Elizabeth Báthory's company.' Before Jack could say anything she rattled on. 'I mean, it makes sense if you think about it. If borrowed time leaves you balanced on the edge of all your organs packing up, surely she would be interested in investing in that research. It might have kept her healthier than you, you said she didn't need the circles or the herbs or anything. They did a lot of research on Jewish prisoners during the war. Horrible. But maybe they created some borrowed timers and learned from them.'

'I can't have treatments tested on concentration camp victims.' Jack was shocked, the revulsion ran deep. But somewhere in the back of her mind, Saraquel noticed her disquiet.

'But Sadie will die if we don't,' Charley said.

'And Báthory lived on blood. It's a huge energy boost.' Charley leaned forward to stress each word. 'She lived for four hundred years, more, even. If we can strengthen you and Sadie with this drug, maybe we can get this thing out. Exorcise it.'

Jack searched inside herself for a reaction to the threat from Saraquel, squeezed down inside her like a dormouse. Nothing. 'I don't think we can, somehow. It's not a demon, Charley, it's an angel. Whatever that is. I can't say it behaved much like an angel when it took over.'

'What do you want me to do?' Charley held out her small hand, and after a moment, Jack put her brown fingers into it again.

'Tell everyone I'm all right. Tell them I'm safe here, and keep working on the plan. And look after Sadie.'

Charley squeezed her hand, then let it go as Bea came across the grass towards her, carrying a large tray of teapot and mugs.

'I'm guessing you are the real Charley Slee.' She put the tray down on the grass and pulled up a garden chair, left in the shade where some of the older nuns liked to snooze in the afternoon.

'Guilty. Oh, let me . . .' Charley knelt on the grass and poured three teas and put a dribble of milk in each.

Bea settled herself into the chair and, for a moment, shut her eyes as she lifted her face up to the light sunshine. 'I'm Bea Armstrong. That's lovely.'

'You're speaking, isn't that breaking the rules?' Jack smiled at the older woman's blissed-out expression.

'That's probably why I'm the ex-nun,' Bea said, opening her eyes to look at the two of them. 'I can't help breaking the rules. Jack believes she's possessed.'

'You can tell Bea,' Jack reassured her. 'She's the nearest we've got to an expert here.'

Charley handed her a cup. 'She is possessed –' the simple statement of fact was more compelling that all the arguments Jack had been making '– by an angel called Saraquel.'

Bea opened her mouth, then closed it again. 'You're not joking, are you.'

'It's a really long story,' Jack said, then sipped her own tea. It was hot and comforting, and when Charley sat down she leaned against her for a moment. 'I'm so pleased to see you.'

'I know. You used to be a nun, Bea?'

Bea nodded, staring at Jack. 'I've never really believed in demons, or angels for that matter. But the church is training more exorcists than it has for a hundred years. Possessed by an *angel*?'

'Called Saraquel. He can't function in churches or on holy ground. I don't know why.' Jack could feel the slight breeze lift a strand of hair, the scent of a few hyacinths halfway across the garden drifting towards her.

'I might know,' Bea said, putting her tea down with a clunk on the arm of her chair. 'According to the exorcism handbook, possessing demons respond most to the belief systems they have been influenced by through inhabiting people. They pick up religion like measles. Maybe angels – I can't believe I'm going along with this – are the same.'

'There's a handbook for exorcisms?' Jack winced a smile. 'We could probably do with a copy.'

'Mostly the guidelines are to rule out mental illness. The problem is, the way demons get in is supposed to be mental illness in the first place.'

'Or possession drives people mad.' Jack's voice was soft, but Bea reached a hand across and patted Jack's leg.

'Not you, not yet,' Bea said. She sat back, putting her hands squarely on her own knees. 'So, how can I help?'

Charley leaned away from Jack, her almost white hair fluttering around her face, freckles creeping across her nose from the first few weeks of spring sunshine. 'What do you want us to do, Jack?'

Jack took a deep breath, then exhaled, realising for the first time that there was a tiny glimmer of hope. Saraquel reacted to that, squirming inside her like a snake trapped in a bag. 'Call the cavalry. I'll give it one go, but that's all. Otherwise I can't keep doing this, Charley, I can't hold him – Saraquel – back much longer. You need to tell Felix to talk to McNamara, look into Kelley's writings, anything.'

Charley bit her lip and lowered her eyes for a moment. 'OK. But we have to give it everything we have: the Inquisition, magic, science. We'll get the bloody Pope if we need him.'

Charley was invited to stay to the communal supper, and Jack enjoyed the feeling that family was close. She realised how much she had missed all of them as she watched Charley charm each of the retreaters and the nuns in turn. She jumped up to help at every turn, halfway, Jack thought, between a ballet dancer and a bird. But strong, and she knew every time Charley looked towards her that tonight, at least, she had her back.

The nuns had found an old camping bed that squeaked like it was a hundred years old and made it up for Charley in the limited space in Jack's cell. Somehow, with Charley's comical observations about the bed, and the convent, and the daft things Ches was doing up north, Jack drifted off to sleep more relaxed than she had been for weeks.

The dream started innocuously enough. She was striding out with her wolf-dog over the fells near Bee Cottage, a few miles from Lake Windermere, when she heard a whimper of distress. It sounded like an injured animal at first, and Jack whistled for Ches to go and look, but couldn't make him hear. Stepping off the path, towards the edge of an escarpment, she saw the broken body of a red-haired girl. Again, the noise, then the girl looked up with an impossibly distorted neck and mewed, 'Jack'. It was Charley, not now Charley, but the thirteen- or fourteen-year-old who had dyed her hair a different colour every month and drew tattoo designs all over herself until she was old enough to get a real one.

'Hold on, Charley!' Jack dragged off her coat, and held it over the edge. 'Catch the end!'

The girl made no effort to, but cried in pain, both arms twisted unnaturally under her body. Her cries started to be panted out, calling out Jack's name, the sound gasping in her throat as if she was being suffocated.

Jack awoke with a start, to hear the same sound in the room. She was kneeling on Charley's legs, her fingers digging into her foster sister's throat. She could just see Charley's outline in the narrow bed, squirming and fighting, her hands around Jack's wrists. Jack fought to release the pressure but found she was leaning forward, more of her weight on the delicate structures in Charley's neck, the pulse fluttering madly against one thumb. Her fingers were digging into Charley's skin so hard she could feel her nails cutting the skin.

Jack tried to stretch her hands back, to lean her own weight away. She succeeding in taking some of the pressure off, but her hands were gripping so tight she could only cry out in frustration as she felt, rather than heard, the tiny squeak of Charley trying to take in a little air. Jack managed to wrench her fingers back for a moment, just a second before they clamped back on Charley's throat, but long enough for her sister to grab one breath of air and tuck her chin down. She let go of one of Jack's wrists and reached up.

The next thing Jack knew was a searing heat across her forehead, pressed there by Charley's shaking hand, the room lit by some brilliant light, or maybe that was just in her head. She fell back, or was thrown back, into the space by the door, falling in a tangle of limbs, the pain behind her eyes still burning. She reached a shaking hand to the handle and pulled the door open.

The light in the hall was low but enough to see that Charley's face was purplish red, her eyes closed, her hand slumped at her side as she heaved with the effort to get her breath back. When Jack tried to stumble to her feet, Charley opened her eyes and waved her hand in front of her. It held the large wooden cross which had been on the wall above Charley's head. Jack stepped away and switched on the bedroom light.

It took several minutes for Charley's rasping breaths to go back to normal and several more for her to trust long enough to let go of the crucifix, resting it within reach. Charley's neck was dark red and already purpling up; the whites of her eyes were scarlet. She couldn't speak above a hoarse whisper, and terrified that she was seriously injured, Jack ran to get Bea. When she returned, Charley was resting, her head on her knees, sitting up in bed.

'Bea's coming. I'm so sorry.' It didn't seem possible to stop saying it, even when Charley rolled her eyes and mimed for Jack to shut up.

'Come here,' Charley managed to say, opening her arms. When Jack gently hugged her, she could feel Charley's heart jumping in her chest, her whole frame shaking with each breath.

'That – that was – Saraquel?' rasped Charley.

'Well, it wasn't me! But I didn't think he could operate here.'

Charley's head dropped onto Jack's shoulder for a moment, her hair plastered to her forehead with sweat.

'I'd hate to see him . . . at full strength, if that's him damped down by holy ground.'

She rested for a few minutes, Jack trying to feel inside her own mind for Saraquel, but all she got was the impression of distant laughter. When Bea came she brought the girl some ice cubes to sip to ease her sore throat, and dabbed a cold cloth on the bruises on her neck.

'You need to get out of here, if he's going for you.' Jack let Charley go and looked up at Bea. 'I thought she'd be safe here.'

Charley rubbed her eyes. 'You said he was less powerful on holy ground.'

'He is. I didn't know he could do anything.' She looked up at the ceiling. 'Oh, shit. The symbols, the magic. Maybe they help him in some way, too.'

'I'll sleep with the crucifix. I'll be fine.' Charley lay back down, lightly pressing her throat with her fingertips. 'I'm going to have such a bruise.'

'If that's all you have, we'll be fine.' But she was mortified, looking at the marks on Charley's neck.

'Yeah, but we know one thing.'

Jack lay down, putting her hand out to the light, but then deciding to leave it on. 'What's that?'

'It's scared of me and my crucifix.' Charley smiled across at Jack. 'Now go to sleep.'

But neither did more than doze for the rest of the night, and Bea left the door open so she could hear them.

Chapter 22

Present day, London

The woman who sat in front of Felix had her hands clasped in her lap, the knuckles white. The eyes that gazed into his were as light green and straight as Jack's. She had agreed to meet him in a hotel after the police put them in contact.

'The police said you have spent time with her. Tell me what you know about my daughter.' As direct as Jack, too.

'I haven't known her very long,' he said, trying to think what to say. 'I met her a few months ago. Last November.'

'And the last time you saw her, she was well?'

'She was.' That, at least was true. 'She ran away and, well, you have been told about her suicide attempt. I haven't seen her since.'

'And you haven't heard from her.'

There, the question he couldn't avoid. 'No.' It was a painful admission even to himself. Six weeks and not a word. She could already be dead. 'Mrs Harcourt—'

'Olivia.'

'Olivia. The whole time I knew Jack she was unwell. She was very weak.'

142

The woman let her gaze drop for a few seconds, and he could see tears balanced on her lower eyelids. 'The hospital said she was dying. But she got out of a bed and walked out of the hospital. How could that be, Professor?'

'Felix, please.' He took a deep breath, looking at the blank window, reflecting the hotel room back. 'I don't know, but perhaps she was used to being so ill.'

She stared back at him again, her head tilted a little, the way Jack looked at him when she wanted more than he was saying. 'Do you believe she is still alive?'

'Yes.' The answer fell out before he had time to censor it. 'But . . . I love your daughter, Mrs Harcourt. I can't bear to think of anything else.'

'You must be twenty years older than Melissa. Jack. Whatever she's calling herself.'

'Almost.' He smiled wryly, glancing down at his hands for a moment. 'But I don't know anyone quite like her.'

'Tell me.' Her voice was unsteady, and when he looked up a tear had found its way down her face and around the corner of her mouth. 'What's she like?'

He took a big breath before answering. 'She's brave, and compassionate and she's loyal. Once she takes someone on, she will defend them to the end. But you better not ask her opinion unless you really want it, because she's uncompromisingly honest. And . . . she's innocent. She's led a very sheltered life. I think I'm the first person, the first man, she has been close to.'

The tears turned into sobs, and Olivia buried her face in her hands.

Felix felt helpless. He reached out a hand as if to pat her shoulder, but didn't connect. 'I'm sorry. I'm so sorry.'

'I . . . we, my husband and I, we thought she had been abducted by some monster.' She found a tissue in her bag, and blew her nose, mopping her eyes. 'I didn't want to believe she was dead, but then I imagined her in the hands of some sadist . . .' The tears came again, and Felix waited while she mastered them, rocking slightly in her chair, lost in grief. Tears prickled his eyes in sympathy.

'I don't think her life was bad,' he offered, immediately regretting the words. 'I mean, she seemed quite happy. Maybe not happy – content, when I met her. Just ill.'

'Did she ever talk about the abduction?' Olivia tucked the tissues back in her bag and turned to Felix.

'Only that she grew up in a family and was cared for. I don't know what happened.'

'Would you tell me if she contacts you?' She closed her eyes for a second before staring back at him.

'I will tell her I met you,' he replied, more honestly. 'I will tell her you want to see her, I promise. But Jack – Jack is a very private person, and if she's so unhappy she tried to commit suicide, I don't want to put more pressure on her.'

Olivia nodded slowly then reached into her handbag. She brought out a letter. 'Then, can you give her this? I didn't seal it. I thought you might want to read it first, if you know her so well.'

'Thank you.' He took the letter, brushing Olivia's cold fingers. 'If I can, I'll give it to her.'

She narrowed her gaze and studied him again. 'I can see what she sees in you, I think,' she said, her voice rough from the crying. 'There's something very reassuring about you.'

'Not fatherly?' Felix said, his voice cracking. 'I wonder if she just sees me as a father figure.'

Olivia smiled, the expression more sad than amused. 'Fatherly, no. Her own dad . . . It was easier for him to believe her dead than being abused. He left me a year after – I don't blame him, but—'

'You lost a child and your marriage in the same year.'

She shook back her short hair, darker than Jack's and threaded with a lot of white. 'But my memories of Melissa have always been with me.'

Felix was suddenly filled with emotion for this woman who reminded him so much of Jack, excusing the man who gave up on his child and moved on. 'If I speak to Jack, I'll make her promise – when all this is over, when she feels better. She will make contact.'

Olivia stood, lifting her bag onto her shoulder, her shoulders tight. Felix put out a hand, and she took it in both of hers, squeezing it a little. 'Thank you. If she's still alive. I do understand from the doctors that she has been very ill.'

'Jack is the ultimate survivor,' he said. 'And she's got a lot of friends who love her. We're all hoping that she will be OK.'

Her cold fingers released his slowly. 'Please tell me if you hear from her. Anything that tells me she's still alive.'

He nodded slowly, even though it was a promise he knew he might have to break. He checked his watch. It was time to get back to Sadie, to get ready for the hospital the next day. The travelling was exhausting, he would have to catch up with some sleep on the train.

Felix held Sadie's trembling hand. She was ashen-faced, the shadows and hollows of her face suggesting the skull beneath it. Her mother Angela held the other hand, and Sadie whispered something to her. Then she turned to Felix. 'If I die . . .'

'This is so you won't,' he said, as uncertain as she sounded.

'If I die,' she continued. 'I want you to find out why, so you can help Jack. You know, do a post-mortem or whatever they are called.' She grimaced with gallows humour. 'Only make sure I'm really dead, you know, not just half dead.'

'It's not going to happen. If you get worse, we'll improve the symbols on your skin and Maggie will do all the healing spells she knows. You'll be fine.'

Maggie spoke from the end of the bed. 'We can stop the treatment at any time, I promise.'

'Who's looking after Bandit?' the girl asked, already a little sleepy.

Maggie walked up and stroked the fringe out of her eyes. 'I'll go back and look after all the animals every day, I promise. It's only an hour's drive, and I can walk Ches and play with the cat and the raven. Angela and I will get some rest too. And Charley will be able to help when she gets back from looking for Jack.'

Felix nodded through the window to George, who pushed open the door, followed by two nurses and Lexie, the anaesthetist, who would be supervising Sadie's sedation.

'I'm scared,' Sadie whimpered.

'I know.' Felix gripped her hand more tightly, while Lexie leaned over the girl.

'You need the rest,' she said, with gentle authority. 'This will be like a really refreshing sleep. It won't seem like long to you, but you will be better when you wake up. OK?'

Sadie nodded, her lip trembling. Her eyes started to droop before she could say anything, and Felix noticed Lexie had slipped a needle into Sadie's IV. 'We need to intubate,' she added, nodding at Angela, who was already weeping into Sadie's other hand.

Felix took Angela out while the nurses and doctors worked over Sadie's body, connecting her to the ventilator that would breathe for her, putting in more tubes and drips, taking blood. Angela sat in a small waiting room and sobbed.

'I thought she was getting better,' she said, mumbling through her fingers.

'I wish she was but she seems weaker each day. We want to give her the best chance,' he said, feeling helpless.

George put his head around the door. 'We are running further tests, but she's already further stable. Her oxygen levels were dangerously low, her blood sugar was in her boots. We've corrected those straight away. We're going to do everything we can, I promise, Angela. You can go and sit with her in a few minutes. One of the nurses will be along to talk to you shortly, and to make sure you get some food and sleep too.'

Felix followed him into the corridor. 'She doesn't understand all of this, all she knows is Sadie is dying. She's already buried her once.'

'One day you'll have to explain all that to me.' George's face was creased with concern. 'Look, I suspect I'm breaking half a dozen laws here. The other staff don't know, they just think she's recovering from a tropical illness, but Felix – we could all get into a lot of trouble.'

'I know. I'm sorry, George. I didn't know what else to do. But the less you know, the less incriminating it is.'

George looked down at the clipboard he was carrying. 'Let's see if we can help. But you need to look through this research. Bachmeier and Holtz developed a treatment a few years ago, it's not licensed for general use yet. They have a clinical trial authorisation, and they have had some good results. No better than other protocols but—'

'Bachmeier – they don't know who the patient is, do they?' He could feel his heart drop a beat at the name. Maybe they could identify her by her abnormal blood results, the possibility was terrifying. 'Sadie's identity is absolutely confidential. No one can know who she is, what she is.'

'I don't understand.' George looked at the monitors. 'Bachmeier and Holtz are leading the world in some aspects of intensive care. And you were the one that suggested them in the first place.'

Felix took three swift paces to Sadie's door, turned and came back. 'You don't understand. You don't know what they are allied with.'

'Without Respiridol, Sadie will die. The symptoms that seem especially severe in Sadie were the ones helped most by the drug regime, according to their research. I don't know what to do for her other than slow the inevitable. Take her core temperature, for example.'

'She's cold all the time, I know.'

'Not cold, she's severely hypothermic. Down to under thirty-three degrees. Normally I'd rush to warm her up but I'm reluctant to mess with whatever's going on with her. The Bachmeier and Holtz protocol seemed to resolve issues of core temperature.' He tapped the clipboard which had a fat report secured to it. 'Read it through. Any questions, I'll be looking after all the patients whose physiology I *do* understand.'

Felix went back to Sadie's room in time for one of the nurses to explain what was going on to a tearful Angela and hostile Maggie. Sadie had somehow shrunk in the bed, tubes up her nose and in her mouth, a dribble of urine in a bag at her side. He paid attention, learning to read the monitors on a screen at her side. They had turned all the alarms off, and even he knew a heart rate of thirty-odd was wrong. Her blood pressure was almost immeasurably low, but the ventilator whooshed regularly into her lungs and she had a slightly better colour.

'We've starting feeding by drip and a small amount of nutrients via the tube into her stomach,' the nurse explained. 'We're repeating the bloods this evening to see if we can get some improvement.'

'She looks so ill,' Angela whispered.

Felix put his hand on her shoulder and she crumpled against him. 'It's going to be OK,' he mumbled, hoping his tone would reach her, at least, as he patted her back. 'She's getting the best care and the doctors are looking into a new treatment as well. And Maggie will be here.'

Maggie stroked one of Sadie's hands, softly talking to the girl. Then she turned to Angela. 'She can hear you, Angie, I'm sure, if you speak clearly. She needs her mum now.'

Angela fumbled a tissue to her face. Felix could smell the alcohol on her breath. She had been drinking heavily since Sadie's abduction and near death last year.

'I know,' Angie managed, then took Sadie's other hand. 'We're with you, Sades. We're all trying to make you better. I just want my little girl back.'

She dissolved into tears again, and all Maggie could do was look at Felix and jerk her head towards the door.

He walked down the corridor away from the intensive therapy unit, towards the car park. He sat on a bench outside in the fading light and began reading the research papers. When his phone beeped he almost ignored it, but long habit made him check it. There was a message from an unfamiliar number.

Jack OK. In safe place. Will call later. Charley x.

Charley didn't respond to texts or answer her phone and it was a long wait before, finally, his phone rang.

'Charley, thank God.'

'No, it's me.' The voice was hoarse, but unmistakably Jack.

He was stunned to silence, relief surging through him like a wave, leaving a mixture of anger and fear behind. 'God, Jack, we've been so worried. Are you all right?'

'No. I'm really not.' Her voice cracked on the words. 'He – Saraquel, he's been in charge ever since I—' She couldn't say it. 'I don't know what to do.'

All the things he had rehearsed for this moment had disappeared. 'I don't know either.'

She chuckled weakly at the other end of the phone. 'Charley says you have considered exorcism. But you don't know how to do it.'

'If you have any ideas, it would be very helpful.'

'I'm sure Saraquel is an angel. But you know that already.'

He didn't know how to answer, or how much he could safely tell her. 'Kelley wrote about Saraquel, you know that. Look, Jack, there are hints in his journal about this, and about the book of Enoch. I'm reading it as fast as I can because it fits with something his daughter wrote. She encoded a message in her poetry, Sadie and I have been decoding as much as we can. We think Saraquel doesn't possess one person at a time but many.'

She paused for a moment before answering. 'That's crazy – but kind of makes sense. I can almost hear other voices when he takes over.'

'I thought Stephen McNamara might know something, someone. I might be able to track him down through the Vatican number he gave me last year.' He could hear her breathing down the phone. At least she was still breathing. 'Look, Jack, you need to promise me something. No matter how bad it gets, you won't do – that again. Try and kill yourself.' The words failed him.

'I won't have to if you get the Inquisition involved,' she said, her voice stronger. 'McNamara will probably have a stake through my heart the second he sees me.'

'I don't think he will. I think he wants to get Saraquel, not you.'

She broke off and spoke to someone else, then returned to the phone. 'Charley's asking if you've started the treatment with Sadie?'

'We have, just this morning. The first blood tests show a small improvement. They are going to put her on dialysis later to clean some of the toxins out of her blood.'

'Good. That's good.' She spoke to Charley again, her voice muffled, then returned to the phone. 'I'm not ready to tell you where I am, Felix. That way you can talk to Mac but not give away where I am. Do some research into exorcism, and when you are ready, I'll tell you where I am. How's that?'

He could see the logic but was frustrated by the secrecy. Then a thought occurred to him. 'Have you seen a newspaper over the last few days?'

'Why?'

Charley must have kept it quiet deliberately for some reason. 'Let me talk to Charley.'

'No, talk to me.' That was the strident Jackdaw he knew.

'When you were in hospital the police compared your fingerprints and DNA with records they had from twenty years ago.'

'Oh, God.' She sounded dazed.

He waited for a long moment. 'Jack?'

'Did they contact my parents?'

'They had to. There's a nationwide manhunt for you. I spoke to your mother, she's desperate to see you.'

'Oh.' Another long silence. 'I have to go.' The phone clicked and she was gone.

The next day brought the dialysis process, and Felix took over sitting with Sadie while her mother and Maggie went home to rest. The slow whoosh of the ventilator was joined by the soft hum of the machine cleaning Sadie's blood. He started reading the report by Bachmeier and Holtz again. It used words like promising and success but only 14 per cent of the test subjects survived, compared to 11 in the control group.

The door opened and for a moment he didn't look up, expecting one of the nurses, but a pair of expensive brogues came into his peripheral vision. He glanced up and for a moment couldn't recall the face, although the man, perhaps a little older than himself with thick silver hair, seemed familiar.

Of course. 'Pál Bachmeier,' he said.

'I've made no secret of it,' the man agreed, his voice accented with some middle European accent. 'And you are Felix Guichard.'

'And you are Elizabeth Báthory's descendant.'

The man half-smiled, then sat on one of the two chairs by the window. 'Oh, I think you can do better than that, Professor.'

Felix looked at the man, then again. There was something, maybe around the eyes and chin, that was familiar. And he was hard to date, in some ways he looked older but his skin was tight and his hands smooth. The truth came in a rush. Elizabeth Báthory needed to keep her son alive to ensure the succession. 'She made you a borrowed timer – a revenant.'

'A borrowed . . . oh, I see.' He laughed, and sat down in one of the chairs. 'Yes, if you like. My mother had lost two sons, one at birth and one in childhood. I was a late gift for my father.' He shrugged. 'They needed an heir.'

Felix found himself standing between Sadie and Bachmeier. He knew Báthory had kept her life going by draining the blood of another revenant every generation or so.

'You don't have to worry,' the man said softly. 'I know what you did last year.'

'We killed your mother.'

Pál shrugged. 'For me, you released a tortured soul from centuries of captivity. You know she was possessed?'

Felix studied the man. His face suggested little emotion, just interest and maybe a touch of amusement at Felix's defensiveness. 'But you aren't?'

Pál smiled, and he looked at Sadie. 'For the first years – I don't know how many, all my childhood certainly – I was weak, like young Sadie. But gradually I grew stronger. My mother surrounded me with people she knew could keep me alive – she used methods developed by someone you have been researching.'

'Edward Kelley.'

'And we would love to support your research efforts.'

Felix sat by Sadie's side, still ready to jump up if needed. 'You were trying to buy the fifteenth folio. When you couldn't, you tried to steal it.'

'Indeed. But Professor Dennett is an intelligent women, she concealed it somewhere out of our reach. But I'm sure you now know what is in it – or even have a copy.'

'Why would I help you, even if I did?'

Bachmeier looked back at the child and waved a hand at the monitors on the wall. 'Because we have effective treatments for this weakness. Without the help of my doctors I doubt if she will survive more than another few weeks.'

Felix could hear something in his voice, but after four centuries presumably Pál had developed the ability to dissemble flawlessly. 'Why do you think we would ever trust you? Your mother was . . .' Faced with the man himself he hesitated.

'A monster? A crazed, possessed creature who killed countless children and young women? Definitely. But I hardly knew her.'

Felix frowned. 'What?'

'She knew that I was at risk of possession by her personal demon, Saraquel. I was in the room with her a few times in my whole life, and then only on holy ground.'

Felix sat back. 'So how do you survive and stay strong?'

'Ah. I would like to help you, Professor, I really would. But I need something from you first.'

'Folio fifteen?'

Pál smiled. 'Exactly. I would also like Professor Dennett's help, but if that's impossible, I would happily take a copy of the folio.'

'Why? Clearly you have understood your own condition well enough to stay healthy.'

Pál winced. 'But not young. Every time I weaken, even for a day or two, I age. I was in my twenties for almost three hundred years, then last century I started to deteriorate. We managed to do some research during the war but I had aged three decades in just seventy years. We made the final breakthrough in the twentieth century and I've been holding steady but . . .'

Felix shuddered at the thought of the research they must have conducted. 'And you think Kelley knew how to stop the ageing process?'

Pál leaned forward. 'He knew how to stop the possession that goes with the taking of human blood. I'm hunted by Saraquel – I'm vulnerable. He has more hosts than ever. I was worried about coming here – I dare not be in the same building as Jackdaw Hammond. But I'm still human.'

Felix took a deep breath and leaned back, studying the man. 'This Saraquel—'

'Has the power to possess revenants, yes. Hundreds, even thousands at a time. And they are coming to the UK each day – we count two hundred and twenty so far. They are Saraquel's army.'

Sadie made a slight sound, as if she had twitched in her drug-induced sleep. 'Will they – Saraquel – come to take Sadie?'

'She hasn't taken blood yet, has she? She wouldn't be dying now if she had.' He shrugged. 'This Jackdaw – if she took blood and then Saraquel was disembodied, she had no defence against him.'

'She's found a way to stay free of him.'

'Consecrated ground helps somewhat, in the first months. But only exorcism works completely, and I know of no one who has survived the experience in modern years. But I think Kelley knew more than he published. He sent the details to his daughter.'

Felix stood and walked over to the window. The sunshine outside heated up the room and it was hard to believe he was sitting with someone more than four centuries old. A part of him wondered how much history the man had seen, the stories he could tell.

'Eliza Jane Weston.'

'She put those instructions about the nature of Saraquel and how to exorcise him in her poetry. Unfortunately, to tease out those instructions we need the whole catalogue of her published writing and a few pamphlets eluded us.'

'Like the fifteenth folio.' Felix thought rapidly. 'Which contains the key to decipher the other clues.'

'Exactly. It was in the hands of a private collector and his heirs for many generations, then donated to the university.'

'Robert Conway.'

Pál Bachmeier laughed out loud, a soft sound in the quiet room. 'Conway, yes. Who we would like to talk to even more. He had the folio in his family's possession for a long time, and they were as elusive as revenants. They knew the value of Weston's writings. I think they were sorcerers.'

'Did you ever meet this Weston?' The question sounded absurd in Felix's ears even as he said it.

Pál shook his head. 'She died when I was a child. But my mother met her and tried to get the information Kelley had left her.'

'Did she manage it?' Felix could feel his phone vibrating in his pocket.

'Some, but no, not what she needed. Eliza Weston was an extraordinary young woman. That's no surprise, I suppose, being raised by Edward Kelley himself.'

Felix looked down at Sadie. 'I want you to save this child. I want your best treatments, experimental or not.'

'But—'

'And I will do my best to win Professor Dennett's cooperation. But you will back off, leave her alone. You understand? She is elderly, and frightened by your goons.'

'So I'm supposed to give you the benefit of a multi-million-dollar research project – on trust?' He took his glasses off and looked at Felix. His eyes were faded blue like his mother's, almost a pearl-grey.

Felix looked directly at him. 'Because you claim to still be human, you will help save Sadie. You will have to take on trust that I will intervene with Alicia.'

'But you and I need to work together. The child, yes, I can do that, we can try our best. But if revenants are closing in on England, and I suspect your Jackdaw, it must be because Saraquel is weakened by her. The Inquisition will not be far behind.'

'Why?'

'Because this is a rare opportunity to exorcise Saraquel. If an exorcist can evict Saraquel from just one victim, it may be possible to exorcise several more, weakening him further. We could finally end this five-thousand-year-old curse and send Saraquel back where he belongs. I know of only one man who is reputed to be able to do it.'

'What exorcist knows enough to do that?' Felix guessed the answer by the time Pál said it.

'Our mysterious Robert Conway, of course.'

Chapter 23

Journal of Eliza Jane Weston, 23 November 1612

The countess turned to the door as Tomáš entered with a basket of wood, and watched as he laid the fire. Tomáš is but a young man, and the back of his neck seemed vulnerable to her gaze, which was fixed upon him as if greedy for him. I thanked him, and dismissed him. My belly was hard again, and I pressed a hand to my back.

'I am indisposed,' I said, in a gasp. 'You must come back another day.'

'You have time. Your father's letters, then, you have those?'

'I do not.' The pain eased, and I sank into my chair.

She leaned forward and took my face in one hard hand, the long fingers digging into my cheeks. 'Tell me, lady, or I will rip the child from your belly. Do not doubt that I can.'

I looked into her eyes, I fancied glowing blue with her passion. 'I do not doubt it,' I said, my voice weak through a dry throat.

'Tell me what you know,' she ground out through her teeth. She released my face, and I fancied it bruised to the bone, it ached so much.

Edward Kelley, Brindisi, 1586

Izaak and his wife dressed themselves for the town. They had to go in disguise, as all Jews had been ordered from the town many years before. A few had returned from Alexandria, mostly to trade in medicines and currency. It was a miserable life, and the woman, covered from head to toe in a dirty cloth I would not have thrown over a horse, was spat at as if she was a beggar. But no one hindered us, and eventually we came to a simple house unmarked with a name or number. We slipped down an alley so narrow that I reflected it was helpful none of us were stout.

A side door led to a small room as dark as a closet, and lit only by foul-smelling tapers made of some animal fat. Inside it, a man was taking his ease on a low settle, his bearded chin nodding, his bald head marked with brown spots declaring his age.

The young Jews behaved with great reverence, waking him gently, the woman immediately taking a kettle through a door that I judged went through to the front of the building. After some confusion, as the man gathered his wits, he turned his face towards Dee and me. It was then we saw that he was completely blind, his eyes like white pebbles.

'Visitors, you say?' he said in Latin. A smile broke over his face, so welcoming and glad that I was humbled. What could we bring these beggarly people? In stumbling Latin, laced with Greek and what I recognised as Hebrew, he welcomed us into his home.

'My Latin – is small, you understand? Modest.' He waved his hand. 'Sit, sit.'

Dee took the only stool, Izaak sat beside the man on the settle, and I sat upon a box by the door. The whole room stank of fish, and when I looked up I realised why. Hundreds of silvery fillets were strung overhead, drying.

'We are scholars, seeking knowledge of the book of Enoch,' Dee said, in slow Latin. Clearly the old man understood it, although he asked Isaak for a few words as the conversation progressed.

'The books are far too valuable to keep in a humble home like this. They are kept in safety in the synagogue at Krakow,' the old man said, his smile as broad as ever. 'I know the words by heart, of course.'

'It is an older scroll that I seek,' said Dee, surprising me as well as Izaak. 'One written in Abyssinian, the land that you call Ethiopia.'

The old man nodded, but I had the impression he had tensed. 'That is to be found – if it is still safe – in Alexandria. Even if you locate it, you shall find it impossible to read. No one in Alexandria can decipher the language the scrolls are written in directly, although we have copies of the original translation.'

Dee leaned forward to speak gently to him in stumbling Hebrew, which I didn't understand. Whatever he said, the old man looked surprised, leaning back for a moment.

'I understand,' he said, in slow Latin. 'All translations are incomplete. The script was unfamiliar to me when I saw it, but my mentor could read a few phrases. They are spoken in ritual, you understand.'

'What ritual?' Dee asked, looking at me.

The old man shrugged, and reached a hand out to Izaak. He whispered something to the young doctor, who whispered back.

It was Izaak who answered. 'Magic rituals, almost lost to our religion but kept alive by a few of our wiser women and some scholars. Especially Rabbi Loew, who works the holy magic to protect our people.'

'Holy magic?' I couldn't stop myself blurting the word out.

'The magic was given to Enoch in heaven, to bring back to man. The book tells the story of an angel called Shemhazai, or in Christian texts, I think Samyaza. He persuaded the angels we call the Watchers to fly down to earth and take human women to wife.'

'I know this,' Dee said slowly. 'They gave birth to the Nephilim, unclean in God's sight.'

'That mating of divine messenger and human women was spiritual, not physical, in our interpretation of the texts,' the old man said, 'which gave rise to a race of men who craved the blood of children, and their flesh.'

'The biters,' Dee said, looking at me. '"And to Gabriel said the Lord: Proceed against the biters and the reprobates, and against the children of fornication: and destroy the children of the Watchers from amongst men." The biters are the children of angels and mortal women?'

Izaak murmured to the rabbi, then spoke directly to Dee. 'Some members of our sect believe that those are the angels that have become so corrupted by contact with mortals and their base desires that they become monsters. The *dybbuk*.'

Kelley nodded slowly. 'You mean, a person who is inhabited by a – fallen angel? One of the Watchers?'

Izaak leaned forward, his black eyes darting from Dee to myself. 'I cannot believe that an angel itself would do evil things, to hurt others, but perhaps within the sinful form of a human it cannot resist. They might suffer the temptations of man: lust, gluttony, violence. These are the creatures you seek?'

Dee sighed. 'Rather, my young friend, they seek us. One woman, unnatural in her existence, seems to have become contaminated by such a force. She craves blood, even that of her unborn child.

161

She seeks the possession's expulsion. She has our wives and children held captive in Bohemia.'

After a few moments of discussion, Izaak interpreted the old man's speech for us.

'The exorcism you seek is that of Zadok.'

'I know nothing of the exorcism save the name.' Dee looked at me. 'If we exorcise the countess, she dies. For she is certainly unnatural, and haunted by a possessing spirit.'

'Neither God nor angels allow such creatures. If such exists it is unnatural and must be ended. We wish you success in your mission. Our rabbi will give you letters for Rabbi Loew in Alexandria.'

Then Dee leaned forward. 'And what of the golem your people speak of?'

Izaak did not translate until the old man, smiling, spoke to him. Then the old man stopped smiling. Izaak translated.

'This is secret, you understand, but because you are a holy man in your own way I will tell you this. It was given to the Jews, in a direct line from Enoch himself, to do the holy magic that gives life to inanimate creations. It is written that a traveller such as yourself will go to Alexandria, to the temple there, and will destroy the Watcher who haunts mankind.'

'Master,' I said urgently in English. 'Alexandria is hundreds of leagues away, even more via Candia.'

'Hardly a hundred, Edward. We can travel with Marinello to Candia and then onward to Alexandria if the conditions are good.'

'But it will take so long. Perhaps we should return now.'

Dee paused for a long moment. 'Travel by ship is so fast, Edward, we can do twenty leagues in a day with the right winds.' He bowed to the Jews and spoke in his most stately Latin, quietly translated by Izaak. 'We shall take your sage advice, rabbi, and travel to Alexandria. Letters of introduction would be truly helpful.'

After a few minutes, Izaak took the dictation of the old man and helped him sign it. He then folded the paper carefully, and the woman entered carrying three metal medallions and three small scrolls, densely covered with what looked like symbols. Izaak secured the letter with an impression of the rabbi's ring pressed into the wax, then turned to each of the scrolls. Each had to be fastened with a different seal, the woman muttering over each, and spitting upon one of the medallions before pressing it into the wax to secure each scroll. Immediately afterwards, we were ushered to our feet. The woman, who kissed the old rabbi's hand several times, held out her hand for coins, which Dee dropped into her palm.

She nodded several times, transferring the money to a pot beside the old man, then pointed to the door. As we stepped into the alley she finally spoke. 'You need help. Yes? Yes, old man, young man?'

I answered her as clearly as I could. 'We have help, madam, from your rabbi.'

She shook her head and held out her hand. After some muttering, Izaak indicated that she wanted to hold the scrolls.

'See? Here?' She indicated the three scrolls. I bent over and squinted at them in the low light. The seals each had a different design.

'They have symbols on them,' I said to Dee.

'This one,' she said, tapping the one on the right. 'For winds, yes? See birds. This for fire, see flames and smoke?' There was an impression of an inferno. 'This –' She pointed to the one on the left with a strange shape in it '– This one for help from God. Yes? Only use very big danger.' I recognised it as a stylised hand. 'When only death can come.'

Izaak nodded. 'They are spells from our tradition,' he explained. 'My wife sends you with them, but only break them if you really need them, especially the last. Women's magic is hard to control,' he added, 'but God's true name is harder still.'

She tapped the final one gently. 'This one – only in great need, yes? When death comes? This is foretold by Zadok the seer. Only a champion of the Jews may use this magic.'

Dee thanked her profusely, and I placed the letter and scrolls within an inside pocket of my cloak. We escorted the woman back to the alley where their humble house was, and she disappeared without a glance at us. Izaak came to the ship with us, so that he could see Dee's map and make a copy.

Despite the muttering of the few returned crewmen Izaak managed to make a fairly accurate copy both of Dee's map from Venice to Brindisi, and a sketch of Marinello's map. He also made copious notes, his hand as fluent as a scholar – but then, I could not be surprised as he was a doctor. He saw me looking over his shoulder.

'We are taught to write as children,' he explained, 'forming the letters of the prayers and scriptures.' The notes were incomprehensible, which he inscribed swiftly from right to left. 'You must come back and show me the map when it is completed.'

'We will,' said Dee, staring at a group of muttering men gathering on one of the larger ships. 'I'm afraid you must hurry, my friend,' he added.

'I am finished,' Izaak said, looking where Dee was staring. 'Make sure you visit the rabbi at Alexandria, for he holds the original books.'

'We will.' Uncaring of the angry stares from the onlookers, Dee held out a hand to the young doctor, who hesitated only a moment before grasping Dee's forearm.

'Go with God, friend,' he said, letting go of Dee and reaching for my arm, 'whatever you call Him. I wish you well on your journey.'

He scuttled onto the larger ship, up the ladder to the quay and back into the shadow of the wall. A stone skidded after him as he reached the gate and the muttering grew into shouts but he slipped through out of sight. The men went back to their group, now scowling at us. Oblivious to their hostility, Dee returned to the cabin and I judged it politic to join him.

We looked at the three seals, and the first thing I noticed was that each was in a different-coloured wax. I hadn't been aware of them using different tapers, but one was grey, one almost black, and one a reddish brown. Something drew me to them and I was reluctant to let Dee hold them.

Dee opened his journal to copy the intricate shapes. 'This one, upon the left, for fire, did she say?' he murmured, and I knew he was already intrigued by her witch magic, if indeed it was witchcraft. 'Strange,' he said, poring over the fine detail inscribed on the outside of one scroll, the last she gave us, the one she warned us not to break unless death was the only other option.

'What, Master?' I asked, but he shook his head and pushed the three scrolls together.

'Put them in the map bag. I doubt we need to rely on witch magic when we are on the work of angels,' he said.

But I could see the mark plain. It was the sigil of the Archangel Uriel.

Chapter 24

Present day, Hampshire

The quiet nuns, who Jack had barely reacted to before, were seated around the table, Bea among them, after the day's silence. Jack and Charley, who had stayed the day, were invited to sit at one end, their chairs away from the others. The nun in charge, Sister Mary, the only nun under pension age, was a sturdy woman in her fifties.

She stood to start the conversation. 'Beatrice tells us that you believe you are possessed, that being here helps you.'

'Yes.' Jack spoke for herself.

'You understand that we cannot harbour a demon, if there is such a thing, within the holy walls of our retreat.' The uncompromising words echoed around the tiled room.

'I understand.' Jack looked at her hands. 'Come on, Charley. You need to go, I don't want you anywhere near me when I leave here—'

'Wait. You misunderstand me.' Sister Mary looked around her sisters. 'We have all discussed this after chapel. There are advisers at the Vatican who can help. They have experience of this situation.' She turned to Charley. 'We could not help but see that you

166

had been injured. We could not allow this to continue. Somebody could die.'

Charley rearranged the scarf around her neck.

Sister Mary folded her hands in her lap. 'Our order, in its own time, has been associated with exorcisms.'

For a moment a sense of hope flared in Jack's chest.

'But, you must understand, our order does not now take part in such controversial things. Our path is to offer refuge, so people can sort out their own problems.' Sister Mary smiled at Jack, a little sadly, she thought. 'I have never met someone who is genuinely possessed, but I have seen a lot of people afflicted with their own demons. Our research suggests we should ask the Congregation for the Doctrine of the Faith for advice.'

'The Inquisition?' Jack looked at Charley, knowing that she was a target too. 'They will kill me, and they'll use you to find Sadie.'

'No, no,' Sister Mary said, waving her hands at Bea for support. 'No one would hurt you, they just have more experience of this that we do. I would not have believed such things were even possible, but seeing your sister's throat, we have to help if we can.'

'I need to talk to Felix,' Charley answered, her own face pale.

Jack took a deep breath and turned to Sister Mary. 'My life has been different from most. The Inquisition has declared war on people like me.'

'We know you believe that. And we would only contact them if you stay here. But I can assure you, no one at the Vatican wishes you or anyone else harm. We know they will be compassionate.' Sister Mary pressed her palms together, smiled and turned to Bea. 'In the meantime, if it would reassure our young guests, we can make up beds in the chapel.'

Jack felt as if she and Charley had been dismissed. She slid from the table and Charley turned to Sister Mary. Jack could hear her foster sister's voice ringing out as they left through the back door.

'You have no idea what you have just done.'

The two walked out into the garden, the last of the light fading under low cloud. Charley sat on the bench and stretched out her feet on the flagstones, in the yellow glow from the kitchen window.

'What do we do now?' she said, chewing the side of her nail as she always did when she was anxious. 'Jack?'

Jack turned at some tiny noise, perhaps just an animal skittering through the grass. 'We can't just run. Saraquel will take control the second I leave here.'

'Maybe.' Charley's voice was strained, tired, Jack thought from the terrible night. She started tapping on her phone.

'Why don't you book into a hotel, Charley? You can't sleep anywhere near me.'

'I'll be OK in the chapel. We both will be.' Her voice sounded strange. 'Jack – Felix has left a load of messages. Sadie isn't doing well.'

'Oh.' Jack looked over Charley's shoulder at the tiny screen.

Bea scuttled out of the garden door and walked along the path to them. 'I'm so sorry. They haven't been entirely honest – they have already asked for someone to come and help you. Are you quite certain it wouldn't help, going to the Vatican and being seen by the best experts on possession?'

Jack sagged on the seat, too tired even to argue.

Charley shrugged, put her phone away and stood. 'Well, we have contacts of our own. Maybe Felix will come up with something.'

Jack felt the cold creeping in. 'I don't even know if I can safely travel away from here without Saraquel taking over.'

Charley stared at her in the low light. 'I was thinking about that. Wait a minute, let me call Felix.' She jumped up and walked up the path.

Bea extended her hand to Jack's and took it in both of her warm ones. 'I don't know if it would help, but I have some small savings.' She reached into the pocket of her apron and pulled out a wad of notes. 'It's about two thousand pounds, if that would make a difference.'

'Bea – I couldn't!' Jack felt the weight of the money in her hand. 'I don't think it would help.'

'Take it anyway. They have to pay me for managing the place, but I'm a nun in my heart. Chastity, obedience and poverty.' Bea gathered Jack into a hug, squeezing her until she could barely breathe in an embrace filled with the smells of baking. 'I like you, Jack. And the church doesn't understand this sort of thing. I'm not sure I do either but I want to help.'

When Bea released her, Jack staggered.

'Let me know if I can do anything else,' Bea whispered, and turned to walk away.

Charley watched her go before she came back to Jack. 'Felix is going to contact Mac. You know, McNamara.'

Jack sighed. 'That might be a really stupid idea. But right now, they are the only ideas I have left.'

'I'm sure he will help.' Charley's face seemed a little pinker in the dim light from inside.

'Charley?' Jack turned to look into Charley's face.

Charley managed a muffled chuckle. 'I kept in touch! OK? I was . . . worried. Mac was really badly beaten up, you know, when you two killed Elizabeth Báthory. He was in hospital in Rome for weeks.'

169

Jack shook her head slowly. 'So . . .'

'I have his mobile number. I just gave it to Felix, that's all.'

'But how can I travel? Saraquel takes over when I'm even a few feet away from this place.'

Charley frowned as she puzzled over that one. 'Mac and Felix will come up with a plan. I promise.'

Jack, who had persuaded Charley to sleep in her bed in the main house, spent an uncomfortable night on the floor of the chapel, constantly guarded by a nun in prayer, the murmured blessings echoing in the corners of the building like the whispering of bats. A draught from the door blew straight under the lines of pews and into Jack, who couldn't get warm. Nuns came in at intervals to worship, and eventually their prayers lulled Jack to sleep.

Waking in the morning was a shock, the ache in her hip grinding as she sat up, her hair tangled. She tried to straighten it a bit under the gaze of the watchful nuns. She stood, stretching the kinks out of her spine and straightening her clothes. She turned at the creak of the door to see Charley advancing ahead of a tall man, his iron-grey hair short and wearing a black coat over what looked like a suit.

'McNamara,' she said, with a bitter tone, 'of course. Are you the big guns Sister Mary called in?'

'Actually, no.' He hesitated. 'Although I have been asked to find you for . . . neutralisation. No, I'm here because Felix contacted me. I was able to follow Charley's phone.' He stood back. 'We should talk outside,' he said, in a low voice.

Charley put her arm around Jack's waist. 'She's safer in here.'

'No doubt. But it is not just Jack I need to speak to.'

170

Jack looked at Charley and some consensus shot between them. Maybe they would learn something.

The grass was wet with dew on the strip of lawn outside the chapel, and McNamara followed them from the building. Charley stood between him and Jack.

'You can't hurt her.'

He stepped closer. 'You have no idea what you are dealing with.' His voice was hard but it had an edge of sadness.

Saraquel surged through her defences and cackled from her throat. 'The Inquisition, of course.' Jack gasped a protest even as the words were forced involuntarily through her vocal cords.

'Charley, get away from her,' McNamara said, reaching for Charley's arm and pulling her away. 'He's dangerous.'

Charley's face looked white. 'That's – it, isn't it? Saraquel?'

'The monster, yes.' His voice was less impassive than usual.

Jack fought with the thing inside her. It felt bigger than her, stretching her body from within, forcing her back to arch, her mouth to open.

'We meet again, Stephen,' it ground out, past her tightening jaw muscles.

'She is not Báthory,' he answered. 'You have not chosen well, Saraquel. She is not your toy.'

The thing squirmed inside Jack, fighting to launch itself at McNamara. A blinding heat distracted it, and she won. It slid back down, and she fell to her knees. As she came back to herself, she felt water trickling down her face.

'What?' She wiped her face, her hands shaking, shivers riding up and down her spine. 'Holy water? Charley—'

'No!' The inquisitor seemed to be scuffling with Charley, Jack could see them locked together.

'It's OK, Charley,' she stammered. 'Stay back, if you're not sure.' She staggered to the bench under the chapel wall, suddenly exhausted.

Charley wrenched herself from McNamara's hold and put her arms around Jack.

'So will you help us?' she hissed at the inquisitor.

'There's more than you know. I've been investigating assaults in the centre of London,' he said, his face coming into view as he stepped into the low light. 'Assaults I suspected were caused by Jack. Two victims identified her from our photographs.'

Jack covered her face in her hands. 'Saraquel.'

'So I began to suspect. Then a Vatican exorcist contacted me, not through the usual channels.' He paused. 'I don't even know what channels I would reach him on. He has told me the Inquisition are sending an extraction team for you, any day now. He wants me to capture you before you kill an innocent, and he will offer you an exorcism.'

She glanced up at his hard face. He was staring down at her as if she was a monster. 'So you are here to get me? To subject me to some exorcism. Why don't you just follow orders and "neutralise" me?'

'Those were my instructions.' There was a trickle of uncertainty in his voice.

Jack took Charley's hand and squeezed it. 'So what's stopping you?'

He sighed, the sound drifting in the still air. 'Every time I meet you I get the impression . . . there's something about you, Ms Hammond. But it's not your life I have come to save. It's your immortal soul.'

'I did save your life,' she mused, then managed a wry smile. 'Of course, you saved mine, too. So, what happens now?'

He managed a small, tight smile. 'The exorcist believes this is an opportunity to defeat the monster that turned Elizabeth Báthory into a killer. Maybe if we can persuade him to try and get it out of you—'

Saraquel sent a wave of pain through Jack, as if her insides were being crushed. She doubled over, clutching at her midriff. When she coughed, it tasted of blood.

Charley jumped up and reached for Jack.

'Back to the chapel, I think,' she said, and after a moment Mac walked forward and pressed something to Jack's chest. It sent a wave of something cooling through Jack, even as the skin on her breastbone burned. Jack clung to Charley's hands as she pulled her up, then let her guide her towards the side door of the chapel.

Bea was waiting there, and she barred McNamara from entering. 'Who are you?'

'I'm here to help,' he said, then met Jack's eyes. 'I'm here because I have special knowledge from my work at the Vatican.'

'Oh.' Bea turned to look at Jack. 'Is that right? Are you here because Sister Mary contacted Rome?'

'No. He was sent to find out if I was attacking people in London,' Jack managed, the pain easing as she entered the cool space. She sat on one of the chairs. 'He's working for some mysterious exorcist.'

'Prostitutes were being approached by a woman, who knocked them down, bit their necks and arms, and robbed them.' He spoke as if it were commonplace.

Jack winced. 'Do the police think it was me?'

'No.' He paused, looking at Charley. 'Does she know, about—?'

Charley nodded. 'She knows the police are looking for her, and they know she is Melissa Harcourt.'

'That sounds strange, after so many years.' Jack looked from one to the other.

'Sister Mary contacted the Vatican,' McNamara said. 'They will have given the extraction team your location. I may be able to persuade them to wait for an exorcism attempt.'

Charley stepped forward. 'You really believe they would wait?'

McNamara shook his head. 'No. But there is a wave of revenants convening on the UK for some reason. The Inquisition is going to be distracted for a few days. I don't know where else to take you other than straight to the exorcist.' He sighed. 'You probably won't survive it. This unnatural existence of yours is the cause of the possession. Perhaps it is time to put right what witches and sorcery have created.'

Jack sat upright, still feeling sick from the pain. 'How can I travel?'

'We could sedate you. Or tie you up.'

Jack shook her head, a smile creeping onto her face at the thought. 'Saraquel could break my arms getting me out of shackles. Sedatives don't work either, I've tried. He's laughing at you all, even now. You really want him loose in a car?'

Charley shook her head. 'He can get inside other people's minds, too. How can we avoid that? What if he attacks you, or someone else?' She sat on a bench, her arms folded tightly, then undid her scarf. In the dull light from the overcast sky the bruises looked black. 'Saraquel did this to me in a religious building.'

Mac smiled, a grim twist of his lips. 'I know it will be a difficult journey.' He sat heavily beside Charley and looked at Jack. 'There's only one chance for a real exorcism.' He studied the splayed fingers on one hand. 'His name is Robert Conway. He has a reputation as a very powerful and experienced exorcist.' He took a deep breath.

'He seems to know a lot about this Saraquel, and even more about revenants. I looked him up but most of his information is classified. No one would talk about him.'

Charley dropped her small hand over his tense fingers, making him flinch. 'Can you contact this guy?' She let go and he glanced at Jack.

'I have a number for him, that's all. But you have to understand: exorcism is hard, and it's dangerous for both the possessed and the exorcist.'

Jack looked into the night sky, distant streetlights yellowing the underside of the clouds. 'It can't possibly be as dangerous as having this twisted monster inside me.' She turned to McNamara. 'One thing you do need to understand. The evidence so far is that I'm not possessed by a demon. I think it's an angel. Tell that to your exorcist.'

Chapter 25

Present day, Dartmoor

Robert Conway stepped over to the oldest headstones in the graveyard. 'Johan wife of Thos Woodward 1678' was carved into the granite, still legible after hundreds of years of weathering. He took another bite from his vegetable pasty while he walked around the raised burial area, then stepped back onto the path alongside the church. Always a favourite, St Michael's Church seemed to make him feel not just safe from Saraquel, but invisible to him. It was also a good spot for a mobile signal. He read the text McNamara had sent him, which he'd picked up on one of his regular visits into the town, and dialled the number.

'Hello?' The voice was low, as if he didn't want to be overheard.

'I've been thinking about the female revenant,' Conway said.

'Jack. Yes?' The man sounded more tired or more emotional than Robert could imagine.

'Are you all right?' Robert allowed his voice to soften and drop, to encourage the man to speak, one of the lessons he had learned as a priest.

He could hear the man's breathing: tight, strained. 'I can't kill her, and if I leave her the Vatican extraction team will take her.'

McNamara's tone was bitter. 'They won't listen to me. She's a good person, she's doing everything she can not to hurt anyone.'

'They won't listen to me, either.' Again, the sibilant breathing. Robert spoke again. 'Look, I have a plan. It may be the most dangerous approach, but – I do think it may be possible, finally, to exorcise Saraquel. You have no idea how much suffering he has caused over the last few thousand years. You've said it yourself, this woman – Jack – isn't a good host for Saraquel, she's fighting him and he hasn't possessed her for long. Centuries of attempts haven't succeeded, but she may be a window into this possession.'

'She has to leave here, the Vatican already know where she is. The sisters contacted them.' McNamara's voice sounded even more bitter than before. 'I agree we have to try exorcism or this thing will destroy her and move on to someone else. She's already attempted suicide once.'

Robert walked to the edge of the churchyard, and smiled at a woman coming through the gate into the broad meadow behind the church, walking onto the grassy plateau and away from him. The land ahead dropped into a steep valley, then up the wooded hill beyond, and was one of his favourite views.

'You will bring her here,' he said softly. 'Do you know, Stephen, that on a day like today it doesn't seem possible that anything bad could happen in Devon?'

He could hear the explosion of breath at the other end of the phone. 'Well, I'm not in bloody Devon and Jack can't even step away from the walls of a church without being controlled by Saraquel!'

Conway smiled. Always, the short view of the young. 'Listen. Saraquel can be sedated with magical drugs along with the host. Just keep her drugged and chained on the journey, and preferably lock her in some container. I'll text you a postcode and the formula for the sedative. All you need to do is put the location into a satnav and follow the instructions. It takes you to a rather seedy pub, the George and Dragon. About three hundred yards along the road going west is a layby. If you can be there at, say, six tomorrow morning, I can meet you. How does that sound?'

'And you won't harm her?'

Conway winced. Truthfully, he knew no way to disembody Saraquel in a way that would leave the host unharmed, or even alive. 'Saraquel will kill her anyway,' he compromised. 'This is her best chance.'

'There's another thing.' Stephen McNamara sounded better now he had something to do. *Not a patient man.* 'I told you that Jack's friend is Professor Felix Guichard.'

'Ah, yes, the Dee scholar. He managed to get hold of one of Kelley's missing journals, I hear.'

'He has some ideas about Saraquel and has been looking into exorcism.' McNamara sounded stronger. 'I'm bringing him in as well.'

Conway's immediate response was of an increased sense of danger creeping through his spine, a prickling of the skin. 'No, no. You and I must do it alone.'

'Why?' The man's voice was strident now, angry. 'He's a person who understands possession. He's even starting to understand the science behind the life of revenants.'

Conway sighed. Even though his neck felt like a cold wind was creeping down it, he had to overcome his terrors and get Jack to the cottage. 'Very well. But he is your responsibility. If he is unhelpful or difficult he has to go.' He felt a wrench at the thought of using his retreat; his anonymity would be wasted if there were any survivors. It would take years to find as good a hideout.

After a few more moments, while the sun slowly came out from between light clouds and turned raindrops lying on the long grass into a shimmering blanket, McNamara agreed to rendezvous with Conway. 'One more thing – and I find this hard to believe myself. I've always thought this possession was by some blood-sucking monster of a demon but Jack thinks . . .' McNamara paused.

Conway smiled but there was a flicker of fear in it. 'I know. Saraquel is a blood-sucking monster of an angel.'

Chapter 26

Journal of Eliza Jane Weston, 23 November 1612

I stood, holding onto the table as the pain twisted inside me. The countess waited, as I wrestled with the babe trying to push free. When I could move again, I reached within the coffer Johannes Leo had given to me upon our wedding. I brought out, not the letters which I did not have, but copies of my books, given to me by my publisher, Baldhoven.

'Here lie his wisdoms and knowledge,' I said, laying the volumes upon the table. 'I wrote them into my poetry.'

She flew across the room like a velvet bird, her claws grasping the books. Opening one, she scanned one page, then another.

'Nothing,' she hissed at me. 'None but maudlin sentiment.'

My father's face rose into my memory, his instruction to hide the truth from the countess but leave it where any scholar could find it. Forgive me, I thought.

I took one book from her hand, and turned to an inner page.

'This is the key,' I said, showing her the words. The giant gripped my belly again.

Edward Kelley, the voyage to Brindisi, 1586

The men came back, full of the local wine and with coarse speech that, although I spoke too little of their language to be certain, suggested that they had partaken of the local whores. Marinello, however, had not indulged his appetites, but had been meeting with other sea captains.

He threw himself upon his favourite seat, and shaded his eyes from the low evening sun. 'I hope your mission succeeded, for mine has not,' he grumbled.

Dee waved at the awning, now rolled and tied into a bundle beside the cabin entrance. I started working on the rough jute bindings, and when it was loose, rolled it out. As Dee held it I hoisted it up and tied it securely with a seaman's knot Marinello had taught me. I had acquired many skills on the short voyage.

'What mission was that?' asked Dee, once he was seated under the shade. He spoke quietly to one of the men, who first pretended he did not understand, then, at one look from his commander, brought us three cups of the local wine. I sipped it and found it sweet, like fruit juice left in the sun for a few days.

'I hoped some of the local ships would form a flotilla that we might frighten off these pirates,' Marinello grumbled. 'But no, the cravens, the fools, would rather stay in harbour for a few days.'

'Must we do likewise?' Dee asked, and I knew he thought only of our families, left in captivity.

'We must not,' he said. 'But the crew are jittery. We are but three, and these men are fighters. I do not wish to put down a mutiny. That would lose me one or two sailors, and that puts us at more peril. The problem is, they do not yet know me.'

I thought of the sullen faces of the men, that I had assumed were aimed at the Englishmen but perhaps were more about the pirates. 'Let me help,' I said, waving my cup at the sailors.

I commanded the man who had served us, through the captain, to buy more wine, and gave him a few of my dwindling supply of coins. When he returned, with a small barrel over his shoulder, I went to the foredeck where the men sat or dozed in the sun. There, as Marinello watched and translated for me, I announced it was my saint's day, and I wished my new friends to join me in celebrating.

They reluctantly took a cup of my wine, their grumbling in Vèneto even more spiteful-sounding than usual, and then I stood among them.

'It is the custom of my people to tell a story with wine,' I lied, in good Latin. 'And I shall tell you of the great adventures my friend Marinello and I had with a demon.'

That caught their attention and one crossed himself and muttered a blessing.

'Amen,' I said, sure of my audience. 'This was an adventure of great peril, and a great danger. But my Lord Marinello, who was born under a lucky sign, essayed it and triumphed.'

A few men glanced towards their captain, who raised a cup to them then turned back to Dee, to whisper something. Then he stood up, and with gusto, translated the story into their own language with much acting and waving.

'It was because of a woman.' They cheered as we told them of a beautiful succubus who enchanted Marinello until the Inquisition – there were hisses at the mention – formed such a force that Marinello realised if he stepped back into the arms of the demon he would be damned, and if he stepped into the embrace of the Inquisition he would be destroyed. So he fought, hand to hand up the great stairs of his palazzo, vanquishing soldier after soldier until he stood at the top of his fortress, still outnumbered. As the Inquisition forces threatened to set torches to the house, he took his great sword and slashed it at the window, shattering the shutters there, and swung out upon the hangings until he flew above the many boats below. Then, and only then, did he drop into the lagoon, escaping not just the soldiers but the demon as well. They cheered as they heard how he outwitted the soldiers, for none in Venice cared for the Inquisition, and were silent when I described the demon that had at least momentarily enchanted Marinello and told how he had vanquished her also as she sank her demonic teeth into his arm but he threw her aside. Here I embellished my story until they laughed and widened their eyes in fear at her terrible powers and how he dodged them. Then I told them how Marinello was born at a time when the stars were propitious and how his previous crews had all retired to the hills, rich men.

The wine softened them more, and by the time the barrel was empty, they were singing some song, lustily and unmusically. When I led the call, 'Marinello!' they joined me, and spoke to each other of the cravenly local sailors and the speed of *Il Delfino*. Then, and only after they settled in the dark, for dusk had come, did I speak of what I knew mostly they feared.

'Dr Dee is a famous traveller and mapmaker,' I told them. 'And I have to tell you a secret.' I made much of looking back to where Dee seemed to ignore us, though I knew he heard every word. 'Dr Dee is also,' I paused for a moment to let Marinello catch up then lowered my voice, 'a famous sorcerer.'

'This we know,' scoffed one of the sailors, although he too, was quiet-voiced. 'And God puts a curse upon our voyage.'

'No, indeed, my friend. Dr Dee is not allied to the forces of evil, to *Il Diàolo*.' I wasn't sure I had the word right, but they sat back and murmured prayers, and fingered crosses around each neck. Even the Portuguese cook crossed himself.

I waited until the muttering died away, leaving the crackling of the brazier as it lit to fill the air.

'Dr Dee has been visited by angels, my fellows. *Angioli*. Carrying messages from God Himself, and He, my friends, has decreed that we shall go into these dangerous waters to do His bidding. Did not Marinello, under the command of God, pass the pirates in the night unseen? Do we not carry His own emissary?'

I left them with their thoughts, and in earnest conversation.

Dee's dark shadow nodded to me. 'Well spoken, Edward,' he said.

Marinello chuckled. 'Must you have ennobled me with your story? You virtually gave me the power of flight.' But I knew he was pleased, and his hand found my shoulder in the dark in a strong grasp, which warmed me.

'When will we sail?' I could smell the meat the cook was browning over the brazier and realised I had not eaten since the slices of pork earlier.

'We shall slip out of harbour before first light,' said Marinello. 'I would not be surprised if the other ships here tried to prevent us leaving lest we bring down the wrath of the pirates upon the town, so we shall sail on the tide when they sleep.'

He went and spoke to the men in a low voice, then clasped a man's hand here, patted a shoulder there, and I knew that the men, already impressed with his size and vitality, had finally fallen under his spell.

Dee sighed in the darkness. 'I wish I was as confident as the storytellers on the ship, my friend. But I fear we go into great danger. Oh, I don't fear the pirates, they can merely smite my body. No, my fear is that we are being led further and further from God's purpose.' I could just see the flash of his teeth as he spoke, reflecting back the glowing charcoal. 'Paid for with the Inquisition's gold.'

We slipped from the quay before dawn, just a few yards of canvas above my head as *Il Delfino* drifted into the tide and was sucked from the harbour. Marinello had ordered a couple of men to dangle fishing hooks in the water to make it appear that we were just casually sailing up the coast, and had not ordered the men to make the ship ready for a long journey. We had not taken on much fresh water, nor provisions, and by my calculations we had more than thirty-five leagues to sail. Marinello scoffed at my concerns, and promised we would make land in less than three days, but I scanned the flat horizon as the sun built up a suffocating calm about us. It took two hours to be sure we were out of sight from the port, and it took every inch of sail to manage that. The men had caught divers fish, many brightly coloured and new to us, so Dee and I watched the catch with interest and at least we ate well. Finally, Marinello ordered the oars put out, and we all took a turn, even I. Breaking the glassy water was satisfying, as we pulled for Kérkyra and safety. The lighter men, including myself, took turns at scaling the tallest mast and keeping watch, but by the time we reached the first evening shift we had seen no ships, pirate or otherwise.

I fell into sleep tired but content that we had travelled a number of leagues, but was awoken by shouting. Dee's hand was upon my shoulder, shaking it, and for a moment I knocked it away and scuttled away from him.

185

'Edward, my friend, you must awaken,' he said to me, in a voice that did not disguise his concern.

'What?' I gazed around. A lantern was shone upon my face, half-blinding me, and I could hear Marinello's voice speaking sharply to the crew. It was then that I noticed a circle of daggers pointed at me and realised that Dee sat between me and death. Marinello roared something at the men, and the knives dropped a little. In Vèneto, Latin and for all I knew Portuguese, he chastised them. Finally he dismissed them back to the oars and commanded that they row for their lives.

'Are you well, little fool?' Marinello set his warm bulk beside me on the bench. His hand pressed against my face for a moment. 'Are you sun-crazed?'

'No, I don't know what happened. I was just asleep.'

Dee's voice was low, so that we kept the conversation just between us. 'You were shouting out in your dreams, Edward. In some language I did not recognise. I think it was the voice of a being within you.'

'It was not your tone,' Marinello said, his warmth comforting beside me. 'It was like the tolling of a great bell, a deep note. It certainly must have carried over this water.'

'An angel?' I whispered.

'If so, the little I understood seemed to offer a warning.' Dee turned his head towards the crew. 'The men thought you possessed and would have slipped a knife into you and thrown you overboard were it not for Lord Marinello's intervention.'

'What did you dream?' The captain turned his head sharp as a cat and snapped something to the muttering crew. 'Tell us, before I have to knock a few mutinous heads a-cock.'

I struggled to think back to the dream but it was as if wrapped in a blanket of night. 'I know not,' I confessed. 'I remember nothing.'

Dee moved aside so that Marinello might master his rebellious crew. I watched as our captain took the foremost oar, stripping off his jerkin, his white shirt a ghost in the dark. Dee nodded to the helmsman to release him to an oar, and took up the steering position himself.

'You must open yourself to the message, whatever it is,' he said, scowling in the dim light of the helm lantern and fumbling for his eyeglasses in their purse, hung around his neck. 'For I fear we are going into danger without it. The angels themselves warn us and we can't speak directly to them. Unless you allow an angelic conference.'

'Here?' My voice was high, as I could not imagine such a discourse without the appropriate protections and prayers.

'We have essayed it before,' he said, checking the compass. 'Edward, wait.' He stopped, then called out to Marinello in a whisper.

The oarsmen stopped their labours until the only sound was the hissing and bubbling of the water parting before the prow, and the dripping from the oars.

There, I heard it. The sounds of another ship, the creaking of timbers as the hull was dragged towards us, the rustle of sails as they lost their wind.

Then the metallic slither of swords from scabbards and a mutter of orders from Marinello to his crew. Dee placed the lantern between the ship's side and his own cloak. The brazier was rekindled, and I saw by its red light three men, their arms drawn back, then saw what they were doing. Crossbow bolts soaked in pitch were waiting in a bucket beside the brazier, and two men had swarmed aloft carrying heavy crossbows and vanished into the dark.

The chill of the night crept into me: I shivered. All I could think to do was grasp my dagger and hold the ship's side as I crouched low.

A man called across the water to us. 'Christian dogs or infidel ones?' called a deep voice.

'Venetian dogs, by Christ's blood,' swore Marinello.

A laugh rippled over the still waters and I heard the sound of orders upon the other vessel. 'Cargo?'

'Some glass, some oils,' Marinello called back.

'I should like some glass myself,' the voice returned, and this time I saw the ship, its belly bristling with oars – I counted fifteen pairs. 'A little sea tax, perhaps, for safe passage?'

Marinello slipped into his native tongue, and said something that made his counterpart laugh.

'Then name yourself, little flea,' the man scoffed. 'For that bucket cannot match my ship.'

'Are we pirates that we will rob our own countrymen?' called Marinello. 'Send your weaklings and moonlings to their death, if you choose. Marinellos are never vanquished.'

'The son of Admiral Marinello?' The ship's side loomed over us. A man, a fat grey-haired ruffian much beribboned in a suit of red, leaned forward. 'I knew your father, youngling. I would rather rob my own sire. But how could I know a Marinello would command such a wreck? I am Sebastiano Valaresso. Will you come aboard?'

Marinello sprang to the gunwale, reached for the rope dangled within his reach and swarmed up it with easy grace. Our little *Delfino* bumped the side of the other ship and was swiftly tied to it with exchanged lines.

We heard some bartering going on above us, and a few hearty laughs from the captains, but I noticed both ships had several lookouts aloft, and generally speech was low. Finally, Marinello climbed lightly back onto our ship, followed by the other master. Marinello did not introduce us, but snapped a command to two men, who went into the hold and brought up several heavy wooden chests.

'See, the finest Venetian glass,' boasted Marinello. 'The Pope himself drinks from it.'

'I don't care if he pisses in it,' said the other. 'What studio?'

'My nephew's, Garzoni.' Marinello leaned over, turning the lantern up so the glistening gold within could impress the man. 'You would get a fine price in Spain. I swear there is nothing so fine in Madrid.'

'Not a great studio. But I like the gold thread. I would have to see them in daylight. The Spanish like some glitter, the bastards.'

'Dawn is but an hour away.'

'Then we should lift two of your glasses to the memory of your father, and unite against the barbarous Turk.'

The two men sat across the belly of the ship, drinking and talking while the crew remained as tense as cats in a butcher's shop.

Dee beckoned that I should join him in the cabin, cool as it was mostly under the waterline. 'Edward, we must know. If you will be open to a consultation—'

'I will. If we get away. Have you noticed the other ship's men? All armed.'

'And our own men. They are suspicious people, these Venetians. Perhaps because their empire falls around them. Only Candia and Corfu are sovereign to them now.' Dee ran his hand over his head. 'I fear I have led us both into danger.'

'What choice did we have,' I said, 'with our women and children in captivity?' And by the hand of such a creature, I dared not say.

Barely an hour later, while I tried to sleep and Dee kept watch, a shout from above brought us to the deck.

I could hear the exchange between the captains getting louder, and there were more bared teeth than smiles. I noticed in the dawn light that the men on the other ship were openly armed, and our men, lower and fewer in number, were tensed to take up their bows or swords. The other captain seemed unworried, despite being on a hostile ship. But finally, in a flurry of insults too fast to follow, even if I understood their language, they spat upon their palms and joined hands in a hearty salute.

'As much a villain as his father,' said the stranger, his eyes wandering over to us.

'Worse,' agreed Marinello.

'You have greybeards among your crew?' His eyes ranged from Dee to my unguarded curls. 'And runaway slaves?' He tossed a purse to Marinello.

Too late I remembered my docked ears, and reached for my cap. I recalled that runaway slaves were often mutilated to show that they were not trusted. Mine own, notched by a magistrate in Norfolk when I was but a youth, spoke of a crime that I have never confessed to.

Marinello nodded to two of his men, who started closing each box, fastening them with nails. Then they passed the chests up to their comrades.

The old captain clambered stiffly up a ladder knotted from ropes and nodded to his men as they stowed the cases of glass.

Finally, he turned back to Marinello, who had already ordered the ship's ropes to be unfastened.

'About that sea tax, Marinello,' he called down, a gleam in his eyes. 'What other cargo do you carry except my gold?'

'As I said. Some wine, some oils.' He grinned. 'And two sorcerers from England, seeking wisdoms and enchantments.'

Never had a ship been cast adrift as quickly, as Marinello laughed and the sailors on the other vessel crossed themselves and some ropes were even slashed – a sin aboard any ship.

'Go to hell, Valaresso!'

'Go there first, Marinello!'

'Say hello to my father when you get there!'

The shouted insults faded as Marinello turned to us. 'Put out all oars,' he said briskly. 'Edward, all sails. We need to get on our way. Valaresso speaks of a pirate fleet north of Kérkyra, north of the isle of Mathraki.'

I waved to Domenico, the youngest sailor on board and more nimble than me, to run out the sails on my command. Marinello took the helm himself, scanning the horizon as I cast a glance back to the receding ship. It seemed that nowhere upon this azure sea was secure.

Chapter 27

Present day, Manchester

Sadie was losing ground, Felix could see it. She was slipping away like an injured bird, despite every effort to shore up her deteriorating condition. Bloodstained tears oozed from her eyes, and even Maggie's remedies and the circles didn't seem to help any more. Purple blemishes mottled every visible area of skin. Drip sites were stained with scarlet bandages. But she still didn't die. George lifted her ivory wrist in his brown hand as if he needed to feel her pulse for himself.

'She's dying,' he said to Felix. 'We would try dialysis again, but it's risky. She's not clotting properly.'

Angela had already donated platelets but they had hardly made a dent in Sadie's test results.

Maggie, who was sat beside the girl and had barely left her bed, scowled at the two men. 'You know what we have to do. Blood saved Jack.'

'At what cost?' Felix snapped back, equally tired. There was no way he could expose Sadie to the possession that Jack had suffered when she drank blood.

George looked from one to the other. 'We have the Respiridol here. Bachmeier is sending one of his technicians to record her vitals and a doctor will supervise the actual protocol.'

'How can they do that? Sadie has no identity with the authorities, and what explanation would you give for her condition?' Felix touched Sadie's cold, grey hand. It felt as if she was already dead.

'She is going to be recorded as an anonymous patient. It's the best we can do, we have to do everything we can to save her life.' George shook his head. 'Look, I know you, Felix. What you have done to get her this far – I don't even know what you've done but that kid has a day, tops. She could bleed out at any moment. I don't know why she's still alive.'

Felix shook his head. 'You don't, you can't understand. Sadie was declared dead last year, but as you see, she isn't – quite – dead. She's survived because of Maggie's knowledge.'

'You really believe that a few scribbles and some herbs have been keeping her alive? Felix, come on.'

'George, I'm sorry, but if you knew.' He stared at Sadie's body under the flat, unwrinkled sheet. He laid her thin fingers back on the bed. 'They are . . . this company has some really dangerous origins.'

'I read they were funded by Nazi money,' George said.

'Even worse.' Felix sighed as he stared down at the teenager. 'Start the Respiridol. I'll deal with Bachmeier and Holtz.'

Felix was walking in the grounds outside Sadie's room when Jack phoned.

'Felix, we have a problem.'

'We have one here, too. Sadie's fading fast.' Felix sat on a bench in the car park, and rubbed his hand over his forehead. It was incongruous, surrounded by climbing roses on the wall behind him, flowers in a bed under the window, vibrant with bees and butterflies going about their business as if Sadie's life wasn't draining away. 'Now George has decided to use a trial drug from Bachmeier and Holtz.'

'You can't trust anyone from Bachmeier – I mean Báthory's – own company.'

'We don't have any alternative, Jack. I sat down with Bachmeier himself – he knows she's a borrowed timer. In fact, he's one himself.'

There was a long silence on the other end before she spoke. 'He could be possessed. Saraquel might already know where Sadie is.'

'He isn't . . . I'm sure he isn't possessed, Jack. He's also close to understanding Saraquel's weaknesses. We have a research angle, I can't tell you any more.'

'Obviously, or Saraquel will know too.' She sighed. 'You know Mac is here? He wants to get me to this exorcist. Robert something.'

The name created a tickle in the back of his mind but he wasn't sure what from. 'I have to persuade an academic to at least share the information we've been trying to get from the poetry of Kelley's stepdaughter.' That was it – the donor. 'Actually – was the name of this exorcist Robert Conway by any chance?'

'It might have been.' She must have turned away from the phone to speak to someone and Felix could hear a man murmur. 'Yes. Why?'

'The poems we've been looking at seem to speak of exorcism and Saraquel. I think they were donated to the university by a Robert Conway.'

'Charley's arranging transport for me. All we're waiting for is the van.'

'Will Saraquel let you go?'

He could hear a tired chuckle at the other end. 'Of course not, but it isn't down to him. They're going to do . . . something. I don't know what. All I know is we're going to somewhere in Devon. But Mac says he will send a text to your phone with the time and location if you want to be there.'

Felix exploded with the trapped tension of the last few days. 'Of course I want to be there!'

'I know, I'm sorry. I want you there, too. But Saraquel is always listening.' She paused. 'You don't know what he is capable of.'

'I'm beginning to realise how much damage Saraquel has done. The poems speak of the armies of Saraquel, hundreds of people controlled by him, acting out their most sensual experiences for his pleasure. The hosts' inner fantasies and ideas get acted upon to satisfy Saraquel's craving for sensation.'

'Don't tell me any more. But if you can use Kelley's ideas, or his daughter's, bring them with you.'

'I will.'

'McNamara's going to try and get me – and Saraquel – to this place tomorrow. To be exorcised. But that's not the worst thing. I – I nearly killed Charley the first night she was here. I woke up and Saraquel was strangling her, even in the buildings of the abbey. I think the circles strengthened Saraquel somehow.'

'What?' That brought his head up. 'Is she OK?'

'She says so but – I can still feel her throat being crushed by my fingers, Felix. She could have died – she would have died if she hadn't hit me with a crucifix.'

'I haven't been able to find a single mention of specifically angelic exorcism. There are some hints of the early roots of exorcism generally. But I'm not a practitioner, I'm a theorist,' he said.

'I have no idea what this exorcist has planned but he thinks this is the best chance. I can't go on like this much longer.'

'I don't even know where you are, Jack. You could hurt Charley, you could hurt yourself,' he said, almost to himself. 'The exorcism could kill you.'

Her laugh had just a touch of hysteria in it. 'Well, exactly. This really wasn't my idea of a great plan. But it's the best we have.' She paused for a moment and her voice softened. 'Can you leave Sadie?'

'She's in the doctors' hands now. And Maggie never goes away for long. When we have a postcode to meet you, I'll drive down to Devon as soon as possible.' He paused for a moment. 'The doctors are trying this new treatment on Sadie. It's an experimental drug that increases oxygen use in the body, slows down the breakdown of certain cells. Supposedly, anyway. It occurs to me that it might be why Elizabeth Báthory was so strong.'

'I suppose she would have had all that research available to her. Maybe the same research will help Sadie. But I don't trust their motives.'

'I'm sorry, Jack. Sadie has perhaps a day, maybe less. We have to try it.'

'Did you think of giving her blood?'

'She's had transfusions,' he said, 'but no, I'm not going to let her drink blood. I don't know why that makes such a difference, but I don't trust it.'

'Saraquel can't reach her there, I'm miles away.'

Felix rubbed his forehead, just realising what a headache he was carrying. 'Saraquel has multiple hosts, Jack. One could be nearby – damn it, there could be one, maybe a nurse or doctor, working with Sadie now.'

He could almost see her expression, the one she had worn when Sadie was comatose for weeks last year. Partly exhausted but partly resigned, as if she never expected to win. 'Do what you can for Sadie, Felix. I don't think . . . I don't think I can survive this exorcism. Saraquel doesn't think so anyway, he's been showing me glimpses of what happened when others tried. Saraquel killed the hosts from inside, by shredding their organs in some way or burning them from the inside out. He's feeding me memories.'

'We have to try. Maybe this exorcist knows something Saraquel doesn't. I have some ideas from my research but I'm no exorcist or a believer.'

'Don't tell me too much.' He could hear the smile in her voice. 'Remember, I'm the enemy. Or at least, *he* is.'

Felix changed the subject. 'Are you sure McNamara's going to help, not follow orders and take you to the Inquisition?'

Jack's voice was soft. 'We have an idea about that. Felix, I need you to bring Maggie with you.'

He rubbed his hand through his hair and realised how tangled it was. 'But I need her to stay with Sadie. Angela's struggling.'

'I need Maggie because I will need her magical knowledge if we do get Saraquel out. She can keep me safe, she saved my life before.'

He thought fast, running through the theory he had come up with, afraid it would sound crazy if he voiced it. 'I'll get her there. Can you send Charley back to the hospital to be with Sadie and keep an eye on these Bachmeier and Holtz people?'

She paused for a long time before speaking. 'Of course.'

He looked around to see if he was being overheard but no one was around. 'I miss you, Jack. Maybe we can find some time to talk . . .' Just the thought of seeing her choked him up.

'We can't wait, Felix. I have a really bad feeling about Saraquel. It's like he's taking over more and more.' She sounded as if she was close to tears. 'I know this is silly, but I just want to see you one more time before I'm gone for ever.'

'I'll be there. And I'm not giving up, we've got lots of bits of information, things that Elizabeth Jane Weston knew from Edward Kelley and hid in her poetry. I'm going to speak to Alicia Dennett, see if she can give me as much material as she can.'

'Bring it all with you.' Her voice sounded weaker. 'I'm so tired. I need to sleep but I'm afraid to.'

'How are you going to keep Charley safe, or you, for that matter, if Saraquel is still so powerful he can reach into you?'

'We're bedding down in the chapel until we leave. The nuns have been amazing, they just take all this supernatural stuff in their stride. They won't let me draw a circle, though. No sorcery in the church, so I'll be weaker in the morning.' Her voice dropped. 'Do everything you can for Sadie.' Then a long pause. He could hear her struggle with the unfamiliar words. 'I love you, Felix. I know I shouldn't say it because I may not be here after tomorrow night, but I do.'

'I know.' He rubbed his hand over his forehead. 'I love you too, Jack. Don't forget that, whatever happens tomorrow. And tell McNamara to keep you safe on the journey.'

'Alicia? Felix Guichard.' He tucked his phone between his chin and shoulder, while he packed up his notes.

'Felix? I don't know what you've done but those people have backed off.'

He forced another bunch of papers into a folder. 'I'm sorry, Alicia, but I had to speak to them.'

'Why?' There was a long pause at the end of the phone. 'You must have had a good reason.'

'It's the message Eliza Jane Weston was trying to disseminate. It was designed to be out in the world, Alicia. I know their heavy-handed attempts to get it worried you, but I need the whole message. So do they, if we're going to save a child's life.'

She sounded relieved at the end of the phone. 'I always thought it should be published.'

'I suggest you do. But what I need is your version of the message so far.'

'It doesn't make much sense.'

'You've done the most complete analysis, the most work.' Felix tried to find a place for a phone charger and a couple of pairs of rolled-up socks. 'Please – if you could email it that would be perfect. Alicia . . .' He took a deep breath. 'I may not be back, I'm going up against something I don't understand.'

'Felix! What do you mean?' He could hear her moving papers around. 'Is this about Eliza's monster?'

'It is. I know this sounds crazy, I can't explain more, but that monster is a possessing spirit.'

'That's what the message says. Look, I'll email it to you in a minute. It's just fragments so far, I'm afraid.' Her voice sounded a long way away. 'Please let me know how you get on. There's just one other thing.'

'Yes?'

'Bachmeier and Holtz asked if I wanted a research grant to do further work on the manuscripts. I was going to say no because . . .' She took a hissing breath. 'Felix, you need to know Bachmeier's family were high up in the Nazi administration. In fact, the name Bachmeier might be a pseudonym.'

'Do you have any idea what their previous name was? I mean, was it Báthory?'

'I don't know. I think – oh, you're going to think I'm going daft. I looked into Bachmeier and Holtz and they may have been founded by a Nazi general called Hans Kammler. I mean, it can't have been because Kammler would be over a hundred years old, but he could have started the company after the war and maybe his son or grandson is running it now.'

'Alicia, you must decide for yourself whether to work with them, but they have more of Eliza Weston's books, and together you might be able to put the whole story together and publish it. I don't know what this company did in the past – I can't think about that now. But what happened to my friend is so awful – if we can help prevent that in just one person it would be worth it.'

He could hear her sigh down the phone. 'Felix, please be cautious. You seem like a nice man and the story Eliza was trying to tell is so awful, all monsters and curses.'

'I'll be careful.'

'Good luck. I hope to see you again, and I just hope Eliza's code helps you.'

Within a couple of minutes his phone pinged with an email. He scribbled the words down, not sure how much signal he would get wherever he was going. He hefted the flight bag and turned to leave the room. All he had to do was wait for the final location to be sent to him. Maggie was stroking Sadie's head and murmuring to her. He just hoped whatever she was doing would help, because to him Sadie looked dead already.

Chapter 28

Journal of Eliza Jane Weston, 23 November 1612

The countess read aloud the title of the poem that I had encoded as a key to my father's work. "'They shall not taste death". An auspicious title.'

Her eyes ran down the lines, a frown building upon her face, a face that some thought beautiful.

'This says nothing of my situation,' she said, 'of my damnation.'

'It is a key,' I repeated. I sank back into my chair, the sweat cold upon my body even by the growing fire. 'Lady, my child comes. Of your mercy, I beg you, let me take to my bedchamber above. Take the books.'

'A key.' She read the poem again. 'His knowledge must be hidden within a text, then, a cypher.'

'My father taught me to hide words within words,' I said, rubbing my belly gently, as if to quiet it. But I knew the birth was coming.

'What words?' Her breath was upon me, as she pushed her face towards me.

'All his wisdoms,' I answered, but weakly, as the pain started again.

Edward Kelley, Kérkyra, 1586

With the warning that Valaresso gave us, we made good progress into a harbour upon Kérkyra, a mountainous land to mine English eyes. The Venetian garrison had constructed a fortress within the town, and its gateway was surmounted by a great carving of a lion, which seemed auspicious to me. Marinello's money made friends with the suspicious natives, and they softened under his Venetian charm. He damned them merrily for their rudeness and bought them all fresh wine.

We found privacy in a hired room above the tavern. Here I eased my aching back upon a window seat, for I had taken my turn upon the oars several times, driven by fears of Turkish pirates. Dee had had the box with all our papers brought on shore, and opened it, fussing over the salty damp that had invaded the oiled canvas that covered his maps. He asked Marinello to get the lamps in, even though it was the middle of the day, for the room was dark and cool on account of its deep-set windows.

He unrolled the map and opened his ink pot. Making frequent reference to the notes he had made, and balancing his glasses upon his nose, he started drawing in the coastline as we had observed it.

In the dusty silence, broken only by the scratching of his pen on the parchment and the hooves of mules on the cobbles outside, came a distant tolling of a bell. I listened, trying to find it outside, but as it built up inside the room I was astonished to see that Dee did not respond. It was somewhere inside me, beating like a metal heart.

'Master—' I said, the word trembling in my throat.

The sounds built up until I felt the bell reverberate through my whole body. I saw Dee come towards me, one hand outstretched, his mouth making sounds I could not hear, but my body staggered off the seat until I stood before him. My muscles forced me upright as if I were suspended from a rope. I felt a great swelling in my throat until I could barely breathe, the sensation of a great being trying to inhabit my feeble, mortal shell.

Then I was somewhere else. The pressure was gone, and instead I stood within a dream. I was standing in a bright courtyard, sandstone walls glowing yellow in the light. The bells were gone, instead laughter like falling glass rang around the walls.

The smell of flowers filled my senses. Roses, jasmine and then, something spicy. I turned around completely, seeing walls, windows, a doorway half concealed by vines, but no person. A tapping upon stone made me spin back to the doorway and a lamb, barely a few days old, stepped through it on tiny hooves.

'Edward,' it said, in the sweet voice of a child. Its jaw moved from side to side, not like a man, and for a second I looked around to see who else could have spoken.

'You . . . speak to me? Am – am I dead?' English seemed strange in my mouth.

'Not yet,' it said merrily. It clicked on the stone pavement towards me, then stopped, looking up with golden eyes, the pupils a sideways slit. Its nose was pink, the fleece short and soft-looking. I hesitated, then knelt upon the floor so I could see the creature more closely. It did not seem threatening, but put its head on one side to better observe me.

'What do you say to me, lamb? For I hoped to speak to an angel.'

The lamb turned and nibbled its shoulder. When it turned back it looked as if it were smiling. 'I thought that is what you hoped to avoid?'

Humbled, I put both hands on the ground in front of him. 'I fear it above anything; I know not what to do,' I confessed. 'I have done something terrible. I have condemned a woman to a dreadful fate. She lives half-corpse, on the blood of others, and is haunted by a demon.'

'No demon, as you well know,' the lamb said merrily, looking even more amused. 'You helped Saraquel in good faith, foolish Edward. The sin lay more in your terror of death. You stayed nature's hand upon the woman.'

I sat back at that. 'I do not understand.'

The lamb did a little hop on all four feet. 'Look at me. I am born, I will die. How many lambs and sheep have fallen to your knife and those of your butchers, Edward?'

'I suppose — many.'

'And there will be others.' The lamb skipped this way and that, in the manner of new lambs everywhere. 'And I will be taken, and my throat cut, and my blood will fall. It is my nature.'

'Never.' I spoke with conviction. 'I will never slay another lamb.'

The creature put back its head, its ears waving, two small bumps suggesting horns that might grow one day. Its laughter was less musical, and the lamb seemed bigger. 'You will slay many,' it laughed, 'and it is as nature makes it. But you too will age and die, Edward. How will you face the knife at your throat when it is your turn to bleed?'

I swallowed. 'I know not. I hope with grace and faith.'

The lamb stopped moving, and stared straight at me. Its breath, of sweet grass, washed over me. It had grown more, big enough to face me as I knelt. 'But now you know the secrets of prolonging life, Edward. How will you face your own death?'

I could feel my face reddening with heat. 'I shall trust in the mercy of my Lord Jesus,' I said, my voice cracked.

'For your death could be soon,' said the lamb, the golden eyes somehow bigger, amber now, the pupils rounder. The soft fleece seemed to have thickened to a tawny yellow. When it opened its mouth, long teeth were revealed, and I realised I was sitting next to a growing lion.

I shuddered with fear, and shut my eyes. I found within me that knot of faith that sometimes sustains me. 'If God wills it.'

'It could be soon,' it said, the voice rougher and deeper, as if a growl was threaded through it. 'It could be now.'

'Then let it be now.' I said with a moment of courage, a moment of faith. And I fell into a pit of darkness.

I awoke upon a narrow bed, the lamplight flickering over the rough wooden ceiling. I turned my head, my neck aching with the movement, and saw Marinello and Dee sitting close together, speaking low, Dee making notes within his journal. I tried to speak, but a ragged croak was the only sound I could make.

'Ah, my friend,' said Dee, taking my hand in his. 'You rouse at last. We feared you lost to us until morning.'

His hand supported me as I sat up, and I shuffled up to lean against a cushion of sorts. Marinello held out an earthenware cup of wine, and I drank deep. Dee sat upon the end of the bed and smiled at me.

I coughed and looked around. It seemed that Marinello was reluctant to meet my eye. 'What happened?' I said, my throat still rough.

'Uriel spoke through you. An archangel of light, my friend, blessed us all.' His eyes seemed filled with tears, they shined in the light of the flame. 'You spoke—'

'Of death?' I asked, remembering the lamb. My head thumped like a drum. Marinello stepped forward and sloshed more wine into the cup, then he retreated to the dark shadows of the corner again.

'No,' he said, his Venetian accent more obvious in the Latin than usual. 'He spoke of the language of angels, written on a manuscript in Alexandria, guarded by scholars and mystics.' Marinello crossed himself and mumbled a blessing.

'Uriel spoke of the past and the future flowing into one,' Dee said. 'That I did not yet comprehend, but one thing is clear: Saraquel, the same angel that teased and lured us to Transylvania to save the Countess Báthory, has fallen from grace. It is not natural that an angel seeks corporeal life.'

Marinello stepped forward a little, a small smile lifting his sombre expression. 'I am thankful that you did not act as a mouthpiece for an angel on the ship,' he said. 'My crew would certainly have deserted us, even if they had to jump overboard. The room was filled with light, the like I have never seen. They would surely have cried "sorcery".'

'What did you see, Edward?' Dee asked.

I described to Dee my strange encounter with the lamb. He scribbled down notes as I spoke, scratching the page with his tiny marks. As I told how the lamb grew into the lion, he paused.

'And said what?'

'He spoke of death. My death.'

Marinello paced across the room, his boots loud on the timbers. 'We sail upon the next tide,' he growled.

Chapter 29

Present day, Dartmoor

Robert Conway, already sweating in the early sunlight, raised the pump handle. Pushing it down, he could hear the whistle of water in the pipes, bubbling louder until it surged out of the tap into the bucket. The fresh water came from the deep granite fissure below the house, brought up with its hand pump, and it had some energy the spring water lacked. It was winter cold, splashing over the edge onto his bare feet. He lifted the bucket onto his shoulder and topped up the tank just inside the porch of the cabin. He had a feeling he might be besieged, and he would feel better if he was prepared. He had no idea where these intuitions came from – perhaps from his study of distant history, perhaps from his own experiences. But he knew better than to ignore them.

Twelve buckets later and he felt reassured that at least one chore was done. He took the opportunity to strip off and run a bar of soap all over himself, even his hair, and sluice it off again in a few breath-taking buckets of the water, shaking like a dog over the long grass. It made him feel younger, stronger. His skin was reddened by the icy water, except for the scar on one thigh, a twisted white rope of his history running into the knee. The leg had healed, but the missing knee cap would always be awkward. He rubbed himself dry with the towel he had hung on the cabin door.

Slipping on new clothes from the cupboard in the cabin made him feel different. They had a musty smell from a year or more of storage, but also smelled of the incenses he kept with them. He shook them out, the scent invoking years of training in the seminary. He hadn't been a young man when he trained, he had had experience of life to offer, his innocence already gone. His main purpose had been to study exorcism, and he had been lucky enough to train under a master exorcist, and attend several cleansings and tests before his own first foray into the art of communicating with demons. What he had learned had led to this day, and he spent a moment weighing the trappings of an exorcist: robe, surplice, stole. He had learned not to wear the stole as it was too easy to strangle the exorcist with. And, hung up on a bent nail, the most valuable item he had apart from his books, a gold crucifix once owned by St Paul of the Cross. He touched it gently, feeling the need to genuflect, but resisting with his damaged knee. His beliefs, such as they had been, were long spent. He no longer knew if there was a God, but he still had some belief in an Anti-christ. He lifted the cross down, and slipped it over his head. Superstition, maybe, but he felt better with it on. He slid it inside his shirt and turned back to the cottage.

There was a strange excitement, even as he recognised the dangers. Maybe he was just tired of hiding. He lifted the rug in front of the fireplace, displacing a few silverfish that shimmered like spilled mercury and disappeared between the planks in the floor. A single knot in the wood was dark, and he slipped a finger into the hole and under the board to lift it. It was stiff, another year's worth of dust holding it in place, but it came up to reveal a space where he had placed a gun safe. Not that guns could stop a possession by a supernatural agent, but inside the box were two handguns and ammunition, safe in oiled cloths, and two plastic containers of black powder for booby traps. More importantly, a dagger inscribed with symbols along its length. Just touching the hilt made his fingertips hum. It was made by a Saracen who was famous for dispatching demons in the Muslim world.

Laying out his weapons on the table, he felt a shiver run down his spine. He had dreaded this confrontation his whole life, but part of him was tired of waiting. Either he would send Saraquel back where he came from, or he would become part of Saraquel's army of possessed beings.

He opened the book, Kelley's journal, at a much-thumbed page. Here, jotted in Latin with a few notes in Hebrew or even older scripts, lay the answer. Somewhere in the scribbled notes, not in Kelley's hand but in that of a Jewish scholar, Rabbi Loew, was the conjuration that had originally been in the first versions of the book of Enoch. The symbols sketched out the words that could send Saraquel back, not into heaven as that historical Kelley hoped, but into physical captivity. The exorcism of Zadok was witnessed by Kelley in 1586, even though the notes were incomplete. It had conjured a golem, a great clay figure, which had been animated in some way. Conway suspected there was a link to the magic of the borrowed timers. Finally, he reached for the precious box, Edward Kelley's last gift to the Inquisition, but dared not open it. Its contents rattled softly, just a loose roll of parchment with a cracked seal clinging on. He laid the box with some ceremony on the table, and wrapped it with a faded square of silk. Finally, he packed the whole lot except the knife in a sport's bag to keep it all together, the bright logo incongruous against its ancient contents.

Conway rested in the hammock he had slung between hooks screwed into the overhanging roof of the modern cabin, the dagger in his lap. The old house was scrubbed as clean and dust free as he could make an old stone-and-cob building. He had washed again, anxious to be as clean as possible when he confronted the threat. The old woodburner had finally stopped smoking, and a stew of vegetables and tinned lentils sat on the top. A few of the early wild garlic stems had added a bit of flavour, and he had brought the oil with him. He daren't eat meat before an exorcism, he found the clearer his body was of waste, the harder it was for a demon to get a foothold. He had been present when Father Michael, in New York, had exorcised a young woman. The demon had latched on to the steak dinner being digested and shredded Michael's gut from inside. The American exorcist had barely survived the surgery to save him, and now had a permanent colostomy. Robert would top up his energy levels as far as he could with organic vegetables, then cleanse with a handful of herbs made into tea.

The cottage's paved floor was already painted with symbols of protection, but a new triangle had been added to contain the non-corporeal essence of Saraquel – if he could be confined. What the angelic possessor didn't know, hopefully, was that the triangle sat over the borehole in the granite maybe twenty or more feet deep, from which he had drawn the water. Edward Kelley himself had seen a possessing spirit, this one of a violent and jealous human, confined to a well. Kelley had described it, along with his experiences of alchemy, in the endpapers of his first journal, encoded in a strange script and as yet undeciphered by generations of scholars at the British Library. Robert had a version of the decoded text written in his notes, tucked into the back of Kelley's Mediterranean journal.

First, the triangle of conjuring, that gave rise to the triangle of Solomon . . .

It had been many years since he had studied sorcery, even though elements of it were contained in his seminary education. The line between exorcism and conjuring spirits was a fine one. *You must know the spirit's name, and must fast that you be clean of pollution so the spirit will be obedient before you . . .*

The name was simple, it had haunted him since his youth. Saraquel had tried to work his way into Robert's mind many times, but had never been able to stay more than a few moments. It was the last encounter that had terrified him, feeling Saraquel stretching into his consciousness, forcing out his thoughts, his feelings, feeding greedily on his grief. Ethan had been so close to the moment of death that Saraquel had found him, had crawled his way into Ethan's last few breaths and, there, scented Robert Conway. Robert's impulse to save his lover by attempting to bind his soul to his body had nearly cost them both the price of possession. How he had found the strength to stop him he could barely even now contemplate. The dagger, the soft skin of his lover's throat, the instinctive slash that put both of them beyond Saraquel's reach. There could be no lovers now, no possible conduits to Saraquel. Robert had surrounded himself with a barrier of loneliness, and so far it had worked. Saraquel seemed to have finally lost sight of him. He smiled wryly, as he polished the dagger with the silk cloth, wondering if there was some trace of the boy's blood on it. Barely a man, twenty-four and beautiful and the first person who had understood Robert for so long. An impulse led

211

him to touch his lips to the blade, feeling it hum against his skin, in grief, in love.

Saraquel, angel of death. That had been his calling, to soften the separation of soul from body. But at some point, he had found a body that rallied, clawing its way back into life and taking Saraquel with it. Robert's research, with historians and archaeologists, led him to suspect the first victim was Qahedjet, a third-dynasty pharaoh, who was saved by a priest's magical intervention. The legend ran, the pharaoh was thrown from a chariot while hunting, and the wheel ran over his body. The pharaoh was dying when his priests arrived, and they sent the guards and servants away. A few hours later, still injured but breathing, the pharaoh reclaimed the throne being made ready for his infant son. The pharaoh's behaviour changed; he took many more wives and produced a lot more children, to the distress of his first wife. She subsequently tried to poison him, leading to her execution. His people called him the 'stone king', because he had, in their eyes, become impervious and god-like.

Robert's expertise in linguistics had helped take the early translations further, but he kept the final decoding private. What the pharaoh's priests had stumbled on was the ritual that had anchored Qahedjet's soul to his body, and they recorded every step in symbols and carvings. Conway had spent a dozen years trying to decode every last dot and line. He now had, in his notes, the key to life and death.

Chapter 30

Journal of Eliza Jane Weston, 23 November 1612

The countess placed her arm around my waist and half lifted me to my feet. 'Where lies your chamber?' she asked.

'Upon the next floor,' I said, fighting to get away, but the pain tore through my body and I cried out. This was not like the pains I remembered, this was sharp, like a wolf gnawing upon my spine. Tomáš met me at the door, and the faces of two of my children looked on.

Tomáš took my other arm and between them they helped me up the narrow steps. There was no respite, the pain a continuous thunder struck through with lightning.

The countess chafed my hands between hers, hard, cold hands that they were, and repulsive to me so I pulled away.

My man looked inside the door. 'I shall send a boy to get Master Leo.'

I could do nothing but hold onto the bed, moan as the tightness pulled at my entrails, and a cry burst from my lips.

'Get wood first,' she commanded, 'and build a fire. For the babe comes.'

My mind, dazed by pain, was sharpened by the thought of my helpless child, born into the hands of this dead thing, this creature, this revenant.

Edward Kelley, the voyage to Candia, 1586

Leaving the safe harbour of Kérkyra felt like leaving a mother's embrace. We had time to pen a few words to our families before addressing them to the house of Konrad, whom we hoped would be supervising the countess, and sent them homeward on a merchant ship. Then we slipped into the sharp dawn with a mumbling, grumbling crew and shipped oars for Candia.

The water was still opaque with darkness, each stroke of the oar curling it into froth, the men easing their way into the rhythm while the cook stacked his supplies and herded three goats into a pen aft of the rowers. The air was breathless, and Dee able to spread out his maps as the light grew.

He had traced other maps at the house of Marinello using paper made of some sort of rice. This was so fine only the softest of pencils could be used to make a line, and he was transferring the coastline onto sturdy parchment. Here he could make adjustments, adding a few tiny islands as he saw them and sketching them carefully in his journal. This one had a hill upon it like a sleeping dog; this one had cliffs that looked like they were made of honeycomb. Despite his fears for Jane Dee and our children, he seemed younger and browner than I had ever seen him.

'Come, Edward, take an oar with me,' said Marinello, and I was glad to, since he had avoided me since the conversation with Uriel.

I was glad to sit in the morning sun, reaching for the rhythm of the oars. 'Tell me of Candia,' I said when I had breath. 'Is it truly the earliest civilisation?'

He smiled, his sinewed forearm marked by the pink scar, visible now he had removed the bandage. Jane Dee's surgery had healed well.

'Many say so. It is held by Venice, and the Greeks think of it as theirs, but the natives claim it is a sovereign land and they are a unique race. They call it Creta.'

'And we shall take a ship there to Alexandria?'

'We shall, I hope, turn this bucket back to Venice and use my own caravel to get to Alexandria. There is a great demand in the Arab lands for such ships, built by the Portuguese, and sturdy.'

'Why is your caravel in Candia?' I asked, heaving upon the oar, which sucked greedily at the sea, spawning a dozen mouths.

'My partner, Antonio Alighieri,' he said, spitting loudly over the side. 'He borrowed it for a venture of his own, sailed into a storm and lost two masts.' He stretched back into the oar. 'She is an old vessel, but fine, and only a sailor as bad as Alighieri could fail to get the sails down in time.' He grinned at me, his teeth very white against his dark skin. 'You will like her. We call her *Cachorro do Mar*, dog of the sea. I learned to captain aboard her. She can sail into the wind as no other type of vessel can, so we won't need oars.'

We rowed for some minutes in the sunshine, the heat already gleaming on his sweaty skin and shimmering over the canvas shade Dee was working under.

'Will you be sorry to sell her, my lord?'

He grimaced for a moment, perhaps with his labours. 'I cannot sustain my business with her. She is my last remaining asset except for *Delfino* and the bigger ship in Alexandria.' He shrugged, and shook his black curls from his eyes. 'She is older than either of us. We can survive her loss, and she represents a lot of gold.' He called out something in his own language, and the crew rested for a moment, while the cook brought watered wine around for all. It tasted sweet, far from the rank water we would drink in a few days.

One of the crew called out. '*Patrone*.' And pointed to the flag, just quivering in the air.

Marinello stowed his oar and indicated I should do the same. He called upon several of the men. 'Let us run out some canvas,' he said, grinning, 'and let the wind do the work.'

The winds caught us in their grip as they strengthened, making it necessary for two men to strain at the rear oar and drive her against the currents before a light squall. But nightfall brought calm, and with it fresh food and rest. I saw, in the darkening water, a flash of silver, then another. Before I could call out, the fishes flew up beside the boat and threw themselves across the surface. I was astonished as dozens of similar fish splashed upon the surface then flew a few yards.

The cook snapped out some command and a makeshift net was assembled from canvas, and a lantern held over the sea. I watched, entranced, as dozens of the fish danced across the wavelets and into our trap.

'Flying fish,' Marinello said. 'Sweet eating.'

Dee was as interested as I, holding one of the creatures in his hands, watching it flap and gulp before it was dispatched by a crew member with a quick blow from the hilt of a knife. 'Why do they fly?'

A crew member attempted in halting Latin to explain. 'They sleep on shore,' he said, mimicking laying his head down at night on his hands. 'Safe . . . yes?'

Marinello smiled at that. 'More likely there are sharks or dolphins below us, and they seek to escape them. But they come to our lanterns and that I don't know how to explain.' He ordered the lantern dimmed again, and the 'net' was brought in.

He was right. We gorged ourselves on the little fish, their skin blackened by a few minutes over the charcoal, and the sweet flesh falling off the bones in our hands. One of the men was passed food up the mast, where he was tied as a lookout. He hissed softly, not a sharp sound that might carry, but a low one that attracted the crew's attention. In the dying light, his pale form seemed to gesture and point.

The men threw the remains of the fish overboard, and immediately ran to their oars. We rowed on through the first part of the night. Perhaps it was nothing, but in these waters our anxieties were raised again. I finally slept but was awoken by Dee in the dead of night, shushing me.

'What is it?' I whispered back. 'Corsairs?'

'No,' he said back. 'Just the angel speaking in the dead language of the Jews. The men are afraid.'

After that I sat huddled in a blanket against the night chill and looked over the glints of starlight on the black sea until sleep took me. I awoke again in the light, cramped and stiff. None of the crew would meet my eye, and only Dee would bring me food to break my fast.

'We must be careful of the crew's fears,' he said. 'This will be a long journey and as we leave the safety of land there can be no retreat.'

I had already seen Dee's calculations on the journey. Assuming we stayed on course the journey would be another twenty days. Twenty in good weather, but many more if we were blown off course.

We were fortunate. Twenty-two days with a mostly following wind, all of them with the suspicions of the crew building. I could not speak to them, nor would one sit beside me, and I knew at night the dreams grew more vivid, and the speech louder into the dark. Nevertheless, Marinello demanded that they treat me equitably.

By the twelfth day the wine was gone, by nineteen the charcoal. We chewed biscuit with a ration of stale water, and counted ourselves lucky. Another shoal of the flying fish was caught, and the cook scavenged oddments of wood from the ship and a coil of tarred rope to cook them. The meat stank of tar but we were hungry, and then anything becomes palatable. On the twentieth day rain came, caught in our canvas fish net and drained into buckets. There, brackish and silvery with scales, it gave us as much water to drink as we could hold, and never has water tasted so good. But the rocky shore ahead gave us new heart and strength in our arms for the rowing.

Chapter 31

Present day, Hampshire

Jack waited in the chapel until past two o'clock, unable to sleep. She heard the distant rumble of an engine stalled, then silence.

'Charley,' she whispered in her foster sister's ear, making her jump. 'Is that the van Mac was getting?' She glanced past the last pew where one of the nuns sat dozing.

Charley crept to the porch. 'Black cars, two of them. Shit.'

'The Inquisition?' She suddenly felt cold to the marrow, and realised just how much she wanted to live, at least long enough to see Felix again. 'Let's wait in the road,' she whispered to Charley, pointing to the porch. 'Mac can't be far away.'

She got to her feet, grabbing the blanket to put around her shoulders. Charley had slept fully dressed, and had been using her coat as a pillow, but Jack was in indoor clothes. Charley handed it to Jack and she dragged the borrowed coat on.

A man had got out of the lead car, his shoes loud on the gravel. She could just see him standing there, looking towards the lit chapel. She froze, and he turned to look straight at her. He peered into the dimly lit nave, hunched his shoulders against the cold, and turned away.

219

'Wha . . .?' Jack managed to say, as she turned to Charley, who has murmuring something, her eyes closed, her forehead wrinkled into a frown. 'A spell? Here?'

Charley didn't break the chant, but a tiny smirk suggested she had heard. The spell, called *nihil vident*, required the chanter to be sightless as well as invisible, so Jack had to guide Charley from the church, through a small back door from the sacristy. The path beyond had been paved, so they were able to tiptoe across in silence, Jack looking out for Mac. He met them in the vegetable garden carrying a bag. Jack could already feel her control slipping. All she could do was stare open-eyed up at the inquisitor.

Mac brought his mouth down close to Jack's ear. 'The van's in the lane,' he whispered.

The good news gave Jack power over her limbs for a few moments more.

'Help Charley,' she hissed. 'She can't look.'

He didn't question. She let Mac guide Charley over the dark grass and towards the back of the property where the lane curved around towards a cluster of farms.

Jack paused, glancing back towards the small graveyard at the rear of the church. 'They're in the chapel,' she whispered. Their proximity brought the hairs up on the back of her neck.

'There,' Mac said from directly behind her, and when she jumped, he coughed out what could have been a laugh.

Jack swung around, and even Charley stopped chanting.

'For God's sake,' Jack said, clutching at Charley's arm. 'What is that?'

'It's a mortuary van.'

'You're putting Jack in a . . . hearse?' snapped out Charley.

'I'm sorry, it was the best I could come up with at short notice.' He swung the doors open. Inside was a heavy box. 'It's secure,' he confirmed, stepping out of range of Jack's reach. Saraquel started to fight Jack again.

Charley said, 'Hurry up, the enemy are already here.'

Jack could hear voices at the convent, Bea's voice and a man's reply. 'Can we trust Mac?' she breathed to Charley.

'I don't know,' was the uncompromising answer. 'But so far, he's avoiding the Inquisition.'

The vehicle was parked in the lane, blocking it completely.

Mac had to lift Jack onto the high step as Saraquel locked her muscles. 'Drink this,' he said, holding her against one shoulder. She fought, some of the liquid going down her chin, but some – enough, she hoped – went down. She let Mac guide her towards the back of the van.

Except for a box against one side, it was bare. The container was about the size of a large coffin. Jack found her tongue, even though her words were starting to slur. The sedative seemed to work better on Saraquel than Jack. 'You are kidding! I'm . . . OK . . .' She was slurring her words.

Charley looked inside. 'I think they're coming,' she said in a low voice. 'Just get in, Jack. It's the safest we can do. I'll go around the side of the chapel to draw them off.'

The box, ventilated down one side, had a thick coat at the bottom like a makeshift mattress, and smelled stale, like mould and compost.

'I can't,' she suddenly said, in a panic at least partly fuelled by Saraquel.

'You have to,' said Mac, his eyes reflecting the small inside light in the confined space. She hadn't seen him climb up, but his hands were suddenly digging into her shoulders.

221

The next thing she remembered was waking up. The engine was rumbling in the background and she was warm in a dark that felt like it was pressing down on her. She fought to give in to the fading sedative. Saraquel surged forward with both arms and angel strength, slamming into the top of the box. He kept beating against it, confined by the narrow distance to the coffin lid.

Saraquel only stopped when Jack's howls of pain were stretched into animal screams at the feeling of her bones at breaking point. As he retreated, Jack sobbed, letting her arms rest crossed over her chest.

You think you can win this battle? The voice in her head was tempered with a growl of frustration.

'I already am, you psychopath,' she muttered, struggling one hand up to wipe her face.

Saraquel must have completely taken over for a while because she drifted in and out of awareness, hearing the echo of the angel's shrieked frustration, a mixture of languages echoing around the box. Her human body was cramped for space, but he was crushed by the box, his body trying to expand hers to shatter the confinement, but something was weakening him with each effort.

In moments of lucidity, Jack could hear something scratching on the lid of the box, something sharp.

'What's going on?'

'This is a sigil we used to supress demons. I wasn't sure if it would work but I'm worried Saraquel will kill you.' Mac's muffled voice came from the other side of the box.

She heard him jump down, slam the back door shut and the little light that had come through the ventilation holes was gone again. He got back in the driving seat and started the engine.

'Where's Charley?' she shouted, before he pulled off.

'Gone to the hospital to be with Sadie.'

The engine rumbled again, and found a comfortable pace on the road. Saraquel started to fight back and Jack dozed off.

The van shook her awake. It seemed to turn off the main road and rumbled over a hard, uneven surface before it stopped.

'We're here.' Mac opened his door and got out, crunching over gravel.

A gleam of dawn crept into the box as the van door creaked open. 'He's coming,' Jack mumbled as Saraquel pushed forward.

This time he was stronger. Jack could feel him crush the breath in her throat until she could see nothing but a blanket of black shot through with stars. She gasped a single breath when he let go for a second, then he overcame her again as someone lifted the box at each end.

Whoever was carrying the box was struggling with it. At one point they dropped it, and Mac swore, while Jack fought for every gulp of stale air.

'How is she?' someone said, and the coffin levelled out. Slowly the voice became familiar. Felix. 'Is she all right?'

'Put her in the back of the estate, please.' A new voice, soft, cultured. The angel inside her stopped so suddenly Jack felt dizzy for a moment, back in charge of her own body. It was a relief to get herself back for a moment. Jack felt like her arms, shoulders and chest had been strained beyond their normal limits, they hurt so much.

She was able to croak. 'Felix. Felix!'

'Don't worry, Jack, we'll get you out soon,' he said. Then he spoke to someone else. 'We'll follow you in the van.'

Finally, a thump as a blanket was put over the air holes, dimming the little light. The door slammed.

223

The engine started, and the vehicle rumbled for a short while over a road, then turned, jolting her into the side of the box as it bumped over an unmade surface. Stop, then start, then a long shaky progress downhill, uphill again, then finally curving to a stop. Another car pulled alongside.

Jack could feel Saraquel retreating. She started shouting. 'Felix. It's me, he's gone—' She heard a buzzing sound and the lid seemed to ease a little up one side, letting in a slit of light.

'Wait a minute,' said Felix. A few more whirrs and, finally, the lid was lifted off.

Jack sat up with some difficulty, her arms heavy and painful with each movement. She looked around what seemed to be a garden as overgrown as her home in the Lake District, except for a narrow boundary around the walls of a tiny house. The stone walls felt familiar, like the priest hole she had been confined to as a child.

Felix put out his hands, and she touched his warm fingers before Saraquel started to fight for control. She whimpered with the effort to keep the possession at bay, but Felix scooped her up and pulled her out of the box. She staggered but could balance on her own feet, distracted by the sensation of Saraquel trying to balance as well.

A man came forward and smiled at her. He was a little older than Felix, or maybe a lot, she couldn't tell. His hair was streaked with grey but his skin looked youngish. She could feel the angel inside rock back in shock, completely stunned.

'It's good to meet you, finally, Miss Hammond,' he said. 'But we must get you inside before Saraquel acts.'

Felix half-carried her into the cottage as the man held the door open. Once inside there was an immediate relief from the resurging force of Saraquel's control. She slumped to the floor with relief the second Felix let her go.

The older man crouched down in front of her. 'Better? Come further into the circles. They will make you more comfortable.' He was short and slight, hardly bigger than her.

She crawled forward and felt the warmth of the circles as they enclosed her – much stronger than she had ever felt them before. 'Wow. Thank you.'

She looked around for Felix who was smiling down at her. The house was a stone shell, flagstone floor made of granite, the roof open to the rafters, old beams snaking across the top of the building. Felix sat beside her and she let him gather her into his arms and for a long moment was content. The unknown man cleared his throat.

'Welcome. My name is Robert Conway, and I am an exorcist. Don't worry about the magic in the circles. It will release Saraquel somewhat but it will strengthen you more.'

He bent down and held out a hand. She shook it, and smiled back. 'You know about Saraquel?'

'Saraquel and I are old adversaries,' he admitted. 'And it is my duty, even my vow, to exorcise him.'

She let go and hugged her knees, resting her forehead on them. How much was Saraquel influencing all her decisions, her feelings? It seemed like years since she had been herself – cold, empty, lonely years. But Felix had changed all that; the moment she met him something about him had pulled her into his warmth, his light. Her feelings for Felix were definitely hers, she decided, even if Saraquel had pushed her to behave strangely around him and awakened her dormant body to longings she had never had before. *I do love him.* She felt Felix's arm around her, and smiled. She loved Charley, too, and Maggie and Sadie. She had people. It was worth the battle.

225

Chapter 32

Journal of Eliza Jane Weston, 23 November 1612

> As Tomáš built a fire I leaned upon the bed post and thought as
> fast as I could, between the pains gripping my flanks and back.
> The countess moved around the room, looking on shelves and within
> a press, where she drew out a few sheets.
>
> 'You will tell me what I want to know,' she said, and nodded
> towards the window, where I saw the small pile of books. 'You will do
> so over the torn body of your babe or before. I care little which it is.'
>
> It seemed incongruous that she talk of rending my unborn child
> for her vile appetites, even as she prepared for his birth.

Edward Kelley, Candia, 1586

Candia was a fortified port on the island of the same name. It was
a place where many peoples came to trade and to gather supplies
for longer journeys. On land, my legs were as unsteady as if the
earth was heaving in a storm. I sat upon a bollard and heard
a dozen languages spoken around me in banter, trading and

argument. I found, mixed with French and Latin, the accents of an Englishman, and hailed him. Dominick Smith he called himself, and he limped over to my station on what I saw was a wooden leg, carved in the shape of a mermaid.

'An Englishman? What is this?' he said, looking over our boat, which was dwarfed by many a fine galleon and xebec.

'A traveller, heading south,' I said. 'Are there many English here?'

'A few,' he said, 'passing through. Few venture so far east, but some, like me, have escaped slavery.'

I could see the roughness of scars criss-crossing his brown arms and neck. I had seen a few such marks upon the skin of Marinello, who had spent two years in the service of the Turks, and grieved for such agony. I commiserated with him, and we passed a few minutes talking of Somersetshire, which I knew a little. He had been captured aboard an English ship travelling to Rome, and had spent a dozen years working for the Sultan in chains before that ship was captured by Dutch sailors. I could see that despite his long years he was watchful and curious about us. Before long he knew our names and I saw in his eyes a recognition of Dr Dee's name, although he said nothing.

Marinello was swept ashore in a group of sailors and merchants who either knew him or his father, and I followed into the town, named Heraklion, with my new friend. I was curious about the place, a great fortress still under construction by a gang of builders who swarmed upon its walls on ropes and wooden scaffolds. Here Smith took me to his home, a small house under the shadow of the castle, and he introduced me to his Greek wife. She was young, a dark-haired and buxom beauty who plied me with sweet meat in stews and much wine. After so many days with short rations, I ate and drank until my belly was painfully swollen and my head swimming as if we were at sea. Then, as I knew they must, came questions.

What ship did we travel on? What were our cargoes? When did we sail? Fortunately, I could not share information I was not privy to, and he kept serving me wine and dishes of eggs and honey. What was the news of the queen, and London town? Here I could share the gossip, and titbits were translated for his wife, who laughed at each and exclaimed. For her I exaggerated some of the court's excesses and we spent a merry evening. Finally, I left with Dominick and we walked into the town to find my master.

Marinello had bought lodgings for us at the port, and here I found Dee, fresh from examining our new vessel. He was slightly amused but more irritated by my excesses. My mentor was right – the rich food and wine had sat uneasily upon my starved belly and made me queasy. He foretold that I would suffer in the morning, and the last thing I recall was lying upon a fat straw pallet listening to Dee and my new friend exchange pleasantries. Here I fell into sleep, but a word awoke me some time later. The room was dark, the tallow guttering in holders around the room. I looked around, to see the two men still leaning upon the table, their speech low. What word so disturbed my slumbers? I sighed, and turned a little upon the pallet that they would not suspect I was awake.

They had stopped their conversation, a dying candle hissing in the silence. I made my breathing slow, and strained in the darkness to hear them.

'Walsingham could consider your travel treasonable,' came the soft voice of my new friend Dominick. 'Then it would be my duty, no, my pleasure, to stop you.'

'What do you propose then?' asked my mentor, his words as calm as ever.

'Perhaps if you were to write to Sir Francis, and pay me a sum of money that would ensure its delivery, we could agree that your activities are not treasonable,' the man said. 'A letter that outlines your present ship, its commander and men and the cargoes, perhaps.'

Dee's chair creaked back as he moved a little, and under the cover of its tiny sounds, I reached within my shirt for my scabbard. 'I have little money of my own,' he said truthfully. 'I am on a personal journey to advance my research, and I have always been known as a loyal subject of Her Majesty. She herself would vouch for me, as I was her adviser since she was a child.'

'I must assure myself of your loyalty, nevertheless,' Dominick said, his voice harder now. 'Your commander is covering some whore in the town, your crew would think themselves lucky were you to end in the harbour with a slit throat. There are those who might pay for such, for they tell of sorceries and demons.'

I slipped the covers from my shoulders, muffling the sound of the knife sliding from its sheath.

Dee seemed unsurprised by the man's response. 'In every port is a rogue who will do anything for money,' he said. 'I would be saddened to discover that in Heraklion it was an Englishman.'

The varlet jumped up, the sound of his boots on the floor and the hiss of a sword sliding free covered my own lurch to my feet. He swung around, just a black form in the dark room, to meet me and my dagger. But Dee's chanting filled the room and wove a paralysis that netted us both, frozen like statues of gladiators, my puny point inches from his short sword.

Dee, his eyes glinting in the low light, advanced, his spell weaving a spider's web of enchantment.

Too late I recognised a tone in the room, a chiming that did not come from our plane. My hand shook, even in its frozen state, and the handle of the knife became hot in my fingers until it near burned me. Finally, with a great swell inside my chest beyond my own breath, the presence arrived, forcing my shoulders back from the ensorcellment. And it spoke, its tone grinding free from my throat although I could taste blood.

'Saraquel, begone,' it said, in a rush that hurt my ears and throat.

Dominick Smith strained against the enchantment, the knife slowly cutting the air between us.

'You cannot protect your puny champion,' he said, his words forced out against the stranglehold of Dee's chanting, the paralysis persisting despite his widened eyes and shaking hand. The sword crept down my arm, creasing the shirt, then started to stretch my skin. I felt the searing of it entering my body, then I started to shake as he forced it forward. Dee caught the blade and it clattered to the floorboards.

I felt my own muscles swell as if inflated like a bladder, and with a moment of freedom, my arm swept against the man, pushing him back into the wall with a crack that broke Dee's spell.

I felt my body lifted into an unnatural curve, and pivoted upon my very toes. 'John,' it breathed, as if trying to moderate its tone. I heard no more, my soul forced back by the invading angel, until I awoke to the soft sound and motion of the sea.

'Gently,' warned Dee, as I saw him bent over me, Marinello behind him. 'Smith lies insensible in a gutter in the town for the moment, but time will restore him. I believe it was Uriel himself who intervened for you, else Saraquel would have killed you. Aye, and Smith too.'

Whether it was the rich food or wine or the invasion of the angel I do not know, but I was vilely unwell, and Dee held the bucket for me. I looked around me to see a small stateroom all bound with carved wood beams at odd angles, the narrow bunk I lay upon tucked within the ship's curved wall. Marinello held out a goblet, and I drained it. Some herbal concoction in wine, I thought, one of Dee's physics, but it settled my stomach.

'We must sail anon,' Marinello warned as he took back the goblet. 'There are whispers of devilment ashore, and such rumours are dangerous.'

'The men?' I croaked through a rough throat.

'We change crew here, I have a full complement aboard *Cachorro do Mar*. She can run closer to the wind than almost any vessel in Candia and she is nearly loaded. We simply exchange some goods into *Delfino* and she can return to Kérkyra, then straight back to Venice.'

'Loaded?' Dee helped me swing heavy legs out of the bunk, to sit trembling on the edge.

'We carry local oils – some of the finest in the Mediterranean. Honey and wax, also, and perfumes. High-value cargo that should sell for enough in Alexandria to release my ship.' He grinned. 'And this old bucket. I will sell the *Sea Dog* and partners be damned. They would stick a knife in my back as willingly if it brings a profit, and they know I will share the money eventually.'

I swallowed down a mouthful of the water and wine, which threatened to return. 'I should like to learn how to sail her,' I said, choking a little.

'And you will, my young friend. But sailing a caravel is a master's business. Come and watch them tow us out of harbour, get your sea-legs back.'

It was a great sight, high on the foredeck, feeling the sea sway under our deep keel. A barge with as many, I dare say, as sixty rowers heaved us out against the slight tide, and then the new crew, more Venetians I judged by their language, swarmed into the lines and sails, and the great lungs of the ship unfolded. A single breath of wind pushed against the first of the sails and the ropes between the ships – straining and shedding water at each stroke – fell slack. Marinello gave a number of whistles and orders and at his hand the ship started to pull free of the barge, which raised its oars on one side to allow us to pass. As I looked down into the belly of the barge-tug, I smelled the first wave of stench and saw on many benches the shackled captives that worked there. Row upon row, three to a bench on each oar, chained so close that if one row leaned back the one behind was obliged to also. I saw men burned oaken-dark in the sun, Moors pulling with fair-haired Christians, old men and boys matched equally against the weight of the sea.

'Slaves?' I asked Dee, but I knew the answer. No free man would be chained so.

'I believe so. They are traded here if their masters are licensed – that is, if that they are not corsairs but legitimate brokers.' Dee looked away. 'The trade is vile, certainly. Despicable. Yet the queen has rewarded Drake and Hawkins for bringing slaves from Africa.'

I looked away and covered my face as we drew away from the ship. 'But the smell . . .'

Marinello joined us, one hand braced against the rigging. 'The men are chained to their station unless they are taken ashore to sell.' He spat into the sea, then raised a hand to the ship in salute. 'I have spent two years chained abaft like those men, sat in my own ordure, sores on my rump, my hands raw and back striped from endless floggings. But the alternative – forced to convert, to be castrated and work as a man's servant – I would have rather died. God bless the name Marinello that at last brought my freedom.'

Dee had not heard the tale of Marinello's kidnap in childhood from the great siege of Cyprus and his suffering thereafter, and was entertained by his story of the rescue by his father, Admiral Marinello. The great ship strained against the wind in its sails, the wood moving and creaking around us.

Then, a call from amidships from a tall man. He pointed at the way ahead, and in rough Venetian held conversation with his captain.

'The better weather takes us onwards,' Marinello said, 'but the distant hills are on the island of Karpathos. It is infested with pirates and held by the Turks.' He bit his lip while he thought, his dark lashes veiling his eyes. 'We shall steer instead straight along the Candian coast to Alexandria, away from merchant routes.'

The man below simply nodded and gave orders that it should be so.

Marinello shaded his eyes, looking in all directions before jumping down from his lookout at the side of the ship. 'And now begins our greatest challenge,' he said, his sudden grin flashing white against the brown of his face. 'For there are a thousand corsair ships that would like to see me back on a bench, rowing for His Majesty the Sultan.'

And with that, a great bellow of laughter.

Chapter 33

Present day, Dartmoor

As soon as Jack was settled in a chair in the middle of the cottage, a woman walked in.

'Maggie!' Jack struggled onto her feet, meeting her in a hug. She was overcome, tears tightening her throat as she felt Maggie's strong arms around her, holding her up. 'Oh, I'm so glad to see you.'

'Good.' Maggie held her a little away so she could stare at Jack's face. 'Because we're all here to help you.'

'I know.' She sighed, pulled Maggie close for another moment, then registered a dark shadow by the doorway. 'How's Sadie?'

'Charley is on her way to the hospital. We are doing everything we can, but—'

Jack pulled away, aware she was rumpled and in yesterday's clothes. She took a step towards the edge of the circle and could just see Felix standing outside, turned away to speak to someone. He looked older, shadows under his eyes, stubble on his cheeks.

Jack stepped back into the circle, to find Maggie holding out a bag. 'Toiletries, fresh clothes. Hairbrush,' she added pointedly.

'Thank you. It's a bit primitive here.' Jack grabbed the brush which was on the top, and dragged it through her hair. 'And I did travel in an old box. Ow. Grooming hasn't been a high priority.'

'Conway says you can leave the circle if you feel strong enough. There's a kind of bathroom outside.'

Jack took the bag through the cottage to the tiny back door, which led to the hut that housed the primitive but effective earth loo. In the few minutes she took to wash in the small rainwater sink there and change her clothes, she allowed her heartbeat, which had started looping in her chest when she first saw Felix, to settle down. 'It's just Felix,' she whispered to herself. 'It's OK.'

The second she stepped out of the hut, she almost ran into him. He didn't speak, he wasn't even smiling, but when he opened his arms she went into them, leaning against him. He hugged her a little too hard, his breath hot in her hair.

'I'm sorry,' she managed, at the same time as he mumbled something similar.

'I just wished you had trusted me.'

'You don't realise – I have no control over Saraquel.'

He huffed his frustration into her hair and it tickled her ear. 'I know,' he mumbled after a moment. She pulled back a little.

She kissed him, and for a moment she could hear and see nothing, just feel him, feel herself. He broke the kiss, and she slowly opened her eyes.

He looked concerned. 'Where is Saraquel?'

'Gone for the moment. There's something strange about this place, something that he can't cope with.' She took a deep breath, and it came out as a shaky laugh. 'I've missed you so much. I didn't realise how much, until you were gone.'

'When this is over, if we both survive—'

She stopped him with a kiss. 'OK. But no ifs. We're both going to make it.'

Her hand curved into his for a moment, then they both let go. Jack turned to enter the cottage.

Maggie was sitting at the table with a cup of tea in her hand and a pot of herbal decoction for Jack bubbling and hissing on the woodburner. Sunlight was reaching across the doorway but the windows were set in walls too deep to let much of the morning in. The scent of familiar roots and leaves in the steam and the hint of woodsmoke was familiar.

'That smells terrible,' Jack said, her nose wrinkling up. 'But I really need some potion.'

'We thought you would have a better chance if you were as strong as possible.'

'Won't it feed Saraquel too?' Jack gave it a stir. 'It did at the convent. That's really strong.'

Robert Conway, who was scribbling in a notebook, looked up over half-glasses. 'We think not. The main thing is to make you well enough to survive the exorcism. It is an ordeal, physically and mentally.'

Jack shivered for a moment, and turned to Maggie. 'Tell me about Sadie.'

'She's in a coma. She's slowing down. The doctor, George, says she's dying in really slow motion. She's on a ventilator now.' Maggie's shoulders squeezed up. 'She's started the treatment but—'

'Don't say it. Don't even think it.' Jack turned to Robert. 'Do you know anything about borrowed time, the things revenants do to stay alive?'

'I do.' Robert looked from Maggie to Jack. 'Who made this Sadie?'

Jack frowned for a moment. 'I did – well, I saved her from dying, if that's what you mean.'

'There will be a connection between you and her that is unique. You have more power over her fate than anyone else. When you are free of Saraquel you may be able to help her.'

Jack watched as Maggie lifted the pot of decoction off the stove. She found an old coffee pot on a shelf and rinsed it out, tipping the decoction in carefully, using the pot lid to strain off the roots and fungi.

'Maggie saved me. Does that help?'

Robert raised his eyebrow and looked at the older woman. 'It might, but not in the way you think.'

'I don't understand.' Jack could see the tension in the man, as if he were deciding to conceal something.

'I don't think we should talk about this in front of Saraquel.'

Maggie placed the pot on the table to cool. 'I think you don't want to talk about this in front of me, either. I know what you were going to say.'

'What was I going to say?' The man looked up at Maggie as she stood over him.

'"The witch that made us." That's the quote in Kelley's journal. Felix and I have been working on deciphering pages. That's why Elizabeth Báthory killed the witch Zsófia, isn't it? Her blood can be used to contain the essence of the revenant.'

He pressed his fingers onto the pages of an old book, which Jack could see he had been working from. 'So it was rumoured. But she also sought out the sorcerer who made her, for the same reason. His blood could also be used to undo the magic. It made her vulnerable.'

'Should we be telling Saraquel this?' Jack could feel Saraquel squirming in the back of her mind.

Conway's smile was half grimace. 'He already knows all of this. He knows far more than we do.'

'OK.' Jack sat back. 'But if the magic was undone?'

He seemed to hesitate. 'Yes, the revenant could die. But you need to understand the nature of death. The moment of death is bypassed. The longer the person gets from that time, the better they can potentially get. If we removed the magic right now, medical science might be able to save you.' He lifted the book up. 'I have details in here. This is by Edward Kelley, the unpublished details of his journey to find the secrets of Saraquel in Alexandria.'

Jack frowned. 'Are you serious? How did you get that?'

He smiled a little crookedly. 'I have contacts in the Inquisition who have been researching what Elizabeth Báthory wanted from her medical research company. The company run by her son, Pál Bachmeier.'

'Her *son*? How old is he?'

He shrugged. 'Almost as old as the countess. But as far as I know, he was never possessed by Saraquel, and his existence does not rely on blood.'

Maggie snorted. 'And now he's helping Sadie. Talk about doing a deal with the devil. Felix tells me his family were prominent Nazis, and some of the research was done on concentration camp inmates.'

'Oh, great.' Jack turned back to Conway. He had a nice face, she decided, he looked like he was smiling even when he wasn't, laughter lines making him look genial. He was a shade taller than her, and almost as slight, but he gave off an aura of confidence. 'So, Mr Conway, how are you involved?' Her eyes were drawn to the small book in his hand.

Maggie passed him a cup of tea – regular and black, not the decoction she was sipping reluctantly.

'Call me Robert, please. Would you like a few dried berries to help you with that concoction?'

He stood up, rummaged in the single cupboard and put half a dozen dried berries in her cup before she could answer. The fragrance from the fruit started to wind itself into the steam.

'Thank you.' A cautious sip confirmed a slight improvement.

He sat back at the table and closed the notebook. 'I am an exorcist; I specialise in cases that might involve Saraquel. Actually, I'm more of an academic, training other exorcists and continuing research into Saraquel. I'm an expert in medieval texts on magic.'

Felix walked in carrying a couple of bags. 'I brought the things you asked for,' he said. Jack went over to help Robert put the supplies away. The teabags, milk and sugar were all pounced upon by Maggie, but he also had bottled water, biscuits and pasta, with a few tins and bags of vegetables. 'You said vegetarian,' Felix said, unpacking a packet of rice and a bag of cashews.

Robert tucked the book away back in its case. 'Yes. Thank you. I'm not a bad cook but the opportunity out here is a bit limited. You're the first guests I have had for some years.'

Jack nudged Felix. 'He has an undiscovered book by Kelley.'

Felix stared down at the older man. 'You do?'

'It's a journal, but as an antiquarian book it's priceless.' He put the case under his arm. 'I have extracted all the knowledge we need from it and made notes. But we don't want Saraquel knowing what it says,' he said pointedly.

Jack could see Felix's enthusiasm bubbling up. 'OK, I'll go and chill outside while you discuss the book behind my back.' She picked up the packet of biscuits. 'Any objection if I take these with me?'

'Don't eat them all,' mumbled Maggie, sorting through the shopping.

Jack walked out of the cottage, shutting the tiny door behind her. The clearing that surrounded the house was barely a few metres from the buildings. Beside the cottage, a painted wooden studio had all its doors and windows open in the sunlight, which was starting to burn off the dew. Inside the cabin was a hammock hung from the rafters, covered with cushions. Jack felt sleepy just looking at it. Stephen McNamara was working on making something out of wood in the corner, and barely glanced up at her.

She lifted herself into the hammock and swung her feet up. She sighed as she lay down. The cloth smelled nice, like fruit and dust and probably Robert Conway. She wriggled her toes and closed her eyes. She felt better than she had for weeks.

Sleep eluded her. After a few minutes, she looked across at Mac, now measuring something. 'What are you doing?'

'I'm making a template.' His tone didn't welcome further comment, but Jack, swinging gently in the sunlight coming through a skylight in the cabin roof, didn't care. This might well be her last day on earth but Felix and Maggie were close by and she felt strangely happy.

'Template for what?'

'For the ritual. Which I can't talk about so don't ask me.'

'OK. Let's talk about you, then. Married, single, straight, gay?'

There was a long silence during which the pencil scratched whatever wood he was working on. 'Celibate, religious,' he said.

'OK. Dog or cat?'

'What?'

'Dog or cat. Which do you prefer?'

There was an exaggerated sigh from McNamara before he started sawing. It went on for a couple of minutes then the silence returned.

'Well?'

'Dog. I had a border collie when I was growing up.' He started sanding the edge of something and she let her attention wander. A bumblebee had flown in and was tapping against a window. While she wondered whether to help it, it buzzed closer and closer to the door before finding its way into the slight breeze.

'You? Cat or dog?' He wasn't looking at her, and she jumped at the long-delayed question.

She gave it some thought. 'Cat, I think. Even though I have a dog. But he's wild like a cat, sometimes. I like wild things.'

Another long silence. He was in a rhythm now, sanding around the edges of what looked like a curve. 'What will you do, if you survive?'

She thought about it. 'I don't know. Contact my mother, I suppose. I nearly spoke to her last year. I drove all the way to Yorkshire in a rental car just to see if I could speak to her, but . . . you know.'

'A life in secret. A prison.'

She smiled. It wasn't funny but with the sun on her legs and the quiet of the cabin nothing seemed so intense. 'I didn't want to get Maggie into trouble. And there would be questions, you know, she really did abduct me from the gymkhana. And they would want to know why I didn't call the police, why I didn't run away.'

'You could have tried telling your parents the truth. It was an open secret in our family.'

'Of course, I forgot. Your sister was a borrowed timer, too. What happened?'

He put down one rounded piece of plywood and picked up a second, more curved one. 'She was born with a genetic defect. No immune system. Our older brother had already died from it when she was born. I was conceived to be a bone-marrow donor, but she couldn't wait. They found out about the magic.'

'Where from?'

'I don't know. It was common knowledge in my parents' occult circle. But no one they knew had ever survived.'

'Maggie said that. Most people can't be saved. She used a seer to find me, and we used one to find Sadie.' She lay back on the worn cushion behind her head. Conceived to be a bone-marrow donor. She hoped his parents loved him anyway, but didn't like to ask. When she was taken, Maggie's daughter was dying of leukaemia. A healing spell could save her, but it used borrowed-time blood, and they didn't know anyone who was a revenant, one of the 'saved from heaven by sorcery' community. Jack had spent twenty years resenting it, but for what? She adored Charley and would have done anything to save her life. She had grown to love Maggie, and death from a broken neck at the age of eleven was the alternative. Now death loomed again, she was under no illusions as to the probable outcome of the battle to come. And yet she wanted to live, more than at any time in her past.

McNamara picked up the templates and walked to the doorway. He turned back to her before he went out. 'Stay out of the cottage. We'll come to you when we're ready. Shout if you need something.'

She understood: they didn't want Saraquel to know what they were doing. She relaxed into the hammock, the sun brushing her legs as it swayed gently.

She must have slept. When she woke, the sun had moved away, and she was a little cold. Felix was looking down at her, his eyes crinkled at the edges, a small smile lifting his lips.

'They want to start the ritual soon. I thought you and I could talk.'

She extended her arms as far as they would go above her head until her shoulders creaked. 'OK.' A yawn caught her mid-stretch.

'I don't think I have ever seen you this relaxed before.'

'Well, this is the calm before the storm, isn't it?' She reached out a hand, and he put his in it. He was always so warm, his fingers so strong. She ran her thumb over the back of his wrist. 'I wish you weren't going to be there. I wish you were safe and looking after Sadie.'

He stepped so close she could sense the warmth of his breath. 'I am going to be here. Even if –' He swallowed, leaning on the side of the hammock lightly '– even if we don't make it.'

'Die together? Very romantic.' She tried to smile, but her eyes stung with tears. 'All those years wasted.' Apart, she thought silently, years when we lived in the same world and didn't even know. 'I didn't know love was like this.'

He smiled down at her. 'Don't count us out yet. Conway seems to know what he's doing.'

'Does he, though?' Jack let go of Felix's hand and struggled upright, sliding to the floor. The bare boards were cool under her feet. 'We don't know anything about him, except that he has a book he won't show us that may or may not be written by Edward Kelley. Who couldn't deal with Saraquel either.'

'Mac knows of Conway. He's a very senior exorcist, and has been involved in an exorcism of Saraquel once before.'

Jack opened the holdall Maggie had brought from the cottage, and pulled on a fleece. 'What happened?'

Felix hesitated then looked at the floor. 'The subject died. The chief exorcist was badly injured.'

Jack sat down to pull her socks on, but paused at that. 'Injured how?'

'Conway told us about it. The demon – or angel – reached inside him and ripped his gut to shreds. He was in hospital for months.'

'You are definitely not going to be there,' she said, appalled at the thought. 'How could a non-corporeal being do that?' He sat back. 'I shouldn't be telling you anything about this. Saraquel is listening.'

'How about telling me we're sure it will work, and you and I will live happily ever after.'

The smile was even more crooked. He looked down again. 'I thought we should be honest with each other.'

'But optimistic.' Jack looked at Felix, seeing new lines on his forehead. There were a few more grey hairs at his temples too, although that could be the poor light.

She moved closer, and he put his arm around her shoulders, kissed her forehead. The dull light spilling in the open doorway caught her attention. Something was moving, something at ground level.

It was a young badger, curious about the smell of food emanating from the cottage, now Jack could smell some savoury stew. It lifted its head, peering at Jack, then scuttled back into the bushes.

'I want to live in the countryside,' Jack breathed. 'I don't want to live in the city.'

'OK. We'll sell my house – we could move into your Devon property now it's been renovated. As long as you have broadband, I could commute to work three days a week.'

She looked up at him, trying to read him. He meant it, he would give up his safe urban routine for her. She reached up for his kiss, felt his arms pull her closer.

The moment was lost when Maggie entered, carrying two plates of food.

'Eat up, you two, you're going to need the energy.' She waited for Felix to let Jack go, a little frown on her forehead. 'I've been talking to Conway. We have a plan. But Jack can't hear it in case Saraquel does, too.'

Chapter 34

Present day, Dartmoor

Felix found a little time to himself before the ritual, just long enough to follow one of the rough paths through the wilderness to breathe, and think. The ritual Conway had described made no sense to him at all, even as a social anthropologist. It was if they were trying to find words that would appeal to the being that had possessed Jack. He had seen the words in their original script, some long-dead Ethiopic script that had been found on a few scraps of papyrus with the Dead Sea scrolls. More than half the words were missing, but he could see the meticulous research Robert Conway had done over the last twenty or thirty years. He was hazy on that subject. It was hard to place Conway, with his strange international accent, somewhere between educated English and American with an Irish twist. His Latin was pure church, and his linguistic research impeccable. His age was a mystery, too. Some part of Felix reacted to him as if he were older than his sprinkle of grey hairs and lined face would suggest. Felix would put him at a trim, well-preserved fifty, yet he talked as if he'd been around a lot longer. When Felix finally asked, he shrugged and smiled, looking younger still.

'Does it matter?'

'I just want to understand where this knowledge comes from.'

Robert put down his pen. 'You need to understand the Vatican. We are trained by priests who continue teaching into their eighties and nineties, who have been priests since they were barely out of childhood.' He shrugged. 'I had access to the wisdom of people who were born in the late eighteen hundreds, and they were trained by people who were born at the turn of the nineteenth century. It's not unusual to be given a text to study that was last read by someone three hundred years before.' He smiled up at Felix. 'I think it's where my love of old books comes from.'

So Felix had let the lingering doubts go, and gone to catch a few minutes by himself, resisting the urge to spend them with Jack. But she would want to talk, and he wasn't sure that the questions didn't come from Saraquel, nor that it wouldn't give him some advantage. He had the strange ache in his chest that had been his substitute for tears since he was a boy.

'Felix?'

He turned to see Maggie. She had never warmed to him, but there was a strange expression on her face now. 'Can I help you?' His voice was rougher than he meant it to be.

'I just wanted to say thank you. For what you are doing for Jack. For caring.'

'I love her.'

Maggie looked away. 'I love her too. I grew to after the first year or two. She was so brave, but so ill. I thought we would lose her every winter until she was fifteen, then I started to hope she would make it.'

'She's a fighter.'

Maggie smiled. 'You don't have to tell me that. If – if I don't make it, will you look out for Sadie and Charley for me? I know I have no right to ask, but Charley is so young, and Sadie's just a teenager. I don't know what will happen, and Angela won't be able to cope with Sadie on her own.'

'Do you feel you're in danger?'

Maggie shrugged. 'The ritual includes untangling the magic that I started twenty-odd years ago. That will affect me and I'm not as young as I was.'

'How . . . what do you mean?'

'Robert's going to undo the original sorcery that made Jack, so he can exorcise the angel.'

'But – that will kill her!' Felix was shocked that Conway had kept that much from him.

'He has a plan to keep her safe but she will get very close to death. A natural death. Then when the angel is out, he will reinstate the spell, only hopefully better.'

Felix rocked back onto his heels. 'That's too much stress for her, surely.'

'She doesn't have another option. She could stay here, but Conway thinks Saraquel will find a way to the surface, and then she's in his control again. How much longer do you think she can cope with the impulse to attack and maybe kill people?'

He turned to look down at her, her white hair seeming to glow in the dying light. 'She didn't experience those attacks in London—'

'Saraquel could make her fully aware, an observer who feels, sees everything. He could even force her to feed off Sadie to increase her energy. We really don't have a choice.' She dropped her head forward for a moment, breathing harshly. 'Do you think I would consider this for a second, if I could avoid it? I made this situation, I'm responsible for Jack.'

He turned to go back to the cottage. Maggie had always been defensive around him. He glanced at her, seeing the tension around her eyes, the brightness of tears.

'You have to trust Jack,' he said. 'This is her decision, she doesn't want to live with Saraquel. She made that plain when she jumped off the bridge. However grateful I am that she survived, never think for a second that anyone else is responsible for Jack. She is completely her own person, and you should respect that. Even if she chooses to risk death.'

Maggie nodded slowly. 'Well, just do your best. Neither of us wants to lose her.'

Jack, her feet and hands shackled and connected by chains to a ring in the floor, was installed in a chair inside one meticulous, ink-drawn triangle within a circle of symbols. Felix recognised some of them from Dee's texts but many were new.

Jack waved at him, clinking the metal restraints. 'It's to stop me getting loose and killing you all,' she called.

'You seem to be in very good spirits for a woman chained up,' Felix replied, his heart aching with something, maybe terror.

'I'm keen to get it over with.' She looked at Robert Conway, who was drawing another shape on the floor with McNamara. 'Stay off the circle.'

The cottage was so small there was little room to stand outside the two circles, except at the area by the woodburner.

Maggie joined him, her eyes running over the symbols as they drew them. 'There's something coming,' she murmured to Felix.

Her eyes flickered to the windows, her arms around herself although it wasn't cold. 'I can feel it. Something . . .'

Robert Conway stood, brushing the dust off his knees. 'Can you tell what?'

She shrugged. 'It's just a feeling.'

The room was lit by candles in sconces on the walls, each inside a glass jar, presumably to defend against draughts. A large battery lantern was in the middle of the half-drawn circle and another hung from a hook in the ceiling.

Robert squeezed past McNamara and joined them. 'Tell me if you feel anything odd, any impression, idea. We need all the information we can gain from our senses, even ones we don't normally listen to.'

Maggie leaned down and picked up her bag. 'I have some charms for protection here, do you mind if I hang them up?'

Robert inclined his head. 'I have no objection. Anything to assist.' He smiled at her, and ran one ink-stained hand through his rather long hair. 'I've been glad of witch magic before, and know how powerful it can be.'

Felix wrapped his arms around himself, looking at Jack, now whispering to Mac. 'I don't think witch magic will save us from something like Saraquel,' he said.

Robert leaned over the woodburner and started sharpening a pencil with a small knife. 'Actually, magic from any source is energy moving on the plane Saraquel operates on. What's surprising is that it works at all on ours. But I have seen it change lives.'

Felix winced. 'I have seen it take a life,' he said, thinking back to when Maggie had created a fire in a man's chest.

McNamara, pale-faced in the light, stepped away from the second circle and joined them. 'Saraquel is already here,' he said simply, then closed his lips so tight they went white. 'Beware what he says, he is looking for a reaction at any cost.'

Felix reached out a hand to steady the younger man. He was trembling under his stoic exterior.

'We're ready?' Felix said, wondering if that could ever be true.

Mac nodded, and Felix released his elbow. They turned to Jack.

She was smiling in the chair, her eyes almost glowing in the overhead light. Which, as Felix watched, seemed to dim.

'Felix Guichard,' it purred through Jack. 'We have so nearly had the pleasure.'

Felix turned to Conway, who was pulling on a surplice. 'Are you ready?'

Conway took a deep breath, and nodded. 'I need a few minutes of prayer, I think. Try not to engage with Saraquel.'

'Felix,' Jack's voice rang out. 'She wants you, you know. She would die for you, isn't that amazing? And *she* actually knows what death feels like.'

Felix locked eyes with Maggie, who was pale again. The room had grown strangely cold. He glanced up at the lantern, which had retreated to a yellow dot. Most of the remaining light was from the candles.

'Do you think you can deal with me in the dark as well?' Jack's voice called out, and in an instant, all the candles went out.

In the silence, Felix could hear Conway's soft voice praying in Latin, while Mac shadowed the prayer a second behind.

Maggie's voice rang out with something she was repeating under her breath. Not Latin, not prayer, some kind of fighting tone and a jumble of words. There was a small bang, and some of the candles relit. Shattered glass fell from one of the jars.

251

Jack's face in the half-light was strained, her eyes bulging and her lips stained with her own blood. She started to breathe loudly, a rasp turning each panted breath into a growl.

Conway beckoned to the other three who stepped into the larger circle. Felix, as had been agreed, took up one cardinal point to the east, Maggie went to the south, Mac to the west. Conway stood facing into the circle, his back to Jack, holding out his hands to the other three.

'Once the circle is completed we cannot leave it until the first ritual is over. Do you understand?'

They all nodded. Felix couldn't take his eyes off Jack, who was now convulsing in her chair, the chains pulled taut.

Conway bent to complete the circle with a brush and the ink he had ready.

Jack responded by shrieking as if in agony. Maggie jumped, even Mac looked round.

'Hold hands!' Robert Conway's voice was stronger than Felix had yet heard it, with the authority of an exorcist in it.

'Felix, Felix!' Jack moaned as if in more pain. 'He's . . . . Oh no, don't . . .'

Felix shut his eyes, knowing Saraquel was tormenting Jack to get him to break the circle. Maybe this meant the angel was under pressure.

'In the name of our Lord Jesus and Christ and by all his power . . .' The words rolled over Felix, as he tried to shut himself off from Jack's screams and groans. Mac seemed to be echoing the words, and Maggie was silent, listening to Jack relive Saraquel's experience of attacking women in London.

'And the one who weeps for himself—' Jack's cries turned into something else, something sexual and unrestrained, something Saraquel must have experienced.

Felix found himself mumbling, not the prayers of his childhood, but speaking directly to Jack. 'This won't touch you, Jack, this is all lies to hurt you and me. Think about Ches, think about how you feel walking with him, with me. Remember how my hand feels in yours, think about Sadie laughing over some video on the Internet, Charley hugging you. That's our future.'

Maggie gripped his hand more firmly, and then she too started talking. 'Remember the first crow we saved, Jack? How Charley wanted to call him Bumble but you insisted on calling him Duke? Eleven years of freedom and love you gave that bird, and at the end we watched him fly on to the next world. That's life, Jack. That's love for something smaller and weaker than yourself. That's what Saraquel can't do.'

'We cast you out, foul dragon,' Conway called out.

Felix's attention was suddenly drawn to something flashing in his peripheral vision. He glanced up and realised a light was pulsing on Conway's perimeter alarm board. Then a second.

'Mac,' he whispered, and the inquisitor looked up at the lights.

'Someone's trying to get into the compound,' he murmured back. 'They're still half a mile from here, though, back on the road.'

Jack was now curved like a bow, her body only touching the chair at the nape of her neck, her feet on the ground. She sounded as if she was drowning.

As the exorcist finished the first reading of the ritual, her body relaxed.

'Quick,' said Conway. 'We need to open the circle and stop the intruder.'

'Why? Whoever it is must be a while away,' said Mac.

Jack's voice cackled in a laugh. 'You foolish child. It is my army.'

Chapter 35

Journal of Eliza Jane Weston, 23 November 1612

The countess continued to order the room, stripping off the good covers and placing rough cloths down for the birth. My mind ran upon our survival.

My childhood was populated with tales of monsters. Demons, men that lived like wolves, corpses with unnatural life breathed into them, witches that lived half in our world and half in that of ghosts and goblins – these tales had given me nightmares since I was a girl. Indeed, was I not the target of an incubus so strange and powerful that it almost destroyed my father? I had little time for such thoughts, but I had to use my father's knowledge to protect myself and my family.

The bed lay within a circle of hidden shapes, carved into the boards and casting the shadow of protection over me. The countess seemed unaware of it, and only I knew where the other circle lay, the snare of confinement, an open trap for demons and fiends. I had never used it. The monsters of my childhood had left with my father, and I was out of the habit of reciting the spells of protection that he had taught me. But now, in peril of my life, they sprang into my mind.

Edward Kelley, the voyage to Alexandria, 1586

It seemed that the possessed Dominick Smith was an informant, not just for the English spymaster but the corsairs as well. We noted the first mast coming upon us out of a clear morning not five days out of Candia, and Marinello put everyone to the sails, myself included. Each of us held as many inches of canvas to the wind as we could, catching every scrap of air, and for some hours we fought to stay ahead of their fast ships. It was only as the wind began to turn that our captain was able to take advantage of the caravel's 'beating', as he called it, cutting across the wind.

'We'll sail as close-hauled as we can manage,' he shouted to me in Latin, then whooped like a boy, pulling his whole weight on to the rudder. This was a great piece of wood, hung upon a post at the stern. As the winds picked up, it took two men to hold it, and the ship leaned out until I feared it would capsize. But Marinello laughed at my fears, ordered me below or lashed to the side if I would stay, and he ran the ship before the pirates for league after league, even into the night.

After that, we were becalmed a little, the great sails catching a breeze now and then towards evening, but flapping uselessly in the heat of the following day. At these hours we had three or four lookouts in the masts scanning the horizons, for the corsairs could row in any conditions. We never saw them in open sea, and although Marinello grumbled at the slow progress, Dee's observations built us a carefully plotted route. Dee grew tired as the food stock fell low, most of the hold being stuffed with rich cargo, but he rested more as the days passed. I was reminded of his great years, and spared him a little of my own rations, as did Marinello on occasion. I knew he was fretting about the safety of our children and women, in the confinement of the Emperor and the countess, and I prayed that Konrad could keep them safe.

We knew we were close to Egypt when suddenly we were surrounded by a great shoal of fat fish as long as a child, leaping from some monster in the dark waters below, some even into the boat. We feasted that night, Marinello ordering a cask of wine to be opened, and all were refreshed by food and drink. It was then, heartened by the appearance of weed in the currents, that we saw the xebec.

At first I could not see it, as it had its sails down and just the slender masts sat above the water. But the man aloft hissed down and Marinello uttered orders in a mutter that spread quietly from man to man. More sails were set aloft but alas, the wind was soft against them and they hung weakly.

Marinello leaped into the rigging and scaled the great mast, shading his eyes at the top to see further. Abandoning all pretence that they might not have seen us, he cried aloud that eight ships at least had turned to cut us off, in two groups.

A faint wind swelled the sails but slowly, and pulled us towards what we knew must be the coast. I took a sail myself, with a Greek boy who spoke no Latin, and by signal we managed to catch a few more puffs of Zephyr's breath.

There, the first grey-yellows of the shore far away.

Dee was below decks, but at last he emerged. 'Are we beyond help?'

I was too out of breath to answer, running around feathering one sail then another, my skills at gathering the weak winds well respected by the crew.

It was Marinello who answered. 'We are spent,' he said, his voice hard. 'We must yield and hope to live another day. If we were closer I could put her aground and we could fight but with this wind . . .'

Dee looked at me, and in a rush I remembered the witch's seal. 'One seal was for wind, was it not?' I said.

Dee nodded, looking at the vessels advancing rapidly. They were great ships, I could see the glitter of the sunlight on helmets and on swords.

'Get the sails in, reduce them, I don't know the correct term,' said Dee.

'Are you mad?' Marinello bellowed. 'Our only hope is a wind upon the shore that might catch us and take us in.'

Dee looked at me. 'Edward.'

I thought of the warning of the rabbi – witch's magic was unpredictable. 'Reef all the sails to one third,' I called out to the captain. 'And let the Jewess's magic do the rest.'

A few of the crew looked askance at the word 'magic', but Marinello, perhaps remembering the power of the foul sorcery that made his arm fester, shouted out the order. There was some muttering from the crew, but I noticed that many had already laid down their arms in case they were seen defying the Turks. They were only a few minutes away.

Dee squinted at the marks upon the seal, even with his eyeglasses on. 'I cannot see,' he said, and handed it to me.

It was as if the tiny words, just strange squiggles pressed into the wax, blazed straight into my mind. I held it aloft and words I knew not flew into me like the wind we sought. As I broke the seal I cried them into the sky, again and again. Those words sprang into the small sails we had left.

The force of the first gale almost capsized the ship, the masts screeching with the tempest and the lower sails dipping into the water upon one side. I was thrown against the bulwark; the Greek boy I had come to know was lifted into the sea and lost before we could save him. Marinello set his shoulder against the rudder and shouted for help, and the wind tore across the ship, carrying it forward.

Before I could regain my balance, the wax of the seal was blazing, burning in my hands and dripping down my forearms and the deck, setting all aflame. A burly man dipped a pail into the foaming water almost running over the side, and doused us all, but it took several buckets before the fire was slaked.

I clung to a rope with my forearms, my hands burning with pain, and realised I was still chanting the strange words, my voice hoarse and small under the roar of the air ripping into the ship. With a crack, the canvas of one sail split, then another, and finally the ship was upright, racing like a great horse, breaching each wave and surging into each trough.

Dee struggled his way to me, shouting over the storm. 'Think of Alexandria!' he shouted, then his next words were lost, '. . . intent!'

I understood, of course. It is a magician's task to bend the natural forces to his will, and I tried to ignore the agony of my palms and focus on Alexandria. As if given a new heading, the ship skewed itself into a new race, and danced forward over the tumultuous waves where calm had reigned just minutes before. I glanced back as we tore parallel to the shoreline and saw, in a floating field of debris, where the xebecs had been. I knew the slaves would have had no chance, chained as they were into their stations, and prayed for their deliverance to a gentle and merciful Jesu.

Chapter 36

Present day, Dartmoor

Opening the circle took a few minutes of Felix scrubbing the oak floorboards with a stone and some wet sand. Conway was first to the door, and to open it to the darkness outside. There was nothing, no sounds of intruders.

'Who's out there?' Felix asked, standing next to him on the step to the cottage.

'I don't know. However many of the possessed people Saraquel could assemble, I suppose. I knew they were coming but I didn't think they would find us so fast.' Conway stepped into the garden and towards the cabin. 'I have some weapons.'

Felix followed him. 'We can't just kill them. They are as innocent in all this as Jack.'

'Well, what do you suggest? They only have to come with a can of petrol and a box of matches and we are all dead.'

'Can't we restrain them in some other way?' He turned to face Conway. 'Maybe Maggie can think of something.'

Conway laughed but there was no humour in his voice. 'Using magic, you mean? I can't think of any spell that could bind so many people. Our best course may be retreat.'

'You think Saraquel will kill us, through these people?'

Conway unlocked the cupboard and pulled out a handgun. 'Yes. Better to step back and fight on a day we can win than die today.'

'And abandon Jack?'

'I would rather see Jack dead than in the grip of that monster much longer. She will lose herself, you know. She will go mad, they all do.' He started loading the gun. 'We know more about him now. It might help in a future battle.'

Felix stopped him with a hand on his chest. 'We are not giving up. We're *not*.'

Conway met his gaze, his eyes glittering in the low light. 'I have to survive this, and pass my knowledge back to those who can continue the fight. That's my part in this. No one knows more than I do.'

'You are going to go back in there and do everything you can to save Jack.' Felix spoke through clenched teeth.

Conway smiled, this time with humour. Felix could see his longish hair flopping into his eyes, sweat damped. His skin was pale from the effort in the circle. 'So you say. But I'm the one holding the gun.'

Felix's hand snatched at the weapon but the older man sprang back with unexpected nimbleness.

'I won't engage the enemy unless I have a good chance of winning,' Conway said. He shrugged, the gun still pointed straight at Felix. 'It's our training.'

Felix could hear someone moving outside the cabin. Maybe it was Mac.

'I can't leave her.' Felix felt cold at the thought.

'You love her. It's your weakness.'

'Love isn't a weakness.'

Conway's laugh, this time, was bitter. 'The last time I loved someone, Saraquel took him. I had to cut his throat to save him from that travesty of a life that is all Jack has left.'

'Doesn't that make you want to defeat him even more?'

Conway glanced past Felix. 'You don't know what you are asking; you don't know what I risk. My life, my soul.'

Felix could feel his temper rising. 'I'm asking you to win for once and for all. Put Saraquel back where he belongs. I want you to use all the knowledge you have locked up in that book of Kelley's, and all the ideas that Eliza Weston encoded in her diaries. Christ, all the knowledge you have gained from fighting him. You said, no one knows more than you do.'

Conway pointed the gun at the floor. 'Look behind you.'

Felix glanced back, then froze. In the light spilling out of the doorway was a slim figure standing in the grass.

'Felix?'

For a moment he didn't recognise her in the shadow. Then her face came into the light. 'Gina?' He stepped into the doorway. He hadn't seen his ex-lover since she had gone to Paris.

She smiled, the saddest quirk of her lips. 'It's me. The cancer is gone.'

'I didn't know if you were OK. You didn't answer my calls.'

She shrugged. 'I was fighting for my life.'

The cancer was gone. Slowly he realised what she had done. 'You let them turn you into a revenant. You let them turn you into a blood-sucking monster, like Ivanova. That means Saraquel is inside you now.'

She smiled, this time with more amusement. 'I feed from willing donors, just like a patient with sickle cell, or haemophilia. I just need a few blood products once a month and I'm fine.'

'But you're possessed. By Saraquel.'

She took a step towards the cabin but Mac stepped in her way. 'I don't think you'll survive my knocking your brains out,' he said, a snarl in his voice.

She stopped and considered the tall man in front of her. 'The blood does make us . . . more resilient,' she said. As he stepped closer she darted in. Felix could see a moment's scuffle then Mac was thrown out of the pool of light. A crashing of foliage suggested he had fallen – or been thrown – into the hedge. 'Stronger, faster,' she said, moving into the doorway. 'Practically immortal.'

Felix could feel Conway moving on the timber floor behind him, flexing the boards under his feet.

'He has a gun,' he said, without looking back. 'Can you survive being shot?'

She smiled. 'Felix, I'm me. *Me*. The woman you made love to just a few months ago. I'm the same person, I'm just not booking a hospice bed.'

'She's Saraquel's thing,' Conway said behind him. 'Even contained in the circle, most of Saraquel is still free. He will defend himself. We have to kill her. We have to kill as many as we can.'

Gina stepped close enough that Felix could smell her perfume. It reminded him of gardenias, of whispers in the dark, of the softness of her skin. As her hand reached for him, he managed to flinch away, fall back a step.

'No, Gina—'

The shot was deafening. A flower of blood spread on Gina's chest, her body crumpled to its knees. She reached up to Felix.

'Stop him,' she said, struggling up. The second shot went through her palm and knocked her back.

Felix leaped in front of her. 'Conway, no!'

Maggie's voice, shrill with alarm, made him look over his shoulder. 'Stop whatever you're doing! That hurt Jack.'

Conway seemed unmoved. 'I'm sorry. Jack's lost to you,' the older man said. 'We can't save any of them.'

Gina was crumpled on the flagstones just outside the door. She turned her face to Felix. 'You don't know who he is,' she said softly, 'or what. Don't trust him.' She pressed her injured hand to the wound on her chest. 'I would never hurt you.'

Some instinct made Felix draw back. There was something unnatural about the way she spoke, as if she was unaffected by the bleeding wounds. She should have been dead – not speaking as if she didn't even feel pain.

Conway stood over her, pulling back his sleeve. 'This is what you want, isn't it? Or, should I say, what Saraquel wants?'

The expression on her face changed. 'Felix, help me. A few drops of your blood will save me.'

Conway stared at Felix. 'You understand that if I wasn't here she would tear your throat out in an instant.'

Gina panted as she struggled to sit up. There was little blood flowing from the wounds which already seemed to be less raw. 'She's fed recently,' Conway said. 'And she's not just Saraquel's.'

'What do you mean?' Felix glanced out of the door, looking for the inquisitor, who had staggered to his feet, and was holding his shoulder.

'What he means,' Mac managed to say, 'is that she's a colony of any entities that happened to be passing when she was turned into a revenant. She's become possessed by demons too.'

Robert Conway put one hand on Felix's shoulder, making him jump away. 'Your friend is mostly demons, Felix.' He pointed the gun at Gina again. 'And she's been hijacked by Saraquel to get to you.'

Gina's face twisted as if in pain. 'Felix, help me. You're helping Jack, you could save me too.'

Felix flinched. 'How do you know that?'

Mac leaned on the doorway. 'Just do it, Robert.'

Conway hesitated. 'We need to be agreed.'

'Why? I thought you were giving up?' Felix ignored the gun and stood back.

Conway looked at Gina, or whatever she had become. 'Now I am face to face with the monster I find I don't want to run away,' he said softly. 'Do you know how many men, women, even children he has taken over? More with each generation. Well, Saraquel, I'm not running away this time. Felix is right, we do have the advantage. With Eliza's knowledge and mine . . . it's the best chance we have had for four hundred years.'

'Felix, please—' Gina put a hand out to him, still stained with blood. The edges of the wounds were already healing. 'Stop him.'

'No. No.' Felix stared into her eyes. Seeing something else there, little of the woman he had once known.

He shut his eyes as the gun sounded again.

Chapter 37

Journal of Eliza Jane Weston, 23 November 1612

Within the corner of the room, beside the small fireplace, lay the inscribed symbols of a triangle of summoning. My husband hated it, and over the past years it had become scuffed and concealed, lest the servants gossip and bring the charge of sorcery upon us. Originally, it had stood beneath a linen press but when my daughters were born, it had been moved to allow pallets to be laid out for them. I had no idea if it would still work, or if I had recalled the strange symbols as they should be drawn.

'Lady,' I said, my voice hoarse in my own ears. 'Of your kindness, I would ask you to attend the fire. For I am cold unto death.'

The pain took my words away, and she did not move. 'Your man returns shortly; he will tend it.'

I lay back on the folded sheets and cried out with the pain, trying to recall the words that would open the trap. I had no idea if they would confine the fiend. I called out in English, no longer the first language to spring to my tongue, as I prayed for help in the litany my stepfather had taught me. Edward Kelley, that adventurer who had fought for me, more tender than my own father whom I barely recalled. Of that natural parent I remember just a scent, a loud laugh and rough hands throwing me into the air: the nobleman who took my gentle mother and made her a creature of shame and me a bastard. Upon his death, cast away by his widow, she was married to my new father and given her honour back. He had always come to our rescue, but he could not return from Heaven to save us.

Edward Kelley, Alexandria, 1586

Alexandria was almost twenty leagues away but we made it in but five hours, the winds barely dying at the low towers that stood in the entrance to the port. The harbour was much run down, not at all what I had expected, but many ships were tied up along its low quaysides. Two square towers guarded the entrance, with huge bronze guns following our arrival on pivots.

I had never seen such a range of ships as were moored in the harbour in Alexandria. Marinello pointed out galleons and galliots, caravels and xebecs, brigantinos crewed by Moorish sailors, trabaccolós laden with bales of cloth, all with their guards. He talked of different sails and masts until my head spun, and I could see their grace and power even as they rocked on the small waves. Here was a veritable navy, which surely could survive any pirate fleet.

Marinello laughed at me. 'Here are men from every corner of the world,' he said. 'Their allegiance is to their cargo first, their king second. Look, an English ship riding at anchor – do you imagine her men think only of your queen's business?' He observed one ship, one he called a carrack, with his standard atop its main mast. 'My ship,' he murmured. 'She has been in harbour too long. I need to get aboard to make certain she is seaworthy.'

I looked across at her, seeing the cracks between planks along her sides, uncaulked and silver grey with salt. 'What does she need?'

'She needs her timbers wetted, so that they might swell. She needs a carpenter to inspect every beam and rib and the masts, and men to caulk her. And the sails are rotting up there.' He looked down at my charred shirt cuffs and hands. 'Are you injured by the fire?'

I turned my scorched palms to the light. They were pink, as if they had been healing a week. 'Not much, my lord.' I flexed my fingers, evoking an echo of the pain. 'It was an unnatural fire, perhaps it does not injure the living as would a normal flame.'

Dee bustled up from the cabin, his shirt no doubt bulging with our letters and notes, and perhaps his maps too. 'Edward,' he said. 'Carry the letter for the rabbis and the last scrolls. Do not touch the seals, but keep them safe.'

He knew that I had various secret pockets within my clothing, and I went below to stow the letter from Izaak's rabbi and also the remaining two scrolls. The first one had been charred as if it was burned away by the force of the magic raging through it to make the gales.

It was a timely thought. When we tied up, there was a crowd of interested men looking at us, and watching Marinello's men unload our cargo, sparse though it was. Men talked in small groups and more glances came our way.

'They are telling stories of the storm,' Dee said, some uneasiness even in his placid voice. 'These are not good Christians, Edward, they are all sorts of travellers. Some our enemies.'

'Good Christians,' I scoffed. 'Like the Inquisition of his Holiness perhaps?'

Dee gave a half-smile, his eyes shaded by his bushy grey eyebrows. 'Perhaps sorcery is always unwelcome in these lands.'

Maybe it is not even welcome in our own, I dared not say, but placed my borrowed sword and scabbard upon my belt. My dagger was pressed tight against my breast in its sheath, for who knew what ruffians lived here.

Every effort to find the synagogue of the Jews was met with misunderstanding and comment in their own language. Dee, who spoke some Arabic tongues, muttered a translation here and there, and Marinello sent one of his men into the town to find out more. Alexandria, although once a great town, was now very poor, with many collapsed walls. Within the harbour, stoneworks had fallen in some ancient times. It was run partly by janissaries, the Sultan's own troops, who watched from the port buildings in their silk uniforms.

The man returned and spoke harshly to Marinello, shaking his head when commanded, I suppose, to escort us to our destination. Finally, with an angry exchange and a mighty buffet from our captain that laid the man to his knees, he sullenly nodded.

We followed his hunched shape as he walked quickly through the stinking streets, sweeping aside a horde of small children who begged with hands cupped, their faces as thin as if the town had been besieged. Dee smiled vaguely at them, but neither of us could spare any money, and besides, we had no small coins. More than one hand crept within our clothes and needed to be brushed off. I clung to the letter and seals through my shirt and shouted at them, scattering them for a moment.

At the end of the main street, the sailor pointed down a side alley even more noisome than the road, and shouted something at us. Then he darted away, back to the ship, I supposed.

Before we could travel down the side street, a group of brightly clothed men filled up the wider road. We stepped back in respect, but they stopped before us and I was intrigued to see a litter being carried by four giant men, or so they appeared to my eyes. The litter was adorned with gold leaf and covered with a canopy of what looked like sumptuous silks, fluttering in the slight breeze. The whole equipage smelled, as it was carried closer then set down, of the most musky roses.

A curtain was raised by a servant, a beautiful boy, and a man emerged wearing a preposterous hat, to step onto the road in velvet slippers. We bowed, an elaborate obeisance, but nothing like that of the entourage. Every man, woman or child in the street lay upon their faces in the road, in that dirt and ordure. We stood like two trees remaining in a storm-flattened forest.

The standing man shouted, nay, screamed at us. Dee bowed again, and I followed suit, this time resting my nose close to my knees. The man fair steamed with anger and, at his command, the four great men who had carried his litter leaped up, and two more followed suit, drawing swords.

Dee looked at me. 'I cannot understand many words,' he said. 'Although I hear the word "infidel".'

Infidel. St Paul's letters to the Corinthians. *What parte hath he yt beleveth with an infidele?* Did they mean us?

One great man swept an arm out and knocked Dee to his knees. I dodged a similar blow aimed at my head and slipped under the elbow of one of the guards. Using the monkey-like skills I had acquired upon Marinello's ships, I swung myself onto a crumbling wall of some tumbledown house, long abandoned, and ran as nimbly as I was able with my sword swinging upon my hip, onto still higher walls. Even as I paused to look down in triumph, I saw the movement of a man throwing some knife as long as my forearm at my heart. I slid down inside the roofless building even as the missile clanged overhead, followed by the thud of two cross-bolts. Knowing they meant to kill me, I scrambled from the rear of the place into a narrow alley and ran for my life.

It came out upon a quay, one of a complex I judged more used for fishing boats. I looked about me, but hearing the heavy footfalls of my pursuers I barely had time to cram my letter and the scrolls into a space in the crumbling mortar wall over my head before I ran along the narrow walkway between the boats.

There one of the guards found me as I crouched miserably beside a boat too low to fully conceal me, and I watched as he raised a huge curved sword, a *kilij*, as I later learned they were called, or a *scimitarra* in Venetian. I had little time to wonder at it, and I could do nothing but throw myself head first into the arms of the sea.

It is a strange thing that men who live by the sea do not swim, I always thought. Yet throw a cat into a pond and it will splash to the shore with no difficulty. I first found I could swim when I was a small child and I fell into the river Liffey at Kilcullen Bridge in Ireland. I was trying to drive some pigs to the market, but they overwhelmed me and ran down to the river's edge. When I tried to drive them back, just a small boy with a stick, one of the beasts shouldered me into the water. There, the river runs deep and fast and I was soon, just a child of eight or nine, in its hold. My instincts made me paddle like an animal, my hands trotting like a horse, pulling my face half out of the water. I was washed into the shallows and made my way up mud flats, arriving on the shore completely covered in silt but glad of my new accomplishment. A boy was drowned there but a summer later, and after that I was old enough to travel from the land of my birth to Dublin and thence to England, but upon hot summer's days I have practised the craft in ponds and streams.

The sea was quite different. My fall carried me far below the surface, knocking the breath from my body. I could see beside me the planked wall of a fishing boat, all covered with sea-grass or weed, emerald in the sunlight and bejewelled by silver bubbles. I wriggled down it to where I could see the very base of the keel, not a man's height above the sandy bottom. I swam, kicking vigorously, under the ship. My lungs burning, I struggled to the surface, a silver mirror above me, breaking free and gasping a breath. I looked up into the crossbow of my follower and dived back down, much as I had seen dolphins do along our journey, this time feeling my way along the boat. A bolt shot past my shoulder but with a wavering power that was lost as it fell onto the sand, kicking up a little to cloud the water. I looked around me, and saw another boat, this one flat-bottomed, and I dived beneath it. When I broke the surface there was a great outcry above the water, as the owners of the boat refused passage to the man following me.

I swam along the boat, ducking between two new vessels to put as much distance as I might between the man and me. Finally I found a small set of steps within the stone wall, and behind it some bales of something. I crept to land, and hid among the bales. When I finally looked around them, the man was gone and I was looking up at a group of black-haired, brown-skinned men, holding many sticks and pitchforks.

Chapter 38

Present day, Dartmoor

Felix stepped back into the cottage from the cool of the garden, now slightly lit by a crescent moon. Conway had secured Jack inside the circles, and he and McNamara were working on something in the cabin. Maggie was trying to rest there in the hammock. Felix could smell the gun smoke that hung in the still air.

There was a rusty scent in the doorway from a puddle of Gina's blood on a flagstone. He took a bucket that Conway had left outside and filled it with water. Jack was slumped in the chair, apparently asleep.

The sound of the water splashing in the doorway seemed to wake her. 'Felix?' Her voice sounded drowsy, unsure. It was hard to believe there was any part of Saraquel when she was like this.

'Go back to sleep. I'm just cleaning up.'

She moved in the chair. 'It's hard to be comfortable shackled to a chair. Can you at least get me a cushion from the cabin? There are some in the hammock.'

Conway had made it plain that stepping into the reinstated circle, the symbols inked over the healing ones Jack relied on, was to Saraquel's advantage. 'I can't. I'm sorry, Jack. Or Saraquel.'

The low laugh suggested he was right. 'I'm sorry about your lover. But we had to test your defences – and your resolve. My army will be here at any time. You will all die.'

Felix walked over to the kitchen area. Under the small sink was a scrubbing brush and some detergent. 'Maybe.'

'You know so much,' the soft voice continued. 'It will be a shame to wipe you away. Conway will be ours, and all his wisdom and experience will be at our disposal, and you will be gone.'

'That may be.' Felix lifted the water and started sloshing it over the flagstone.

'There's a clear alternative. I could release Jack.'

Felix's hands stilled for a second, then he crouched down to scrub away the red water. Some of the blood had splashed onto his shoes. 'In exchange for what?'

Conway had warned him not to speak to Saraquel. His heart was already beating faster at the thought of saving Jack.

'Conway will try to nullify Jack's enchantment. She will die.'

Felix stopped moving altogether, his breath stilled in his throat. 'So he says.' He started scrubbing again.

'He hasn't been honest with you. He will kill her and then try and attack me while I am still trapped in her body.' Felix couldn't resist glancing at Jack, her eyes seeming to glow in the low light.

'Let me speak to Jack.'

Something changed in the room. Jack sighed, and sat up. 'He's telling the truth but—'

The words were strangled into a cough. 'I mean it, just Jack!' he said, knowing Saraquel was at least partly in control.

After some struggle, Jack seemed to win. 'He thinks Conway is some über-exorcist that will do anything to get rid of him. Not just from me. He wants to kill me to get Saraquel out in the open so he can save all the other hosts.'

Felix stood up abruptly. 'No! I—'

'Don't say it, Felix, whatever you are thinking. He doesn't know everything.' She seemed to struggle again.

Felix stepped to the edge of the circle. 'I don't trust Conway – he seems to be keeping a lot back.'

'All I know is Saraquel is afraid of Conway and someone called Andreotti more than anyone in the world.' The words were gasped out as Saraquel seemed to take her back. She struggled to squeak out a last few words. 'Let me . . . go. If it has to be . . .'

A sound made Felix turn back to the doorway. 'Professor,' Conway said quietly. 'Come. Jack is gone for the moment.'

Felix followed him to the door of the cabin, stepping over the water still draining into the grass from the flagstone. 'That's true, though, isn't it? You will sacrifice Jack?'

'I cannot tell you everything. You must trust me. Jack may be lost anyway. But if I can save her, of course I will.'

Felix followed him into the far end of the cabin, away from a settle where Mac was resting and the hammock where Maggie was still sleeping. 'If you have some secret weapon, I need to know about it.'

Conway brought out a phone. 'There is one man who knows as much, maybe even more about Saraquel. We have just spoken by satellite phone. I'm afraid it's the only device that works out here.'

'This – Andreotti?'

Conway nodded. 'He has managed to confine many of the hosts that are in the country. About a dozen are unaccounted for.' He smiled. 'To be honest, I feel better just knowing he's in the country.

But he risks his life – we both do in this battle. And we are all here to wrest Jack from Saraquel, and release hundreds, maybe even thousands, from his possession.'

'So, what do we do about this last dozen?'

Conway nodded to an old wooden box on a shelf. 'We use that. McNamara?'

Mac rolled off the settle. 'I'm awake.'

'Wake the witch. We'll need her.' Conway turned to Felix. 'My research suggests you know a fair amount of sorcery, between the three of you.'

Maggie clambered out of the hammock and stepped between Mac and Conway, her white hair standing on end. 'I know more about the application of it. Felix has theory. I don't know about McNamara.'

Mac rubbed his short hair with one hand. 'I recognised Báthory's sorcery and was able to turn some of it against her. I don't have a working knowledge of witchcraft.'

Conway brought the box over to the table. 'Saraquel is calling all the people he has possessed. This is to our advantage.'

'How?' Felix strained to look outside into the dark, but the drive twisted along most of its length, shadowed as much by the undergrowth as the night. The moon was shielded by low clouds scudding above the moor.

'He struggles to influence fully alive people. I suspect all the poor souls out there are revenants, borrowed timers, as Jack calls them. If he is trying to bring them here, they will resist.'

'How many could be out there?'

Conway shrugged. 'More by the hour, I'm sure. If they frighten the neighbours, they will call the police, and then we're in real trouble.'

Felix looked down as Mac opened the box. 'So what do you plan to do?'

Conway grinned. 'Good, old-fashioned sorcery. A magical sleep, both for my neighbours and the intruders. The trick is making sure it doesn't affect us too.'

Interested despite his anxiety for Jack, Felix leaned over the box. The smell of decayed flesh immediately repelled him. Inside, what looked like a twisted handful of roots gleamed in the low light from the candle lantern Mac carried.

'I can't touch it,' the exorcist said, looking at Maggie. 'This is not of God, this is black magic. I need to be cleansed for the exorcism.'

'Let me see,' said Maggie briskly, leaning over the object. 'I've read about these, of course. Needs must—'

'—when the devil drives,' finished Conway, with a wry smile.

Felix's breath caught at the back of his throat. For a moment the brooding presence of Saraquel seemed to invade the cabin, as if he was looking over their shoulders.

Conway leaned over the box, his fingers over the objects inside but not connecting. 'Although I don't believe in the devil,' he said, his voice quiet.

'How can you not, when you have seen what I have seen?' Mac was as impassioned as Felix had ever seen him. 'Demons in people, perverted angels, if you like, but look at what they have done! How can you not believe in the devil, when you believe in God?'

There was a long silence before Conway looked up, first at Felix, then at McNamara. 'I don't believe in God either, not in your Christian sense.' He held the box out to Maggie.

Mac's mouth opened in shock but he didn't speak.

Maggie reached into the box and took the bundle in one hand.

Conway continued, stepping away from the thing Maggie was holding. 'I know, I have seen and felt the presence of beings beyond our own experience. Call that God, if you choose, but when I call upon the authority of the Lord, it is an angel I am speaking to. He is shaped by belief in a higher authority over him, he literally is formed by that belief. He cannot deny that authority, if we can compel him to listen. He can retreat from Jack by killing her, of course. But if we anchor him in that circle, he has to yield to an exorcism if we can keep him there long enough to complete the ritual of Zadok.'

'Why that version?' said Felix, stepping closer to the stinking object. It looked like a skeletal hand, wrapped in greasy skin. 'Is that real?'

Conway glanced at him. 'Zadok was a Jewish mystic. He was present at the death of his son, and he recognised Saraquel's presence. He is supposed to have supported Solomon, who was a sorcerer and an exorcist in the Christian Apocrypha. It doesn't really matter what we believe, this is the ritual that *Saraquel* believes.'

In the flicker of the candlelight, Felix realised he was looking at the cut wrist of a withered human hand.

'It's a hand of glory.' Maggie lifted the box into the light so the men could see it. 'It was described in the *Compendium Maleficarum*, the witchcraft manual. Careful with that candle, it's supposed to ignite very easily. Did you make this?'

Conway nodded. 'Many years ago. I hope it's still fresh enough to work.'

'I thought that was just a superstition.' Felix leaned back as the smell reached him again. 'The hand of a hanged man?'

Conway wrinkled up his nose. 'It doesn't need to be a hanged man at all. Francesco Maria Guazzo who wrote the compendium was also an exorcist. He thought making it harder to obtain the ingredients would reduce the incidents of witchcraft from his book. This is from a man who drowned in Naples.'

McNamara stepped away, out of the light of the lamp. 'Do you really believe that you can exorcise a monster who threatens hundreds of people without faith?' His voice was shaky, as if he was trembling.

'Guazzo himself was an exorcist as well as a practitioner of magic,' Conway said. 'My faith is not in a paternalistic God, but in the totality of all. I just happen to call it God, or Jesus.'

'But you believe in magic?' Mac frowned at Felix. 'Can an exorcist be apostate?'

Felix shrugged. 'Is Saraquel real? I think so, you think so. Whatever he is, if he believes in an anthropomorphic being called God he's vulnerable. It's that argument, if I understand Robert properly, that will force him out.'

Mac turned abruptly to Conway, his face taut in the light. 'But you prayed.'

'Oh, I pray.' Conway glanced at Felix. 'I pray because my intent, that energy of mine which extends beyond me into other planes of existence, can influence the outcome.' His voice softened. 'Perhaps I pray to my much-neglected God also. It is that part of me that calls to Him, from childhood. I blessed you, in the hope that your faith will protect you.'

Felix nodded to the withered hand. 'And how will you use that?'

'It will send to sleep everyone in the farmhouse and around the perimeter, leaving just the cottage.'

Felix could see the shiny surface of the bones and skin were some sort of foul-smelling grease. 'Human fat?'

Conway's smile deepened. 'Humanity has infused the superstition with power. Animal fat just wouldn't work for me,' he said, a little chuckle in the back of his voice. 'I just wouldn't believe enough myself.'

'But your belief in the circles, and the ritual, can save Jack?'

Conway nodded slowly. 'I hope so. I truly do. But she is, in many ways, already dead. I can make no promises.'

Chapter 39

Journal of Eliza Jane Weston, 23 November 1612

As I lay in a stupor of pain, my children's voices cut through my delirium and recalled me to their peril. The countess had retreated from the bed and a new voice spoke, the midwife who had attended my previous births. A rough and motherly woman, Madame Běla had great skill and experience, and she clucked her tongue when she saw me.

'You should have called me sooner,' she scolded, but the warmth of her touch upon my brow was welcome. 'It goes hard with you. But it is ever so when the babe comes quickly.'

She bustled the men out, both loyal Tomáš and, I realised, my own husband, whose voice I now heard outside the door. I caught her hand and clung to her before I could look around. The countess, unveiled, stood on the other side of the bed, her hands twisted into claws as if she would make good her threat and tear the child from me.

'Don't leave me, madame,' I cried out to Běla, but she just tutted.

'A matron of your experience to make such a fuss,' she soothed. 'And with a great lady here to help you, as well. Remember your manners, mistress.'

There was some conversation between the women, but I could not discern it, crushed again by the pain.

Edward Kelley, Alexandria, 1586

My new friends – as they proved to be – were from that land called Sicilia and were Christian fisherman trading wheat as well as fish. They spoke some Latin and some Spanish, so we were able to communicate. One of them, named Niccolò, explained that in Alexandria they stayed close to the docks and were out upon the soonest tide. They spoke to me of Ottoman slavers, monsters that would pounce out of the night and raid villages along the coast. They had no love for the Turks or Egyptians, and identified the man whose guards had wanted to cut off my head as the son of the ruling pasha. I feared for Dee, and begged Niccolò to find out what had become of him. He sent one of his boys, as thin and lithe as a gazehound, to ask in the town. He then followed me back to the wall where I had stuffed both the letter and the seals.

They were still there, praise the saints. I explained to Niccolò that they were of sentimental importance, and that I had to seek help from the Jews. Immediately, the Sicilians drew back, and I had some difficulty persuading them to help me. Slowly, a story emerged.

The Inquisition had ordered all Jews driven from Sicilia in the past century, and a few remained as converts to Christianity. The Spanish Inquisition had rooted out some who were deemed poor Catholics and perhaps secretly practising the Jewish ways, and they were cruelly tortured and executed as an example to those on the island. But all was not lost. My new friend knew where the Jews resided, and I managed to persuade him to take me to the home of the rabbi, who might read the letter and advise me. I was sick to think that my friend, my teacher Dee, was in the hands of the Turks, of whom I had heard no good.

The house I sought was in the outskirts of the city, and we walked through some areas of great poverty and some of wealth. Niccolò, alone now but for a boy who had returned to show us the way, was nervous. We kept our hands upon the hilts of our daggers. The boy led us to a wide gate where a low building lay beyond.

I recognised by the sign by the door, a clay holder, that a Jew lived within. Niccolò, who was jumpy as a cat, shook his head and indicated to me that he did not want to associate with a man of Hebrew but would wait outside. I could do no more than nod, and beat upon the great gate with the hilt of my knife.

At first no one came, then voices muttered on the other side of the door.

'I come to speak to Rabbi Loew,' I said in a bold voice. 'I come with letters from Rabbi Eleazar of Brindisi, and his grandson Izaak the doctor.'

I heard the grinding of a bolt, and the creaking of hinges, as if the gate was rarely opened, and saw three men with sticks and clubs, and several children. They jabbered at me and beckoned me in, and within a few moments I was locked in with them, my weapon removed and all my clothes searched ruthlessly, down to emptying my boots. When they found the packet enclosing the seals they peered at the scribbled inscription inside and one of the men carried them gently at arm's length. Finally, I saw the door to the house open and the rabbi himself emerge.

Far from being an old man as I had expected, Loew was perhaps in his late thirties. An imposing presence, with an ale barrel of a chest and slightly bowed legs, he looked more like a sailor than a man of religion. I bowed.

'I am come from Prague, thence to Venice, Brindisi and Candia to consult with you,' I said, wishing Dee was with me. 'I brought Dr John Dee from the court of Queen Elizabeth in England, to meet you.'

'And where is he?' the rabbi asked in the language of Prague, his lips curving, perhaps at my dishevelment.

'A lord of the town – a pasha – took offence that we did not know the customs of your land. They took my master.'

The rabbi took the proffered documents from the man who had searched me. He read the covering to the seals carefully, then, to my surprise, handed them back to me.

'This is for but one man, perhaps the man who carries them,' he said, his voice deep and his face frowning. 'Such sorcery is dangerous. Be very careful.'

Then he turned to the letter Rabbi Eleazar had written to him, and broke that seal with a long thumbnail. After a long wait, while he read, then prayed, then read aloud a few words for his companions, he finally turned to me.

'You are welcome within my house,' he said, with a small bow. 'As is your master.' He snapped out some orders to his adult companions, and they ran to do his bidding. 'My sons will find out where he is being held, and see if we can speak to him. But it is possible he has been sold.'

I couldn't believe Dee would be of any value to anyone, a man of sixty years and barely knowing the language. Loew beckoned me to follow him inside, and I was shown to a cool hall where a woman, veiled from head to toe with only her eyes showing, offered me a bundle of clothing.

'If you care to wear clean clothes, the women can launder yours,' he suggested, and I realised how salty and dirty my own suit was. He showed me, with rare delicacy I thought, to a small chamber where I could wash in a basin of scented water and dress in the rabbi's own clothes. A simple shirt, a robe and underclothes with a pair of loose sandals and I was comfortable again. A girl, not veiled but her hair tightly covered, waited for my clothes, which she took away with care. Before she left, she indicated the open door through which I hoped to find my host.

It was a room with a roof far above, tiled on the floors and walls in all colours, the windows without shutters and open to a court-yard. Unlike the outside, which had become stifling in its heat, the room was cool, and my sandals slapped on dazzling colours beneath. Within were several young men, two older ones, and the rabbi. He waved me to a wooden bench covered with cushions, onto which I sank with relief.

'I have studied the words of Rabbi Eleazor,' he said. 'They speak of Dee, some, but mostly of you. And they speak of texts that we do not show unbelievers.'

To come so far and be denied was impossible. I shook my head. 'It is not I that ask for this, nor Dee,' I explained, 'but it is an angel of God who visited me in my sleep, nay, even by day. It is he that asks.'

The man had to restrain a young man, who perhaps enraged by my seeming blasphemy, tried to dart forward.

'It cannot be,' the rabbi said simply. 'I have no doubt that you yourself believe it . . .'

The distant chiming and shimmering of bells caught me unaware for a moment, and then I realised what was happening. My mouth was dry, my words cracked like an old woman's.

'Rabbi Loew, I beg you,' I began, the ringing deafening yet the men before me seemed unmoved. Only one of the older men lifted his head, as if he smelled something or heard a little of what I felt. Then the familiar sound and sensations, the agony only half-built before I was taken into a swoon.

I awoke in a darkened room, I judged at night, with an older woman bathing my brow with rosewater. She murmured something in her own language, and a shadow fell over me as Marinello took my hand.

'Easy there, little man,' he said, sitting beside me.

'How did you find me?'

'Your friend Niccolò,' he said. 'He is here too. The people here talk of you being afflicted again by your madness.'

'No madness,' said a distant voice from the shadows of the room. 'But the words of an unearthly presence.' I recognised the Rabbi Loew's voice.

'Hm.' Marinello looked into my eyes, his own dark, searching. 'They say Dee is in the hands of the slavers. What use could they have for an old man?'

I tried to speak but could not, my throat dry and seared by the encounter. Marinello lifted me to his shoulder and put a cup to my lips. Not wine, but some sweet juice. I drank eagerly, being very thirsty. He lowered me back to what I could now feel was a soft bed with feather cushions.

'We must rescue him,' I managed to croak.

The rabbi stepped forward. 'From the garrison? Not with a hundred men. It would be easier to buy him.'

'Buy him?' I must have looked confused as the rabbi explained.

285

'He is old. Unless he has something of great value about him, he will not be expensive.'

I rested a little easier. I did not think his great reputation as a mathematician and occultist would serve him here.

I was wrong. Far from being one unknown old man, Dee's name had travelled as far as Alexandria, where we found a small number of bidders for him. He looked a little dishevelled, and his forehead was bruised, but he stood in the row of slaves with dignity. At least he was clothed. So many of the poor wretches were displayed like prize cattle, stripped to the waist or completely naked.

He saw me, and waved with both hands tied together before him. When he finally came before the auctioneer, a thin Arab man close to Dee's age stood and spoke. An exchange of words ensued, with a final announcement from the front.

Marinello took counsel from Niccolò, whose Arabic was more sure than his own, then shook his head.

I could hold my tongue no longer. 'Bid, my lord, or Dr Dee is lost!'

'I cannot, my friend. The price is too high, more gold than I have, even if I sell my ship.'

I was silenced, and watched as Dee was helped down to his new owner, the words paining me even now to write. He looked at us, one glance perhaps of understanding, certainly of sorrow.

'Who is the buyer?' I asked of Niccolò. 'Perhaps we can speak to him.'

Niccolò pushed his way through the chattering crowd, getting black looks from many of the men there but finally coming back after talking to one of the guards.

'His name is Sulaymaniyah Masuk, and he is from a city far from here. He stays in the town, and he invites you to join him and your friend there.'

To my amazement, Dee and his new owner bowed courteously to each other and my mentor was led from the market.

Marinello spake into my ear thus: 'Go with Dee. But I will keep watch and make ready my ship. The caravel has already got a buyer, and I have money for the taxes.'

I nodded, and with Niccolò going with Marinello I had little choice but to follow Dee. For only he could save our children from imprisonment and the countess.

Chapter 40

Present day, Dartmoor

Jack was exhausted, her chin dropping onto her chest, but she was aware of someone coming in, so wearily lifted her head. It was Maggie. She tried to smile but her face hurt. Saraquel's words had forced themselves through her resistance.

'Are you OK?' she managed to say, though her voice was hoarse.

Maggie pulled one of the chairs closer to Jack, although both knew she couldn't breach the circle and touch her. 'I wanted to talk to you.'

Jack was thirsty, he – Saraquel – was tormenting her with it, hoping someone would break the protection spell.

'Is everything all right?' Jack leaned back in the chair, her back and shoulders in spasm.

'No. Not really. I need to tell you something.'

The pain in Jack's back was getting worse. Another of Saraquel's minor torments.

Maggie spoke so only Jack could hear. 'That day, the one when I took you. Do you remember it?'

Jack looked up at the older woman. This was one topic they never raised. 'Of course I remember.'

'You were thrown off your pony. Your mother comforted you.'

'I remember. Tinker was a bit scared of the planks. I loved him, though.' Anger squeezed in, even through the tiredness. 'I missed him.'

'I know.' Maggie looked at the hands twisting her lap. 'When I saw you, so beautiful, so healthy, I couldn't bear it.'

'With Charley so ill? I know—'

'No. Not Charley, you. You, Jack. You were a beautiful child, so vibrant, so alive. I knew in a few minutes, you would do something and your spinal cord would be damaged and you would die. I was going to say something to your mother, I really was, even though I knew it was hopeless. But then you went to the horse box.'

'She told me to sit down. I went back and sat on the ramp.' Jack could recall the pain in her neck. It was similar to the feeling she had now, the vertebra aching. 'She went to catch Tinker, he was loose in the ring.'

'I saw you there, and I couldn't let you die. Not for Charley, not for the magic, for you. In a few minutes, you would have been dead. I just couldn't stand it. Could you have walked away from Sadie?'

'No.' Jack remembered the wet bundle of jacket and teenager that she had bundled into her car less than a year ago.

'You saved my baby's life, Jack. You lay in that priest hole, in the dark, for two years. I did everything I could to keep you alive, but – I'm so sorry. I know I took away your childhood.'

'Of which I had, what, eight minutes left? I know why you did it.'

'But I kept on looking after you because I grew to love you.'

Jack was silenced by that. Maggie wasn't demonstrative normally, but now her eyes were wet.

'You were so brave, so determined. Even when you were trying to escape. You know, when you did get out, you even tried to take Charley with you.'

'I remember.' She had been about twelve, her legs wasted from many months of immobility, but one day Maggie had left the door open. 'I didn't get very far.' She had collapsed a few yards from the circles, Charley still wriggling in her arms.

'But you kept trying. Right up until we brought Duke into the house.' Maggie looked across the candlelit room. 'He'd been hit by a car. The man at the post office in the village knew I had had animals before.'

Duke had been an adult rook, aggressively wild, but with a shattered wing. Jack had never managed to tame him, but he had tolerated her caring for him.

'Then we got the twins.' Jack smiled, Saraquel fading for a moment into the background. A chimney sweep had brought a pair of baby jackdaws, which Jack had fed every few hours until they fledged. Both were hopelessly tame. Jack had called them Spit and Spot and looked after them for years. They cached food everywhere. There was hardly a book in the cottage that didn't have peanuts wedged between its pages when she was a teenager. When Jack decided to give up the name Melissa, she took Jackdaw instead.

Maggie rubbed her hands over her face. 'But every day, I thought, what is that poor woman going through? At least if you had died she would have known. And your father – he thought you were dead, you know, according to the newspapers. It was easier for him than thinking you were in the hands of some sadist.' She sniffed. 'What I put them through.'

Jack thought about it for a long moment. 'If I do make it, and I know that's a big if, I will be able to see them again. I know that's not much comfort for them, I mean, they've been through hell. But at least they get something, at the end.'

'Something priceless. It will be comforting, Jack, I promise.' Maggie lifted her head up, and the candlelight in the room flared. 'Now, listen and listen carefully. I may not be here to tell you this after – well, none of us can be sure we'll make it through. The cottage in Devon is yours, if anything happens to me. Charley can have the Lake District house. There's some money too, split between you and Charley.'

'Maggie.'

'Don't. We don't have time. There's just one thing I don't trust you to look after properly.'

That stung. 'What?'

'Felix.' Maggie half-smiled. 'I haven't given you and Charley much of an example, have I? He's the man for you. I don't care how old he is, or how strange your existence is, you are right for each other.' Before Jack could get a word of protest out, she interrupted. 'Stop running away from him. You need him, Sadie needs him too. Promise me.'

'OK.' Jack didn't know what else to say. 'Anything else?'

'If anything happens to me, go to George Pierce. He has a letter for you.'

'Pierce?' Jack couldn't imagine what the dodgy magic dealer could possibly be trusted with.

'I have things on Pierce, things that he wouldn't want to get out. He'll do as he's told. He may be a nasty little man, but he's completely a creature of his word. It's one of the strange inconsistencies that make him manageable.'

'What?' Jack said. 'And what's in this letter?'

'Everything I know about magic and sorcery. Just to give you a head start if you set up in business somewhere new.'

'Maggie, you won't be as much danger as me.'

'My death is foretold,' Maggie said simply. 'Your death is always unclear, because in many ways, you've already had it.'

'We'll survive. I know it.' Jack's words surprised even her. Maybe they were Saraquel's.

Chapter 41

Journal of Eliza Jane Weston, 23 November 1612

Beyond reason, I strained against my child, the midwife's hands and the whole world. I called out again and again for Johannes, but they would not let him come. The pain was tearing my spine in half, and the midwife, her face running with sweat, could do little more than pass a cloth soaked in poppy juice and water between my lips.

'The babe is placed badly,' she said to me, 'but he is coming. You must push with all your might, my dear, for all your children's sakes.'

'But the babe must be crushed, he must be dead,' I sobbed, in a lull in the storm.

The child and I were beyond tired, the flickering candles were being dimmed by sunlight creeping over the sill and through the shutters. Yet still he tried to be born, and still I strained for his life. Then, in one sudden rush, his head came, then the wet slither of his body. I lay back, sobbing, too afraid to see his still face.

But I was mistaken – after a few moments, he gave a wavering cry, then another. I turned my head to see the midwife cradling him in a cloth.

'A girl, mistress,' she said, and I could not believe it. As the midwife moved to lay her in my arms, the countess stepped closer.

'You attend to the cleansing,' she commanded, 'and I will take the child.'

Edward Kelley, Alexandria, 1586

To my surprise, I was allowed to follow Dee and his captors, though I was not encouraged or even looked at during the walk through the paved streets. Before me, people would bow to Dee's new owner, although they ignored me. As I came to what I assumed was the home of Sulaymaniyah Masuk I found the way finally barred by two burly guards holding swords that looked wickedly sharp. I crouched down against a wall opposite, where the shade was deep, and waited until fate intervened. I did not have long to wait before a harried little man burned almost black, I judged, by the sun, bustled through the guards to my side.

He babbled something in which I managed to find the syllables 'Kell-ey', and beckoned to me to follow. I slid between the unmoving guards and was shown to two great ornamented doors.

If I had thought the home of the rabbi grand, then I was mistaken. The floor before me was adorned with such intricate patterns I could barely take it in, and it was flooded with light from a wall of narrow windows reaching from the carved wooden ceiling above almost to the ground. The servant indicated that, like him, I should take off my boots. He was insistent, so I did so, turning my back that I might transfer the contents of one boot to a space within my shirt. I eschewed the proffered slippers.

The mosaic floor was cold against my bare toes and wondrous smooth, and I followed the man across to, I judged, an inside door. It was so carved into a lattice of flowers and birds that I felt it would crumble at my touch. But it survived the encounter, and I saw it was much reinforced with silver inlays and wires.

The door opened onto another room, this one housing low couches much like beds but draped with fine cloths of every colour. The Arab, a spare man with a thin beard, arose upon my entry.

He bowed a little, and I judged it better to bow deeply, my hands before me as his were.

'Master Kelley,' he said in scholarly Latin, his speech barely accented. 'The esteemed colleague of Dr Dee himself. You are most welcome.'

I looked around but Dee was not present. 'Thank you, my lord,' I answered. 'I seek my master.'

'He is well, and is being bathed and dressed by my servants. You have come, I hear, from the house of the Jew Loew.'

He wrinkled his nose a minute amount, not noticeable to a man of lesser perceptions perhaps. 'I have, my lord,' I said.

'You wish to read texts from Ethiopia,' he said cordially. 'That much Dee tells me. And also to learn of this monster – the unnatural life infused within a clay statue? It sounds like a story to scare naughty children.'

I did not know how much to tell him but there was something of the father about this gentle man. Not my father, you understand, who took my mother and left her to bear her shame, but a father like Dee. I began to describe the sorcery itself.

'We happened upon people, much cursed with frailties and ailments such as to threaten their lives,' I began. 'And they were only sustained by the knowledge of pagan women, witches of the forest, perhaps bringing knowledge from Egypt itself. They burned symbols into the skin of these sad creatures to enliven them. Have you heard of such in your world, my lord?'

Rebecca Alexander

He shook his head. 'Such practices are abominable to Allah,' he began, in a soft voice. I knew Allah was the name given to God by the Arabic races, and bowed my head.

'Indeed, my lord,' I said. 'Abominable in the eyes of God-fearing men everywhere. For life is for God to grant or deny.'

He smiled. 'Yet facing one's own extinction, would one not be tempted? At my age, I wonder if paradise will truly be my reward.'

We were interrupted by the entrance first of a bowing slave, who was, I thought, better dressed than I, and then by Dee. The slave folded to the floor in respect of his master, then shuffled out in reverse.

'Edward! I feared you captured or killed until I saw you in the market. You have seen Rabbi Loew?' said Dee, in English.

I saw the Arab's eyes dart from Dee to me and I fancied he knew a little English. I replied in good Latin. 'I have seen the rabbi.'

Our host turned as the door opened and a servant entered carrying a great round tray and almost bent in half by the weight. He placed the food – for my nose detected roast meats and spices – upon a low table. 'First, my honoured guests, we should eat.'

We were set great cushions upon the floor, at which Dee winced a little. A servant was sent upon a word – and returned with a low chair for Dee while our host and I availed ourselves of the floor.

So we ate. Ducks roasted in honey, dried fruits rolled in spices and served with a grain flavoured with herbs, fish charred without but sweet within, all served with a fruit drink called sherbet or with tiny glasses of a spiced tea. I ate my fill – there was no assurance of my next meal. Dee kept his counsel, instead speaking of the city and its great history, and of mathematics.

This whiled away the hour as we feasted, and only then was the tray taken away.

We all moved to the couches and disposed ourselves comfortably.

Sulaymaniyah Masuk was a man who seemed to notice everything, from Dee's discomfort to my bulging shirt front. His eyes upon one, then the other, he cordially asked what we wished to do.

'I would meet with this rabbi,' said Dee. 'And ask that he show us the scripts he holds, and translates them for us. For we have been guided to a great mystery.'

I felt the gaze turn to me, I fancy, even before I looked up to meet his eyes. 'We were directed towards certain symbols in a land far away,' I said. 'In Transylvania.'

'I know it well,' he replied. 'The Turks inhabit more than half of that land, I have travelled there.'

I hesitated, hearing in the very back of my skull a rumble from an angel, like a question I could not discern.

'Indeed, my lord, there we were visited by a spirit falsely calling himself an angel.'

'Tell me of this being.' The man's presence seemed to fill the room now, even as my eyes saw his small frame.

Dee answered before I could dissemble. 'He called himself Saraquel. But we are now visited and advised by an archangel called Uriel.'

'*Saraquel*?' The man seemed different than the kindly, scholarly creature I had first observed. I found my limbs tensed as if they wanted to flee. 'A prince among angels. The angel of Death, indeed, gifted with separating the soul from the body.'

My breath was caught within my chest, I was panting like a cornered mouse but could not understand the threat. I looked around the room but there was no one about.

'We need to go, to speak to this rabbi,' I repeated, my voice strangled in my throat into a squeak.

'Tomorrow,' Sulaymaniyah Masuk said, smiling and bowing. I caught my breath.

Dee smiled at him, more polite than warm. 'I do not know how I can ever repay you,' he said. 'You must have paid a fortune for my pitiful self.'

The man bowed. 'Indeed, *effendi*,' he said, 'the honour was mine. Perhaps you will reward me with your wisdoms in conference before you leave Alexandria.'

A soft chiming ran around the room for a few seconds, leaving the air still when it had finished. We were shown to an upper chamber to rest overnight. I was miserable with suspicion, and no sooner had the door closed behind us than Dee turned to me.

'Edward, I am concerned,' he said in English, rubbing his temples. 'We must take care who we trust. Your angelic visitor warns against the vessels of Saraquel, like Dominick Smith.'

'I do not understand,' I said, for weariness infused me deeply, and I could see the bed.

'I see now that Saraquel has many slaves, Edward, who will do his bidding mindlessly.' He paced around the room for a moment, his robes swaying. 'A servant, the rabbi, even our host could be one.'

I lay myself upon the bed and pressed my hands over my eyes. 'The angels are warning me,' I said, half-asleep already. 'But I can see no other course than to stay here. He owns you, body and soul. He does not have to let you leave, you are his property.'

Dee sounded pensive. 'We must get word to Marinello.'

298

I had no idea how this was to be achieved, and felt a soft throw drawn over me before I fell into an unnatural sleep.

This time I dreamed I was on a mountain looking over a lough, in Ireland as it had been when I was a boy. But everything was warm and green, so green it almost hurt my eyes after the muted greys and yellows of Araby and the endless sandstones. I looked about me for the lion or the lamb, but all I heard was the songs of birds. One, a robin, bounced upon the ground before me and I wished I had some crumbs to share. But when I put my hand inside my jerkin I found a cake wrapped in a cloth, still warm from the baking. I broke off a crumb for the bird and took a taste myself – it tasted like summer kitchens and feast day sweets rolled into one. The bird hopped unheeding at my feet as I sat down, and eventually perched upon my knee. And it sang, like a choir of birds all singing, the sound a delight.

'Are you here to speak to me?' I said, when it stopped.

It cocked its tiny head upon one side, its beak as black and sharp as a needle. He resumed his song, which formed strange words in my mind, almost as if I were reading them from the air.

'You are in great danger,' it trilled merrily, turning its head one way and the other, until I broke off more crumbs, my own appetite gone.

'I feel it,' I said, recognising the patch upon my hose, darned many years ago by my mother.

'Yet you have been guided to the right place,' the robin continued, as it flew into the air, fluttering above me like a dragonfly, darting this way and that.

'Who are you?' I cried out, and jumped to my feet. I snatched at it this way and that, flailing my arms but he was always nimbler than I.

"Ware treetops,' it called to me as I redoubled efforts to catch it, and I looked down. My body quivered in terror as I realised I had left the rock below me and now dangled many yards above the mountain peak.

I cried out in terror and flapped my arms like a bird, and every movement seemed to lift me into the sky.

'Look!' cried out the bird, its trilling more like laughter than words. So clumsy in my slow flapping, I endeavoured to follow its easy floating.

I looked about me, and there beneath me lay not Ireland now, but a long lizard-shaped piece of blue, dotted with islands. I could see, not just Candia and Kérkyra, but the world laid out below me, turning this way and that as I clambered into the sky.

'Now,' called out the bird in a longer, deeper note, and I looked at it. It was darker, almost grown three times, four times its size and still expanding as it sprouted glossy black feathers. 'Follow.'

I tried to do so, but the creature plummeted towards the world like a peregrine falcon, although when I caught up with it it was a raven, black as night.

'There,' it croaked. I looked below me to see a ship in port, a strange shape from the air.

"Tis Marinello's ship?' I wondered. And all over it were men in some sort of uniform, not Venetians, I feared, but janissaries.

'Will you follow me?' the bird screeched. As it turned into the sun I was blinded, shielding my eyes against its silhouette like an eclipse. 'Will you follow me?'

I was afraid. If this was an angel, was it our enemy Saraquel or a great angel like Uriel? 'I know you not,' I sobbed, trying with heavy arms to stay above the masts.

'You know me well,' the bird shrieked in a strange and familiar voice. It was white now, its wings scything the air. 'You know me now.' Somehow within my mind I did know this creature meant me no harm and meant mankind well.

'I have sinned,' I said, tears streaking down my face as I fought with a sea breeze. 'I simply seek to undo the evil I have done.' We were over Marinello's ship now.

'You cannot undo it,' the great gull said, landing upon a spar even as my own feet settled upon it and held on, with my clawed feet. 'But you can spend your life repairing the damage you have wreaked.'

'I cannot,' I said, suddenly humbled before the yellow beak and eyes of the angel before me. 'I know not how.'

It opened its beak and clacked it a few times, then turned the other eye upon me. 'Go back,' it said, 'and spread your knowledge like seeds over the land. The time of belief in miracles is past. Now man will find God through understanding.'

'I cannot!' I cried.

'Yet you have the means.'

I didn't understand such words entirely, but they seemed right. But my foot could no longer grip the curved wood of the spar, and screaming like the gull, I fell backward, my arms too heavy now to lift me.

I awoke alone in the room Dee and I had retired to.

The dream had left my mind filled with words, some in a strange language that I almost understood, but just eluded my thoughts. But a picture was growing in my mind as I listened, finally, to the messages I was being given. I recognised that it was not Saraquel that haunted my dreams this time, but another angel of a different order. Or, at least, so I hoped, having been foully deceived by Saraquel.

I washed thoroughly, for these Easterners were a finicky race, and drew on the clean clothes I had been left. Taking a few bites from some figs, ripe and dripping with honey, I opened the lattice door to the chamber with some caution. A servant stood waiting without, and beckoned that I might follow. We progressed to the room where we had passed the evening, me licking my fingers and straightening my shirt. Rabbi Loew was there with Dee, poring over a scroll.

Dee glanced up at me. 'Edward. The rabbi has come to speak to us. Come and see.'

I walked to the table, and was immediately struck with the fineness of a papyrus, the grasses still evident under the text. The scent of many fine spices emanated from the single page, laid upon a fine silk cloth and held down by strings of carved ivory beads. The rabbi clearly venerated the text, not touching it himself, but bowing before it and uttering blessings from time to time, in his own language.

The text was strange to me, curved and ornate, and suddenly my brain saw it. The symbols the witch had taught us in Transylvania, that she had carved and burned into the dying flesh of the Countess Báthory, were ornate forms of these symbols.

'Where do these letters and words come from?' I was almost whispering, the man seemed to revere the text so intensely.

'This,' said the rabbi, touching his fingers to his forehead and bowing, 'is the manuscript given to the true believers by the descendants of Enoch himself.'

I looked at Dee, but he was studying the script through his eyeglasses, miraculously preserved during his capture, though one lens appeared scratched. His lips moved slowly as he tried to decipher the script. 'It is a form of alphabet without vowels,' he said slowly, 'I think. Like some Eastern texts, from India. I have never seen anything like it before, except . . .' He lifted his head and looked straight at the rabbi. 'What does this say?'

Rabbi Loew pressed his palms together. 'These words describe secrets told to Enoch by angels.'

'About magic?' I prompted, as if in response to the softest of chiming in my head.

'About the nature of heaven and earth, and the wisdoms of the angels, yes,' Loew interrupted. 'Secrets revealed only to the children of Israel.'

I noticed we were joined by our host, his slippers silent upon the polished floor. I bowed, and noticing my actions, Dee and Loew did likewise.

Sulaymaniyah Masuk bowed deeply, the top of his head a patch of mottled baldness. 'With respect, my lords, it was given to mankind before anyone thought of themselves as children of anyone but one God. The secrets, if that is what they were intended to be, were wisdoms given to all.'

There was still something about our host that I found disquieting, and the whispering voices behind my eyes grew louder when he spoke. I tried to decipher what they were saying.

The strings of shapes before me seemed less strange as I sought the designs we had been given by that monstrous imposter, Saraquel, in communion with me far away in Transylvania. He had shown us how to anchor a soul that belonged to God to a dying body, an unnatural business that had led to the most vile appetites in the countess. She had learned that her vitality lay in the consuming of human blood, especially from children. Somewhere in these curves and lines lay the magic we had used, perverted to Saraquel's purpose.

Dee sighed, his beard almost touching the text so he swept it back. 'I begin to see,' he murmured. 'Edward, you must take notes . . .'

The rabbi moved so fast I jumped, to cover the text with another silken cloth. 'We cannot allow copies.'

'No, no, not at all,' protested my mentor. 'But our scholars can help explain certain lines, certain words.'

The Jew conferred in their own language, with Dee and the Arab. Perhaps I was the only one in the room who did not understand. I turned instead to recalling the conversation in my head, started in the dream.

Finally, the rabbi uncovered the text again with great care and started answering Dee's questions. It was a slow process: Dee did not speak good Hebrew, and the Jew spoke broken Latin, so the translations flew left and right over the text, interjected occasionally by our host.

I thought back over the bird's comments – that knowledge was like seeds to be spread across the land. I looked up to see an expression upon the face of Sulaymaniyah Masuk that seemed familiar. Even as I tried to place it, Dee called my name. I shut my eyes and let the memories flow into me. Where I saw a dark room, a noisome smell of garlic and rancid oil, smoke . . .

My eyes flew open. Dominick Smith, Sulaymaniyah Masuk, they shared an expression with the countess. Saraquel was within the room, reading what we read, slyly laughing at our pathetic efforts to defeat him.

'I have it,' Dee said, his voice strong again. 'We must perform the ritual again, Edward, but in reverse, as I thought! But first, the exorcism of Zadok, partly preserved in this scroll.'

I knew from the smile that we had spoken not to our host but straight to our enemy.

Sulaymaniyah Masuk turned to me, his face open with laughter now.

'Oh, my English friends,' he said in my own mother tongue. 'You are really too clever to be allowed to live. I had not expected such persistence. You were beyond foolish to come here alone, and with the text of Zadok.'

I felt within me an enlargement, a presence within my chest as if something much larger than I was crammed within my body. I took a deep breath, then another.

'They are not alone, Saraquel,' my mouth said.

Chapter 42

Present day, Dartmoor

Felix watched Maggie carry the burning hand of glory around the outside of the cottage. She wasn't squeamish, and seemed to relish the role as she carried the stinking thing, trailing a slick of smoke that seemed to hang in the air as she chanted a spell that she said had been traditionally used to activate the hand. Conway was clearly interested in her knowledge, and had compared it to versions of the spell he had studied. Not for the first time, Felix wondered at how a priest – and exorcist, even if he had lost his faith – knew so much about sorcery and witchcraft. He stepped back into the cottage to see how Jack was doing. She looked exhausted, the shadows from the candle lamps and the couple of twelve-volt lights casting deep shadows on her face. He realised just how thin she had become.

She turned towards him, and for a moment he could tell who was looking back.

'Saraquel's not going to let me go,' she said, more resignation than sadness in her voice. 'He'll only let me go if you back down.'

'Then he would always be there,' he said, sitting on one of the chairs at the edge of the larger circle, Jack being confined in the one with the triangle. 'We'd be haunted by him. Once we have no hold over him, he'll do what he wants.'

'He's not afraid of any of you. Not really.'

Slowly, Felix started to suspect it wasn't Jack that was speaking. 'Well, he should be. We know what we're doing.' He let his voice rise, hoping Jack would be able to hear it. 'We're going to win this one. Remember what we did with Elizabeth Báthory. Four hundred years of possession and slaughter, wiped out in an hour of Mac and you and me. We're a good team.'

Maggie and Mac came in, looking to Felix, uncertainty on the older woman's face.

The face before him took on an amused twist. 'A good team? A lapsed priest, a doubting inquisitor, a witch and an academic? I'm quaking in my boots, Felix.'

'How does an angel become a torturer? That I would like to know.'

Jack's shoulders shrugged, but the angel replied. 'Erzsébet? She was already a monster, I just got hooked in for the ride. Before her, I had known the pleasure of killing experienced by warriors. But nothing like her. It was shocking, at first, how she could weave together the flaying of a child's skin with such lust.'

'They were violent times.'

The angel nodded, jerking Jack's head back and forth as if the movement was unfamiliar. 'But not godless. Erzsébet's contemporaries were harsh but bounded by their faith. She believed in her God above all that. She had no compassion for her victims. That, I think, is what she was born with.'

It was surreal, cordially exchanging views with the monster that had tortured Jack.

'So why do you hurt Jack by making her hurt others?'

Conway entered, dressed in a simple robe like a monk's habit. 'I warned you about trying to talk to Saraquel.'

The creature shrugged again. 'She craves the blood. They all do.'

Felix knew he was being manipulated, he could feel his anger rising. He sidestepped his emotional reaction and tried something else. 'You are spread thin, though, whatever you are. Angel or demon.'

The corner of Jack's mouth twitched. 'You know my nature.'

'I know you feed on people at the moment of death. Not very angelic.' Felix clenched his fists.

The twitch was more like a sneer now. 'I ease the passing of the soul.'

'But you help them cling to life, when possible, don't you? Recruiting your army of people who feel for you. Because you can't, can you? You have no feelings or sensations of your own.'

For a moment, the air in the room seemed to stop moving, become hotter and heavier. Across the back wall of the cottage, a shadow started to grow along the plaster, growing, stretching – opening. Wing shapes that shaded the roof and spread right to the edges of the circle then beyond, almost to Felix and the woodburner.

'The only thing that confines me is her body,' the creature said softly. 'If I wish, I can burst through her and consume you all.'

'Can you?' Felix jumped to his feet, letting his anger out. 'Can you really? Because except for a few shadows, you haven't shown me anything else beyond the circle. Even your other slaves can't reach you because you need them to breach the circle physically, don't you? And we aren't letting you out.'

'I will consume her!' The voice was deep and ragged, as if coming from somewhere beyond Jack's vocal cords. Jack screamed, holding out hands that were turning red before him.

'And then we will have no reason not to trap you for ever!' Conway shouted. 'You are confined over a sink hole, and there will be no escape until it weathers away. You hurt her, and we will confine you for millions of years. Do not doubt me, Saraquel! You know the lengths I will go to to beat you.'

Jack's face tilted to one side. 'The boy, of course. Ethan, your lover. In your terror for yourself you cut his throat.'

Conway beckoned to Mac and Maggie to follow Felix into the circle through the gap in the ink. 'I killed Ethan because he was already dying. And because to spare his life, at the expense of hosting you, was too high a price.'

Conway stepped through the space in the outer edge of the circle and crouched to complete it again. Then he dug in his pocket for a small object. When he unfolded the blade, Felix could see it was a penknife. Without flinching, Conway drew the knife across his palm. He smeared it crudely over the join, then ran his finger around the rest of the circle, squeezing his hand to pump more blood to the oozing cut. Jack licked her lips from her own circle. Felix wondered whether it was Jack or the angel that needed the blood. He had an awful feeling it was both.

'This time, the full rite,' he said. Felix knew that the hand of glory would keep burning as long as the fat lasted and hopefully that would keep the other hosts asleep.

'Ready?' He nodded to Mac, who took up his station at the west, Maggie already standing in the south. Felix, with some reluctance, stepped over to the inked mark that represented the east.

'Now.' Conway looked at the other three. 'We are using a ritual given to Enoch by the angels themselves. Sorcery, at its very heart, comes from the same place as angels and demons. After our first attempt I asked my old friend Andreotti to help refine the ritual.

Whatever we think of Saraquel he is a being of magic, and with magic we can control him.'

'Can't we just destroy him?' Maggie had wrapped her arms around herself.

'Nothing is ever really destroyed,' Conway said gently. 'He is more controllable as an entity than as formless energy.'

'Well, let's get on with it.' When she took Felix's hand, her own was shaking as if with cold. He squeezed her fingers and she clung to his for a moment. When Felix's hand touched Conway's it was sticky with blood.

Conway faced them. 'First, we will call upon the assistance of the archangels. They have some influence over other angels, and if they help us, it will make it easier.' The lights flickered again.

'It's feasible.' Jack spoke from her chair in the smaller circle. 'Saraquel says without the angels' help it's impossible. But they won't intervene. They never do, up on their ivory towers.'

'Don't listen to anything Saraquel or Jack says,' Conway said. He started the invocation of the angels, letting his voice ring out in the rafters of the old cottage. 'I invoke the mighty and powerful archangel Michael to stand at my right-hand side. Please grant me the strength, courage, integrity and protection I need to accomplish my purpose. Smite with your sword to cut away the darkness. Surround me with your protection, so that I may always work on the side of God.'

Jack arched back in the chair, her shuddering feet just inside the smaller circle. Felix shut his eyes, trying to echo in his mind the words that Robert was speaking. Mac seemed to be on more comfortable ground, and joined in the invocations, in turn, to the archangels Gabriel and Raphael. A cold breeze drifted over Felix and made the candles flicker. The electric lights buzzed for a few seconds then blinked off, leaving them in darkness.

Robert changed the words when he reached Uriel. 'Uriel, I humbly ask you to hear our plea . . .'

The atmosphere in the room changed. The air became still, so still it felt like an effort to breathe out. Jack sounded as if she had collapsed in the chair. There was a slight glow through his eyelids, so Felix opened his eyes. The room was bathed in a glow coming from Conway himself. His face was tense, his eyes screwed shut, and he was shaking. He dropped Felix's hand.

Conway threw back his head so hard it sounded as if his neck cracked. His lips seemed to be mouthing something but it wasn't in sync with the words that slowly built up in the room. Felix could only understand fragments, the voice was coming so fast. Then it slowed.

'Saraquel,' it said. It was deeper than Conway's voice, louder. Conway's mouth kept working when the voice stopped and waited.

'Uriel.' Jack's voice was deeper too. It was a conversational tone, as if two old acquaintances had met by accident.

'The experiment is over, Saraquel.'

'I disagree.' Saraquel was quite calm and sounded dispassionate. Felix glanced over to Jack, her body folded in the chair, but the words seemed to come from somewhere else. He looked back to Conway.

'This child is not yours. She belongs to a higher power.' Felix could feel Maggie's hand, limp and cold in his.

'There is no higher power.' Saraquel stretched Jack's shackled hands up to the limit of the chains, her head still lolling on her knees. 'I can snap her bones like sticks and let her scream.'

'You can.' Conway/Uriel's voice was so soft it crept into Felix's mind like a warm blanket of memory from childhood, the scents of roses and stephanotis in the garden in Yamoussoukro, and the honeysuckle outside his bedroom window in England. He had to drag his attention back to the words drifting over his head. 'But you won't.'

Felix caught his breath as he looked over his shoulder at Jack.

'I can kill her and be gone from this puny circle. An angel, confined by a few human magics?' Saraquel's words rang out, and echoed as if he'd rung a bell with each syllable.

'No . . . no!' The second word was in Jack's own voice as she rattled her arms against the chains. 'Maggie!'

The exorcist's hands did some movement, and he put his head down on his chest, mumbling something in his own voice. Felix could see a knife, the blade quite thin and short, the penknife he had used earlier. Then Conway stepped forward and before Felix could respond, plunged the knife into the side of Maggie's neck and pulled it across.

'No!' Felix shouted and only a violent slash of a hand from Mac made him stay still and not breach the circle.

Maggie let go of Felix's hand and slumped onto her knees. Robert supported her in the circle as she gripped her neck, the blood spurting between her fingers. Jack sagged in the circle, her breathing gasping in the quiet cottage, the light dimming to almost nothing. Mac grabbed the knife out of Robert's unresponsive fingers and pulled him away from Maggie. The shock rang through Felix like a bell, and he stared at the other three in the circle.

'What? Why!' he shouted, bending down to help Maggie. Mac laid her gently in the centre of the circle. As Felix placed his hand over hers, he could feel the hot blood pumping slowly against his fingers. 'Hang on, Maggie.'

Maggie's eyes, dark in the low light by the floor, were locked with Felix's. One hand, black with blood, covered his for a moment, even as the rasp of Jack's own breaths slowed. Her mouth formed a word, but he couldn't hear anything. The light in her eyes was fierce, even as her body started to relax. 'For Jack,' she mouthed.

Jack's breath rattled in her throat as the tension went out of Maggie's body. Felix closed her eyes and lowered her hand to the floor. He heard Jack's breath stop, her body only suspended in the chair by the shackles, her head slumped forward.

He realised what had happened. Robert Conway had killed the witch that made Jack, and Jack had died with her. 'You killed them all.' He stared up at Conway, restrained by Mac, who looked as appalled as he felt. 'You killed Jack, and Sadie as well.'

The scream that came from the circle was not confined to the limits of a human voice. It roared like a train going overhead, the air blazed in Jack's circle, and Robert wrenched himself out of Mac's restraint, the knife clattering on the floorboards.

'We have taken away the witch that trapped her soul in her body,' Conway shouted at Saraquel, rage making his voice strident. 'We deny you her soul! Out, creature of the heavens, out of your earthly hosts! Release them. Release them – now!'

Another, deeper voice added a parallel timbre to Robert's own.

Saraquel shrieked in some language, the sound sweeping into Felix's head even as he covered his ears. Grief seemed to be locked in his stomach like pain, and he doubled up. Mac was crouching over Maggie's body, praying.

The light was growing into a fire in Jack's circle, flames licking over her body, forming the shape of the intruder, so tall his head brushed the beams of the cottage, his body filling the space. His wings, like smoke, unfurled from his back and spread around the walls, only his body restrained by the circle.

When Robert spoke again it was with Uriel's soft tones. 'Leave them, Saraquel. Must we kill all of your hosts? Your time here is over.'

'Death!' Saraquel moaned, swaying in the cylinder of flame. 'It is death to feel nothing, to sense nothing.'

Uriel pressed Conway's hands together. 'And yet you have a purpose. A purpose that allows you to experience what they experience.'

'For a fleeting moment,' Saraquel snarled, fighting with the confines of the circle. As Felix watched, it seemed to bulge. 'When I have had a thousand lifetimes of love and fear and hate.'

'It is our nature.' Uriel, in Robert Conway's body, turned to Saraquel face on. As Felix watched, the glow that seemed to emanate from Conway's skin started to exceed it, and Conway slumped to his knees beside Maggie and Mac. The second angel began to take shape over him, in a cool russet glow, rather than the scorching orange of Saraquel.

The phantom of its radiant head swept the rafters, blazing wings drove back Saraquel's shadow until they lit the whole cottage. As the light grew, it encompassed Felix and the others. It felt like calm warmth, filling Felix with a sensation that swept his grief and rage away, sucked it out and left him filled with an impression of . . . peace. He could feel the others too, as if his mind was somehow overlapping Mac's and Robert's. Mac's was filled with certainty as he yielded to the angel and prayed. Robert's was fighting the angel, trying to guide it to defeat Saraquel. Yet there was something gentle and insidious about Uriel. Uriel, he was inhabiting the same space as an archangel, for Christ's sake! He was overwhelmed by it even as part of him reached for his agony over Jack. He turned towards Saraquel and opened his eyes.

314

Saraquel's screaming had given way to a smouldering silence. The column of red flame now obscured Jack's body, perhaps it was burned away. Blended with black smoke which coiled around the red it seemed to be filling the space it could force itself into, bulging the confines of the circle into new shapes. Heat boiled across the air from the smaller circle.

When he spoke, it was so loud it seemed to vibrate in Felix's head. 'I have a mission, Uriel. Do not deny me my purpose.'

Uriel seemed to shimmer and contract, back into the middle of the circle, centred around Robert. 'I deny you your victims, Saraquel, not your duty.'

It squeezed down into the confines of the kneeling body, even as Conway howled in agony. 'No! Uriel!'

'It is the only way,' Uriel said, his voice soft. 'If we are to put right what is wrong.'

'Don't kill me.' Conway's voice was anguished. 'I know what I did was wrong.'

'You started this storm. It is for you to end it.'

Conway's voice was tormented. 'I don't know how, without dying.'

'The way you started it. With the help of an angel.'

Felix stared at the bulging Saraquel, the columns shot through with oranges and yellows as if it was a chimney filled with burning logs. He couldn't see whatever was left of Jack at all. The heat was burning his face. 'Do what he says, man! For all our sakes.'

Robert staggered to his feet, his face tormented as if housing the angel was agony. 'All right!' he shouted. 'To end it!' He turned to Saraquel. 'Come on, you psychopathic bastard. Come and get me, it's always been me you wanted!' He turned to Felix. 'I need your blood, just a taste of it.'

315

'You . . . what?'

Mac stood, holding out the knife, still scarlet with Maggie's blood. 'Take mine.' He drew the knife over his own forearm, and after a moment of hesitation, Conway bent his mouth to the proffered arm.

'You,' Felix stammered. 'You are a revenant.'

Mac pushed the man away. 'Enough.'

Felix had seen Jack when she had first taken blood. She had a look of exultation, too. Conway, the glow of Uriel still rippling over his skin, turned to Saraquel. 'We banish you, Saraquel, by the power of the Lord your God, to the heavens of your birth, in bondage to your duty, in perpetuity.' The words rang out like sledgehammers on stone.

The glowing creature, now scorching the ceiling, finally breached the smaller circle.

Robert/Uriel stepped out of the larger protective circle and the two angels collided. Felix was thrown to the edge of the floor, Mac hunched over him, pressing him to the boards in the stink of Maggie's blood. In the light of the angels he could see the white fingers of the dead woman, and hear things smashing around him. He screwed his eyes shut and hid them in his forearm. Even through his eyelids he was blinded, the roar of Saraquel and the hammer blows of Uriel's words almost too loud to distinguish. Then an explosion hit Felix and darkness folded around him.

Chapter 43

Journal of Eliza Jane Weston, 23 November 1612

As I cried tears of despair and the midwife took away the afterbirth in a gush of heat I knew unnatural, excessive, I watched my babe cradled in the arms of the creature.

'Madame, I beg of you,' I said, and the countess turned to me, her face twisted as she fought with the monster within her. 'My child.'

The midwife stepped to the lady, her hands held out. 'I shall take her downstairs to the kitchen to keep her warm,' she said softly, 'for I think the lady needs a doctor. And the priest.'

I knew it already, felt the life blood pulsing from me even as I watched the countess wrestle with Saraquel within. She handed the baby to the midwife and stepped to the fireplace. The door closed. I heard some rejoicing words from my husband as he beheld his daughter, then some quiet speech. I was alone with the countess as her nostrils flared in the scent of blood in the room, the stench of death already gathering around me. Father, I prayed, not to the Lord Jesu as perhaps I should, but to mine own beloved father. Tell me from beyond the grave, what should I do to destroy this monster?

And into my mind came, not his magical voice, but the words he had made me repeat a thousand times lest I be trapped by our enemy. I muttered the words in the tiny whisper that remained to me.

Edward Kelley, Alexandria, 1586

As I stared at Sulaymaniyah Masuk I knew that the angels, Saraquel in his body and Uriel forcing his way into mine, could simply destroy us all. Yes, and destroy the ancient text that gave us the knowledge of exorcising an angel. It was that knowledge we must defend at all cost. I held up my hand and looked at Dee, his gaze caught by the movement. He made a tiny nod, and stepped back beside the Rabbi Loew. He moved as if to cover the vellum, to save it from the sight of Saraquel.

'Lord Saraquel,' I spake, my voice shaking as much as my hands. 'We know we cannot defeat you.' I moved to attract Sulaymaniyah Masuk away from Dee. 'We entreat you to remember your angelic duty.'

'My duty?' The voice of Saraquel was mixed with the Arab's, as if he stood behind him, taller, greater than the mortal man. 'My existence as a statue, unmoved by joy, love, anger, hate? My touch that of wood or stone?' He sounded anguished, and I hoped that his emotion might distract him.

I stepped towards the door, watching as the other players moved as if in honey, their arms and faces moving slowly. 'I am the vessel you seek, Saraquel. Take me, leave them. I am the greater sorcerer.'

I was big with bravado but I knew I would fight such a possession to the last. I slipped my hand inside my shirt for the scrolls.

Which one was the one to be broken in extreme danger? I could feel both, the one for fire and the one for God's own assistance. But there seemed no difference that I could feel. I could see Loew and Dee poring over the text, though still slowed by whatever stupor Saraquel had created.

Lord, I prayed, though to God or angel I know not. *If you were ever guided to help me, help me now.*

I could feel the growing of an influence inside me, not the invasion of something larger than me, but just a part of the angel perhaps. My mouth began whispering, words that flashed before me as the symbols upon the scrolls the rabbi had brought. They were unfamiliar in my mind yet somehow I knew their meaning. 'Ha'ar t'chevnic a fa gralaa Micah bro-han ya hibbab hraleye . . .'

I invoke the mighty and terrible Archangel Michael to fight at my right side. I humbly beseech thee . . .

Saraquel twisted the old man's head around so hard I could hear the snap of the joints in his neck stretching.

'You think to defeat me with an incantation? Puny child . . .' He approached, until he was so close to me that his breath was unnaturally hot in my face. 'I *wrote* those words,' he hissed. 'We should never have given them to you mortals. What can you understand of magic?'

He stretched out his hands and held them palm up. A flame began to dance in each, the skin blistering and blackening before me, the stench of burning flesh filling my nostrils. I could see the agony of the man behind the angel.

My mouth continued to mumble the unfamiliar words as my head filled with ritual of the invocation of the archangels Gabriel and Raphael. Yet when I came to Uriel the litany changed.

'H'havna Uriel t'chevnic, ha'na Uriel, fragrna u l'hah . . .'

By authority of Uriel, the sword of Uriel, cast out foul dragon, brother-beast . . .

The clothes of the Arab began to smoulder around his wrists, then his sleeves caught in a flash of flame. The smoke began to billow away from his sides, forming two shapes, two great wings, growing solid as if made of stone. I stumbled back a step as they grew, stretching up to the roof, over my head. On the joint in each was a claw, as long as a sword.

The man's face was turned towards me, agony twisting his mouth and making his eyes bulge, yet there was something ecstatic about him too. He screamed, a sound like worked metal. Saraquel seemed lost in the sensation of the fiery destruction of the man, his skin blackening and peeling back from the scarlet meat below. My eye was momentarily caught by a movement behind him, as Loew and Dee crept forward with something held between them – a silken cord, unravelled from a robe perhaps. But it glistened with the light, gold, the purest of metals. As they came behind the man/angel, they crouched and I realised they had formed a shape like a U behind him. If I could get him to step back – they could complete the circle.

As the last words died in my throat, I threw my arms up and clapped my hands above my head. Perhaps Uriel added to the sound, for it seemed to echo and grow, spinning around the room, gathering pace with its brassy echo. The angel grew beyond the confines of the man, the gleaming torso and arms reaching below the wings to the roof. But he was still attached to the Arab's feet, which faltered back against the sound of my hands. Saraquel grinned at me in a parody of pleasure, while the flames lapped at the mortal's mouth and nose, flashing into the old man's hair and catching his headdress alight. Loew uttered some words – I know not what – and he and Dee scuttled forward and overlapped the ends of the tiny barrier. Dee knotted them even as the Arab fell to his knees and screamed again, dwarfed by the monster above, now struggling for release from the body. Perhaps it was Saraquel's rage that burned him up, I do not know. But the heat made me fall back and the others run for the edges of the room, and in the time it took to take one searing breath, the body of the poor man was consumed and fell into glowing cinders and ash.

Now a single thread confined the form of Saraquel, and as I watched from the floor, he started to take full form. A creature shaped somewhat like a man but with the hunched shoulders of a vulture he stood square on the embers of his host. His hair, a mane of molten obsidian that seemed to form itself from the air, brushed the tiles on the high ceiling above some eight yards high and his naked feet, curved like the feet of an eagle, almost touched the thread. Between, a great naked giant, not muscled or gendered, his body rolling and changing like the sea at night. The smell of an angel? Like molten iron, like blood in battle, all together. I was lost in terror for a moment, but Uriel shifted within me, soothing me with his presence. I could see Dee praying, hunched against the wall, and Loew crouched beside him, dumb with fear or wonder. He stared at me, then climbed to his feet and retrieved the smouldering papyrus that must have been spun onto the floor. He followed the text with a finger and intoned quietly in his own language. I saw the ashes within the circle shift as if they were blown by an eddy. They started to form a shape, compelled by the rabbi.

The angel turned to me slowly, tightly confined within the circle. 'You think the words of a man can defeat me,' he said, his voice, unfettered now by the constraints of a human throat, like a great

321

peal of bells ringing in my head. My ears hurt, I clapped my hands over them but to no avail. The words mocked me, even as I felt blood ooze into my fingers. 'I can burn your puny thread to smoke. Yea, and you with it with a single word.' The ashes were, I saw, growing into a hand, a thing many times as large as it should be, called up by the rabbi. It seemed insubstantial beside the great angel.

As Saraquel took a deep breath-like movement, stretching his chest and lifting his chin to burn us with his words, the ash hand smote his face. He staggered back momentarily and the last words of the exorcism leaped into my mind. I knew, somehow, that they had to be spoken by me, not the angel. The magic was given to mankind that we might have some influence over angels, that was what Enoch was shown. To control these behemoths, if we needed to.

Loew stood as high as he could, reaching up his own hand. As the angel opened his lips to speak, the hand of ashes stretched high over the angel's face, fingers reaching towards his neck as if about to tear out his throat from inside. It was enough to distract Saraquel again and I shouted.

'Yy-he crahe u a dwahk a yw-e-ha fla'fruh . . . joh'kha!'

In the name of God that made you . . . depart!

Something changed in the room, and changed in me as well as I felt my chest squeezed from inside.

Saraquel shrieked, the sound of the wind ripping trees apart, the sound of the sea battering the cliffs. No words, just an axe of sound to my head, the air rushing from his rage, filling my face with the Arab's ashes. I saw him writhe, his form once man, then beast, a serpent coiled within the tiny thread, then a huge toad, squatting inside. I watched as the creature broke apart into a host of creatures all as the angel had been, monkey-sized men with the leathery wings of great bats. They shrieked, and dived against the invisible confines of the circle. I saw the thread glisten on the floor, stretched tight now.

I spoke the words again, each one like a stone spat out with a gasp of breath.

'Yw-e-ha . . . fla'fruh . . . joh'kha . . .'

There was an explosion of light that seemed to burn through my fingers, clapped to my face. For one moment, it felt like the taloned foot of an dragon grasped my belly and crushed me, at the same time as something within me fought for my body. Agony threw me to the ground, writhing as if in a seizure, bending my limbs back until I felt they must break. My screams were the only way I could breathe, before blessed darkness took me.

Chapter 44

Present day, Dartmoor

Conway's body flopped in Uriel's grasp. For a few moments the two angels strained against each other. The effort seemed to be more that of purpose than energy, and Conway realised he couldn't breathe while Uriel was distracted, and tried to pull his body free. With an impatient swipe, Uriel swatted him away and he landed in a heap half on Maggie's body. The angels swung around, half-melded into each other, the softer glow of Uriel giving way to the fiery brightness of Saraquel. Conway saw the terrifying presence reach out a wingtip in his direction. He scuttled back along the wall, but it crawled towards him. Uriel seemed to grapple Saraquel back a few feet, over the well.

'We need to contain him,' seemed to form inside his head, like a slow whisper. 'We need to distract him.' The chair on which Jack's body was chained, strangely unaffected by Saraquel's conflagration, had toppled over. Mac, who seemed to come out of nowhere, darted over to push her away from what Robert could now see was a smouldering hole in the floorboards. Mac then turned to the writhing forms in the room and held up a crucifix. 'I charge you, in the name of Jesus Christ . . .'

As he spoke, the wingtip shot towards Conway again, who could do little but shout a warning and wriggle further along the wall. Felix seemed unconscious, lying beside Maggie's body.

Mac carried on, his shouts shrill. 'In the name of the Lord God, I command you to depart . . .'

The Saraquel half of the half-merged form of the two angels wrestled with Uriel, and the tentacle, at least, retreated. McNamara carried on calling on the angel to leave, but it had little effect. Conway knew the modern exorcism couldn't work, what the young man needed was Zadok's own, first form of exorcism, and the Irishman was probably the only man alive who knew all of it.

He pushed up the wall until he was standing, shaking in the heat and fury of the writhing shapes.

'By the power of God and the one who weeps for him, and the one who holds him and succours him, lift the curse of Saraquel, the dragon of death, that dwelled in the heavens and was tempted to the earth,' he shouted. The roar of the two angels rattled around the room, smashing the glass in windows and lamps alike. 'Grant me power in exorcising and banishing this angel back to the place where he should dwell, under the eye and fist of the Lord . . .'

For a moment, Saraquel shrank back into a yellow flare within the reddish glow of Uriel, while Conway took a breath. Mac leaned forward and stabbed the crucifix into what was left of the wing that had reached for Conway. It flickered back, then slammed Mac across the room and against the wall.

With the air being sucked from him, the heat in the room rising so fast Conway could feel the skin on his face burning, he wheezed out the final words: '. . .as ordained by Almighty YHWH, Almighty God.'

The room pulsed with heat and energy, knocking Robert onto one knee. The pain seared as Saraquel's presence started to force itself into his body, against his whimper of protest and desperation.

'Uriel!' he shouted, feeling the presence push back as the two angels fought over him as they had done many years before. He felt the flicker of flames inside him and screamed as Saraquel forced himself into his chest. It felt like his body was expanding, as if it would rip in two before it was burned up in the heat. He could feel Uriel being squeezed backwards – there was barely enough room for one angel, he realised, let alone two: he must surely be destroyed.

The attack seemed to take Saraquel as much by surprise as Robert, even as he felt his body reel back into the centre of the room, held up by two presences locked together. McNamara must have leaped forward, and Robert could feel Saraquel's rage burn as it turned outwards upon Mac. With a feeling as if his spine was breaking, Saraquel was gone, Uriel a protective presence soothing the burning, the pain in every inch of his body. Robert opened his eyes in time to see Saraquel manifest as a corporeal being, in its alien nakedness, the wings brushing him back with the softest of feathers and an irresistible force of air. Robert reeled against the wall, the rough stone exposed as the plaster had been blasted off, and watched Mac face the physical angel. Its head barely under the eaves of the roof, its skin the colour of polished gold, Saraquel loomed over the human.

Uriel called out a warning, or maybe it was Robert, but it was too late to stop the angel picking Mac up by his chest – and squeezing. Mac screamed, his hand batting at the monster, fighting the force that was slowly crushing his chest.

'Well, Uriel,' the angel said, the voice ringing through the building loud enough to crack the remaining plaster and drop more fragments to the floor. 'Shall we spare the little zealot?'

'It matters little,' said Uriel in a softer rumble. 'But he is no threat to you. And it is not your place to call death to them, but to soften the transition.'

For a moment, Mac slumped back in the giant hand, staring into the face that turned to examine him.

'And yet . . .' Saraquel sang. His fingers tightened, crushing the man's chest with a wet crunching sound.

Mac's face looked as if he was caught between wonder and terror, but as his head fell back, Robert could see he was gone.

'No!' Suddenly Robert's fear gave way to anger. Saraquel shuffled in the restricted space around to face him.

'Finally, it is you and me,' the angel said, in his ringing words that forced Robert to cover his ears. Saraquel seemed to shrink, and his voice became softer.

'And Uriel,' Robert said, feeling the gentle presence banked down inside him.

'Ah. So Uriel has taken my place. You are possessed after all, your greatest fear.' The angel didn't smile, didn't frown, as if his face was a statue. 'And you think you can force me out of all life, all sensation and feeling. You would make me, as you thought, an effigy filled with duty?'

'I didn't start this,' Robert managed to say in the face of the great being. 'You chose this thousands of years ago.'

'And you think you can stop me? Even with Uriel the Peaceful within you . . .'

Conway reached inside his shirt. The scroll was crushed into a ball, the seal barely clinging to the vellum.

Saraquel, for a moment, hesitated. Then he roared, growing to fill the cottage, bent like a hunchback against the walls. The confining sigils glowed like stars, but held him. The cottage walls shook, and Conway was thrown back against the juddering stones, barely able to keep his footing.

He snapped the seal.

It was as if a desert wind had filled his chest, then forced new words out in a high-pitched rant. Robert didn't recognise the litany, but Edward Kelley had been told that the scroll called upon God directly. He also suspected that the scroll would guarantee his own death, but after a lifetime of being cautious it was time.

'Kill me now, Saraquel!' he yelled into the glowing fiery being now a foot from him. Saraquel's face, distorted by confinement to the space, opened its giant mouth and bent forward as if to consume him whole.

Robert shut his eyes and screamed out the words he had memorised. *H'havna Uriel t'chevnic, ha'na Uriel, fragrna u l'hah . . .*

For a moment, he imagined he could feel the mouth, the great teeth of the angel grating against his head and shoulders. When he threw up the hand holding the smouldering scroll the monster shrieked, a sound like someone tearing a metal sheet in half. When Robert dared look again he found Saraquel once more confined to the triangle and contracting, a misshapen goblin, just stumps where wings once flared.

Uriel, his wings feathered to the floor, stood over him, hands out as if forcing Saraquel down.

'Now!' Uriel shouted in the cottage, like a peal of bells. It echoed through Robert's soul as well.

Robert spoke the true name of God, as known to the ancient Jews, as taught to them by Zadok, as told to Enoch himself.

In a flicker, Saraquel faded into a ghostly image sculpted in flame, then was sucked into the sinkhole with a final wail.

Robert staggered forward to Jack's slumped, chained body.

Chapter 45

Journal of Eliza Jane Weston, 23 November 1612

The words of enchantment, even from my feeble throat, changed something in the room. A sound, like a cat hissing at a dog, made me open my eyes and turn my head on the pillow.

The countess had been standing, not as I had hoped over the magical trap but with one foot within it. She was caught by that leg, and I struggled to repeat the words, knowing their power was short. I knew that my father intended, one day, to undo the magic and release her tortured soul and therefore dispossess Saraquel. This would be my only chance and alas! I was weak.

She screamed then, a great cry of anger as she twisted this way and that, her body arching in unnatural postures as if she was caught in a great convulsion. She started speaking her own spell, in some language I knew not, but with the sound of my child's soft cries still in my mind, I repeated the words, again and again.

Edward Kelley, Alexandria, 1586

I awoke, not in the house of Sulaymaniyah Masuk, but being much shaken, my head hitting the flank of a rough animal. I recognised the hairiness of a mule or donkey, and came to understand I was bound like a saddle pack over the withers of such an animal.

'What . . .' My first words went astray, as I was bundled into a blanket, and I realised I was half suffocated by the heat. 'Dr Dee,' I managed to croak. The animal slowed and I heard voices – thank the Lord, my friend and mentor and the deep voice of the rabbi.

I was relieved of my captivity and lifted down to the road. As my eyes adjusted to the light when the rough blanket that covered me was removed, I hardly recognised my old mentor. His skin was darkened, his beard dishevelled and he was wearing the clothes of a beggar rather than a scientist of England. He brought me drink from a leather flask.

'Water, Edward,' he said, supporting me as I felt unnaturally weak.

I sipped and felt better. The water was not improved by being inside the bottle, but at a word from Dee, I drank it all.

'Where . . .where are we?' I managed to stammer. I felt within me but could not feel anything that was not me. In fact, I felt strangely hollow, like a polished glass that had known that wine rested there before.

'We are outside the walls of Alexandria. Your friend Niccolò was sent to find us by Marinello. Rabbi Loew hopes to guide us within its walls, but we don't know how to get to the harbour. There is an uproar in the city about the escape of a slave.' He smiled suddenly, his teeth light against his brown skin. 'Myself, actually. And stories of demons travelling as Englishmen.'

Loew stepped forward. 'What you essayed,' he said to me, in ponderous Latin, 'was extraordinary. You are truly a great sorcerer.'

'Not me . . .' I said, reluctant to take the credit for such destruction. 'I am but a conduit of an angel. But you – you gave life to dust.'

'For a moment, perhaps.' He smiled. 'Such is the brief life of a golem.'

I could see a cloud raised on the road ahead, and pointed it out. I was bundled back into my blanket and lifted, head first, onto the mule again. He squealed and brayed his discomfort, but as the horses advanced I heard Loew shout something, and after a brief stop they galloped on.

'We have told them you are sick unto death,' Dee said. 'They will not wish to expose themselves to some plague.'

I knew that story would never work at the gates of the city, for they would not let the sick in, but it worked twice more against travelling parties.

Before we reached the gates, I was allowed to sit astride the beast and was wrapped in the blanket as if I were a servant. Dee painted my face, neck and hands with walnut juice, and Loew claimed that Dee was a merchant travelling by ship to sell nickel. The Turkish guards, obedient to the ruling pasha, examined our humble belongings closely. Since I had secreted my remaining seals on their scrolls within my undergarments, they did not find it, nor did they search Rabbi Loew.

They demanded a fee, which Loew paid while complaining and bartering with them, but finally they took the coins and opened the western gate to the city. Loew took us to the gates of the port, but told us he could go no further, Jews were forbidden to travel without permission and papers.

'I shall return the scriptures to their safe place,' he said, looking at me with some respect. 'And I shall write the words your young assistant spoke, in our own language, as I recall them. For that was a mighty spell, given to us by the angels themselves.'

Dee bowed to him. 'I thank you, rabbi, from the heart. Your help was invaluable. If I can ever help you . . .'

Loew smiled through the dust and sweat of the journey. 'When you help any Jew, you help me,' he said simply. 'But I thank you for giving us a window into the the the old wisdoms, forgotten in our modern world.'

We watched him leave, leading the mules behind him. 'That is a great man, Edward,' said Dee. 'And he has told me how he raised the golem. I can report back to Konrad that none of that wisdom will help us in our battle against Saraquel or the countess.'

I turned to the port guards, staring at us suspiciously since we were seen with Loew. 'We must get Marinello's attention,' I said, 'perhaps he can get us through the gate.' I sighed. 'I wish I were truly a sorcerer that could conjure us within his ship.'

Dee thought for a long moment. 'Perhaps conjuring is what is needed, Edward.' He stepped forward and addressed two bored-looking guards with wickedly shiny lances, standing within the gatehouse. 'Gentle lords,' he called, in Italian, then in Latin. They looked at each other, and one drew a sword and the other pointed his spear at us. He shouted some order in his own language. Dee said something in that tongue, then turned to me.

'Behold,' he shouted in Latin. 'My assistant has money within his ear –' and he drew a coin from my tangled hair '– and his nose and mouth.' Each time he brought out a coin they looked at him, not me. He showed them the coins and gabbled in their own language. I heard the word pasha used several times, and then they snapped to attention. One snapped a command to Dee, who imperiously waved to me and I followed him through the gate.

'What did you tell them?' I muttered, in English.

'I told them we come from entertaining the pasha's guests on the occasion of his wedding – Loew says that is why security is higher – and that we are engaged to take ship to the sultan's court.' He turned away from where I knew Marinello's ship was berthed, and along the waterfront to where the Arab ships were tied up. I looked behind me, the last guard was watching, and I ran to catch up with my master. In a moment, I observed him turning to a new traveller and Dee and I slipped behind some bales ready to be taken on board a long xebec.

Within seconds, running soldiers in crisp uniform had surrounded us, each with tall turbans atop and curved swords drawn. The leader, or so I judged him, called out something in first his own language, then in Latin. His skin was paler than some of his men, and he stared at me from under golden brows.

'Halt, on pain of death!' he called.

I froze and Dee lifted his hands as if in blessing. 'We are men of peace, men of God,' he said.

'Where from and where are you bound?' snapped the man, who had a familiar ring to his own accented Latin. I stepped forward.

'We are English travellers hoping to reach the safety of our ship,' I answered in our own language. 'May I respectfully ask who you are, sir?'

His brow creased, as if the words were unfamiliar at first. 'My name is Bayezid, captain of the janissaries,' he said, in slow English. 'Why do you address me in this barbaric language?'

I knew many of the sultan's troops were the children of Christian slaves, some taken from English ships. 'I recognised your speech, your accent. You were born an Englishman,' I said.

Dee nodded. 'We are but humble travellers seeking our return to our homeland,' he said. Perhaps he hoped to draw upon the

Rebecca Alexander

man's earliest memories, of being nursed by an English mother or dandled by an English father. He was wrong.

'My life is to keep Kılıç Ali Pasha, the Grand Admiral's, troops and ships safe in this shithole of a harbour.' He drew his sword, shiny against the bright reds and green of his uniform. 'And since you are two Christian dogs, I think you are better beheaded and tossed into the sea.'

I took a step back, which just brought the sword above my head, both of his hands around the hilt and his eyes staring at my neck. 'Wait,' I managed to say though my voice shook. 'Do you not recognise my master?'

The captain of the janissaries froze for a moment. 'Why should I?'

'Why, he is the great Queen Elizabeth's own astrologer and magician,' I managed to choke out. 'He is beloved of the queen herself.'

'What do I care about a queen of dogs and infidels?'

One of the other men asked him something in his own language. Dee stepped forward, fearless of the raised swords about him. 'My death is already foretold,' he said, 'in my own garden in England. Perhaps your admiral would like to know what great deeds and honours await him by consulting the stars?'

'I can disprove your prophecy with a single swing,' the man said, but something about his stance suggested he was unsure. Finally he snapped back to attention, his men following, and they sheathed their swords. He spoke rapidly to one of his men, who ran off with some message. We waited for a number of minutes, sweating in the rising sun as it approached noon. Finally, the man came back at a run, bowed to his captain, and spoke rapidly.

'It seems the great Kılıç Ali Pasha wishes to see you,' he said. 'You will humble yourself before him like the dogs you are when you see him. Understand?'

334

We had already suffered through not knowing the custom, so I nodded immediately. Dee started to mumble something about crawling only before his God and his queen but I glared at him with such a hard gaze that he stopped.

We were escorted by the soldiers, who stood back lest our dusty rags despoil their uniforms, and were taken onto a gangway covered with shading silks and hung with many flags. We removed our shoes and outer clothes. Then we were taken to a room where we were ordered to strip, wash and put on clean robes. I feigned modesty before the guards in order to protect my precious sealed scrolls, wondering if this were the time to use them, for surely our lives were spent.

Dee was less afraid. 'Come, Edward, are we not beginning a new adventure?'

'We are likely to end as slaves in the Turkish navy,' I grumbled, tucking in my loincloth as best I may.

'That too would be a great adventure.' Then his brow creased. 'But I cannot think how this will end for poor Jane and my precious children.'

'Then you must impress this pasha,' I said, pulling the robes about me. They were a little long for me, and a girdle was given to me to hitch them up. Dee's fell short of his ankles. 'Come,' I said in English. 'This must be your greatest performance.'

And it was. The pasha was a handsome man in his sixties, who was easier in his courtesies than his captain of guards would suggest. He was an educated man who greeted Dee with polite-ness, and even enquired as to my name. Fearless in the presence of the guards, Dee asked questions of the pasha, who spoke excellent Latin and I suspected was Italian in origin. The horo-scope was cast on vellum with fine inks and pens provided and

Dee made some accurate assessments of the pasha's past and character.

'I have some faith in such devices,' the pasha said to me as Dee mumbled over his calculations. 'For my father's horoscope was drawn when I was a boy in Calabria. It said he would die by water, and he did, drowning in my ninth year.'

'This is strange,' Dee said, leaning back so he could see his own calculations, his eyeglasses still in his belongings back at the ship. 'Here, it is said that you shall end your life at sea, but this conjugation says on land.'

I could see the man was impressed from his eyebrows flying up his forehead, but his voice was drily unconcerned. 'And how go my campaigns in Syria?'

'Your peace holds in all the sultan's lands,' Dee said, making a small correction with his pen. 'No, it is read in the stars, pasha. Your death will come within a year, a gentle death among your family but both on land and water.'

The captain of janissaries uttered an intemperate oath and half drew his sword, only halted by the pasha's waving hand. 'Wait, Bayezid,' he said. 'He means no disrespect, nor tells me anything I do not know.'

Dee stood back and bowed. 'I am sorry to bring you such news, but the horoscope tells a story of illness.'

'Already, I feel the crabs gnawing at my stomach, and my appetite is weak,' the pasha said, smiling. 'I wonder – I sailed into the Crimea not two years ago, and fought a hard campaign. There a young woman climbed onto the city walls to avoid being taken by my troops. She hailed down curses upon the janissaries, and I was singled out for her viper's tongue. I felt the curse settle in my old bones.' He waved the soldiers to stand back. 'I know not where you go or whether you will survive but tell me this: do you go against the ships or armies of the empire?'

'We do not,' said Dee, and when the gaze turned to me, I repeated the pledge.

'Then go in peace,' the pasha said simply. 'And if Allah wishes it, we will meet again in heaven. For I have built a great mosque upon land claimed from the sea, and I shall die there.'

We found ourselves, clutching our bundles of clothes, on shore, and started to walk towards the foreign ships' part of the harbour. I heard running feet behind me and turned to see Bayezid, sword in hand.

'Tell me,' he said. 'Is England green, like the sultan's garden?'

'Always,' I said, looking at Dee.

'Thank you. My mother said – but I could not believe there was a land like heaven on earth,' he said. 'I was born in Cairo, to an English slave. When I went to the janissaries' school I was told to forget it, that it was all falsehoods, but I like to think that she was not a liar.'

He saluted us briefly with the sword and turned back. We hastened our steps to the quayside.

Chapter 46

Present day, Dartmoor

Felix awoke to the sound of someone talking, a male voice. Conway's.

'Come on, now, breathe, damn it.'

He lifted his face off the boards, struggling to push the weight of someone – Mac – off his back. Conway was pumping on the chest of someone lying beside him. Slowly, he realised it was Jack.

'Leave her alone,' he tried to say, although his words were slurred. 'She's dead.'

'Not yet.' Conway looked up at him. 'She was down, what, ten minutes? Revenants are harder to kill than you think.'

Felix crawled over the scorched boundaries of the main circle towards Jack, laid on the floor. Her face was bone white, her eyes closed. Conway puffed a breath into her. 'Help me, damn it,' he gasped. The sweat on his face suggested he had been doing CPR for a while.

Felix struggled to kneel up, placed his hands on Jack's chest, reaching for the memory of training he had done maybe twenty years ago. Press, press, press.

'She's dead,' he managed to say, tears spontaneously running down his face.

Conway sat back, and the two men stared at her. A quiver under Felix's hands, then another, made him flinch away, as if he had imagined it. Conway stared at his own fingers. 'Where's the knife?'

Felix looked around. The inquisitor was still unconscious – or dead – and he leaned over him for the pocket knife, stuck in the floor beside Mac. 'What are you going to . . . oh.'

Conway cut a finger with a grimace, then trickled a few drops into Jack's mouth. 'I think that's the best I can do for the moment. She has a pulse, and she's breathing a little.'

'How can that be?'

'We released her soul by killing Maggie. But it was contained within the circle, along with Saraquel. Her body was held in suspension until the angel was drawn into the earth.'

Jack sighed as if to confirm his words. Felix pressed his finger against Mac's throat. Nothing. 'What happened to McNamara?'

Conway looked at the younger man. 'He tried to help me with Saraquel. He stood up to him. He was killed after you were knocked out.'

Felix was feeling dizzy and his head was throbbing. 'How did you beat Saraquel?'

'I gave up something I have been trying to hold onto my whole life.' Conway shrugged. 'My independence. I'm an amanuensis for an angel now. It was the only thing he couldn't have predicted or understood.' He grimaced. 'A sacrifice.'

'I don't understand.'

Conway smoothed Jack's hair off her brow. 'I'm not sure I do, either.'

'So – Saraquel is out?'

'No, no. Saraquel's back where he belongs. He's unable to enter anyone who might be dragged back into life at the last moment. That part of him is locked underground.' He looked at Felix in the dim light of the first blues of dawn and a couple of candles. 'The problem was blood. First sorcerers started using it in rituals, then medical science started using transfusions. It saved many lives but opened the body to angels and demons. A few unlucky people got stuck with Saraquel.'

Felix looked around the cottage. It was almost destroyed inside, the floor charred through in places, the plaster off the stone walls, the dawn sky visible through a few holes in the roof. Maggie's body was resting under one of the windows.

'Maggie, Gina, Mac.' He rubbed the tears off his face with a hand covered in plaster dust and drying blood. 'What do we do now? What about the other people Saraquel called?'

Robert Conway bent his head for a moment. 'Maggie knew what we – she – had to do. You must know that. It was her own choice, she had made peace with her role. Saraquel's other revenants will wake up with amnesia in the UK. Most were confined safely in London, a few made it to Dartmoor. Uriel will soften the transition for them, let them all form reasons why they might be away from home.' His brow creased as if listening to something, then smiled.

'But what do we do with the bodies?'

'Normally I would have a Vatican clean-up team who come and help, but this was off the clock. Maggie asked that we lay her to rest in the garden at her cottage in the north. Apparently, the garden itself knows what to do.'

Felix winced. 'I've seen it take a body down in a week or two. Wait – Maggie spoke to you about it beforehand?'

Conway looked, even through his exhaustion, interested. 'She chose death. She was powerful, her death spell threw Saraquel out of Jack by effectively removing the magic that was keeping her alive. Her sacrifice was strongly healing, it kept Jack's body viable for long enough to revive her.' He looked at his palm, which was black, and winced at he moved the fingers. 'I'm fascinated by green magic, I'd be interested to study it. But first, we need to get Jack to the hospital where your other young revenant is being treated.'

'Oh, God. Sadie.' He fumbled in his pocket for his phone, luckily undamaged. 'No signal.'

'My satellite phone is in the cabin.'

It took an hour to load Maggie, Gina and Mac's bodies into the boot of Conway's estate car and Jack into Felix's. He looked back at the wrecked cottage. Conway heaved a box of books onto his passenger seat and a couple of guns and boxes of ammunition into the glove compartment.

'Don't you ever worry about being pulled over?' Felix said, tucking a blanket around Jack as she lay in the boot.

'Never.' Conway blew on the hand of glory, almost burned to the palm, and threw that in the back too. 'I'll sort out the cottage another time. This house of Jack's – you'd better give me the address.'

Felix still felt shaky after handling the bodies. There was something unnaturally limp about the dead. Mac's body had caved in around the chest when he tried to pick him up, the grating inside making Felix vomit in the grass beside the car. Conway, who was sanguine about the task, seemed remarkably nimble. Felix watched him dart around the property and wondered again how old he was.

'You aren't injured in any way,' he said, watching Conway pack his few belongings on the back seat. 'Mac is dead and I have –'

he gently rubbed his side '– broken ribs and was knocked out. But you are fine?'

'I'm a revenant. I think we established that we're more resilient than most people. I'm now the sorcerer that has bound Jack's soul to her body. If the magic takes, she will be free of possession, as long as she stays well, and away from taking blood.'

'But she will die eventually . . .'

Conway slammed the back door on his bags. 'Get her to your hospital. Look after her and she should start climbing away from death.'

Felix folded a sweatshirt from the back of Mac's car under Jack's head to cushion it. 'So, how long will she live?'

'She'll outlive you, if that's what you need to know. You will be an old man and she will still be young.' He smiled. 'Don't question it.'

Felix frowned, looking up at Conway. 'What?'

'I can tell you, having been around a lot longer than you, that when love comes it's precious. Take what time you have with her, make her happy, leave her with friends and family.'

Felix stared at Robert. 'You mean she could be . . . immortal?'

Conway managed a grim smile as he shut the boot on the bodies. 'Maybe. I don't know. The countess lived for more than four hundred years.' He grimaced. 'Which reminds me, we have to deal with her son now.'

'Why?' Felix thoughts flew to the white face of Sadie, back in the hospital under George's care.

'He owes us.' Robert leaned forward, his hand, still bloodstained, extended. Felix grasped it on reflex. 'Just tell him Saraquel is gone.'

Jack didn't seem to move all the way up the motorways to the hospital six hours away. Felix didn't dare put his foot down in case someone pulled him over and wanted to know why an apparently dead woman was locked in his boot. He worried the whole way that she was being smothered by the exhaust fumes, or knocked about as he took curves and bends on the road. Or had just died of shock or whatever she was suffering from.

He drove into the car park at the hospital and negotiated his way underground to the doctors' parking area, where George was waiting with a trolley and some equipment. He stopped the engine, then found he couldn't stand up, and watched in the mirror as George opened the boot and leaned in. He gave the thumbs-up to a nurse or doctor with him – Felix wondered what kind of hospital would have such unconventional patients who arrived comatose in the boot of a car, but couldn't do more than lean over the steering wheel and shake.

He felt even more sick than he had in Devon. When he moved his head it throbbed, and his neck went into spasm. He jumped when someone opened the driver's door.

'Felix.' George was crouching down beside the car. 'She's made it here, anyway. What about you? You look terrible.'

Felix couldn't speak for a second, then he realised how thirsty he had become. 'I'm OK,' he croaked. 'What—' He swallowed hard. 'She's still alive? Are you sure?'

'Just about. A bit like Sadie. But I have some new treatments for her to try. Come on, out you get.'

He reached out an arm to help pull Felix to his feet. The concrete ceiling of the underground car park spun around, and Felix would have fallen if someone hadn't pushed a wheelchair forward. He caught one of the arms and clung to it. 'Thanks,' he managed to say, before he realised it was Charley who was pushing it.

'Sit.' Charley's face was calm but filled with sadness. 'I'm assuming . . . Mum?'

All he could do was shake his head, setting off more waves of nausea. He managed to murmur, 'I'm sorry, Charley.'

He slumped in the chair and George touched his face in a few places, then gently explored his hair. 'That's one hell of a bump. You may have a more serious injury. CT for you, my friend.'

A few hours later Felix felt better, a patient himself, in clean pyjamas and in a bed by a window. Charley had wandered in a few times to let him know Jack was stable in intensive care, but any attempt to leave his bed had resulted in vomiting, so he was trapped in his room.

When someone entered he hardly looked up.

'Professor Guichard?' His accent was familiar, and made Felix scoot up the bed.

'Bachmeier.'

'I can hardly believe it. You won, and saved Jackdaw as well. And Saraquel – is gone.'

'Gone. Yes, for the moment.' Felix shuddered. 'He was . . . terrifying.'

Pál Báthory looked sadly at Felix. 'My whole life, I was kept away from anyone who might be possessed by Saraquel. My own mother, my sisters.'

'I don't understand.' Felix rested his head gently on the pillows and the pain surged over him again.

Pál closed the blind and the pain eased a little. 'My mother had buried three children before I was seven, and knew she needed a son to survive for the estate to be passed on intact. The Báthory name, the Báthory lands and gold – it was all essential to her.'

'So she made you a revenant, what we call a borrowed timer.'

'Borrowed time?' Pál smiled, as Felix watched him walk around the room. 'I do like that. Yes, she could see I was sick, as a baby. She started the rituals on me, experimenting with different formulae through my nurses. But whatever Kelley and Dee had used on her, she had been too sick to remember. She followed Kelley's daughter to demand more details, and eventually she passed on the details she needed for the sorcery to save me. But I struggled because she knew enough to keep me away from blood. I only had small amounts in holy places, so she could be as sure as she could that Saraquel or other demons wouldn't find their way in. I had to be protected at all times.'

Felix's tired brain called up a question but it faded almost as fast as he caught it. Pál seemed to pick it up himself.

'Oh, my mother was never in a room with me. I never saw her again. She knew Saraquel would find me. She never knew exactly where I was, and I was protected by spells, a horde of witches as guardians. Our relationship was conducted almost entirely by letter – and latterly, phone and email. For more than four hundred years she loved me enough to keep a couple of countries between us.'

'Love?'

Pál's mouth twisted. 'As far as she was able, yes. As I said, dynasty came first, and I, well, I was the heir. I had to fake my death at forty, but it got easier as our fortunes grew.' He stood over Felix, looking down. 'If she could have saved any of her children through choice, it would have been my sister Anna. She was a good woman, much like my grandmother. But she couldn't be saved, and Saraquel was always watching in case she successfully transitioned to revenance.'

'So what do you do? How do you live?'

Pál shrugged. 'I do what many revenants do. I pretend to age, then develop some mystery illness and my grieving widow lays me to rest. Then I reappear as a nephew or son and start again. That way my children have stayed close to me.'

Felix ran a hand over his forehead, catching a fingernail on a dressing over his eyebrow.

'But – your mother was supposed to have died in 1614.' He looked up at Pál, wincing into the remaining light. 'How did she get out?'

Pál shrugged. 'I received word that she had been found dead – even twenty miles away we still took most of a day to get there. My fear is they would burn the body, but when we arrived she was in a coffin in the village church, and the peasants were forming into a mob. I knew instantly that she wasn't dead.' He sat in the chair beside the bed and sighed. 'You saw a lot of corpses at that time. Her skin was unmarked, her body wasn't bloating.'

'So you took her.'

'Back to the family castle at Ecsed, yes.' He half-smiled, his eyes hidden below dark lashes. 'We very formally buried the empty box in the crypt, while witches worked on the body of my mother. With enough time and treatments she gradually came back to herself.' He glanced up. 'You have to understand, before she was possessed she was just a woman.'

'With a history of cruelty.'

Pál nodded slowly. 'They were cruel times. Saraquel brought out something in her – something my father liked. If you are looking for a monster, blame him. For the last few hundred years she has lived life as a successful businesswoman. Occasionally she needed to create a revenant child to sustain her life, but that child's life was only possible with her intervention.'

'She would save the child and then drain their blood. You can't rewrite history. Your mother was a monster.'

Pál spread his hands out. 'She only took children that would have died anyway.'

Felix ground his teeth. The man had probably thrived through the Nazi regime, among others. His perspective was skewed. He moderated his tone with some difficulty. 'Which you don't need to do?'

Pál didn't answer. 'Kelley knew an alternative,' he said instead. 'He worked it out. But before we could catch him, he had escaped from a castle in Bohemia.'

Felix tried to remember the details of Kelley's death, but his head was pounding. 'At Hněvín? That's where he died of his injuries.'

Pál shook his head. 'We made enquiries at the time. There's no grave, we couldn't find two stories that matched up. In fact, that's what they sounded like, stories. No, I don't think Kelley died there. He definitely fell trying to escape from a window, I think that part is true. Perhaps he was spirited away by one of his friends – he had many contacts, you know.'

Felix settled his aching head on a cool part of the pillow. 'So, he carried on researching it?'

'And sent the information back to his stepdaughter, Eliza, yes. She managed to persuade him to help me with my mother's treatment before Hněvín, but we never found him after that. We only had some of the required information, and we got that from the stepdaughter, Eliza. The rest was hidden.'

'In her poetry. So you stole folio fifteen and put the pieces together, just like we did. But we never worked out how to save Jack. Not for sure.'

Pál leaned back, folding his hands over his stomach. 'Because Kelley kept something back. I'm hoping you now know what that was, if you defeated Saraquel.'

Felix felt another wave of nausea curl into him, and he gagged. The memory of the fight between the angels was still reverberating through him. 'You don't need to know any more, surely.'

'Possibly not now. Let me get you a nurse.'

He returned with George, accompanied by one of the junior doctors. 'You've got a bit of bleeding in your brain,' George said. 'It's small, it may not need any further treatment. But it needs careful watching. To be honest, Felix, you might be better in a NHS hospital. Further CT and MRI scans are going to rack up a hell of a bill, even with my staff discount.'

Pál interrupted from where he was standing by the door. 'I will cover all the bills,' he offered. 'And, of course, the Respiridol is part of a clinical trial. There will be no charge.'

As he left, George handed the notes to his junior, then sat on the edge of Felix's bed. When everyone else had left, he met Felix's eyes. 'Sadie has made some progress today,' he offered. 'She had a bad moment back there, she crashed last night. I couldn't believe we got her back but Charley wouldn't let us give up. But she's warmer, she's more stable.'

'And Jack?'

'It's early days. She was very cold, and she's not responding yet.' George's face looked tense.

'What aren't you telling me?'

George looked at his hands. 'I'm sorry – I just don't know if she's going to make it.'

Felix flexed his hand. 'My fingers are numb,' he said, starting to feel floaty. 'Did you give me something?'

He wasn't aware of George, just of the lights, the sounds of running feet, a squeaky wheel that rattled when he was shunted onto a trolley, then falling into blackness for a few minutes.

It seemed as if he had bounced off the bottom of the darkness to slowly rise up through it. Every part of his body seemed to ache. He could see a light through his eyelids but couldn't open them more than a slit. His hand was stinging, and he could feel someone probing it with something sharp. He tried to breathe, and couldn't, and in a moment of panic swatted at his face with the other hand.

A few minutes of confusion and people shouting and telling him to cough, and something was dragged out of his throat. Finally, he could open his eyes. A hand covered his, and a face moved in front of him, blurry at first. Slowly she came into focus.

'Jack.' At least, that's what he mouthed, his throat was so dry he couldn't do more than croak. She turned away, and came back with a small cup. It was filled with lukewarm water, but it was a relief.

Tears surged into his eyes and slipped down his face before he could move. He couldn't believe she was alive, and the memory of seeing her apparently lifeless body slumped in the circle floated up.

'You worried us for a while,' she said. He squinted up at her, wondering if she was real for a moment. 'They put you in an induced coma for three days.'

'I thought you were dead.' He swiped a hand towards his face, but she lifted a tissue to mop his streaming eyes.

'Shh. I thought I was dead for a while, too. But now I'm fine.' She smiled, but it was shaky. 'Sadie's improving too. She'll be able to go home in a few days.'

'I thought you were dead.' Tears itched as they oozed out of the corners of his eyes again.

She leaned over and touched her lips gently to his for a moment. 'I know. I'm sorry. But I'm back – I'm really back. And so are you.'

It unfolded in his mind slowly. She was free. She had a life before her, more than a life. She might have hundreds of years ahead of her. He was already middle-aged.

'What happened?'

'You had a bad bang on the head. They had to suck some blood out of it.' She smiled suddenly. 'That's been the theme of our whole relationship.'

Her fingers were so warm. Her skin, almost twenty years younger, looked smooth and soft next to his.

'Jack—'

'I know what you're going to say, and I have arguments against it. I'm going to win, so let it go, OK? I've run this a hundred times in my head.' Her voice was soft. 'I'm going to –' she dropped her voice even further '– be around a long time. Longer than you, probably, but that's because you had a head start. And every one of those days is going to be more precious because we nearly didn't have any of them together.'

He stared up into her eyes, looking for something that he'd always associated with Jack, some holding back that she always seemed to do. But Jack was still smiling at him, her lips curving as if she could read his confusion.

'OK.' He squeezed her hand. 'What else?'

'And you are going to have to deal with Sadie and my animals and Charley. And I will get used to having my family back.' She looked back over her shoulder. 'Mum, he's awake.'

Olivia Harcourt appeared beside Jack. 'So I see. I hope you are feeling better, Professor.'

'Felix,' he managed to say through the dryness. Jack passed him the cup, and this time he managed to wobble it to his own lips.

'And she's already said everything you were going to say.' Jack seemed bubbly as she looked at her mother. 'And, before you ask, she knows everything. All about Sadie and Maggie and me.' A shadow fell over her smile for a moment.

Felix handed the cup back. 'I'm glad. I'm so pleased you found each other again.'

'And she was there when I woke up. Like I've dreamed for twenty years.' A moment of pain flickered across Jack's face. It was soon banished. 'And I'm meeting up with my dad and my half-brother next week.'

'Good. Good.' Felix could feel his eyelids drooping, and despite his best efforts, sleep took him again.

Chapter 47

Journal of Eliza Jane Weston, 23 November 1612

*The enchantment that confined the countess could last only as long as
I spoke, and in my great weakness, I knew it would not be for many
minutes. It seemed that the very house grew quiet, and the words were
whispered against a backdrop of the countess's struggles to free herself.
She began to speak, her words beguiling me as my father had warned,
but I tried to ignore them. A log fell to cinders in the grate, a draught
whistled between the shutters, and still I chanted, my weakness growing
with the little gushes of hot liquid that spelled my doom.*

*Then I realised, with a growing dreaminess, that my husband,
my great and wise husband who had been warned of the countess,
had taken the children, our children, away from the house and
would conceal them within holy ground. I hoped that he would
take my newest child and baptise her, lest she precede me to heaven,
small as she was. My words faltered, but I smiled.*

Edward Kelley, the harbour at Alexandria, 1586

Niccolò had escaped to his ship while we were entertaining the
pasha and it was already showing sail.

'Hail, Kelley,' he shouted before his ship was pulled through the narrow gates that confined the old harbour. 'God's speed, my friend!'

'And you!' I cried, waving even as the first sailor dispatched by Marinello reached us, his liquid Venetian words flowing over us.

'Come, come,' the man said urgently. 'Time is short, you understand?'

I leaped as nimbly as I could upon the gangway, and came aboard Marinello's ship. He greeted me with a roar. 'Edward!' and embraced me, careless of my dignity, until my toes just trailed upon the deck. I felt tears in my throat and a sense for a moment of being home, safe, in my mother's arms. That childish thought was lost when a cannonball or some other missile crashed into the deck not five yards from where we were standing. For a second I thought it must have hit Dee, but he was thrown to the deck much bloodied and covered with splinters, some the size of my hand. I looked around, dazed, and saw that the soldiers upon the towers at the entrance of the harbour had turned the great bronze guns upon us.

'What is happening?' I shouted, the explosion still ringing in my ears.

'A little business disagreement,' he shouted back. 'Push the gangway into the sea! Take Kelley below deck with Dee,' he cried out to his crew.

I was snatched from harm's way and helped carry my poor mentor below decks. Although we were above the waterline, here and there cracks revealed the light of the sky and sea shining through. I could see that the ship was not fit to leave harbour, had not Marinello seen that?

Dee sank to the deck and my next few moments were spent in drawing out oak splinters and binding his many wounds. The

353

shock seemed to have addled his senses, so I made a bed for him from our clothes and covered him with a blanket. The ship lurched, and lurched again, listing somewhat to the right, or starboard. I climbed the narrow ladder to the deck to see what had happened.

The second cannon shot had failed in its purpose, and hit a Spanish ship instead and it was rapidly sinking. Since we had been lashed to it, Marinello's men were casting the ship adrift and putting up the first few yards of sail. We were drifting out on the tide, starting to pick up speed as the water was funnelled between the two towers, now busy with soldiers loading the two great *bombards*. A report, a single musket shot, made me look aloft and then I saw him. Our captain Marinello, lying on a spar high above the deck, almost level with the towers. A man cried out, and I saw he had managed to hit a gunner, an almost superhuman shot at more than fifty yards with a *caliver*, a sailor's form of the harquebus.

I saw Marinello spit out the smoke that sooted his face and pass the weapon down. He reached for a new one – I saw the match-lock smouldering, and he turned about, sitting astride the spar. He took slow aim at the other tower. The men there ducked, and two broke away behind the fortifications. I heard one cry out, and Marinello took careful aim.

I wanted to cry 'no' for he was balanced upon the spar, and the recoil must surely throw him off his perch to certain death below. As he lowered the smouldering rope to the flash pan I could not drag my eyes from him. There was a flare, and a great bang and he dropped the weapon. He fell, as he could not help but do, but was caught by a rope through his belt. Then an explosion knocked me off my feet.

The captain had not been aiming for the cannoneers at all, but for the barrel of powder they were using to load the great muzzle-loaded *bombard*. The explosion showered us with stone debris, but when I looked through the great cloud of smoke drifting around us, the top few feet of the tower was wrecked.

A cry above made me look up as Marinello was being lowered to the deck. A sailor pointed at the wall of the other tower, as we drifted towards it.

'More sail!' shouted Marinello, although it was somewhat of a croak. A man I didn't recognise took the great tiller with two others and forced it to one side. If we gained even a little steerage we might avoid the wall. I feared the ship would break apart if it collided, but I was wrong. We turned but a few degrees before the ship nudged the wall, its timbers creaking and screeching in protest, but it then drifted prow first through the opening, and the men did not need to be told again, but scampered into the rigging like monkeys. They unrolled more and more canvas until the ship was pulling forward like an old hound at leash, groaning and panting but still eager.

'Man the pumps!' Marinello shouted in several languages and men rushed to do his bidding. When we were maybe a hundred ship lengths from the harbour, I looked back and saw the nose of a xebec hauling out. As we made ponderous headway, I saw another of the sleek greyhounds pulling out.

'Look abaft,' I shouted to Marinello.

'I know,' he said, free from the tiller which was now manned by a burly pair of sailors. 'Worse lies ahead.'

I dared to look and saw what I most dreaded – a fleet of the slave-rowed ships, already coursing towards us. 'Holy Mother,' I said, hastily crossing myself, then thinking what a Catholic gesture it was. No matter, we would need all the saints and angels we could find to save us from the battle.

'We cannot win,' Marinello said to me, grinning from a face burned by black powder. 'Yet I would rather die in battle than yield to those Turkish slaver whoresons. What say you, Edward?'

My mind flew back, as if guided by an angel still lurking in my soul, to the scrolls. 'I have another idea.'

'Do you have more of the great winds you raised?' he asked, as I rummaged under my robes.

'Better,' I said, looking at the rumpled and battered scrolls, barely the length of my palm but sealed securely with the great wax imprints. 'But I know not how they work.'

'Do you not just chant the spell and break the seal, as you did before?' he asked.

I dared not say that my knowledge came from an angel residing in my heart, and he might not aid me this time. The ships were advancing, and our vessel was listing more.

I felt certain the spell should be cast up high, and thrust the scrolls into my robes and made my way to the crow's nest in the foremast. My feet slipped in their shoes until I kicked them off and let my soles grasp the wood. There, I braced myself against the rolling of the labouring ship, seeing the pump water pouring over the side below me as four men hung on a handle.

'God help us,' I breathed, then pulled out the two scrolls. One was still inscribed with the symbols for fire, but what could fire do upon the sea? The other had the hand of God upon it – but was this the right moment, when all was lost? Something drew me to the fire seal. I pushed the last scroll back inside my clothes, reasoning if the fire one did not work, and if I was not incinerated, I could still use the other.

I thought about the intent. What intent could I seek that would win us the impossible battle? An image crept into my mind, of a drop of water in a pool, all still in the centre but ripples running out from the middle. And my fingers snapped open the seal.

This time my lungs filled with air like scalding water and burned the words in my throat. I concentrated on my intent, seeing myself as the still point, surrounded by water, by cool safe water . . .

The rumble was deafening, the light blazed through my closed lids and I covered my face with my free hand. My other was locked onto the scroll until the burning pain made me shout and I was able to move my fingers to drop it. My mouth screamed out the words again and again against a roar like a thousand beacon fires. Water, ripples like tiny waves, the centre calm and cool. The sound faded back to a crackling.

I looked around me.

Men below knelt or sat or lay in terror and prayer, and a sky made of flame arced overhead and slowly spread across the water. Screams pierced the roaring flame but for an instant. I looked down at Marinello, not prostrate but staring up at me, his face somewhere between fear and triumph, his hair burned short. The walls of flame pushed out further as I brought my mind back to the still pool, the cool water. They pushed at a steady rate, until all that was left in the water was a scattering of debris, a few burning corpses and the stench of death.

I climbed down slowly, one hand burned and blistered. As I descended the last few rungs Marinello reached up and helped me down. I rested in his arms for a moment, my heart pattering like a child's. We had survived.

'Let the Lord be praised,' he shouted, and a few men lifted their voices to say 'yea'.

Then we knelt there, my giant captain, his rag-tag crew and I, and prayed in gratitude and in relief in many languages, then teams of men resumed the pumping that kept our battered old lion of a ship afloat.

What of that last journey home? We reached Brindisi, for we sailed straight, in thirty-three days. Of that time there is little to say. Dee recovered his senses and became one of the stalwarts upon the pumps. My hand festered for a time and I feared it would become a scarred claw, but one of the sailors showed me how to massage oil into the palm and stretch it out a hundred times a day. And always, I dreamed of home. Home was where they were, my beloved children John and little Eliza, and Jane Dee, that queen of women.

We talked of the exorcism, and the fear that we would once again meet a vessel of Saraquel, and I knew I could never face the angel again. I felt no trace of Uriel, yet knew if I called, he would be there. Instead, we planned to work on our alchemical experiments and Dee's mathematicals.

Of Marinello? Well, the shocking events of the spell left him subdued, but not for long. He chivvied and chided us when we fell into despair and worked harder than any of us. My memory of that journey as we half died of thirst, ate little but what we could catch and stumbled into exhaustion between watches was of Marinello, standing at the prow of his lumbering ship, his face turned towards the north and home.

Chapter 48

Jack sat in the hospital garden with Sadie, the teenager wrapped up in a fleece blanket, and they watched a group of sparrows squabbling in the bushes that surrounded the car park. Felix would be ready to leave in a day or two, and the future seemed painfully bright. She had Olivia back, she was going to meet up with her father, Sadie had survived. Jack was going to at least have a normal lifespan. But she had many more questions than answers, and there was a gap that was just a well of pain. Maggie.

Jack felt she had hardly known any other parent. Melissa had had Olivia and Robert Harcourt, until she, well, died. Jackdaw Hammond had been born out of the dank cellar in the cottage in Devon, the place that called to her, the place she still felt was home. Maggie had fought for her life through those years, when death swept like an ice storm through her again and again. Only Maggie's determination, magic and love had kept her alive. At first, it seemed like gratitude that because of her Charley was safe. But over time it became about Jack. With each crisis, Jack had felt more part of the dark magic that Maggie had used, closer to the

359

animals around the cottage, closer to the rooks in the trees whose calls formed the soundtrack to her life.

She had developed a story with Charley to explain her abduction to Olivia, and to the police. She had been kidnapped by a crazy woman, and when she escaped had lived rough with some teenagers in an unspecified city. She had grown familiar with a part of London, maybe she would say it had been that area. Then Maggie had found her, and she had offered her a refuge that eventually became a home. Maybe Jack had lied about her age. Now she felt as much part of Charley's family as her own.

It was stupid story, really, full of holes, but she knew that now her mother knew the truth, she would support whatever lies she came up with. The truth was simple. Jack had been changed profoundly by the magic, and was as much Maggie's child as Olivia's. And now she was grieving the loss of that mother.

Sadie threw a few more crumbs to the sparrows that bickered and pecked for them. 'How are you feeling?' she asked, her voice rough from the airway they had used when she was ventilated.

'Sad. Tired. I don't know, how about you?'

Sadie shrugged one shoulder, then folded her feet up onto the bench, under the blanket. 'I don't feel like me any more,' she said, her voice slow. 'Does that sound silly?' She turned to look at Jack, her eyes deeper blue in the evening light.

'Maybe everyone feels like that when they've been really ill,' Jack said, wondering herself.

'What happens now? I mean, who's going to look after me?' There was a touch of the old defiance in her voice.

'I was wondering whether we could get you and your mum to live together again.'

Sadie snorted, but behind the derision, her eyes looked sad. 'I'm supposed to be dead, remember? I can't just go back to Exeter, back to school.'

'I just thought Angela might get a job up in the Lake District, you two could live in the cottage there. Together. If Charley doesn't mind.'

Sadie turned her shoulder away from Jack. 'I suppose you and Felix want to be on your own now.'

Jack put her hand on Sadie's shoulder, only to have it shrugged off. 'It isn't like that!' Only, it was, just a little. 'OK, we could do with some time on our own, to sort things out. But you're part of my family, you don't get rid of me that easily.'

'The family of dead people.' But there was a twist of Sadie's lips that suggested a smile.

'Mr and Mrs Dead and their adopted revenant teenager, Sadie. It has a ring to it.' Jack's heart seemed to tango in her chest for a long moment at the thought of being with Felix. 'Not that anyone is getting married, necessarily,' she added.

'He looks like the husband kind,' Sadie observed, her words drifting over the lawn as if she was thinking about something else.

'What is it, really? There's something – you seem upset. What is it?'

Sadie tucked her knees under her chin, then turned her head to see Jack. 'Mum's great, she really is. But all this magic stuff just freaks her out.'

'I'm not surprised. It's a strange world even when you have to live in it.'

'And she's been drinking. I mean, she always drinks, but now . . .'

361

Jack thought back to the times she had seen Angela at the hospital. In the car park, chain-smoking, or at Sadie's bedside, helpless with tears. The doctor had mentioned that Angela was coping with the help of a lot of drink.

'I know she's struggled, but maybe we can help. Pál Bachmeier, he's given Felix some money. I didn't want to take it, but Felix has it tucked away. If we let you stay at the house Angela can spend some time with you. Maybe she'll be able to get her drinking under control.'

Sadie hunched her shoulder in her blanket. She mumbled something.

'What?'

Sadie turned to her again. 'She doesn't understand this. She wants me to go to school, have a normal life.'

'Well, that's understandable—'

'You don't get it!' There were tears running down Sadie's face until she rubbed them off on her arm. She buried her face and started sobbing.

Jack was appalled. In all the difficulties they had faced, through all the pain and discomfort of being dragged back from death, Sadie had never broken down. Got sarcastic or stroppy, yes, but never this. The crying had an edge of despair to it.

She put her arm around Sadie, and such was the teenager's pain that she curled up against Jack, the sobs rocking them both. When the paroxysms released Sadie a little, Jack murmured to her. 'Explain it to me.'

Sadie pushed herself away and wiped her face on her T-shirt. Her breaths started to even out, her body relax. 'That night, the night I was supposed to die.'

'Yes?'

'My cause of death was going to be choking, drowning on my own vomit.' She sniffed, and slid a sideways glance at Jack.

'You were drunk.'

Sadie stared at her. Her lashes had clumped together, her eyelids were swollen. 'I was. I was really unhappy. Mum was drunk all the time.'

Jack looked out over the lawn. The sparrows had finally moved on, to wherever their nest was, she supposed. A bat fluttered over the car park.

'I'm sure lots of kids do daft things.'

Sadie shook her head. 'I took some pills. I didn't care what happened.' She laid her head down on her knees again as if she was exhausted. 'I was so angry, and so upset. Everything was going wrong. I was suspended from school, Mum went nuts and slapped me.' She touched her fingers lightly to her cheek as if the stinging was still there. 'She said – she said she wished she'd never married my dad and had me.'

'She was angry.' Jack couldn't think of anything else to say.

'She was drunk. She's always drunk. My dad left because she used to hit him. He left me with her even though she used to go on benders.'

'So you took some tablets.'

'I took all the tablets. And drank all the vodka. I didn't care any more, I just couldn't think what else to do.'

Jack was shocked. But she remembered the utter desolation of knowing she had no other future than hurting the people she loved, the moment when she stepped over the barrier and dropped off the bridge.

Sadie carried on, as if she was talking more to herself than Jack. 'I was doing crap at school. I used to be really good at science, I wasn't bad at maths.' She looked down at the fingers twisting in her lap. 'But then I couldn't concentrate. I started getting told off all the time at school.'

'I'm so sorry, Sadie.' Jack reached out one hand, hesitant. But Sadie took it for a moment, her fingers cool and thin.

Sadie's voice dropped to a whisper. Jack struggled to hear it and, then, comprehend it.

'I'm scared I'll end up like her. Do you understand?'

Jack didn't, but she could imagine. There was something weak, broken inside Angela, that was strong in Sadie, despite everything she had endured. 'I think you're amazing to have come through it all so well. I don't think you'll ever do anything else you don't want to. And you'll be there to look after Angela.'

'But I . . . I did try to kill myself.'

'That was a lifetime ago.' Jack put her arm around Sadie, pulling her into a hug, and after a moment, Sadie let her. 'I did the same, remember? I really thought there was no other way out. I felt like I'd been forced into a corner, and everything I tried to do made things worse.'

'But you're the strong one.' Sadie relaxed against her, and Jack hugged her harder, feeling a fierce protective impulse, feeling something of what Maggie must have felt for Jack.

'I didn't realise that you make me strong,' Jack said. 'You, and Charley and Felix.' She let Sadie pull away as she heard footsteps crunching over the gravel. The light tap of a stick gave away the identity, as Robert Conway walked into the pool of light now brightening the dark.

'Ah, the famous Sadie,' he said, looking older than Jack remembered him from the cottage. He must have been in the firing line more than anyone else, she remembered, but he looked well. 'It's nice to finally meet you. Robert Conway, exorcist.' He held out a hand and Sadie took it reluctantly.

'Sadie Williams. Revenant,' she added with a spark of her old sharpness.

'Well, that's all three of us. I assume Felix told you about me? I just stopped by to introduce you to someone who helped enormously – and is still helping. Saraquel's army in London and on Dartmoor are all rather confused at waking up in English churches. Free of possession.'

'You are a revenant?' Sadie looked up and Jack turned to see an old man approaching.

'Not only am I a revenant, but so is this gentleman,' Conway said.

The newcomer was very tall but a little stooped. He walked with a cane too, but quite swiftly, and very upright. He wore a dark suit, a shadow in the evening light, and his hair was pure white, flowing back from a V-shaped widow's peak. He looked like an aged Dracula, Jack realised, holding a giggle back.

He stopped in front of them. Conway smiled, and when the older man put out a hand with an ornate ring on it, Conway bent to kiss it. 'Eminence,' he murmured. 'This is Jackdaw Hammond and Sadie Williams.'

The older man smiled warmly at them all. 'My name is Cardinal Andreotti,' he said, 'and you have, between your courage and resourcefulness, removed a threat to mankind that grew with each year. We knew Saraquel overshadowed many hundreds of people, but now we count as many as fourteen thousand, including people in positions of great power and wealth in the world.'

'That many?' Jack turned to Conway. 'You didn't know that, did you?'

'To be honest, Miss Hammond, I don't think I would have dared face Saraquel if I had known.'

'Which would,' Andreotti said, 'have been a mistake because his influence was divided between so many hosts, and therefore he was distracted. Would you mind if I sit? My old legs are tired at this time of day.'

Jack stood, and he sank onto her seat with a smile.

'I often wish I had taken advantage of the sorcery when I was still a young man,' he said. 'Alas, I resisted the temptation until death was almost upon me. But I had vowed to see the Countess Báthory put in her grave finally, and it was the only way I could see my vow carried out.'

'You really are a revenant too?' Jack stared at him, his skin mottled and blotched with age. 'How long ago?' she blurted out.

'Oh, I have been an old man for a long time,' he said, his white eyebrows lifting like tiny wings against his forehead. 'But the process did give me a last burst of energy. Not enough to tackle Báthory herself, unfortunately. That I had to leave to you, and McNamara, and Professor Guichard.'

'And Sadie,' Jack added. 'We wouldn't have won without Sadie holding out as long as she did.' She bit her lip. 'What about Mac? I know he's dead, but—'

'He has been restored to his family. They only know he was killed saving a life in a tragic accident.' He sighed. 'A better man than an inquisitor. Perhaps like myself.'

'What now for you, Eminence?' asked Conway, leaning on his stick.

'I shall make my confession, make my peace with the world and end it in repentance and humility.' He sighed, stretching out long feet in shoes that caught the twinkles of light from the hospital windows. 'I just wanted to meet the heroine of the hour and tell her that as far as the Vatican is concerned, she need have no more concerns. Being a revenant, by itself, is no longer a matter for the Congregation for the Doctrine of the Faith. They shall go back to fighting heresies and conspiracies.'

'Thank you,' said Jack, her voice quivering with reaction. A lifetime of secrecy and hiding was fading, and the world seemed blindingly bright.

'There is one small, remaining problem,' the old man said. He turned to Sadie, made a strange gesture in the air, and murmured something so simple Jack had to look again.

'Did you just say, "sleep"?'

Sadie's head had dropped onto her shoulder, and her eyes seemed closed.

'Just a trick I learned in my younger days. Jackdaw – may I call you Jackdaw – you have spent time with Robert Conway. What do you know of him?'

'He's a revenant, he works for the Vatican as an exorcist . . .' She frowned. 'What else do I need to know?'

'That we are both very grateful,' Conway said promptly, as if cutting off anything Andreotti might have said.

A strange idea crossed Jack's mind. 'You know an awful lot about Edward Kelley,' she guessed. 'And you have one of his unpublished journals.'

'I do.'

She squinted at him in the low light. 'How old are you, anyway?'

Conway stepped in front of her, close enough for her to see his face in the light from the porch to the hospital reception. 'I am older than you think.' His eyes seemed to grow larger in the light.

'But I am grateful to you. And if you ever need me – you will remember me.'

Jack felt tired. She looked down at the sleeping teenager, and nudged her to wake her up. What was she thinking? Yes, Sadie had obviously been through a lot. There was something else, something about the Irishman, Robert Conway. She looked around as she almost remembered something, but there was no one there.

Bee Cottage was warm in the early summer sunshine when Jack finally got out of the car after a journey beset with caravans and tourists. Sadie was bouncing, Jack had never seen her so well. She was the first out of the car, shouting 'Charley' before the barking told them that Ches was alive and well.

Charley opened the door and Ches charged down the path and into them.

'Stupid puppy!' Jack laughed, as the dog-wolf couldn't seem to decide whether to fall at her feet or knock her flat. He looked thinner and older; Charley said he had been pining.

Sadie, locked in Charley's arms, was in tears. 'I didn't think I'd come back here,' she was mumbling.

'Well, we had more faith in you.' Charley let Sadie run back into the house and hugged Jack. 'I can't believe Mum's not here too,' she said in a small voice. 'Hi, Felix.'

He was getting bags out the boot of the car, and Jack let go of Charley to help him. 'Let me take Sadie's . . .' Ches was fawning around her feet and she shooed him back into the house. 'Daft dog,' Jack said, grinning. She led the way into the newly renovated house, bare plaster in the hall reminding her that she needed to get around to decorating. Sadie came out of the kitchen holding a kitten, black and white, with the dark markings over his eyes looking like a mask. He looked about three months old.

'This is Bandit,' Sadie said, smothering the cat in kisses. 'Close the door, Felix, I don't want him going on the road.'

He looked at Jack and she smiled back.

He nodded towards the stairs. 'Where do you want these bags?'

'Well, yours and mine in the front bedroom over the living room,' she said, realising what she was saying as the words came out. She put her head on one side. 'Sadie can bunk in with Charley.'

Charley shut the door behind Felix and Sadie. 'Actually, Sadie and I are going into Ambleside to the B&B you stayed in when you first came here. I'm sure you would prefer to be alone, and Sadie and I have some clothes shopping to do now she's feeling better. And, you know, I need a break from being here. Too many memories of Mum.'

Jack reached out for Charley and they hugged for a long moment. 'I'm so sorry.'

'I know. It's all horrible. And Mac, too.'

'He died a hero. Conway saw him take on Saraquel personally.'

Charley sniffed, turned away. 'I know, Felix said. So, are you going to be all right here, just the two of you?'

'Oh.' Jack smiled but nervous butterflies started circling under her ribs. Sadie opened the door. 'I suppose so.'

'I need a complete makeover,' the teenager said, the kitten in her arms. Jack stroked its head.

'Great. Enjoy your shopping, Sadie. Where's your mother?'

'She's back in Exeter. She's packing, she's going to come and live up here, like you suggested.' Sadie kissed the kitten again. 'We thought – me and Charley thought – that you and Felix would need to live in Devon. You know, with both your jobs.'

That reminded Jack that Pierce had some paperwork for her. Magic from Maggie. A lump seemed to have formed in her throat.

Charley blinked, her face going red. 'I know, I know,' she said. 'But Mum knew all about it – she warned me years ago. We're just going to be really sad for a while – well, I am. I suppose you've got your mum back finally.'

Jack sighed, and put down the bag she was carrying. 'Maggie was my mum too, Charley, it's not that easy. I think we're all going to be a bit wobbly for a while.'

'Which is why we're going to be nice to each other and spoil each other a bit. Retail therapy for us girls, and you and Felix can finally – well, you know, get on with it.'

Jack could hear Felix's footfalls above her and feel her face flushing. 'There are a few issues . . .'

'I know, immortality and all that.' Charley took the kitten from Sadie and the teenager opened the door onto the garden for Ches. 'If there's one thing we've all learned – there are no guarantees, are there? We could all be dead tomorrow. Enjoy today.'

Jack climbed the stairs into Felix's arms, hearing the clatter of the raven in the back room, hearing the bird start to squawk as he recognised her step and voice. She kissed Felix then pushed him back a little. He released her, frowning down at her.

'Are you all right?'

She nodded, too choked to speak at first. 'I need . . . I need to do something.'

She turned to the door to the back bedroom, where the raven waited. When she let herself in, she shut it behind her.

'I'm sorry,' she soothed, as the bird bristled from the back of the chair. He had demolished the newspapers on the floor and pecked plaster off in various places in the room. He screeched at her, his whole body extended. 'I know, I know. I'm sorry I had to go away.'

She reached out her hand and, as if she hadn't been gone for weeks, he flapped onto her wrist for the first time, as if he'd always done it. He dug his overlong claws in to keep his grip, his weight suprising Jack. He turned to stare at her, intelligence and frustration forcing him to caw, the loud noise deafening in the small room, and he rattled his glossy feathers. Jack walked to the mended window, the new paint already pecked and scratched.

He hopped onto the wide sill, as if he knew exactly what she was about to do. When she forced open the bottom sash, squeaking with disuse, he walked with his rolling gait towards her.

'You can go.' Tears were streaming from her eyes. Grief, yes, even for Mac, who had given his life for hers along with Maggie. But this was a good feeling, even though it made her upset. 'There will always be food for you here, do you know that? If you never even go beyond the garden, you will always be home.'

The bird perched on the sash frame. He cried, one long screech. She wondered if he could even fly, brought up in a house since he was young. But he wasn't imprinted – there was a good chance he had flown before. He clattered his wing feathers, shaking them out, then stepped into the air. For a heart-thumping moment, Jack watched him fall towards the rough grass, but at the last minute he threw out his wings and soared, flapping occasionally, climbing into the air to land on the garden wall. With a last caw, he stretched into the sky again – and was gone.

Chapter 49

Journal of Eliza Jane Weston, 23 November 1612

Maybe I dreamed it in the last weakness of dying. As my last words faded, the countess was free of the magical trap and leaped to the bed. She gripped me between hard fingers, shaking me, screaming at me, raging that I was unable to speak. I just closed my eyes and waited for death. It did not come. Eventually, she left. Perhaps she thought me already dead.

Instead I lay in the bed, my body slowly disappearing, the pain going, and the darkness falling. I heard the fire fall into ash and the room cool. I too, cooled and rested. Then, of God's mercy, I heard the light step of my husband, his kisses and tears upon my forehead and lips. I managed to open my eyes but words were beyond me.

'The babe lives,' he told me over and over. 'Come back to me.'

But I knew it was too late. He built the fire to warm me, and the room grew darker even though he brought candles to light it.

Finally I heard new footsteps, the soft voices of men, and my husband retreated. I could not open my eyes but I knew, with a fluttering of love in my chest, the arms of my father.

Epilogue

Present day, off the coast of Italy

Robert Conway sat back in his seat at the helm of the *Marinello*. The yacht was usually moored at Amalfi, in the marina, and he had taken her out for a spin. His physical wounds had healed but the psychic ones would take longer – nightmares of the angels battling within him left him gasping. And banked down, a tiny flutter of observation from Uriel kept him safe.

Cardinal Andreotti lifted a glass, a sixteenth-century *millefiori* masterpiece, one of only two Conway had left. 'Do you think she knows who you are?' He sipped the sweet wine and hummed with pleasure. 'A great vintage, my old friend,' he said in Latin.

'Like yourself.' The exorcist toasted him back, letting the boat ride at anchor. 'I think she will seek me out some day to ask questions.'

'Whether Edward Kelley sought life over death at Hněvín? That it was Kelley who defeated Saraquel, finally?'

Edward Kelley smiled. 'I think she first has to find a way to live with centuries instead of decades. It is the lonely world of a revenant, my friend, as you know.'

Konrad shielded his eyes against the sun, then fumbled to unfold his sunglasses. 'Sometimes I wish I had sipped the poisoned chalice *before* arthritis twisted my fingers,' he said, sighing. 'I can't even hold a sword, you know. Hardly a warrior for God, these days.'

Kelley took the glasses, straightened them and put them back into the older man's hand. 'Yours was a heroic quest,' Kelley said, 'for God's purpose. Mine was mostly driven by fear and self-preservation.'

'Your destiny was always to be a conduit for angels, my friend. It led you to Dee all those years ago.'

'Uriel, yes.' He could still feel the warm centre where the angel slept. 'And now – will you go on? Or end the sorcery and ascend to heaven?'

'I think I will need to do some penance first. For the sake of my soul, steeped as it is in magic, sorcery and sin.' He shrugged. 'Living in the shadows at the Vatican is difficult enough. I'm astonished no one there has worked out that Cardinal Soranzo was also Cardinal Barbarigo and so on. Perhaps there is more evil in the world that needs my attention. And you?'

Edward Kelley felt inside him for some guidance that he should step either way. 'I think I shall carry on. Perhaps I will enjoy life more when I don't have to look over my shoulder every day for Saraquel.' He looked at the shimmering water, with flashes of tiny fish close to the surface. 'Bachmeier's company has treatments for all of us. We will save many people, and keep revenants safe from possession.'

'I don't think anything will keep revenants safe. We are unnatural. Wandering corpses.' The older man laughed and raised the glass. 'Corpses with excellent taste in fine wines.'

'Indeed.'

Kelley stretched back in his chair. The sun was warm and a flicker of hope, lit by Jackdaw Hammond and her loyal partner, was fanned by an angel.

Historical note

Writing a story rooted in the past is always a balancing act between being as grounded in the evidence as we can be, and trying to tell an engaging and believable fiction. Edward Kelley and John Dee were extraordinary thinkers and travellers, and were in Europe in 1586. I don't know if they went to Alexandria, but I feel it would have drawn them had the opportunity come up.

Marinello and Konrad are fictional, but who can resist writing characters like them? They seem real to me now. Research is a swamp into which a writer can get lost, following pirates, explorers, rogues and heroes through history.

With all this uncertainty about such interesting and sometimes infamous characters, I have stretched history to serve story. If this causes any offence, I apologise.

Acknowledgements

I have a great many people to thank.

Firstly, Michael Rowley and Emily Yau of Del Rey UK for editing this draft into a proper book. It's great to get ideas from Michael. With his help, I've become a better storyteller, and for that I will always be grateful.

Charlotte Robertson, my then agent, for liking the book and giving me so much guidance. All while making me feel good about writing, and inspiring me to write in what were dark months. And Jane Willis of United Agents, who has taken over, for her support and encouragement. I look forward to working on new books with her.

My friend Ruth Downie, author of a series of books set in Roman Britain and published by Bloomsbury USA. She, and other writers in the work-in-progress group in Barnstaple, are a constant source of encouragement and not afraid to offer criticism either.

My noisy family, who have cajoled, read, and invented, especially my eldest son, Carey. He is my first editor, and he's usually right. And my brother Guy, who reads early drafts, argues for the characters and pushes me to finish.

My husband Russell, who is already asking where Kelley and Konrad and Jack and Felix go from here. I tell these stories mainly for him, usually in the car on long journeys. Who knows where they will end up.

And finally, for those who read my stories. I hope you enjoy reading them because I love writing them.

Thank you all.